Praise for Eva Marie Everson and G. W. Francis Chadwick's "Shadows" series. . .

Breakneck pacing and picturesque setting. Everson and Chadwick's tangled plot and endearing characters do not disappoint!

DEBORAH BEDFORD,
Best-selling author of *A Rose by the Door*

I love a good contemporary mystery. . .filled with intrigue and suspense. What a joy to read *Shadow of Dreams*. From page one I was hooked. Fresh and vivid in its portrayal of a challenging mother and daughter relationship, I laughed and cried at the poignancy of the issues these two women faced head-on. This cliffhanger left me wanting more. Move over Mary, Jim, and Patricia. . .Eva Marie and G.W. have arrived!

ALLISON GAPPA BOTTKE,
Editor of the *God Allows U-Turns* Series

Shadow of Dreams left an imprint on my heart. Everson and Chadwick have the amazing ability to bring their fiction to life in such a way that you will convince yourself you know the characters intimately—they simply must be real.

LAURA SABIN RILEY,
Author of *All Mothers Are Working Mothers*

Candid, unvarnished, ripe with characters who move from hollow to wholeness. If you like riveting plots that keep you reading, *Summon the Shadows* is waiting.

JAN COLEMAN,
Author of *After the Locusts*

I always love a good fiction book to take my mind off some of the heavy load of counseling I do. *Shadow of Dreams* is one of those books you just don't want to put down until the very end. I can't wait to find out what happened to Ben in the sequel.

LESLIE VERNICK, Christian Counselor and
Author of *How to Act Right When Your Spouse Acts Wrong*

Shadow of Dreams is an engrossing read guaranteed to keep you up long past your bedtime. Everson and Chadwick's ability to get inside the character and to successfully take readers to diverse locations is what makes this book a winner. I can't wait to see what happens next!

CARMEN LEAL,
Author of WriterSpeaker.com

Here's a book that deeply touches real life and real people. It's a book of encouragement and hope to anyone who has ever been or had a prodigal child. Having experienced both—I can say that personally, with such detailed descriptions and transparency, the characters of *Shadow of Dreams* took me anew to the very heart of love, forgiveness, and God's grace. I can hardly wait for the sequel!

SHARON HOFFMAN,
Author and Conference Speaker

In *Shadows of Dreams,* Everson and Chadwick write a compelling plot with powerful characters. Live the adventure as prodigal Katie Morgan searches her past in an effort to survive the present. A must read!

LINDA EVANS SHEPHERD,
Author, Speaker, and Host of "Right to the Heart" Radio

Shadow of Dreams is a brilliant work, intertwining great literature with glamour, mystery, dread, anticipation, and personal relief. *Shadow of Dreams* offers healing light on secrets that have long been covered by God's redeeming love.

CRISTINE BOLLEY,
Author of *A Gift from St. Nicholas*

There's nothing quite like a well-written mystery full of intrigue and characters you care about. *Shadow of Dreams* has it all! You won't be disappointed.

KARI WEST,
Author of *Dare to Trust, Dare to Hope Again*

SUMMON THE SHADOWS

Sequel to *Shadow of Dreams*

EVA MARIE EVERSON AND
G. W. FRANCIS CHADWICK

PROMISE PRESS
An Imprint of Barbour Publishing

Member of the Evangelical Christian Publishers Association

Printed in the United States of America.

Dedication

Eva Marie Everson dedicates this book to her parents
Preston Purvis and Betty Purvis
For their years of unyielding belief in my purpose and talents!
I can never thank you. . .or love you. . .enough.
. . .and to my brother.

G. W. Francis Chadwick dedicates this book to his sister
Minna Chadwick Egan
Because you had the courage to move on with your life.
I love you.

Special Dedication

This book is set in New York City in the fall of 2001.

On September 11, 2001, Dennis and Eva Marie Everson were in a Midtown Manhattan hotel when terrorists attacked the World Trade Center. That afternoon, they visited Fifth Avenue's Saint Thomas Church, where the public was beckoned to come in. . .to pray. . .and to join together during a time few could understand. For the next five days, they wandered about the city, observing the enormity of what had happened, and the effects it had on the people who either lived and worked there or had come to visit during what would be our darkest days. They witnessed the comings and goings of the fearless, tireless, brave men and women who served their city and country in the efforts of rescue and recovery. They spoke with and embraced citizens who simply didn't know what to do. . .where to go. . .who to blame. . . .

Because of this, Eva Marie Everson and Francis Chadwick would like to give a special dedication to those who have risen to the occasion of terror, fought valiantly, and won the battle. Therefore, a percentage of our profits from this book will be used to help Saint Thomas Church in its efforts to rebuild the hearts, minds, and spirits of those who enter their doors.

God bless America.

Soul Dance

Lord,
Teach my soul to dance—
Move me with the power of the Holy Spirit.
Cleanse my heart
And carry me away in Your direction
To the beat of Your precious instruments.
Amaze me with the anointing of
Your glorious presence
And surround me with Your everlasting,
Indescribable peace,
So that I may have the courage
To defeat my enemies
In this temporary hell,
Until the day I go home
Forever.

© SARAH RUTH WOODCUM

THE HAMILTON PLACE FLOURISHES
UNDER INTERIM CEO
By James Preston Kicklighter
© Hotel Times Magazine

NEW YORK CITY, NEW YORK (June 2001) – Under interim chair and CEO Katharine Morgan Webster, the renowned five-star The Hamilton Place (THP) chain of hotels experienced significant growth over the past year, defying the odds and the predictions of industry pundits. When William Benjamin Webster, who had helmed the group since 1981, mysteriously disappeared twelve months ago, the experts forecasted that THP would flounder following the loss of its charismatic leader. Yet the hotel chain, famous for its luxury and its tender catering to A-list clientele, has not only survived but has also thrived.

Mrs. Webster, who had never held such a position before, was an unexpected choice as chair and CEO, with many feeling she would not be able to continue the work her husband had begun. But surprise apparently runs in the Webster family.

William Webster had earlier amazed everyone by taking over the presidency of the one-hundred-year-old international THP when his father, Donald Webster, suffered a massive heart attack, and restoring the original opulence and grandeur to the aging buildings, revamping the business models for the hotels. Despite low expectations, Mr.

Webster's improvements increased revenue by 125% in the first year. By 1985, THP was renowned once again as a five-star hotel and was the choice hotel of the world's most glamorous jetsetters. Business continued to increase and plans were made for additional branches.

Then, last June, just after exposing a crime ring operating in his hotel, Mr. Webster's car exploded outside his Hamptons home. His body was never found. Though the story mesmerized business communities and the social elite of two continents, the FBI is no closer to unraveling the pieces of this complex and fascinating story than they were twelve months ago. Nor have they been able to locate the brother and sister duo behind the illegal operation, Brandon "Bucky" Caballero and Mattie C. Franscella, who remain the prime suspects in the car bombing.

Mr. Caballero and Mrs. Franscella had owned and operated the upscale women's boutique, Jacqueline's, located within New York City's THP, and which was used as a front for an illegal escort service catering to some of the world's wealthiest travelers, as well as some of New York's most illustrious politicians and diplomats.

Just after Mr. Webster contacted the FBI, he sent his wife Katharine to her hometown of Brooksboro, Georgia, for her safety. Apparently his concerns were well founded. Shortly thereafter, Mr. Webster's 1999 Jaguar XJ6 exploded, with Mr. Webster allegedly inside. Mrs. Webster immediately returned to New York with FBI agents. Later that night at the Hamptons residence, Mrs. Franscella's husband, David, attempted to take the life of Mrs. Webster, but was shot and killed in a struggle with the Webster's housekeeper.

In her husband's absence, Katharine Webster was appointed the CEO and president of The Hamilton Place chain. James Harrington, general manager for the flagship NYC hotel where Mrs. Webster has her offices, made a recent public statement saying, "Mrs. Webster continues to hold firm to the hope that her husband is not dead and that he will return home soon. Until then, she will do his job in the same manner of professionalism as he would." The love and devotion from Mr. Webster's personnel continues to be apparent. "He is missed," Mr. Harrington said.

When asked if the events of last year had affected the hotel's business, he replied, "Business has increased since last year. There were the curious, of course, but they have since stopped visiting us. We accredit our continued success to exceptional customer service in a premiere hotel."

When asked how Katharine Webster was doing in her new role, he said, "Mrs. Webster is doing a wonderful job."

PROLOGUE
October 2001

The old neighborhood had changed. Katie had heard about it, of course. She'd seen it on the news and read about it in *The Times* and *The Post*. Mayor Giuliani had vowed a major cleanup of the area just off Times Square. . .the place called Hell's Kitchen. . .and clean it up, he had. But more than twenty-five years ago, it had been her home. *Her* hell. Now, after all these years, here she was again, standing on the edge of it, gripping a shiny vinyl shopping bag in her hand.

This was the neighborhood that had left such an indelible mark on her soul. No matter how hard she tried, she could not truly disengage herself from its baneful effects. And yet, here it was, looking so completely different, although the change could not alter anything about her history there. Gone were the filthy, littered sidewalks, the roach-infested apartments, the spiritless vagrants, and the underfed hookers, who stood lolling against the walls by the street corners. Katie could still hear them calling to the drivers of the cars crawling by, who looked as though they were observing a tourist attraction and wanting to make certain they hadn't missed anything.

"Hey, baby! Wanna talk to me? Wanna play tonight? What 'chu got for me, baby?"

Katie closed her eyes momentarily, reliving the sound of one of the

15

girls calling out to her one cold, February evening in 1977 as she passed by the corner of 44th and 10th.

"Hey, Katie, baby. Goin' to work, sweet baby? Why don'chu join the real ladies of the evenin' instead of just dancin' for your dollars?"

The memory was still sharp, even after all these years. Katie had stopped in front of the young black woman with the piercing green eyes who called herself "Mittens," though her real name was Margaret. At the time she had been. . .what?. . .maybe eighteen. She had looked ten years older. She was underfed, underpaid, and Katie remembered wondering if she, too, looked older than her real age of twenty, which, around Hell's Kitchen, was old. That evening she had worn a too-short blue polyester, summer dress that clung to her willowy figure and only served to make her long legs look even longer. It was one of the few dresses she had owned at the time, and she often covered it with a fake-fur dark blue jacket she'd gotten at Goodwill though it hadn't done much to keep her warm. Back in the day, not much could.

"Excuse me."

Someone bumped Katie from behind, jarring her out of her daytime reverie and into the present. She spun around and squinted against the bright sunlight.

"Oh, I'm sorry. Excuse me," she said. She pointed herself toward the area of the borough where she had once danced and began to walk the now unfamiliar sidewalks of her old home, stopping here and there to peer into the narrow shops and small cafés. Yes, the neighborhood had changed. There was a new ambiance. It was clean, artsy, and inviting. Shoppers moved in and out of the storefront doors, chatting to those around them, laughing and pointing to things in the windows. Most of the cafés with patio seating were filled to capacity; it was still warm for October in the city. Some of the patrons ate salads, some sipped on hot tea or coffee, still others ate specialty sandwiches or pasta. As Katie passed them, she inhaled, drinking in the aroma of coffee. Coffee was one of her passions.

Along the way she purchased flowers from a vendor, and, enticed by the scent emanating from a hot pretzel stand, she purchased a pretzel.

"How long have you had your stand here?" she asked the vendor while pulling two bills from a wallet she had thrown into the shopping bag.

"Five years," the man answered.

"Since the cleanup?"

"A little after. Certainly doesn't look like it did in the old days. Not that a lady such as yourself would know."

Katie looked down, suddenly uncomfortably aware of the expensive suit she wore. "It's very. . .um. . . ."

"Yuppie-fied?"

Katie laughed. "Yes. Yuppie-fied. That's a good word for it. Did you live here before?"

"Yeah. About ten years before they cleaned it up. Ran a dry cleaning service down on Fifty-third. Mr. Giuliani really meant business, didn't he? Just why, who cares? Not me, that's for sure. I just know the neighborhood is. . .what would be the word here. . .*gentrified* enough that my landlord took down that old, black security gate around the entrance to my building and several others have done the same."

Katie looked around. "It looks nice. It really does." Then she smiled. "I noticed that you even have a Starbucks."

He grinned back at her. Another customer approached and ordered a cheese pretzel. Katie stood silent, taking small bites of her pretzel and continuing to take in the sights and sounds around her. When the customer had completed her purchase and walked away, the vendor turned his attention back to Katie. "Can I get you anything else?"

"No. I'm just enjoying my pretzel. I see most of the bars are gone." Katie shifted the shopping bag from her hand to her shoulder.

"Bars, hookers—begging your pardon. Every so often you see a bum, but, hey, they're everywhere. They're sleeping on the steps of the New York City Public Library for pity's sake."

"Sadly."

Another customer approached. Katie reflected on the number of vagrants who had littered the streets in the days when she had lived here, and when the customer left, the vendor said, "What'd you say?"

"I said it was sad about there always being vagrants."

"Oh. Yeah. But we have some fine eateries and wine shops—not liquor stores, mind you—nice places where you can get wines and cheeses and fancy crackers." Then he laughed out loud.

Katie really laughed then. "You're funny."

"Ah, it's just the way of it." Then he pointed straight ahead. "If you go up a block and turn left, you'll see blocks and blocks of the buildings that were burned out—you know, vacated—and renovated. One bedrooms that were slums back in the day are going for nearly two thousand a month now."

Katie pressed her lips together. That was her old street. . .her old slum. . . .

"Mercy." The shopping bag was getting heavy.

"Looking for something in particular?"

"Yes, actually. Do you remember a place called Private Dancer?"

"What does a lady like you know about a place like that?"

Katie took another bite of her pretzel and swallowed hard. "I'm a reporter for a local magazine. Thought I'd do a piece on the cleanup." The lie came easy. Too easy.

"And on Private Dancer?"

She looked the man in the eyes. "That's right. Someone I interviewed mentioned it." She wondered how many lies she would be able to tell in one day before she stopped counting?

"Private Dancer's not there anymore. None of the clubs are; they ran them out. But the man who used to run it. . .I knew him before he died—"

"Leo died?"

The vendor's eyes narrowed. "How'd you know his name?"

Katie paused before answering. "I remember the name from the girl I interviewed."

"I imagine." The man didn't sound convinced, but he continued. "Yeah, he died. But his son opened a dance club in Chinatown." Another customer interrupted them.

When he had left, Katie quickly interjected. "Where might I find it? The son's club?"

The man fiddled with his money belt before looking up. "You're really going in there?"

"I want to interview the son, if I can."

"Oh, I'm sure Sharkey would love to be interviewed! Yeah. . . ." The vendor chuckled. "It's on Canal Street. Between Little Italy and Chinatown. They call it Mist Goddess."

Katie was down to the last bite of her pretzel. "Thank you for the pretzel."

"No problem."

She glanced around and easily found a trash can where she deposited the pretzel's wrapper and the small napkin she'd wiped her hands on, then began to walk toward the block where she had once lived. She wanted to see the renovations. . .wanted to know if they were as extensive as the one that had been done to her soul.

A lady like you, she thought. *I'm not such a lady. I just managed to escape. . .*

. . .from Private Dancer to the West End Men's Club to the law firm of Mosley, Carter & Troup, where she had met the man who would truly take her away from her old life; her husband, William Benjamin Webster. *Ben.*

Those first few years in New York City had been bleak indeed, but in other ways they were of watershed importance. The turning point that followed made her always appreciate what she had, never taking anything for granted.

When she was eighteen, she had run away from her hometown of Brooksboro, Georgia, and like thousands of other young people were known to do, ended up in New York City, where life offered few career choices to girls with no education and few skills. She hadn't wanted to dance, but it was easy money and, unlike the streetwalkers, she didn't have to do anything she didn't want to do. They were a class unto themselves, these dancers.

She'd tried to keep the hard truths from Ben, but in the end, she learned that he had known the truth after all. Her pattern of hiding the truth from people, most of whom were actually superficial acquaintances rather than friends, had even carried over to her "surprised by joy" relationship with Ben.

After Ben's disappearance, his cousin, Cynthia, told her that he'd hired an investigator before they married. Unbeknownst to her, the truth about her shadowy past had been exposed. Still, Ben loved her. The fact that they had never broached the subject of her unsavory background seemed like the easy way out, and it made her feel comfortable at the time. Deep down, she began to realize she couldn't truly move on without leveling with this man who meant everything to her. . .and for that she still harbored a dull gnawing chagrin that was impossible to shake. The failures and indiscretions of her past were somewhat overshadowed by her lack of courage, fueled in part by a fear of loss. . .the loss of one who meant more to her survival than the air she breathed. The irony was not lost on her.

Even now she didn't want to be in this part of Midtown, just around the corner from the glitz and lights of the most famous square in the world. To her, the cleanup was just paint on sin. In spite of it, she could still smell the past, mingling with the faint scent of urine. Try hard as they may, Mr. Giuliani's cleanup team couldn't scrub that away. Too much of it had been left in the cracks of the sidewalks and between the cement and the buildings. Drunks, whores, and vagrants don't care where they are when nature calls. They just go.

Completing her self-guided tour of the old neighborhood, she walked back to where her chauffeur waited for her and told him to drive to Canal Street.

"Mrs. Webster? Canal Street?" From his place in the front seat, Simon turned his nearly shaved blond head and looked at her. At twenty-nine, he was ruggedly handsome in a bullish sort of way. He looked intimidating—more like a bodyguard than a driver—but Katie knew what a teddy bear he could really be. Still, she wouldn't want to be on the other side of a fight against him.

"Canal Street, Simon. It's between Little Italy and Chinatown."

"Yes, Ma'am, I know—"

"The club is called Mist Goddess. Look it up on the laptop you keep up there if need be."

"But Mrs. Webster—"

"Don't ask any questions, Simon." The tone in her voice changed. "Just look it up, please."

She wasn't usually so brusque, especially with Simon, but she had to stay true to her purpose, the purpose she had been led to since hearing about the death of her former boss, Mr. Mosley. Mr. Mosley, who had lifted her out of the West End Men's Club to his law firm, enabling her, finally, to change her life.

As Simon wove in and out of the city traffic, Katie reflected back to Mr. Mosley's funeral where Mrs. Mosley had approached Katie and whispered in her ear, "Don't forget what he did for you. Do it for someone else. That will be your way of paying him back, my dear."

Katie had managed to hold back her tears until she slipped into the privacy of her limo; then they came like a torrent. It took her days to comprehend what Mrs. Mosley had said to her. . .days to fully understand. . .and then she knew all too well what she was to do. Go back to the neighborhood and bring some other young girl out of the shadows and into the light.

Only there were no shadows in the old neighborhood, and now she was on Canal Street at the entrance to Mist Goddess, still holding her shopping bag with the flowers peeking out coyly from the top. If the outside advertising was true, the club was what was known in the business as a cage club, where most of the dancers performed in cages away from the patrons. *Good,* Katie thought. Her job here would be easier. She took a deep breath and opened the door.

The room was well lit; it was only three in the afternoon and the sign outside indicated the club opened at five. The old but familiar scent of ammonia, beer, and vomit permeated the room. Music blared. Last night's cigarette smoke lingered in the air, casting a haze across the room. A man was standing on top of a bar stool in the center of the room adjusting a light. Another was pulling chairs off the tops of the tables and shoving them underneath. Two bartenders, one male and one female, were stocking up for the evening. A large young man Katie assumed to be a bouncer approached her. "Too old, Lady," he said.

"Excuse me?"

"You're too old for an audition. You're good looking, but you're too old."

Katie squared her shoulders. "I'm not here for a job."

"What are you here for?" The man crossed his arms over his massive chest.

"Is Sharkey here?"

"Who wants to know?"

"I want to know." Years in the business had taught Katie one thing: You have to be tough when you are dealing with the tough. From the corner of her eye she saw the bartenders come to a stop in their work. *Ringside seat,* Katie thought.

"Who are you?" He shifted his weight from a full stand, to his left foot, then to his right, and then back to both feet.

"Someone who used to know his father."

"Oh, yeah? What's his father's name?" His chin jutted forward.

"Leo. Leo was his father's name." Katie's chin did the same.

The man paused. "Hold on. I'll go get him."

A few minutes later the bouncer returned with a man Katie had no problems believing to be Leo's son. Like his father, Sharkey was a bit of a greaser. He was short and small. His hair was dark, slicked back, and curling on the ends. His eyes were a little too wide set, he had a large mole near his chin, and a cigar was secured between his teeth.

"You want me?"

"I knew your father," Katie said by way of an introduction. "My name is Katie."

The cigar came out of his mouth as he gaped up at her. "Egad, how tall are you?"

22

Katie sighed. The age-old question.

"You're too old, but I wouldn't mind an audition just to see what you can do." His smile was crooked, and his eyes glazed over in hopeful anticipation.

Katie stood firm and cocked an eyebrow. "I'm not here for an audition. Like I said, I knew your father."

Sharkey popped the cigar between his teeth and crossed his arms as he examined Katie again. "Yeah, yeah. I remember you. You and that other girl. . .what was her name. . .Abby. . .came in about the same time?"

"That's right." Katie remembered him, too. But she recalled a boy who wasn't allowed past the front room and never allowed in the establishment after certain hours.

"Man, I used to have some wild thoughts about you." He puffed on the cigar a few times, blowing the smoke directly toward her face.

She didn't flinch. "Save the compliment. That's not why I'm here."

"So what can I do for you then? My old man's dead you know."

"Yes, I heard. I'm sorry."

"For what? You here for money. . .nah, you aren't here for money. What'd that suit cost you?" This century's answer to Napoleon laughed and stroked her sleeve. "Nice. Nice."

Katie felt like white trash. After all these years, men like Leo and Sharkey could bring her back to Private Dancer and Hell's Kitchen by speaking but a few words. She moved her arm away from his touch. She had to stay focused. "I want to see your girls."

The bouncer laughed then. Sharkey turned around and looked at him. "Don't you have somewhere to be? Something to do? Do I pay you to be my shadow?"

The man hung his head and walked off. Sharkey returned his attention to Katie. "Now why don't you tell me what you would want with my girls?"

"I have some gifts for them," Katie said, indicating the shopping bag.

"What kind of gifts?" Sharkey leaned over as if to steal a peek.

"Cosmetic gifts."

"What for?"

"Can't a woman do something nice for another woman?"

"No."

"Sure we can." *Don't play games with me, Sharkey. I know too much about people like you.*

"You want them to come up here? They can't. They're busy getting ready."

"I'll go to the back. I have no problems with that."

Sharkey looked up into her eyes. "Yeah. Yeah. I 'magine you wouldn't. But only for about ten minutes, you hear? And I get to go back there with you. No funny business."

Katie felt her face flush. Apparently, Sharkey was just like his father; any excuse to be in the dressing room would do. "Let's go," Katie said.

Sharkey eyed her one last time. "No funny business," he repeated.

Katie smiled slowly. "You've already said that."

"I wanna make sure you heard it."

She merely stared down at him. "I heard. Would you be so kind as to lead the way?"

Sharkey Garone removed the cigar from between his teeth one last time before turning toward the back. "Follow me, Lady. Right this way."

CHAPTER ONE
Monday, December 3, 2001

Katie wanted to go home. She simply wanted to go home.

She sat primly at her desk—Ben's desk—across from her brooding general manager, James Harrington, and the young but savvy comptroller, Byron Spooner. She glanced at her Vivian Alexander desk clock and sighed. It was barely after nine o'clock, and already she felt as though she'd put in a full day. Meetings with James Harrington did that to her.

Eighteen months ago, after her husband disappeared, Katie had begun to shoulder the responsibilities of president and CEO of The Hamilton Place hotel chain. Initially she'd been as clumsy in her new position as a sweet bride on her wedding night, but eventually she'd taken hold of the reins and done what, she felt, was a remarkable job.

And it was an enjoyable job, with the exception of the dreaded weekly meetings she was forced to endure with her GM, a silver-haired, handsome, sophisticated man, who made no efforts to hide how he felt about Katie taking over Ben's position at THP since. . .the accident, and whose job was to bring her up-to-date on all events occurring in the hotel, no matter how minor. They covered everything from employee changes to convention bookings, and, joined by Mr. Spooner, the three of them often bounced around ideas for the future. She had similar meetings with the

GM of every hotel in the chain, usually by phone, but these—at the flagship—were especially stressful to her.

Still, the meetings are part of my job.

When Katie stepped in as acting president, it had been purely by default, and her transition from adoring wife to executive had not been an easy one. There were the legal battles—not only did she stand to inherit Ben's share of the business if he were dead, but he had made her an ex-officio member of the board—and she had dealt with vehement opposition from James. He had protested fiercely during the board meeting where the decision had been made, basing his opposition on how little she knew about the hotel industry. But Katie had pointed out that Ben was most likely not dead—would be home soon—and the business should be disrupted as little as possible. Therefore, she would only be acting as an interim CEO for a short period until he returned.

But it wasn't very soon at all. An entire year and a half had gone by, and Katie's second Christmas as president was looming ahead of her. New York City had prepared itself in a soaring display of recovery and resiliency after the attack it endured just months before when the World Trade Center was destroyed by terrorists. Rockefeller Center lit its famous tree; Saks, Macy's, and Lord & Taylor had decorated their storefront windows to holiday perfection. The good Lord Himself sent an early dusting of snow on the first day of December. But other than the usual Christmas banquet served in Bonaparte's, the hotel's famous restaurant, and the elaborate seasonal tree, ornaments, and greenery, nothing special had been prepared.

She turned to James. "Mr. Harrington, I believe Prime Minister Blair is expected to arrive soon?"

"In two weeks."

"Is everything in order?"

James Harrington's face remained stoic. "Of course."

"Security?"

"I've had our normal security measures increased by one hundred percent. In addition to his usual staff, Mr. Blair will be well watched by two members of our security team."

"We can't be too careful, especially after September," Katie remarked. "What about security agents posted in the lobby at all times?"

Harrington nodded. "I've already spoken to the head of security about that."

"And it's been arranged?"

"Of course."

"Very good. I'll leave this matter in your reliable hands. Now, gentlemen, I'd like to talk to you a moment about Christmas. I want to do something special this year," Katie now announced to the two men sitting across from her desk.

"Define special." James's voice was arrogant and haughty.

Katie slid her palms across the burgundy leather inset of the desk top before she spoke, which gave her reassurance to say what was on her mind. As she moved her arms forward, her Chanel suit tightened over her square shoulders, revealing a stunning—albeit deceiving—picture of relaxed sophistication. Two years ago, she had worn silk pantsuits or linen skirt ensembles. Smart, but not imposing or authoritative. If she was to hold down the fort until Ben's return, she must—at the very least—appear to be both. And she knew the way she dressed on the outside said a lot about how she felt inside. In the past two years she had grown closer to her family, deepened her faith, and become a powerhouse in the business world. Initially referred to as William Webster's wife, she was now—at least professionally—Katharine Webster, president and CEO of The Hamilton Place. Her letterhead said so.

In an effort to gain support, Katie looked to Byron, who had remained a loyal friend over the past eighteen months. "The idea came to me when I went to my mother's home in Georgia during the Thanksgiving holidays. She and I were having an afternoon tea with a few of her friends and my girlfriends from high school. And I thought, wouldn't it be lovely to have a mother-daughter tea during the season? Especially in view of the events of the past few months. . .I think families are of paramount importance right now."

Both men looked down.

Katie's lips twitched slightly, in memory of the tragedy. "Of course, this would include grandmothers and granddaughters, mothers-in-law and daughters-in-law. . . . The only requirement would be that they attend as a couple."

"We don't have time to plan anything," James interjected.

Katie took a deep breath and exhaled slowly. "I realize this is very last minute. . .and next year we will have more time. . .but if we get on this right away. . .well, it will be exclusive. We offer tea in the lobby every afternoon, Mr. Harrington. We'll just make this one a little more special—and we'll have it in one of the smaller banquet rooms."

"I am quite certain none of the rooms would be available at this late date."

Katie reached for the phone beside her. "Vickey," she said, when her assistant answered. "Could you call downstairs please and see if any of our banquet rooms are available on any date between now and the 25th of December. . .I want to host a holiday tea in addition to the tea we have each afternoon. . . ." Katie smiled warmly. "Yes, something like The Plaza's, but solely for mothers and daughters, that sort of thing. . .thank you. Let me know what you find out." She replaced the handset of the phone, turned her gaze back to Mr. Harrington and raised her eyebrows.

"What about additional staff?" Mr. Spooner asked. "We don't have anything budgeted for that."

"I can have my girls help."

"Your. . .girls?"

"Yes, Mr. Spooner. The three young women I brought in to work in housekeeping a few months ago."

James looked out the window. "Now there's a point to talk about. Ex-call girls serving tea to the socially elite."

Byron Spooner jerked upright. "Call girls? They were call girls?"

"They were not call girls, Mr. Harrington," Katie interjected, returning her gaze to him.

He looked her in the eye. "May as well have been. I continue to find

28

it difficult to imagine what you were thinking."

His patronizing, condescending indignation nearly caused her to lose her composure. "I was *thinking* I wanted to give them a chance at bettering themselves."

"So you gave them jobs in housekeeping. What a step up."

"Believe me, it is. And I don't intend to stop there." Katie leaned forward, resting her forearms against her desk. "Do you know, Mr. Harrington, that Ashley is an absolute whiz at research and development? Or that Brittany has a mind for sales and fashion. These are two young women who simply lost their way for awhile, who had a bad break and made some wrong choices, but who have all the capabilities of becoming—"

"Their pimp was in here again the other day, you know," Harrington interrupted.

Katie felt her backbone straighten. "What did he say this time?"

"Another scene in the lobby. Fortunately, security was able to escort him to the end of the block before he caused too much of a stir." James pointed a pen he was holding at her. "That's the kind of thing you are going to have to deal with when you bring women like that in here. Pimps in The Hamilton Place."

"He isn't a pimp, Mr. Harrington. Still, he can cause us problems, I'll admit that." This made Sharkey's fifth visit to THP in a little over a month. His threats toward her alarmed security, and Simon never let her go out alone. So far, however, Sharkey hadn't carried out any of the threats. "I'm sure this will all blow over soon."

James leaned over. "See to it that it does."

"Mr. Harrington, are *you* threatening me?"

"No, Mrs. Webster," he retorted, as though her name were a curse word. "I'm not threatening. But as the *president* and *CEO* of this hotel, you must get a grip on what goes on here."

Byron Spooner shifted slightly in his chair and cleared his throat. "Aren't there three girls?" he asked.

Katie looked at him. "Yes. Ashley, Brittany, and Candy."

James rolled his eyes. "The ABCs of THP."

Katie sighed. She was almost too tired to continue this argument any further. "Can we get back to the tea, please?" she asked, just as her desk phone buzzed. "Yes, Vickey," she answered. "Really? How fortunate for us. Thank you." She replaced the handset and smiled across the desk. "Gentlemen, a small reception scheduled for December 16th was cancelled, and one of our banquet rooms opened up not two hours ago."

Byron shifted slightly in his seat as he opened the DayTimer that was resting in his lap. "I think if we begin planning now we can do this. After all, this is December 4th. The 16th is just a week and two days before Christmas and on a Sunday. I can check and get some figures together for you as far as cost. How does that sound?"

Katie smiled. "Thank you, Mr. Spooner. I will leave it up to you to delegate the necessary details, then. Please keep me posted."

"I'll be happy to, Mrs. Webster."

"Mr. Harrington, do you want to be a part of this?" Katie asked, shifting her gaze to the man.

"I am the GM of this establishment, so I suppose I have no other choice. Mr. Spooner would, of course, handle the financial end of things."

"All right then," Katie concluded. "Mr. Harrington, I will leave you with the task of delegation. I will tell the girls they will help with serving. This will be a wonderful opportunity for them to learn about social teas."

"By all means. Let's educate them about *teas.*" The way he said the last word made the very idea sound ridiculous.

Katie bit her tongue and counted to three before speaking again. "Is there anything else we need to discuss today?"

"Should we go ahead and discuss the annual Valentine's Ball?" Byron asked.

Katie closed her eyes for a moment. Her head was beginning to throb. "Mr. Spooner, can it wait one more week?"

Byron pulled a sheet of paper from his portfolio and extended it toward her. "Why don't I leave you with these figures, and we can discuss them after you've had an opportunity to go over them."

Katie smiled in appreciation. "That would be perfect."

"I have one other item," James offered.

"And that would be?"

"Jacqueline's."

Katie felt herself stiffen. Her hands slid from the top of the desk to her lap where one clasped the other. The past owners of Jacqueline's, the upscale fashion boutique located on the first floor of New York's The Hamilton Place, had been the brother and sister business duo who had taken her husband away from her.

Has it only been a year and a half? Katie asked herself. *Ben! Ben! Why haven't you called me? Why haven't you let me know you are okay? And where is Andi?*

A year and a half ago, Katie and her husband had unearthed the notorious business of Bucky Caballero and Mattie Franscella. Though Caballero had owned Jacqueline's and the business did well by itself, his true purpose was to use it as a front for his escort service. Andi Daniels, the beautiful black-Asian woman who managed the store had also served as its "Madame" of sorts. Adding insult to injury, this woman had been Katie's friend. When Ben made the discovery of what really went on at the boutique, he had obtained a confession out of Andi in exchange for protection. At the same time as he placed her on a plane for an undisclosed location, he had sent Katie back to her hometown of Brooksboro, Georgia. This was for more than mere protection for Katie. It provided Katie and her mother, Carolyn Mills Morgan, an opportunity to heal their twenty-five-year estrangement. But while Katie and Carolyn were working out their differences, Ben's car was bombed. He alone had knowledge as to where Andi was located, and since she had not resurfaced in all these many months, Katie assumed she wanted to stay well hidden, an idea she understood all too well. After all, she had disappeared for over twenty-five years before returning to her hometown.

Katie also understood that most people believed Ben to be dead. But she didn't. He had practically told her in his last letter that he was alive.

Where was he?

What's more, where were Bucky and his sister Mattie Franscella, who had owned the large, moneymaking businesses of B. Caballero, Inc., and Jacqueline's? If nothing else, why hadn't they returned to seek revenge on David Franscella's death? Was there anything more James Harrington could possibly bring up about Jacqueline's? What more could it take from her. . .demand of her?

"The owner who took over the lease of the store after Caballero's disappearance has ended his contract and has decided to leave. We already have someone new to lease it." James spoke deliberately.

"I see."

"The new owner. . .a Miss. . ." James shuffled through the papers in his lap. "Zandra McKenzie. . .wants to meet with you at your earliest convenience."

Katie's brow furrowed. "Why me?"

"That's what I wanted to know. She said you two actually knew some of the same people."

"Vickey is my assistant; why didn't she just contact her? Why call you?"

"She didn't call me. I saw her in the boutique—went in to introduce myself—and that's when she told me."

"I see," Katie repeated. "When will she be taking over the store?"

"She already has. She's bringing in a few new lines. The store was closed for a day or two, but other than that, there wasn't a problem."

"When you see her again. . .*if* you see her again. . .tell her to call Vickey. In the meantime, I will call you again tomorrow afternoon about the tea. Now, unless there's anything else?" Both men shook their heads. "I believe we've covered everything that needs to be covered for THP New York." Katie stood. "Gentlemen. Thank you, as always, for your good work."

The men stood. "Mrs. Webster," Byron said with a nod of his head, then turned and headed for the door.

James stood in his place and stared at Katie for a moment before following Byron. When he had closed the door leading to Vickey's office, Katie shuddered. How she despised working with that man!

Katie reached for the phone on her desk and buzzed for Vickey. Instead of answering, Vickey walked through the door. She was clutching a bottle of Ibuprofen in one hand and a frosty bottle of cola in the other. Without a word of instruction between them, she walked over to the wet bar, reached for a small Waterford glass, poured the cola, then returned to where Katie had plopped into Ben's large, black leather chair. Vickey extended the pain reliever and the drink, which Katie took like an obedient child.

"Thank you," she whispered, closing her eyes.

"You are quite welcome. What did the old stick-in-the-mud have to say this time?"

Katie shook her head. She didn't want to have to repeat it.

"I can imagine what he had to say about the Christmas tea."

Katie opened her eyes and rolled them.

Vickey laughed. "That excited, huh?"

Katie smiled. Vickey was not only her assistant as she had been Ben's, but her dear friend. "When I gave the responsibility to Byron, James immediately rose to the occasion."

Vickey patted her on the shoulder. "Just think, a year ago if you'd suggested the tea and Mr. Harrington had argued against it, you would have allowed him his way."

Katie grinned facetiously. "Aren't I just the bad ole boss?"

Vickey crossed her arms. "Not so bad. Your husband will be proud."

Katie sighed at the thought. "Oh, Vickey, where do you think Ben is?"

Vickey returned to the wet bar and retrieved the empty soda bottle. "I don't know," she whispered.

Katie's eyes followed her. "Keep believing with me, Vickey. I have to believe. Otherwise I won't be able to endure this."

Vickey swung around and faced the wife of the man she had sworn her professional allegiance to so many years ago. "Of course, I believe he's still alive. William Webster is a wise man, not a foolish one. If he has stayed away this long, it must be for good reason." Vickey, like family, friends, and business acquaintances, used the formal name "William" while Katie always called her husband "Ben."

Katie stood and walked over to the high-rise window overlooking the seemingly endless panorama of the city. "If only we knew what might have happened to Andi—where Ben might have sent her."

"You know as much as I do, Katie. Andi flew with William to Atlanta before he returned here. From there, he could have put her on a plane for anywhere in the world." She paused. "My offer to hire another private investigator still stands."

"I know. . .I know. . .I don't know." Katie couldn't help but laugh. "I guess I should just do it."

"Why haven't you?" Vickey leaned against the counter of the wet bar.

Katie smiled. "You've been wondering that for the longest time, haven't you?"

"Me and every other staff member."

Katie walked back to her desk and picked up a framed photograph of Ben and her together. It was an impromptu shot, snapped outside a ski lodge in Aspen by a passing guest of the resort.

She smiled at the memory of that moment, then held the photograph to her chest. Even in the frigid cold, Ben's handsome face looked warm and loving. She wanted him as close to her as possible. Until he decided it was safe to return, she would have to settle for his photograph and the note he had left her before his disappearance, an excerpt from a song by Mary Frye and Wilber Skeels.

Do not stand at my grave and weep.
I am not there. I do not sleep.
Do not stand at my grave and cry.
I am not there; I did not die.

Had it not been for the poem, she would not have been able to believe for so long.

"Phil Silver—Ben's friend with the FBI—did what he could in the beginning. After awhile, they have to move on. And you know as well as I do that the two investigators we initially hired came up with little to nothing," she said to Vickey.

"Didn't Phil Silver leave the FBI to become a PI?"

Katie shook her head. "Not so much an investigator—though he does some work on the side. He took a professorship at John Jay."

"The criminal justice college?"

Katie nodded.

"Back to my original question; why not hire another private investigator?"

"I guess I felt as though. . .it meant. . .I don't know, Vickey. . .he's done something underhanded, or something."

"Underhanded? William?"

Katie replaced the photo. "Vickey, *why* hasn't he called?" Tears welled up in her eyes. Vickey crossed the room and wrapped Katie in her arms.

"Shh. This is no way for the president of a five-star hotel chain to act."

Katie nodded. "No, but this is how the wife of a missing man acts."

"Katie, let me call an investigator for you. Please. Maybe we can find Andi, and maybe she knows something."

Katie stepped back. "What would she know?"

"I don't know. But maybe William said something to her in Atlanta. Who knows?"

"*Who* indeed. Vickey, did you know about Sharkey coming in again?"

Vickey nodded. "I didn't want to alarm you, Katie. His threats are becoming more and more. . .how can I say this. . .*vivid.*"

"What do you mean?"

"He's describing in detail what he's going to do to you if he catches you out alone. He wants his girls back, Katie."

"Not really." Katie shook her head knowingly. "It's his pride that's been wounded. Girls are easy to get."

"I think you took three of his best."

Katie nodded. "I don't want the media to get a hold of this, but pretty soon he'll probably get smart enough to call them." She looked away, continuing in her thoughts. *Then everyone will know the truth about me, too. About my past.*

Vickey placed her hand on Katie's arm. "Don't even think about it, Katie. You've got enough to worry about right now without adding something else to it."

An hour later, Katie was at her desk, going over the monthly financial report from her comptroller, when she heard a light tap on the door. Then it opened just a crack.

"Katie?" It was Vickey.

Katie looked up. "Yes, Vickey."

"May I come in?"

Katie gave a look of surprise. "Of course. Why not? And what is that mischief I see in your eyes?"

Vickey stepped in; her right hand was behind her back.

"What are you hiding?" Katie's eyes narrowed.

"Apparently, an early Christmas gift." Vickey swung her arm around, displaying a small package, wrapped in silver foil paper and topped with a silver and gold bow. "A delivery boy just brought it in. Who do you think it's from?"

Katie stood and extended her hand for the package. "I don't know!" She felt like a little girl again. "Maybe Mama. Mama used to do things like this."

Katie remembered the Southern Christmases of her past. The twelve days before Christmas were filled with wonder and delight. Carolyn used to hide little packages around the house. She and Katie made a game out of finding them. When Katie came down for breakfast, she would find a small note with clues to finding that day's package. If school was still in session, she had the long hours to try to decipher the note. While on Christmas break, she would call Marcy, her best friend in the whole wide world, ask her over, and the two of them would scurry around like little detectives trying to find their gifts. On those occasions, there would be two gifts: one for her and one for Marcy. Carolyn had always treated Marcy like a second daughter, and Roberta, Marcy's mother, had done the same with Katie.

Katie took a deep breath and sighed. How she missed those days, especially around the holidays. She especially missed Marcy, now more than ever.

"Well, aren't you going to open it?" Vickey asked.

Katie jumped slightly. "Oh! Yes." She gently slipped the bow away from the box, then popped the tape with a manicured nail.

Vickey shifted one hip. "Oh, for goodness sakes."

Katie smiled. "It's part of the fun, Vickey. Opening a gift slowly really prolongs the excitement. The moment is only that: a moment. Why rush times like these?"

The wrapping paper fell away, landing on top of Katie's desk and the neglected financial report. Katie cupped a mid-sized black box in her hand. She lifted off the top to reveal a black velvet jewelry box. "If Mama is behind this, she's outdone herself," Katie whispered.

"Open it. Open it."

Katie did, then gasped. "My gracious!"

"What is it?" Vickey came around to the other side of the desk. "Oh, my goodness. Is there a card?"

Katie looked at the wrapping and bow, then inside the tiny box. "No note."

"What is it? I mean, what is the stone? Are those *diamonds?*"

Katie shook her head. "I don't know." She let the top of the jewelry case snap shut as she reached for the phone and dialed. Moments later, her mother answered.

"Hi, Mama."

"Katie! What are you doing calling me in the middle of the day? Why aren't you at work? Are you ill?"

Katie smiled briefly. They had become estranged when Katie ran away as a teenager and had reconciled as adults, and it felt good to banter with her mother again. But now was not the time. "I am at work, and no, I'm not ill. Mama, did you send me a gift today?"

"Noooo."

"Are you certain?"

"Katie, I would certainly know if I'd sent you a gift."

Katie shook her head slightly. "I know. I'm sorry."

"Why do you ask?"

"Someone has sent me the most exquisite pearl and diamond necklace."

"Is it real?"

Vickey retrieved the case from Katie's hand and opened it again. "Reminds me of Princess Diana's tiara," she said to no one in particular.

"I think so, Mama," Katie answered, peering over the top of the opened case. "I don't know. I think I'll take it to Mr. Simmons at Tiffany's. Ben always trusted him. He'll tell me."

"Maybe it even came from there."

"No. If it came from there, it'd be in a little blue box. I'll let you know what I find out."

"Call me later."

"I will."

Katie hung up the phone and stepped around her desk. "I'm going to see Mr. Simmons."

"Now?"

"Yes."

"I take it your mother didn't send it."

"No." Katie reached for her cashmere coat and slipped it over her arms, adjusting it around her throat. "I hate the thought of going out in this weather."

"Don't be silly. It's a balmy twelve degrees out there."

Katie smiled again, but only briefly. "Who would do something like this?"

Vickey handed Katie the velvet box, and Katie's eyes fixed on hers. The answer was clear, and they both knew it. They only knew of one person who would ever pour such extravagance over Katie, and he was dead. Or presumably so.

Katie took a quick breath and exhaled. "I'll be back soon."

Katie stood in the warmth of Tiffany's, handing Mr. Simmons the box. "I know it doesn't come from here. But can you tell me something about it?"

Mr. Simmons gingerly opened the box. "Ah, lovely."

Katie smiled. "It is. But I don't know where it came from. . .or more importantly, *who* it came from."

"Just a moment," the diminutive, balding Englishman said. "Let me have a look."

Katie watched him disappear through a door behind him. She turned to look about the luxury that filled the glass and wood. Even after all these years of living in the city, and after all the times of opening the coveted blue-boxed gifts from Ben, the thrill of Tiffany and Company remained just that. A thrill.

"Mrs. Webster?"

Katie swung around to see Mr. Simmons standing before her, extending the box.

"They're real, my dear, though not flawless. The pearls are Akoya cultured and of fairly good diameter, and the diamonds are of good quality. But, as I said, they are not exceptional with regard to color and clarity."

Katie took the box and tucked it into the pocket of her coat. "Thank you for your honest assessment. Do you have any idea where they might have come from?"

"Have you tried Saks?"

"No. I came to you first for your opinion."

Mr. Simmons smiled. "Apparently, Mrs. Webster, you have a secret admirer."

Katie didn't return the smile. "Any idea how much this might be worth?"

"An educated guess?"

"Yes."

"Only a guess, mind you."

"I understand."

"Four to five thousand."

"Dollars?" The amount caught Katie by surprise. "Of course, you mean dollars. My goodness. What I mean to say is, no one I can think of would be so extravagant in their gift giving. Especially for no apparent reason. Not anymore, anyway." Katie looked down.

"I wish you luck, Mrs. Webster," Mr. Simmons said respectfully.

"Thank you, Mr. Simmons. I suppose I'll walk down to Saks."

"Your driver is not with you on such a day as this?"

"Yes, but it seems silly to drive a few blocks. I could use the walk to figure this out anyway."

"Take care, then. I'd keep my hand in my pocket if I were you. The crowds out there are already madding."

" 'Far from the madding crowd's ignoble strife. . .' " Katie quoted.

"Ahh, Thomas Gray," Mr. Simmons said with a knowing nod. "Great English poet."

"Indeed. Thank you again."

Katie left the renowned store. She informed Simon of her plans, asking him to follow her in the car while she walked. Heading toward Saks and Company, she looked up at holiday garlands and wreaths hung from the third-story windows and trios of miniature trees perched on second-story windowsills. Directly across the street, at Rockefeller Center, scores of visitors ducked their heads against the blistering cold to stroll toward the famous tree and skating rink. She glanced over briefly, then pushed open the door leading into one of her favorite stores.

"Mrs. Webster." A young female attendant, dressed in black slacks and the classic red blazer, properly addressed Katie as she entered.

"Jenny, I see you're here greeting the holiday shoppers as usual."

Jenny smiled a smile of perfectly straight, white teeth. "I have to earn enough for college, Mrs. Webster."

"You're a senior this year, aren't you?" Ben had taught Katie the importance of noting the faces and names of everyone, no matter their position in life. "It keeps us in our places as human beings," he had told her. "And it lets them know we really do care."

Now, Jenny nodded as another set of customers came into the store. "Yes. Marketing."

Katie patted Jenny on the arm. "Jenny, come to see me when you can. We need to talk about your future. I may have a position for you when you're done if you're interested."

"Thank you, Mrs. Webster. I'd like that. Are you looking for something special today?"

A passing shopper bumped into Katie, made apologies, and kept going. "Goodness, it's busy, isn't it? Yes, I need to see if a necklace delivered to my office today came from here."

Jenny turned slightly to the right. "Just over there, Mrs. Webster. Then again, you know where the jewelry department is, don't you?"

"I should say so, Jenny." Katie moved forward and to the right, past the floor-to-ceiling columns wrapped in white branches secured with red ribbons and decorated with ornaments, to the center of the fine jewelry department. An employee Katie had never seen before approached her.

"May I help you?"

"Yes." Katie pulled the box out of her coat pocket. "Can you tell me if this is a part of your merchandise?"

The employee took the box from Katie and opened it. "Yes, it is. As a matter-of-fact, I sold this just a few hours ago. Are you Mrs. Webster?"

Katie's eyes widened. "Yes, I am. Do you know who purchased this for me?"

The employee smiled knowingly. "Of course, Mrs. Webster, though I'm not so sure I should give it away."

"Please. It's important that you do."

"All right, if you insist. It was your husband who purchased it for you."

Katie's face blanched as a rush of emotion poured over her. "Are you certain?"

"Yes, Ma'am. It was definitely your husband. The man *said* he was your husband."

CHAPTER TWO

Katie grasped the counter for support. "Where?"

"What? I mean, Ma'am?" The young attendant behind the jewelry counter seemed at a loss, and the bewilderment showed in her face. "Ma'am, do you need help?"

"Where. . .how? Tell me!" Katie knew her words made no sense, but she couldn't seem to get her thoughts together. This was the news she had waited to hear; something that confirmed her beliefs about her husband being alive. She hadn't thought he'd choose such a method. Then again, this was Ben. Ben, who showered her with gifts and trips to exotic places. Perhaps he was trying to reach her without shocking her so severely. Is that what he supposed? That walking out of the blue into her office. . .*his office*. . .or their home would shock her any more than this had? Was he here? Was he watching her now; waiting for the right moment to draw her into his arms and tell her he had returned? Her eyes darted around the store, searching for the familiar face, the comb of his hair, the broadness of his shoulders. Anything.

"Is there a problem over here?"

Katie started as an older woman approached the sales clerk from the other side of the cash register corralled within the glass and chrome cases of jewelry.

"I don't know what I did!" The clerk turned in panic.

Katie opened her mouth again, but nothing came out.

"Mrs. Webster, isn't it?" the woman asked.

Katie nodded and gasped for air. The older woman turned to the young clerk. "Quietly now. Let's get Mrs. Webster to the break room."

"Yes, Ma'am."

The two women came around the counter and took Katie by the arms, gently leading her away from the jewelry department and the small crowd of shoppers who had begun to stare in curiosity. "I want you to call for an ambulance," the older woman spoke quietly once they were inside the elevator and the doors had closed in front of them. "Let's make her comfortable first. She's one of our best customers. God willing, we can get to the third floor before someone else gets on."

Katie closed her eyes as she tried to block out the conversation about her as if she were absent; she felt the surge of the elevator as it rose forcefully through the shaft, heard the gentle "ding" of the bell, and the doors opening. Her eyes opened, but she couldn't seem to focus. *Ben. Ben was back. Ben had sent her the necklace.*

Breathe, Katie. Breathe.

"Mrs. Webster, we're going to just go in here. . .right here, Mrs. Webster. . .to the left. . .that's it. Just sit here. Cassie, get Mrs. Webster some water, then call for an ambulance." Katie felt herself being lowered to a large, overstuffed, brown leather chair.

"No, no," she said, having managed to find her voice. "No." She didn't need an ambulance, thank you very much. She was a strong woman. She had endured so much in her lifetime; surely this wasn't going to send her over the edge. She needed to be strong. . .for herself. . .for Ben.

"Mrs. Webster?" The voice seemed to come from within a tunnel.

"Should I get the water?"

"Yes, Cassie, get the water. Mrs. Webster, who may we call? May we call someone for you?"

Katie looked up at the attractive woman with perfectly coiffed blond hair and almond shaped blue eyes. "My driver. My driver should be just outside."

Cassie returned with the water. "Here, Mrs. Webster," she said meekly, reaching for Katie's trembling hand and placing the plastic tumbler in it.

"Oh, Cassie," the older woman said. "We have better glasses than that in here somewhere, surely."

"I'm sorry."

Katie took a sip of the cold water, felt the wetness drench her parched throat. She looked over at the older woman and read the plain name tag that contrasted starkly with the busy Christmas sweater draped fashionably over the older woman's shoulders. *N. Taylor*, it read.

"Ms. Taylor, please," Katie said quietly. "This is fine." She took a deep breath. "Could you have Cassie go out the front door and look for my driver, please? His name is Simon. He's a rather large man sitting in a white limo. I don't think she'll have any problems finding him."

N. Taylor patted Katie's arm, then turned to Cassie, who quickly said, "I've got it. I've got it."

Katie watched as the young woman started out of the break room. "Wait." Katie stopped her.

Cassie turned from the door. "Yes, Ma'am?"

Katie looked expectedly at the young clerk. "Can you tell me—are you certain he was my husband? What did he look like? Was he tall?"

"Yes, he was tall."

"Dark hair?"

"Yes, Ma'am. It was long. Pulled back into a ponytail."

"A ponytail? Ben?"

Cassie shrugged.

"Then again," Katie looked away from the clerk, toward a wall nicely decorated with gold leaf framed mirrors and copies of Monet prints. "He's been gone a long time. . .maybe he let his hair grow out. . .to change the way he looks."

"Ma'am?"

"Mrs. Webster, why don't you allow Cassie to go and get your driver."

Katie turned her attention to N. Taylor. "Of course. Please," she returned her gaze to Cassie. "Thank you, Cassie."

The sales associate nodded, then hurried out the door, leaving Katie alone with N. Taylor, who stepped over to a small chair and drug it next to where Katie sat so that she could sit next to her. Tugging on her wool skirt, she crossed her legs, then rested her elbows on her knees as she leaned over.

"Mrs. Webster, are you certain I can't call an ambulance for you?"

Katie took another sip of water and nodded. "Yes, I'm certain. I've just had a bit of a shock."

"Would you care to talk about it?"

"I'm not sure I should. . .perhaps I should call someone. . .I'm not sure. . .I brought this necklace. . .oh, no!" Katie jumped from the leather chair. N. Taylor rose quickly as Katie threw her hand over her mouth. "I left it on the case!"

"What, Mrs. Webster?"

Katie grabbed for the woman's arm. "Ms. Taylor. I brought in a diamond and pearl necklace that I received by messenger a short time ago. I wanted to know if it had come from here. . .the young girl. . .Cassie. . . she said it did. . .but I left it on the counter! Oh, please, Ms. Taylor. Call down there! I can't lose that necklace!"

"Now, Mrs. Webster. Don't excite yourself. Sit down. I'll call."

N. Taylor watched Katie return to the brown leather chair, then stepped over to a wall phone and dialed the extension for fine jewelry. "Steven? Nora Taylor. I'm in the break room with Mrs. William Webster who left a very expensive piece of jewelry on the counter. . .a necklace of pearls and diamonds. . .well, look for it, please."

"He can't find it?" Katie sat up straight.

"We'll find it, Mrs. Webster. . .Steven, if you can't find it, ask someone to help you. . . . Did you see it at all? Oh, dear. I'll send Cassie back down there as soon as she returns." Nora Taylor replaced the receiver of the phone firmly in place, then turned to Katie. "Don't worry, Mrs. Webster. We'll find it."

Cassie burst into the room with Simon on her heels. "Mrs. Webster, are you okay?" he asked dutifully.

"Cassie, get back downstairs and see if you can't find the necklace. Mrs. Webster left it on the counter."

Cassie let out an audible gasp. "Oh, no. Oh, no. With that crowd?"

Nora grasped Cassie's shoulders firmly and turned her toward the door. "Oh, Cassie, just go!"

Simon reached for Katie, who grasped his strong hand in turn. "Get me out of here, Simon," she whispered near his ear when she had risen to her feet and allowed herself to be supported by his strong arms.

"Yes, Ma'am."

"Mrs. Webster." Nora Taylor was no more than a step behind them. "We'll find your necklace and have it brought to you. I'll personally bring it to you."

Simon turned to look at the doting saleswoman. "Send it to The Hamilton Place," he instructed.

Nora Taylor stopped in her tracks. "I *know* where to send it, young man."

Simon helped Katie into the back of the limo, then straightened and studied her for a moment. She was ghostly pale. Her lips, typically full of color, were drawn thin and white. He noticed her trembling hands, her short, shallow breaths, and how difficult it had been guiding her out of the crowded store, into the icy coldness of the New York City air. She sat in the back of the limousine, as rumpled as she was disconcerted. He frowned at the sight of her, shook his head slightly, then spoke quietly. "I'll get you home, Mrs. Webster."

"Thank you, Simon," she whispered.

As soon as he slipped behind the wheel, he checked to make certain the glass partition was closed. It was, and Katie's eyes were closed, though he noted a single tear slipping down her cheek.

"What happened in there?" he asked no one. He picked up the phone, dialed the number to the hotel, and waited for someone to answer.

"Happy holidays, The Hamilton Place," the phone operator answered.

Simon recognized the voice. "Trina, it's Simon." He glanced in the side mirror and slowly made his way out into traffic.

"Hi, Simon!"

"Let me have Mrs. Webster's assistant, please."

"Sure. Are you all right, Simon?"

"I'm fine, but I need to speak to Vickey."

"Hold please."

Energetic, techno holiday music by Mannheim Steamroller filled the gap between speaking with Trina and being connected to Vickey.

"Mrs. Webster's office."

"Vickey, it's Simon." Simon spoke quietly.

"Simon?"

"I'm with Mrs. Webster. We just left Saks." Simon slowed the car to a stop at a red light.

"Did she find out who sent the necklace?"

"I don't know what you're talking about exactly, but something has upset her terribly. I had to go in and get her. She's pale. She's shaking like a leaf. She keeps saying something about Ben sending a necklace."

"What?"

"She's crying—"

"Crying?"

"Yeah." The traffic light changed to green, and Simon proceeded through the intersection.

"Are you on your way back to the hotel?"

"Yeah, I just wanted you to know before we arrive so you can—"

"I'll call Maggie."

"Yeah, that's what I was thinking you ought to do."

"Hurry, Simon. Hurry home."

CHAPTER THREE
Monday, Late Afternoon

Special Agent Philip Andrew Silver had been one of the FBI's best. At least he liked to think so. Not that he was egotistical or anything remotely close to it. He just liked to think he had done well in his chosen profession. Especially since his career choice had caused such a rift between him and his father.

Logan Silver, a Harvard Law School alumnus, had wanted his only son to follow in his footsteps. And, in some ways, Phil had. Like his father, he had left his home on the Upper West Side of New York City and headed for the hallowed halls of the over three-hundred-year-old Harvard University. His father had patted him on the back and his mother had dabbed around her teary eyes as they stood before the 1969 L71 Corvette Logan had purchased for his son. "Make me proud, Son," Logan had said. "Study hard, make good grades, and call us often. Be sure to speak to Professor Ingram. He and I were in a fraternity together; he'll remember me for sure."

"I will, Dad," he said, shaking his father's hand before turning to his mother for a goodbye kiss on the cheek and her reminder to find a good laundry service.

"For heaven's sake, don't go to a public laundromat," she admonished. "Take your *dirty clothes* to one of those places where they do it for you." She had downplayed "dirty clothes" by whispering them, as if to suggest a whimsical disassociation. Her son would never dirty his clothes.

"I will, Mother."

"And don't drink too much. Your father drank too much in his college days."

"I did not!"

"Yes, you did, but it's neither here nor there," she directed her scolding words toward her indignant husband. "Therefore, please lower your voice."

Phil had lovingly laughed at her. "Heaven forbid anyone should know about *our* dirty laundry."

"Philip, don't be impertinent. I am, after all, your mother."

Phil had leaned over and lovingly kissed a smooth cheek. At forty-three his mother had the soignée charm of a twenty-year-old beauty. "I'm not, Mother," he whispered in her ear. "I love you." He kissed her cheek again and she blushed.

In reality, Logan Silver *did* drink too much. How much he had consumed as a student at Harvard was open to conjecture, but since the rape and murder of Phil's younger sister, Megan, Logan had frequently buried his grief in a decanter of malted Scotch. A very large, crystal decanter of Scotch.

Megan Silver had been only nine years old when she was brutally murdered. Phil remembered the day vividly. He and his sister had accompanied his mother to Central Park. They were going to visit a childhood friend of his, William Webster, and his mother. The two women sat on a park bench chatting merrily while the three children played happily near the lake where the odors and scents from hot dog vendors tantalized them. The three children went for hot dogs, then Megan had wandered off to pick some flowers. She had never returned.

Phil instinctively knew something was wrong when he couldn't find her a few minutes later. He had alerted his mother, who screamed for a policeman. Within half an hour a search was in full force; by that evening it was over.

Phil wasn't sure what the transient in the park had done, but it must have been too horrific to speak of. All he knew at the time was that his sister was dead and a void that could not be filled had taken her place.

It wasn't until he was sixteen that he had learned the truth. He and William were sixteen and attending the same prestigious private school. They had grown closer than ever and were almost inseparable friends. It was William who told him Megan had been raped and strangled with her own shoelaces.

The image haunted him. Finally, in his first year of law school, Phil made a decision that would change his life—and forever cause a rift with his father. The argument had begun the day he had dropped out of Harvard Law School. He had his undergraduate degree and was working toward his Juris Doctorate. Like all first year students, he studied torts, contracts, and criminal law; the latter stirring and renewing his interest in law enforcement. He called the FBI National Headquarters in Washington, D.C., received the information he needed for the sixteen-week training period required by the bureau, then walked to University Hall where he sat near the bronze statue of John Harvard and composed a letter to his parents.

Periodically he paused to look at the statue, whose face—whether gleaming in the warmth of the sun or frozen by winter's ice and snow—always appeared regal and wise. Perhaps he could glean some wisdom from it, or better still, if he touched the tip of Mr. Harvard's shoe (as visitors and students were known to do), he would receive good luck.

He finished the letter, touched the shoe, then ran to a nearby mailbox to drop off his letter. Three days later his father was standing at his dorm door, waving the letter in his face.

"I'll never forgive you," his father had said. To date, even though Phil had left the Bureau for a coveted professor's position at John Jay College of Criminal Justice, he never had.

Now, Phil, his wife Gail, and their two children, Phil, Jr., and Megan, made their home in Long Island where Gail worked as a CPA and their children went to school and participated in competitive sports. And he loved everything about their life in New York, with the exception of the never-ending antagonism from his father.

The phone on Phil's desk rang, bringing him back to present realities. "Silver," he answered.

"Phil? Dan."

"Dan, how's it going?"

"It's going. The reason for my call is that I understand you're leading a special workshop at John Jay."

"Yes, as a matter of fact, I am." Phil pulled open a drawer of his orderly desk and peered into it.

"What's it on?"

"The Internet and Children. Not my favorite topic, but somebody's got to do it." He closed the drawer and shuffled about the papers and the crystal bowl containing pieces from an old Clue game on his desk. Clue had been his sister's favorite game and the pieces came from the very game they had played as children.

"When does it start?"

"Ahh—Tuesday night. It's going to run three hours. Why? Planning to go?"

"Yeah, as a matter of fact, I was. What are you doing over there? You sound distracted."

"I had a stick of gum here a minute ago." Phil moved the framed photograph of his son's high school swim team, taken just after they had won Nationals the year before. "Oh. Here it is. I knew I had a piece somewhere on this desk." He pulled the gum from the wrapper, folded it three times, then popped it into his mouth. "You were asking?"

Dan laughed. "What time next week?"

"Seven. Seven to ten. It'll be good to see you there. How's Carol?"

"Carol's good, thank you. The chemo is over, and her hair is beginning to grow back."

Phil shook his head. "I think of you, often, Dan. I really do. What the two of you have been through. . .I can only begin to imagine."

"I hope that's all you have to do," Dan said. "She's going back in for reconstruction soon. Hopefully that will bring back some of her self-confidence. I've never seen such a strong woman brought down so quickly."

Phil nodded. "Let's have dinner soon, the four of us."

"Sounds good. Maybe before the holidays descend on us, huh?"

"Sounds good. If not, Merry Christmas."

"Yeah, and a Happy Chanukah to you, too."

Phil chuckled as he hung up the phone, then began the laborious process of research on his desktop computer. The connection was slower than ever that afternoon. He checked his watch. It was getting late, but he needed to finish what he was doing before he went home.

"Knock, knock."

Phil looked up from the computer keyboard. Friend and Bureau Agent John Weaver was standing at the door of his office.

"Weaver, what's up?"

"Got a minute?"

"Sure. How about a cup of coffee, though? I'm nearing the end of my last caffeine fix."

"Sounds good."

Phil pushed away from his desk, slipped his index finger through the handle of his coffee mug, and began to walk toward a faculty break room toward the end of the hall. John sauntered beside him. At six feet, six inches, it was all he could do. There had never been anything graceful about him, least of all his gait. His ears were too big, his hair too thick, his legs too skinny, and his chin too large. He was, as his wife put it, "so ugly you're cute," but she "loved him unconditionally." He was also, as anyone in the Bureau could tell you, a very good agent, especially when it came to missing persons. "I see you still have the pieces to the Clue game in the dish on your desk," he commented as they made their way down the narrow hallway.

"They keep me focused," Phil said by way of explanation. "Sometimes when I was stumped by a case, I'd look at them. . .fondle them. . .until it came together." They passed through the break room doorway.

"Until you find Miss Scarlet in the game room. . .or however it goes?"

Phil laughed. "Something like that. Here we go. Nice black coffee."

John frowned. "How old is it? It looks like oil."

Phil laughed lightly as he poured a cup into the ceramic mug. "Don't be silly. I'm sure it was made today."

John peered into the glass pot. "What time, do you think?"

"No later than six this morning, from the looks of it," he joked. "Do you want a cup or not?"

"I'll pass."

Phil replaced the pot and glanced over to the window. "Want to sit over there?"

"Sounds good."

The men sat at a table near the window overlooking the city. Phil took a sip of coffee as John pulled a piece of paper from his suit coat pocket.

"What do you have there?" Phil asked.

The question caused John to smile, and he waved the paper in front of Phil's face. "Something that's going to make me your best friend for life."

"Oh, yeah?"

"Oh, yeah."

"And just what is that?"

"Remember the missing kid from Long Island?"

"The girl? The fifteen year old?"

"Yeah, her. Her father is Maxwell Griffin—"

"The art dealer."

"Right. The man is convinced his daughter was kidnapped because of a rare piece of artwork he's bringing to his gallery on the Upper East Side."

Phil took another sip of the strong coffee.

"I still think the girl's a runaway, but that's neither here nor there," John interjected his opinion.

"The suspense is killing me. What does this have to do with me?"

"Stay with me, here. I was at the gallery yesterday—nice place, by the way, if you like art, and I know you do—talking to the gallery's curator, when a man walks in. The two of them—the curator and the man—locked eyes, and immediately I knew something was up."

"An agent's instinct."

"Exactly. The curator told the man he'd be with him in a moment. . . to wait in his office. The man didn't say a word. He just turned around and walked away. I asked the curator a few more questions about the painting, then went home. The exchange between those two stayed with me though. . .all through dinner. . .even when my wife and I were trying to relax over a rented movie, you know, the one with Julia Roberts and Brad Pitt."

"*The Mexican.*"

"Yeah. Anyway, I told myself there was something awfully strange about that man. He looked familiar but unfamiliar, you know what I mean?"

"Like someone you know, but maybe this guy is shorter, or taller or has red hair instead of black. Something like that?"

"Something exactly like that. Only in this case, I think it was the man's beard. So today I went over to Deb Lipscomb's office—"

"In Composites?"

"Yeah."

"Now I'm really on the edge of my seat."

John grinned. "Good thing. You may want to slide back though. I don't want you to fall to the floor when you see what I've got for you."

Phil unconsciously slid back an inch.

"I gave Deb a description, she entered the data into her computer and it drew him to perfection." John unfolded the paper and slapped it onto the tabletop.

Phil leaned over and set his mug next to the drawing of a broad faced, handsome man with dark hair and a thick, trimmed beard. He furrowed his brows. "Who is this?" he asked, looking back to John, who was pulling another folded piece of paper out of his pocket.

"If this doesn't make your day, I'll buy your dinner tonight."

Phil reached for the paper as John continued. "I asked Deb to have the computer print out the man again, but without the beard—"

Phil fully opened the paper, then jumped up from his seat, knocking the chair to the floor.

"Yep," John said proudly. "Correct me if I'm wrong, but I'd have to say the man in the gallery was Mr. Bucky Caballero."

CHAPTER FOUR
Monday, Late Night

"Burning the midnight oil?"

Sixteen-year-old Philip Andrew Silver Jr. sat hunched over his bedroom desk. Books of various sizes were stacked up and opened around him; papers were scattered, some secured under his forearms and elbows. In the glow of his computer monitor, his father could see his son's dark brown hair—spiked and damp after a recent shower. Even in the dim light, Phil Sr. could see the countless swimming trophies, medals, and ribbons displayed on the desk's hutch. They were token reminders of the countless workout hours put in by this diligent young man who had an affinity for sports of any kind.

"Hey, Dad." Phil Jr. turned his head slightly before returning his concentration to the computer screen.

Phil stepped quietly into the small bedroom, which was dominated by twin beds, discarded clothes, a desk, stereo system, and childhood and adolescent memorabilia. He noticed the old and scarred football from his younger days—the one he had passed down to his son nearly ten years ago—resting on the foot of the bed, flexed his hand around it and tossed it to the young man at the desk. "Think fast."

Phil Jr. turned, caught the ball and laughed lightly. "Nice throw."

"How'd you see that coming?"

"What? You were going to bop me in the back of the head?"

"Thought about it." There was a don't-dare-me twinkle in Phil's eyes.

Phil Jr. tilted his head toward the computer screen. "I could see your reflection in the monitor."

"What have you got going there?" Phil nodded toward the work.

"Cal-One."

"Calculus, huh? I always hated it."

"Yeah, well, if I don't pass this class, I'm off the team." Phil Jr. tossed the ball back to his dad, who set it back on the end of the bed. For a brief moment he squeezed it lightly. It reminded him of William and their boyhood years. . .and cold winter days of tossing ball in Central Park.

"How are you doing so far?" he asked, returning his attention to the present.

"Barely scraping by."

"Do you need some help? A tutor?"

"Ah, Dad—"

Phil laughed. "Not into that? Rather be into failing?"

Phil Jr. shook his head. "Dad, Coach says I'm Olympic material. I'm not going to let him down."

Phil gripped his son's shoulder and squeezed. "If I know my son, he's not going to let himself down."

"Nah. . .that either. Not to mention you and Mom. The hours you've poured into this. . ." He smiled a crooked smile and Phil noticed his son's straight teeth and the sincerity of his dark brown eyes. His son. . .his handsome, witty, fiercely competitive, precious son.

"You're a good kid. Speaking of your mother, have you asked her to help you with your studies? She used to be a whiz at math, algebra, calculus. . . ."

"Mom was? She hasn't mentioned it."

"Did you tell her you were in need of some help?"

"No, not really. Are you just now getting home?" Phil Jr. looked at his father suspiciously.

Phil closed his eyes and nodded. "Yeah. It's late, I know, but something interesting happened at work today. I called your mother and told her I'd be late. . .didn't she mention it?"

"No. I guess she figured we'd figure it out. We're just not used to you being out so late since you left the bureau. . .except when you teach the workshops."

"Your sister in bed?"

"Last I saw her she was coming out of the bathroom in her pj's, so I'd have to say yeah. Probably."

"I'll look in on her before I head into our room."

"Have you seen Mom yet?"

"No. I'm assuming she's asleep. Is that gum I see on your desk? Let me have a piece, okay?"

"Sure," his son reached for the pack of Dentyne and handed it to his father and winked. "Leaves your breath kiss-ably fresh."

"I'll remember that." Phil removed the small, rectangle of red gum from its wrapper and popped it into his mouth.

"Are you working on a case again? Is that why you were out so late tonight? Can you talk about it?"

Phil slapped his son on the back and grinned as he stepped toward the door. "Nope. You know better than to ask that."

Phil Jr. chuckled. "You are! Mom's gonna be upset. She'd like to think you're happy enough with your work at John Jay."

"Leave your mother to me."

"One of these days I'm gonna go through your files and write a book."

Phil placed his hand on the doorframe as he turned back to look at his son. "Why don't you just concentrate on Cal-One and the breast stroke? Leave the detective work to me, okay?"

"Okay, Dad." The crooked smile returned. "See ya in the morning."

Phil stepped down the hall to his daughter's room. He opened the door just enough to allow the light from a nearby sconce to penetrate the room, slicing its way over to the bed. His fourteen-year-old daughter, Megan, lay curled under a mountain of linen sheets, a thick blanket, and a puffy down comforter. Only her pixie face was showing—she hated the cold and would wrap even her head in the covers. He smiled briefly, then furrowed his brow. Megan had the misfortune of looking exactly like her namesake. *This is what my sister would have looked like if she had lived,* he thought, though he doubted if young Megan would have had the rich, olive tones his children had inherited from their mother's Native-American background, a fact his parents had never quite recovered from.

Phil closed the door gently and continued to the room he shared with his wife.

He had met Gail during a Las Vegas business trip taken with William Webster in 1975 when both men were in their early twenties. He closed his eyes at yet another memory that now carried a twinge of pain since William's disappearance—and probable death.

"My dad wants me to meet a business associate out there," William had told him. "Want to take a trip out west with me?"

It had been a great trip for the two best friends, made even better one night in the famous, nocturnal city, while dining at Embers in the Imperial Palace. Gail had been their waitress.

Phil had looked back as she took a drink order at another table and had been enchanted. He'd asked her out, and for the next five years, they'd engaged in a long-distance, on-again-off-again relationship. Finally, in 1980, without a call of warning, he had flown out to Las Vegas, rented a car, booked a room, settled in, and driven to a nearby florist. When he walked into the accounting firm where Gail now worked, he toted a dozen red, long-stemmed roses nicely arranged with baby's breath, tied with a large red bow and carefully laid in a white box. He'd also tied a ring in the bow. He presented them to the surprised Gail, while a crowd had gathered around her door. Gail had stood, peered into the box, and begun to weep.

Phil had sobered. "You can't say no."

Gail narrowed her eyes. "Then I guess I'll have to say yes."

The small party at the door cheered as Phil untied the bow that held the ring, then slipped it on her finger and kissed his fiancé. "I'll love you forever," he had whispered against her lips.

"I'll love you even more."

And she had. She had dutifully followed him in a career that had transferred him to Los Angeles, then to Dallas, and finally back home to New York City. In 1986 their son had been born, and in 1988 Gail had given birth to Megan.

Gail had left the door open for him, as she always did when he worked late. He padded over to the white wrought-iron queen bed where she lay sleeping on her back. Her dark hair, which still fell to her shoulders, was fanned out against the cream-colored pillowcase under her head. At forty-six she was still petite, tanned, and toned. The skin on her face looked barely older than their daughter's. She stayed in shape with a vigorous daily routine of jogging before work and a strict vitamin regimen. *Whatever it took,* he thought, *it worked.* He couldn't be more proud of her. She was a dutiful wife, doting mother, and exceptional professional.

Phil's jaw flexed. "Gail?" he whispered as he sat next to her. "Honey?"

Gail's eyes opened, but she didn't smile. "What time is it?"

"Late."

"Then why are you waking me? I have a busy day tomorrow. Didn't you read my note on the kitchen table?"

Phil looked back toward the door, as if in doing so he would see the note several rooms away. "What note?"

"I left you a note on the kitchen table. . .it said. . .oh, never mind."

"No, Honey. Tell me what it said."

Gail raised her eyebrows. "I asked you not to wake me. . .told you I was tired. . .had a busy day tomorrow."

Phil smiled. "Oh. Sorry." He bent down and kissed her brow.

Gail shifted to her side, opened one eye and looked up at her husband. "Goodnight, sweet prince. Tomorrow I may kill you for this."

Phil stood slowly, trying not to disturb her. "At least you still think of me as a prince."

Gail moaned sleepily.

"I'm going to do a little work in the den," he told her.

She closed the one eye. "Uh-huh. Goodnight."

When Phil went back downstairs, his first stop was the kitchen table where, sure enough, he found a note from Gail requesting that he not wake her. He grimaced as he laid it back on the table, walked over to the refrigerator, and poured himself a glass of white wine, taking small sips as he prepared a snack of crackers and cheese. Moments later he was sitting on the plush green L-shaped sofa in the den, staring once more at the information he had pulled and copied with John's help that evening on Brandon "Bucky" Caballero.

Bucky Caballero was the third of four children born to Mino and Janice Caballero. Janice, a pediatrician, had died of brain cancer when Bucky was a boy of twelve. Mino had remarried a mere six months later.

After high school, Bucky attended Cornell University, where he studied business. He eventually received his MBA at Columbia and obtained his certification from the NYU Real Estate Institute. His first job, in 1976, had been with Samuel Jordan & Co. Then in 1978, Mino Caballero had been killed in a tragic automobile accident.

Phil leaned over and pulled another file out of the briefcase he had opened on the glass coffee table. This one was marked: Mino Caballero.

Though it had never been openly disclosed, there were questions surrounding his death. The accident had occurred at approximately two o'clock in the morning. There were no eyewitnesses. It appeared that no other cars had been involved. All the evidence pointed to the fact that Mino Caballero had driven his car over a railed ledge and into the dark abyss below, where the car had exploded on impact with the hard earth. No apparent reason.

As Phil flipped through the pages in the file, he glanced only briefly at the evidence linking Mino to the Mafia. Having studied it so many times over the past eighteen months, he had it memorized anyway. Mino Caballero had grown up in the same Bronx neighborhoods as many of La Cosa Nostra. If there were any evidence of his ever having any desire to leave the mob world behind him, it would have been his studious behavior in school and eventual acceptance into law school where he graduated with honors.

When Mino returned to New York, already married to young Janice, then a pediatric intern, he appeared to be on the right track toward lawful and acceptable social behavior. He began his career by joining a small but promising law firm. However, he soon took on a case involving Paul "Pauly Fi" Fino, a small time thug who had been arrested after beating up a man who hadn't paid up on a game of craps. Later records showed that Pauly Fi worked for the notorious mob hit man Salvador Locascio. A month after Caballero won the case, he set up in his own law firm where, again, he appeared to run a legitimate office.

Nearly five years passed before Caballero began to represent Mafia members charged with tax evasion; among them was Locascio, who was later killed in 1974 outside The Blue Pelican restaurant. Sadly, an innocent mother who happened to be strolling her two-year-old son in front of the restaurant's front door was also fatally wounded. The baby had also suffered a slight wound to his left leg, but had miraculously survived.

The representations were few and scattered, but nonetheless they seemed to pad his already thick pocketbook. In 1974, the FBI had begun to suspect heavy association between Caballero and drug lord, John Castellano. In a now famous sting operation, they had placed a tap on Caballero's home and office phone lines as well as microphones and video cameras in Castellano's "office," the Monroe Social Club. By way of the phone taps, they learned two very important—though unrelated—items of information.

Number one: Mino Caballero was up to his eyeballs in La Cosa Nostra. Number two: his second wife Germaine was having an affair with her attorney. But, in the end, the fragile black widow had managed to inherit all the fortune amassed by Caballero. Phil looked over the notes made by the agent who had tried to find some link between Caballero's death and Castellano. When Agent Reese had approached Mrs. Caballero, she insisted that the department let it rest. "He's dead, isn't he? I mean, what do you think you can do? Bring him back? Besides, won't this endanger me. . .or my poor stepchildren?"

Her poor stepchildren. . .obviously blackballed from their childhood home. . .two of them being the young man Bucky and his sister Mattie. Germaine and her new attorney-husband soon opened Germaine's, a chain of ladies' boutiques located in four- and five-star hotels across the city, but in time they went bankrupt and were bought out by a small dummy corporation owned by Bucky and Mattie.

Phil slapped the file on Mino Caballero shut and tossed it back into his briefcase. He snacked for a few minutes on the crackers, cheese, and white wine before turning his attention back to the file on Bucky.

Bucky and Mattie had done well with their boutique business, now called Jacqueline's, the middle name—his records indicated—of their beloved mother. Apparently, the profits were not enough for the Caballero siblings, even when matched with the money they made from Samuel Jordan & Co.

Again Phil set the file aside and reached for a third file, one marked William Benjamin Webster. His lips involuntarily flinched as his fingertips touched the sharp manila edges. He swallowed hard. Who would have ever thought. . .ever imagined. . .that he would be sitting alone in the dimness of his Long Island home, sipping white wine, eating cheese and crackers, while studying a file on his childhood friend? *Where are you, William? Are you really dead? Or is Katie right? Do you continue to watch us from the shadows of truth? And if so, why don't you call us. . .summon us. . .to join you so we can know what really happened eighteen months ago? Ah, but bless you, dear friend, for leaving behind the envelope of information on the escort service Bucky and Mattie were running out of Jacqueline's.*

Phil now looked down at copies of that information. In the end, Andrea "Andi" Daniels, who William apparently hid before his "disappearance," had managed both the boutique located in The Hamilton Place and the private business. In payment for her safety, Andi provided William with records dating back to the early days when a Ms. Victoria Thomas held her position.

Unfortunately, the day after William's car had been bombed, FBI agents discovered that both Bucky and Mattie had conveniently disappeared, though he didn't think for one minute they were dead. He also didn't believe they were living in the country. His best bet was Canada. Phil knew from his investigation that Caballero loved art—especially French art. If what John Weaver had told him earlier today was true, perhaps Bucky had returned to the city to purchase a piece of rare artwork from the Upper East Side gallery of Maxwell Griffin.

If only Andi were here. Perhaps he could talk to her, get more information out of her than what she'd left behind with William. Suddenly a thought occurred to him. Andi's whereabouts were unknown, but Victoria Thomas might still be in the city. Perhaps someone at THP would know. Perhaps a veteran employee. Perhaps even Katie.

Phil leaned over and popped another slice of cheese into his mouth followed by a slow sip of wine. Draining the glass he made a mental note. *First thing in the morning, go see Katie Webster.*

"Thank you for meeting me at such a late hour, Mr. Kabakjian."

"You are one of our most valuable customers. If you called me in the middle of the night, I'd meet you anywhere. Even at the end of a dark alley."

The man sitting behind the curator's desk smiled. "A dark alley won't be necessary. You don't mind that I'm sitting in your chair do you?"

"Of course not."

"I also placed some music in your sound system. One of my favorite pieces."

"I'm afraid I don't recognize it."

" 'Adagio' from *Spartacus.*"

"It's a moving piece."

"Forceful almost."

"Would you care for a drink?"

"A Tom Collins if you don't mind."

Mr. Kabakjian moved from his position in the open doorway toward the wet bar to his left. In doing so, a full shaft of light penetrated the room, making the dark, bearded man sitting in his office chair all the more visible.

"Close the door, will you, Mr. Kabakjian." It wasn't a request as much as a command.

Maury Kabakjian complied, closing the double doors that led into his office with a quiet grace that complemented his cool demeanor. At fifty-three he was still remarkably handsome, tanned and silver-haired with steely blue eyes. He had grown up in the comforts of modest wealth—which paled in comparison to the man across from him. "I'm sorry you felt you had to leave so abruptly before."

"What was that agent doing here?"

"You recognized him?"

"What do you mean?"

Maury finished preparing the two drinks and brought one over to his desk, setting it on one of the four crystal coasters. "I mean do you know who he is?"

"Should I?"

Maury Kabakjian took a sip of his drink and sat in a nearby chair. "You are a difficult man."

The bearded man smiled, reached for his drink, and took a quick swallow. "So I've been told."

"Yes, he is with the FBI. But it has to do with Mr. Griffin's daughter."

"The young lady who disappeared?"

"Yes."

"What do you think about that, Mr. Kabakjian? Foul play?"

"The girl has simply run off with that older man I saw her with. A gold digger if ever there was one. Did I tell you how I caught them practically making love in her father's office?"

"Appalling. Anyone I know?"

"I doubt it. I don't even know the man. Didn't see his face, really. I'm sure he's scum. Changing the subject, how is Canada, by the way?"

"Cold."

"Horribly cold here, too, as you can see. They're predicting more of last year's blizzards within the next two weeks."

"My work here should be done by then."

"And just what is your work?"

The man smiled again, leaned back in the chair, stretched out his legs and crossed them at the ankles. "Why, I'm here to buy art, Mr. Kabakjian. You know my sister and I have a business up north."

"How is your sister?"

"Mattie is fine."

"Please give her my regards."

"You always cared for my sister, didn't you, Mr. Kabakjian?"

Kabakjian licked his bottom lip before taking another sip of his drink. "She's a remarkable woman. But, when you lived here, she was a remarkable *married* woman."

"Yes. But no longer, as you know."

"Mr. Franscella's murder. . .such a tragedy."

"David was a fool."

"Still. . ."

Bucky Caballero straightened. "How is *she* doing?"

"I presume you are speaking of Mrs. Webster?"

"Yes, you know that I am."

"I've seen her from time to time. She's running the business until her husband returns."

Bucky laughed out loud. "So I've heard. That little fool. And yet. . ."

"Yet?"

"Revenge is sweet, Mr. K."

"What is that supposed to mean?"

Bucky stood and looked out the window onto the night lit skyline behind him. He shoved his hands in the pockets of his slacks and narrowed his eyes. "It means, Mr. Kabakjian, that Mrs. William Webster will pay for what she did to me. I am not a man who forgets easily. I have not forgotten."

"What do you plan to do?"

Bucky turned to look at the man sitting in the shadows. "*Plan* to do? Who knows but what I'm not already doing it. Make no mistake about it, my dear man. Time is on my side. Now then, let's talk art."

CHAPTER FIVE
Tuesday, December 4, 2001
Near Dawn

Katie felt the coolness of the Egyptian cotton pillowcase against the heat of her cheek. She opened her eyes just enough to assure herself she was indeed at home in the hotel apartment. . .in her bedroom. . .in the safety of her bed. . .the bed she had shared with her husband. Her eyes fluttered shut again and she rolled onto her other side. While she slept, she was given reprieve from the memories of the previous day. Now, awake, she remembered them again and she frowned. Had Ben returned? If so, would he be proud of her accomplishments over the past eighteen months or would he be disappointed in her? Would he realize the magnitude of strength she'd come to rely upon and would he allow her to continue in her new role, or would he resume his position and insist she become the stay-at-home wife, loyal and devoted to his every wish, as she had been before?

Her brow furrowed deeper. She loved her husband. She wanted him to return. But, she wanted something. . .something deeper still. . .to be seen by him as the strong woman she'd become. Would he?

Katie turned in bed again and opened her eyes just enough to read the clock on her bedside table. It was early. Very early. How had she gotten home from Saks? Simon? Yes, Simon. She remembered him walking her through the back entrance of the hotel, up the staff elevators to her apartment where Maggie, their beloved housekeeper, had fluttered about, helping her into bed. Vickey had occasionally dropped in from her office downstairs, and the family's doctor stopped by.

"That should help her sleep," she had heard him say to Maggie and Vickey, though she could have dreamed it.

"Poor lamb," Maggie had replied, her British accent a comforting sound. "She's had such a shock, I dare say."

Katie couldn't remember any other words being spoken, and she now assumed that she had indeed fallen asleep, though she hadn't rested much. The sleep was fitful and broken, and her dreams a blend of reality and fantasy. Now she yawned delicately and slipped back into her dream with one final thought: *Those who dream by day,* she quoted Poe, *are cognizant of many things, which escape those who dream only by night.*

In the quiet ambiance of Bonaparte's, the hotel's restaurant, Katie sat across the table from Ben. The features of his handsome face shimmered in the flickering glow of the candlelight between them. They had just finished their evening meal. Ben was dressed in his tux; Katie wore a form-fitting, gray-black formal gown she'd purchased from Eleni Lambros Couture. Strategically placed rhinestones twinkled in the pale light from the overhead chandeliers, casting an ethereal effect to all who looked at her.

"You are bewitching, you know?" Ben whispered.

Katie fluffed at the skirt of the expensive dress. "You like?"

He smiled knowingly. "I like."

"I bought it knowing you would."

"You know me so well. And I see you did just as I asked. No jewelry."

"No. You asked me not to wear any tonight. I'm strangely suspicious, though. Will you keep me in suspense all night? Or do you have something hidden away?"

Ben laughed out loud, and it was a beautiful sound to her ears. She loved hearing him laugh. . .especially if she were the source of his joy. "You really do know me well," he said when he had sobered.

Katie placed her hands flat on the table and leaned over. "Like no other, I trust."

Ben took one of her slender hands in both of his, turned it first one way, then another as if examining it. "Such tiny hands for such a tall lady."

Now Katie laughed. "But my fingers are long."

"And sinfully unadorned."

"You said to wear only my wedding rings." Katie lifted her left hand and waggled its fingers at him. "See? I am only here to obey you."

Ben laughed again as he reached into his coat pocket. "You don't have to convince me of your devotion. I've already said 'I do,' you know."

Katie pretended to pout. "You think I'm not sincere?"

Ben pulled her hand to his lips and kissed each finger, stopping on the ring finger and kissing it twice. "Poor neglected little finger," he teased. "So perfectly manicured and nothing to show for it."

"What are you up to, Ben Webster? What did you just pull out of your pocket?"

"Close your eyes," he said.

She did and immediately felt the coldness of metal slipping over her finger. When she opened her eyes, Ben was holding the tips of her fingers, tilting her hand toward her. It was a fabulous ring indeed.

Suddenly Mr. Simmons was standing next to them, examining the ring. "Platinum setting. . .nice choice, Mr. Webster. . ."

"Only the best for my Katie."

Katie glanced from one man to the other.

"South Sea, black cultured pearl in the center. . .simply stunning."

"I thought so."

"How many diamonds do we have here? One. . .two. . .three. . . four. . . twelve? Oh, nice! Nice. Simply splendid!"

"Ben, why is Mr. Simmons here?"

"I asked him to examine the ring, Darling."

"This is ludicrous, Ben. We could have gone to Tiffany's later."

"Yes, Darling. Allow Mr. Simmons to finish."

"The fluted shoulders add such a nice touch," Mr. Simmons continued. "Lovely choice. Just lovely. I'd say a little over ten thousand dollars."

Ben beamed. "Wonderful, Mr. Simmons! You really know your business."

"Ben!" Katie was horrified to hear Ben speak of money so flippantly. "I can't believe you're discussing price like this."

"Oh, I know, Katie, and typically I would never do such a thing. But I think it's important that you understand. This is a South Sea black pearl—"

"Yes, Mrs. Webster. And a perfectly round one, too."

"You see, Katie, round pearls are the most valuable. . . ."

"It takes six years and one hundred oysters to harvest a perfectly round black pearl, Mrs. Webster."

"I want you to understand the importance, Katie."

"I do, Ben. I do. I just don't understand. . . ."

"Have you ever gone to Japan, Mrs. Webster?"

Katie looked up at the Englishman. "Excuse me?"

"Japan? The country?"

"I know what Japan is, Mr. Simmons."

"Don't be rude, Katie," Ben admonished.

Katie stood. "This is insane." She began to walk out of the restaurant.

Ben stood as well. "Darling, wait."

Katie stopped and turned to face her husband. He approached her purposefully, wrapped her in his arms and kissed her. "I'm sorry," he whispered. "I should have waited until tomorrow to show the ring to Mr. Simmons."

"Oh, Ben." Katie leaned into her husband's embrace. "You've never done anything like that. I was so confused."

"Don't be confused. I love you, Katie. I love you so much."

"I love you."

"There's more, you know. There's so much more."

Katie looked into her husband's eyes. "What do you mean?"

"Come with me," he said, taking her hand in his and pulling her out the door. Suddenly they were in the middle of Saks and Company.

"Why are we here?"

Nora Taylor stood before them. "Hello again, Mrs. Webster."

"Ms. Taylor."

"Did you find your necklace?"

A look of horror crossed Katie's face, and she turned to Ben. "Oh, Ben! I'm so sorry! I lost the necklace!"

"The necklace?"

"The one you sent, the diamond and pearl necklace. I placed it right here on the counter, but then it was gone. Ms. Taylor, you didn't find it?"

"No, Mrs. Webster. I'm so sorry. I was hoping perhaps you had."

"No. But now I have this ring. . . ." Katie looked down to her hand, devoid of the ring that had graced it earlier. "My ring. Where is my ring?"

"You've lost that, too?" Nora asked. "Oh, dear. You really must be more careful."

"Katie, where is the ring?"

"I don't know, Ben. I don't know."

"Perhaps it is with the necklace," Nora offered.

Katie slipped to the floor, buried her face in her hands, and sobbed.

"Don't cry, Katie. Don't cry. . . ."

"Katie? Don't cry, Katie. Please don't cry."

Katie twisted only slightly from her sleeping position. "Mm?"

"Katie, open your eyes. You're dreaming. Open your eyes, Katie."

Katie's eyes fluttered open and took in the room around her. It was still dark with only a trace of light coming from one of the brass wall sconces across the room. Even the creamy white linens covering her were shadowed by the blanket of night. The typically pulled-back, heavy draperies of her bed's canopy had been released, forming a sort of fortress about her. For the moment she felt safe, almost forgetting the dream she had just been pulled from.

"Katie, look at me." The voice was Brittany's, one of the girls she had taken from Sharkey's dance club.

Katie turned her head and looked at the pretty black woman sitting next to her.

"Katie."

"What time is it?" Katie's tongue stuck to the roof of her mouth.

"Let me get you some water." Brittany's lithe form rose from the bed, pushed back the draperies, tied them into place, and stepped into the darkness of the room.

Katie heard the clinking of glass on glass and the pouring of liquid. "How can you see?" she asked. "It's so dark in here."

Brittany chuckled, returned to the bed, and extended the drink. Katie's eyes caught a glimmer of light on crystal and reached for it. "You forget my old life. Making my way around dark places has been a way of life for me for too, too long. Whether the alleys of the Bronx or the clubs near the south side, seems I've always been getting around in dark places."

Katie got up on one elbow and drank the water.

"And to answer your first question, it's nearly six o'clock in the morning."

Katie finished the drink and returned the glass to Brittany, who placed it on the bedside table. "I've been sleeping a long time."

"Yes." Brittany sat next to her mentor and friend. Out of the three young women Katie had brought into THP, she felt closest to Brittany, a young mother who'd grown up in poverty and who, in an effort to self-support her young, fatherless daughter, had taken to exotic dancing by way of profession. Now living in THP, she had brought her little LaTisha with her and, with Katie's help, had placed her in a nearby day-care center while she worked during the day.

"Are you standing guard over me?" Katie was only half-serious.

"You could say that."

"Who has been in here? I know I heard Maggie and Vickey."

"Maggie and Vickey, yes. Ashley, too."

"What about Candy?" Ashley and Candy were the other two girls from Mist Goddess.

Even in the dark, Katie could see the frown on Brittany's face. "No. Sit up a bit more and let me fluff these pillows for you."

Katie obeyed. "What's going on with Candy?"

"You don't need to worry yourself about Candy. Candy is gonna do what Candy is gonna do. There now, sit back. How do you sleep with all these pillows under your head? That's what I want to know."

"I worry about all of you."

Brittany smiled. "I know you do. And we appreciate it."

"Even Candy?"

"Sure. She just doesn't know it yet."

"I want to know what's going on with her. . .with all you girls."

"Nothing much. She just didn't come back to the hotel last night. Got here just in time for work this morning. My guess is she's going back to the club to see Sharkey."

Katie closed her eyes. "Do you think she's dancing again?"

"I wouldn't want to venture a guess."

"But if you had to?"

"Then I'd say yes."

Katie sat up straight. "But why? I've given her everything she needs. What more does she want?"

"It's not that—"

The opening of the bedroom door interrupted Brittany. Maggie bustled in and immediately began scolding. "Why didn't you tell me she was awake?"

Brittany stood. "She just woke up."

"I just woke up, Maggie. Don't fret so."

"I'll take care of her now," Maggie said by way of dismissing Brittany.

Brittany looked back at Katie. "That's my cue to go," she whispered playfully.

"I want to finish talking about this—"

"Later," Brittany finished.

Katie nodded, then watched as the young mother left the room.

"And close the door behind you," Maggie called out.

Brittany turned and smiled, her pearly teeth made all the more white by her dark complexion. "Yes, Ma'am."

When the door clicked shut, Maggie stepped over to the bedside table and flipped on the brass lamp. Katie looked over. An arrangement of white roses garnished the table. "Where did those come from?"

"Mr. Harrington sent them. Now then, come with me. Let's get you into the bath. That's what you need. A nice hot bath and a good meal." Maggie jerked the cover away from Katie.

Like an obedient child, Katie swung her long legs over the side of the bed and slipped from the high mattresses to the hardwood floor. Immediately, her feet recoiled. "Where are my slippers, Maggie?"

Maggie looked down. "They should be right here in the bed steps." Maggie bent over, opened the hidden drawer, and retrieved Katie's favorite white velour and satin slippers. "There you go. Put your little feet in there and follow me to the bath."

Katie did as she was told, took a step away from the bed, and staggered slightly. "Oh."

Maggie returned to her mistress immediately. "Miss Katie, should I call a doctor?"

"No, Maggie. I think I've just been in bed too long. You shouldn't have let me sleep for such a long time."

"The doctor said it was best. Lean on me. I'll get you to your bath."

The two women took careful steps toward the plush master bath. "A hot bath, a good meal, and you'll be good as new."

Katie stopped and looked down at the loving woman. "No, Maggie. Not until I know what's going on. Do you think Ben has returned? Do you think he's trying to let me know?"

Maggie, who had been with the Webster family since 1951, resumed her walking, with Katie on her arm. "I don't know, little dove, but your gift of pearls and diamonds certainly sounds like Master William."

Inside the bath, Maggie led Katie to her vanity table and helped her to sit on the moiré stool. "Be a good girl and get out of that gown while I run some water. Would you like a milk bath this morning?"

"Please. That sounds like just what the doctor ordered."

"What the doctor ordered was bed rest and a lot of attention. He's afraid you're going to have a nervous breakdown. And quite frankly, so am I."

Katie reached to the back of her neck and unhooked the lavender halter gown she assumed Maggie had dressed her in. Rising slightly, she allowed it to slip from her form to puddle on the floor near her feet. As Maggie bustled about, turning on the water and pouring in the milk bath, Katie slipped into a chenille bathrobe that hung on a nearby hook.

"I'll be fine, Maggie. I just need to find out who sent those pearls. And more importantly, where those pearls are now."

Maggie stood straight and frowned. "A Mrs. Taylor called. She said no one has seen the necklace, and she apologizes for the loss."

Katie looked down to the painted toenails that peeked out from under the hem of the robe. "It was my own fault. If Ben *did* send that necklace. . ."

"Come on, now. Bath is ready. Let's talk about this later."

Katie stood and walked over to the sunken marble tub where Maggie waited for her. Bending over, she kissed the elderly caretaker on her cheek. "I should be doing this for you, Maggie. *You* should be waited on hand and foot."

Maggie blushed and reached for the shoulders of the robe to help Katie out of it. "Go on, now. I'll serve you till the day I die, I shall."

"I love you, Maggie."

"I love you, dear girl. Now, into the bath with you."

CHAPTER SIX
Tuesday, Early Morning

"Maggie, please stop fussing about me. I'm fine. I promise you I am." Katie had spent the last half hour trying to convince the housekeeper that she was well enough to work and that she wasn't going to spend another day in bed. Should Ben choose this day to return, she didn't want him to find her weak and helpless. She hadn't been weak and helpless in a long time, and she wasn't about to fall back into that old pattern of life today.

"At least let me call the doctor," Maggie insisted, fluttering about the vanity of the master bath where Katie applied her makeup.

Katie caught Maggie's worried reflection in the mirror and winked at her. "Why? Are you sick?"

"Miss Katie."

Katie turned to face the woman. "Maggie, I'm fine. Really, I am. Besides, I have an empire to run. Did you ever know Ben to stay in the bed to nurse a small shock?"

Maggie crossed her arms over her plump middle. "I would hardly call this a small shock."

Katie stood and walked into the small room adjacent to the bath that served as both closet and dressing room. "Help me decide what to wear today, Mags. I'm off to do battle in the real world. I want to look both professional and stunning."

Katie kept her office attire on the left side of the U-shaped room, behind the large glass curio where sweaters, hats, gloves, and scarves were neatly displayed, and across from the more prominent portion of the room, where casual and formal clothes hung from padded and scented hangers.

Maggie grudgingly moved to a position behind Katie. "As though you could look any other way."

Katie looked over her shoulder at Maggie. "Thanks, Maggie."

Maggie reached around Katie and pulled a dark green Kenneth Cole wool suit from the collection of name brand garments Katie so carefully shopped for. She wasn't one to make frivolous purchases. Her taste was cultured and sophisticated, yet the simplest of garments looked like fashion statements on her elegant frame. Ben's influence had been considerable, but in matters of taste things came naturally to her. Katie's upbringing in the more elite circles of southern culture had aided her in absorbing the sheer sophistication of the world's best boutiques.

"What about this, Child? You haven't worn this one before, I don't imagine."

Katie pulled gently at the tags hanging from the sleeve of the jacket. "I hope I haven't. Clip these for me, will you, Maggie? I'll do the rest."

The rest included choosing shoes from her shoe closet, accessories—both jewelry and fashion—from her accessories closet, and lingerie from the lingerie high boy at the far end of the dressing room tucked between the large bedroom and the luxury bath. As Katie completed her tasks, Maggie held the skirt for her to step into. Then Maggie turned back to the closet in search of a blouse.

"Oh, Maggie. The red silk one—in keeping with the holidays," she said, returning to the vanity table.

"You'll look like a Christmas tree," Maggie offered.

"Not the bright red one, Mags. The scarlet one." She peered over her collection of perfumes, pointing until she found the right one for the day, then reached for the bottle.

Maggie laughed lightly. *"Which* scarlet one?"

Katie took the bottle with her as she returned to the dressing room. Because Maggie kept her clothes color coded, finding the scarlet blouse she had in mind wasn't difficult. She did, however, give Maggie a teasing frown. "I guess I do have more than one, huh?" She dabbed the perfume on her wrists and along the lines of her throat. The scent permeated the air.

Maggie walked over to the box of shoes Katie had chosen and slipped off the top. "You'd better be going if you're bent on doing this," she said, extending the leather shoes the perfect shade of green to match the suit.

"I'll be fine," Katie assured her again. "I will. Besides, Vickey will be with me. And I'm sure you'll call her as soon as I step out the door."

Maggie squared her shoulders. "You think you know so much, do you?" she asked, then marched past Katie, out of the dressing room and into the bedroom.

"Are you sure you should be working today?" Vickey followed Katie into her office.

Katie laughed lightly. "Maggie called you," she remarked, throwing her small, efficient clutch purse on the top of her desk and then sitting in the large executive chair. She shuffled the small, square "telephone message" papers. "James Harrington called how many times?"

"Yes, Maggie called, and I'd have to say James called at least a half a dozen times," Vickey answered the dual questions with one efficient answer.

"He sent flowers yesterday. Did you see them?"

"Do you want coffee?"

"Don't I always?"

"Yes, I saw them." Vickey moved toward the door leading to her office. "I'll be right back with the coffee."

Katie noted that one of her calls from the day before had been from Byron Spooner. *Wants to talk to you about the Christmas tea.*

Katie had almost forgotten about the tea. She picked up the phone and dialed the extension for Byron, then reached for a white-paged legal pad lying nearby. "Mr. Spooner? This is Katharine Webster."

"Mrs. Webster! Good to hear your voice. I understand you were a little under the weather yesterday afternoon."

"I'm fine today and that's all that matters."

Vickey walked in with a cup of coffee served in the Noritake Edwardian Rose collection Katie kept at the office for herself and her business guests. Katie mouthed "thank you" to Vickey, who, rather than leave the room and allow Katie privacy, sat in a nearby chair, stubbornly crossing one leg over the other. She began to swing it.

"I'm glad to hear it," Byron continued from the other end of the phone line. "I have a few cost estimates for you on the tea. Would you like to see the figures?"

"Yes, I'd like that, thank you. Have your secretary bring them up to Vickey, and I'll review them later this afternoon."

"Will do. Again, I'm glad to hear you're feeling better."

"Again, thank you."

Katie replaced the phone and reached for the cup of coffee. "I assume you have something you wish to say." She blew gently against the steaming liquid.

"Katie, you shouldn't be here today."

"Where should I be?" she asked, then took a sip of her coffee.

"Resting. Maggie is worried and so am I."

"Hmm. Wasn't it Robert Runcie who said, 'If our faith delivers us from worry, then worry is an insult flung in the face of God'?"

"Yes. . .well. . .Henry Thoreau said, 'Distrust any enterprise that requires new clothes.' "

Katie raised herself in her seat. "You like my new duds?"

Vickey stood, placed her hands on the edge of the desk and leaned over. "Yes, Katie. I like. It looks great on you. But I also know you. I know you very well, as a matter of fact. You'll go to your grave trying to prove you're doing okay."

Katie stood and walked over to the windows against the right of the office. Her eyes glanced about the New York City skyline. "What a gloomy-looking day. I haven't checked the weather. What's the high expected to be?"

"Katie! Why do you do that? Why do you avoid the issue?"

Katie turned back to Vickey, resting against the window ledge. "I'm not avoiding the issue. I really do feel fine, for the hundredth time today. I'm not the scared and intimidated woman I was two years ago. The only reason I stayed in bed like I did was because the doctor gave me something to help me rest." Katie paused for a moment. "I'm more concerned that Ben will choose today to contact me again, and I still won't know where the necklace is."

"*If* indeed it was William who sent the necklace."

"Who else would it be?"

Vickey opened her mouth to answer, but nothing came out.

"What?" Katie asked. "What were you going to say?"

Vickey crossed her arms and returned to the chair. "What about Sharkey?"

"Sharkey? Sharkey could hardly afford a necklace like that."

"Sharkey knows people. You said he said so."

"And no doubt he does." Katie returned to the desk and sat in the leather chair. "Men like Sharkey—whether they run a small operation or a bigger one—know all the wrong kinds of people."

"That's what I'm saying, Katie. What if Sharkey has gotten a loan or knows someone in the jewelry industry?"

"It's not his style. He'll come down to the lobby and rant and rave, but I'm not really worried about him."

"You wouldn't be."

Katie frowned and cast her eyes downward. "For once I regret that I don't carry a wallet stuffed with family photographs."

"What do you mean?"

Katie looked back to Vickey. "Yesterday, I asked the sales clerk what the man who purchased the necklace looked like."

"And?"

"She said he had long dark hair pulled back in a ponytail."

Vickey straightened her shoulders. "That certainly doesn't sound like William."

Katie pointed her index finger skyward. *"But,* what if he let his hair grow in order to disguise himself?" She shook her head slightly. "If I carried photographs I could have shown the clerk. . . ."

Vickey gave a faint smile. "Who carries photos anymore? Besides little grandmothers, I mean."

Katie smiled back. "I know." She looked at the clutch atop her desk, reached for it, and secured it in the bottom drawer as she usually did. "Even when I do carry a purse it's just a clutch purse and hardly large enough for much more than the necessities."

"Like lipstick?" Vickey folded her arms lightheartedly.

"Maybe I should go back to Saks and take a photo of Ben. . . ."

"And then what?"

Katie shook her head. "I don't know. Call Phil? He's not with the Bureau anymore, so I don't know." She shook her head again. "I don't know about anything right now except that I should give this some time and see what happens. I don't want to get the FBI involved if Ben is trying to quietly make an entrance."

"You certainly don't want the media to get a hold of this."

Katie laid her forearms across the top of her desk and leaned over slightly to gain an eye-to-eye advantage. "Hmm. . .indeed. Now, Mrs. McWhorter, don't you have some work to do?"

Vickey took a deep breath and sighed as she rose from the chair. "Yes, I suppose I do."

Katie smiled. "Then go do it and leave me to mine. I have a Christmas tea to plan and, from the looks of these papers over here," she tapped her index fingernail on a manila folder lying nearby, "a new spa in Wyoming to think about."

"Is that the information you asked Ashley to get? She brought the folder in yesterday, and I put it on your desk."

"Yes, it is. She's a whiz with a computer. She told me she's always loved research, and her older brother was a computer science major."

Vickey leaned against the door facing. "Makes you wonder how a nice girl like that ended up. . . ." Vickey stopped short.

"Working in a place like Sharkey's?"

"Yes. I have a daughter, you know? I wonder if *my* daughter could. . . would. . . ."

Katie folded her hands together and smiled warmly. "It happens in the best of families." *Just ask me. I know.* "But I don't think you have anything to worry about."

"I certainly hope not. Well, I'll get back to the task at hand."

Katie looked down at her half-full cup of now-cold coffee. "Vickey, would you mind warming this up for me?"

"Sure thing. Be right back."

Katie reached for the manila folder and opened it. She studied the carefully written notes Ashley had made in the few minutes Vickey took to return with the coffee.

"One more thing, Vickey. Can you call the head of housekeeping and have Ashley sent up as soon as possible?"

"Sure thing."

Katie sipped her coffee and continued to study. She had recently decided to build a resort fashioned after some of the choicest European escapes. She'd asked Ashley to do some Internet research on European castles and chateaux. From the looks of the work, Ashley had divided her search into fifteen main categories based on country, with numerous subcategories based on amenities such as golf, horseback riding, fishing, spa facilities, skiing, and wine tasting. Ashley had written down websites, copied photos, and made personal notes. . .including some written in French.

Katie's desk phone buzzed. Looking over, she saw it was Vickey. "Yes, Vickey," she answered.

"Ashley is here."

"Send her in."

Ashley was a twenty-one-year-old beauty with silky blond hair that fell just past her shoulders. She had a peaches and cream complexion and soft blue-green eyes that gazed at everything around her with a complexity of innocence and too much knowledge for one so young. Katie understood that look, too. She'd seen it reflected in the mirror, oh, so many years ago.

She and Ashley had more in common than their work as dancers. They had both come from small towns, simple places, kinder places; places where everyone knew everyone and everyone cared. New York City could be quite the reality shock for young girls from rural or small town backgrounds.

Ashley, like her parents and grandparents before her, had been raised on a farm in Indiana. Her mother had taught her daughter how to sew, cook, and clean. Her father had taught her how to run complicated farm machinery and told her she was as good at farming as any man he'd ever seen. Her oldest brother had gone to school to study agriculture, then returned to work with their father on the farm. The middle child, another son two years older than Ashley, had studied computer science and, upon being offered a job in Chicago at Holy Cross Hospital, had left home and hearth.

In high school Ashley had caught the drama and acting bug and, at the insistence of her best girlfriend, had caught a midnight bus for Broadway. "Problem was," Katie had once overheard her saying to Brittany, "no one had told Broadway to be expecting me."

Now, as Katie looked at the carefully gathered information about European resorts, she saw that Ashley indeed had a lot of potential. A light tap at the door caused Katie to look up and call out, "Come in, Ashley." As the young woman entered, looking all the more like Gidget with her hair pulled back in a ponytail and dressed in housekeeping's light blue uniform, Katie stood, walked around her desk, and gave her a light hug. "The work you've left for me is excellent. Would you like a cup of coffee or anything to drink while we go over the particulars?"

Ashley smiled. "Sure. Some water, maybe."

Katie returned the smile so as to soften the instruction she was about to give. "Ashley, in business you must always speak as though you know exactly what you want."

Ashley tilted her head slightly. "Yes, water, thank you," she said assuredly.

"Very good." With an almost imperceptible lifting of her left hand, Katie indicated that Ashley should make herself comfortable in the seating area of the office. When her husband had occupied this room, he had arranged two leather loveseats opposite one another, separated by a heavy coffee table. Ben's collection of rare travel books still adorned the table, as well as a leather miniature treasure chest Katie had given him for no particular reason at all.

"No reason?" he asked her. He leaned back against the front of his desk, his long legs crossed at the ankle, teasing her with the boyish twinkle in his dark eyes. She had purchased the gift at a small, out-of-the-way antiquities shop she'd passed earlier in the day. The proprietor had carefully placed it in a box wrapped in masculine, gold foil paper, and topped with a large gold bow. Ben now held the box in his hands, turning it one way, then another. "It's heavy."

Katie bounced with childlike anticipation. "Open it!"

"And it's for no reason."

"No reason."

"Not my birthday."

"Nope."

"Our anniversary."

"Nooo. Open it, Ben."

He placed the box on his desk, crossed one arm over his middle and rested his chin in the other hand. "But I think I should figure this out first, don't you?"

Katie retrieved the box and held it out to her husband again. "No, just open it."

"I know! Our first date! It's the anniversary of our first date."

Katie frowned. "I'd be willing to bet you don't even remember our first date."

Ben took the box and placed it back on the desk, then wrapped his wife in his arms. "That's where you'd be wrong. I took you to Bonaparte's. You wore a short, black velvet dress. The neckline was scooped." He drew out a "scoop" with a fingertip against her chest, causing her to lean into him. "And pearls. Single strand. Matching earrings. Genuine. Good quality."

"You have a good memory, Sir."

He kissed her lightly. "About the important things, yes."

She tilted her chin and whispered, "Are you ever going to open that box?"

The contents of the box now sat on the coffee table, a reminder of their moment. . .their remarkable love for one another. To add a touch of femininity in the masculine office she had refused to redecorate during her interim as president, she had brought in a crystal vase, which was filled with fresh-cut, long-stemmed roses of various colors. Ashley sat directly across from the vase while Katie stepped over to the wet bar to pour a glass of water from the Waterford pitcher Vickey had filled earlier in the morning.

"Again, Ashley, the work you left for me is remarkable." Katie handed Ashley a glass of water.

"Thank you. I have always been really good at research. . .any kind of research and from a multitude of sources. . .especially the Internet. I'm a whiz at that."

"I think we should look into sending you to school," she added, sitting beside the young woman.

Ashley's face brightened. "Are you serious?"

"I am. My only stipulation would be that you work for me for a pre-assigned number of years after graduation."

Ashley pressed a small hand against her breast. "I can do that."

"Something tells me you can do anything you put your mind to. Question is, why didn't you know that sooner? I know you intended to hit Broadway. . ." Ashley's head jerked and Katie continued, "I overheard

85

you talking with Brittany one afternoon."

Ashley took a sip of her water. "I wanted something unattainable for me."

Katie nodded. "Why didn't you go home?"

"I was embarrassed."

Katie nodded. "I understand."

"Something tells me you do."

Katie placed her hands palm down in her lap. "Did I ever tell you I come from a small town, too?"

"No. Here in New York?"

"No, in Georgia; a little town called Brooksboro. I grew up on Main Street."

"For real?"

"For real."

"How'd you get to be so. . .I don't know. . .cultured?"

"A very nice man came along and rescued me from the slums of this city."

"Were you a runaway like me?"

"Yes."

"You'd never know it to look at you now."

"Thank you."

"I want to be like you, Katie."

"Not like me, no. Always be yourself."

"But you're perfect."

Katie laughed out loud. "Hardly."

"You are."

"No, I'm afraid not. There're any number of people who will tell you so. But if what you are saying is that you'd like to learn more about things like etiquette and business, then we'll take it one step at a time."

"Is that what this is about? These sessions you have with Brittany and Candy and me? Our trips to places like Lord & Taylor and dinners out on the town?"

"Yes."

Ashley lowered her eyes. "I'm going to do my best for you, Katie. I am."

"Do your best for *you*. Not me. Now then, let's talk resorts."

The intercom from Katie's desk buzzed, interrupting and startling the two women as they turned toward the other side of the massive office. "Yes, Vickey?" Katie called out.

"Katie, Phil Silver is on the phone and would like to speak with you."

Katie took a deep breath and, frowning, sobered quickly. "Phil Silver?"

"Yes. He says it's important."

Katie's hand involuntarily reached up and her fingertips rested on the hollow of her throat. "Ben," she whispered. "Ben *is* back."

CHAPTER SEVEN

"Hello, Katie," Phil Silver greeted from the open door of her office as Ashley slipped politely past him. "Thank you for seeing me so quickly."

Katie stepped around her desk to her husband's childhood friend. "Do you have some information on Ben? I'm sorry. I didn't mean to jump into that so quickly. Would you like something to drink? I can have Vickey bring us some coffee or tea. How about lunch? Have you eaten? I'll have our café send something up right away."

Phil laughed nervously. "My goodness. All these choices."

Katie turned and walked back toward her desk. "I know. I'm sorry. . . it's just. . .have you any news of Ben?" She admired Phil's sense of dedication and passion. During the eighteen months since Ben's disappearance, she had probably come to know him better than some of his own family members.

Phil followed her across the room, rested his forearms over the back of one of the wingback chairs positioned in front of Katie's desk. "Let's take a step back, shall we?" He glanced at his watch. "It's nearly twelve, so yeah. Let's have some lunch brought in. Unless you'd rather go out?"

Katie's fingertips touched the polished wood of her desk. "No, I'd be more than happy to call down. What would you like?"

"Club?"

Katie smiled warmly. "Fries with that?"

"Sounds good."

"To drink?"

"Diet whatever."

Katie picked up the phone. "Vickey, can you order some lunch for Mr. Silver and me, please? Thank you. Club with fries for Mr. Silver. I'll have grilled chicken salad. . .teriyaki sounds good. . .diet whatever for Mr. Silver and Pellagrino for me. Thank you, Vickey."

Katie took a deep breath and sighed as she replaced the phone. "Would you like to sit here or on the sofas?"

Phil looked over his shoulder to the other side of the office. "Sofas are good."

Moments later, the two were sitting in the same spot Katie and Ashley had sat earlier.

"It seems I can't leave this spot," Katie said resignedly.

Phil unbuttoned his sports coat and leaned back.

"Please tell me you're wearing a heavier coat than that. It must be horribly cold out today."

"I left it in the outer office. You haven't been out?"

"No."

"Bitter cold. Completely bitter."

After a nervous pause they blurted out simultaneously. "How's Gail?" "What'd you mean by that?"

They laughed; Katie slid back slightly on the sofa where she sat and Phil leaned forward, resting his elbows on his knees. "Your question first. Gail is fine. Fine."

"How's the new job, the professorship?"

"It's good. Going very well."

"I still can't believe you left the Bureau."

Phil smiled, nodding his head in agreement. "I know. Sometimes I can't either. But I like it. I like being home more. . .with the kids. . . Gail. . ."

Katie's eyes dropped slightly. "Being with family is extremely important."

Phil reached over and took Katie's hand. "I'm sorry, Katie. That was insensitive of me."

Katie took his hand in hers and squeezed it. "No, no. What you said was true. You made the right choice for your family." She brightened a bit. "I'd be willing to bet the Bureau misses you terribly though."

Phil nodded again. "A man can only hope. Now, back to you. What were you saying about the spot?"

"The spot? Oh! Yes. It seems I can't leave this spot today. Ashley was just here going over some spas in Europe with me, and we sat right here." Katie indicated the two sofas with her hands.

"Ashley?"

"One of the girls I brought out of the club."

"Ah, yes. I remember you telling me about them. How's that going?"

"I think it's going okay. Brittany and Ashley have made the most progress. Brittany is from Harlem, has a little girl who lives here with her, and a mother and several siblings back home. She's a stunning black woman who has an eye for fashion and business." Katie paused for a moment. "A very sensitive soul. Big heart." Phil smiled at her, and she went on. "Ashley, the young woman who was just here, is your typical girl next door. Pretty and blond. Very good with research and the Internet. Has a brother who is a computer scientist."

"And the other one?"

"Candy."

"Ah, yes. She's Asian, right?"

"Yes."

"Not as receptive to your help?"

"I wouldn't say that."

"What would you say?"

Before Katie could answer, the office door swung open. Katie turned to see a young male employee pushing a linen-covered cart toward them. Vickey was directly on his heels. "Where would you like it, Mrs. Webster?" the employee asked.

"Bring it over by the window," Katie said. She looked at Phil. "We'll have lunch with a view."

Vickey turned back toward the door. "I'll get two chairs from the outer office," she said.

Within moments, Katie and Phil were sitting across the small trolley-table, removing the stainless steel lids that covered their lunch plates. "Looks good," Phil commented.

"Dig in."

"So, don't let our food interrupt you. What *would* you say about Candy?"

Katie pursed her lips slightly as she reached for her glass of Pellagrino. "What makes you think— "

"You weren't so quick to offer information about her."

Katie smiled. "Always the detective." Phil shrugged and she continued. "I think she's slipping back to the club at night. She may be working for Sharkey again."

"Why would she do that? All this isn't good enough?" Phil pressed a quarter slice of his sandwich before picking it up from the plate and biting into it.

"That's not it." Katie reached for her fork and speared her salad. "Some girls dance for money. Some dance for attention. My guess is that Candy dances for a little of both. She needs something she's getting only in the clubs. She thinks. . .believes, really, that she is somehow acceptable when she's undressed, for lack of a better way to put it."

Phil reached for the nearby bottle of catsup and unscrewed the top. "What do you know about her background?"

"Very little. Out of all the girls, she opens up the least about her past."

"I'd be willing to bet you'll find some form of abuse in her childhood."

"Abuse?"

"Sexual."

"Why do you think that?"

"Statistics."

"Ah."

For the next few minutes, the two ate in silence, occasionally glancing out the window, then back to the other. Finally, Katie asked, "Do you?" Her voice was barely above a whisper.

Phil wiped his mouth with the linen napkin from his lap. "Do I what?"

"Know anything about Ben?"

"Why would you think I do?"

"Phil Silver, must you always answer a question with a question?"

He smiled. "What'd you expect?"

Katie smiled. "The necklace. Do you know about the necklace?"

"No. What necklace?"

Katie placed her napkin next to her plate of unfinished food. She was finished with her meal. She couldn't eat and talk about Ben. . .not now. "Yesterday I received a beautiful necklace by courier. Diamonds and pearls. . .from Saks."

"How do you know it was from Saks?"

"I went to Tiffany's first—"

Phil sighed. "Katie, why didn't you call me? Why do you always try to solve these mysteries alone?"

"I acted on impulse."

"Okay, so you went to Tiffany's."

"Just to talk to Mr. Simmons. I knew it wasn't from there, but I thought he could help me. He estimated the necklace at four to five thousand."

"Dollars?"

"That's what I asked."

"Of course, he meant dollars."

"I said that, too."

"So what happened?"

"I went to Saks. The girl behind the fine jewelry counter said that she had sold them to a man claiming to be my husband."

Phil stood suddenly, stepped toward the window, and looked out.

Katie clenched her fists and placed them in her lap. "What? What is it, Phil? What do you know?"

Phil turned and leaned against the sill. "One of the agents I used to work with came into my office with quite a story. He's working on the Shari Griffin case."

"The young girl whose father owns the art gallery?"

Phil smiled. "I see you keep up with the news."

"I try."

"The agent, John, went to the gallery the other day to talk with the curator. When he arrived, the curator was talking to a man. . .a man John said looked vaguely familiar. . .like someone you think you recognize, but you don't know from where."

Katie nodded.

Phil reached into the inside pocket of his jacket and brought out a pack of gum. He extended it to Katie, who shook her head, no. "The man had a beard, and later John had our composite artist come up with a sketch of the man he saw with a beard and then without." He pulled a piece of gum from the pack, then peeled away the aluminum wrapper.

"I don't understand. What does this have to do with anything? Why would he zero in on this one man?" Katie felt her heart begin to race. Was the man Ben? Is this what Phil was gently trying to tell her?

"John said," Phil tri-folded the gum and popped it into his mouth, "that the man acted suspicious to him. John's the absolute best when it comes to investigations, so if his instincts tell him—"

"Was it Ben?"

Phil lowered his head as he shook it. "No, Katie. It was Bucky Caballero."

"Bucky?"

"Yeah." Phil looked over at the sofas. "Would you be more comfortable over there?"

Katie stood; her legs felt bloodless, and she grabbed the edge of the table for support. Phil reached for her elbow. "Here, Katie. Lean on me."

Together they walked to the sofas, this time sitting side by side.

"Do you think Bucky Caballero sent the necklace?" Katie kept her eyes lowered. She could see her knees through the veil of her dark lashes, and she focused on them. Anything to stay sane in the moment. To be strong. She refused to give way again.

"Could be."

"Why would Bucky Caballero be here?"

"Could be he was just here to buy art."

"Or to drive me insane."

Katie felt Phil's hand clutch hers; she looked up at him. "Don't let him do that, Katie. Do you hear me? Besides, we have to explore all the options first."

"Like?"

Phil released Katie's hand before he continued. "I want to go down to Saks, talk to the sales clerk." He reached into his coat pocket again and retrieved a notepad and pen. "Do you remember her name?"

"Cassie. Her supervisor is Mrs. Taylor."

Phil scribbled the names. "I'll go by Saks when I leave here."

"Can you do that? Without still being at the Bureau?"

He closed the notepad. "Katie, technically, a crime hasn't been committed, so what I'm doing here is just looking into things. I've got my PI license; I'm registered with the state. I actually have more freedom now than I did when I was with the Bureau."

"I can hire you to look into this for me?"

"You wouldn't have to hire me, Katie. I'm your friend. . .yours and William's."

Katie shook her head, no. "I insist. I wouldn't take advantage of our friendship. I'm hiring you, Phil. That's final."

Phil nodded again. What was the point in arguing with her? "All right. Then let's get started. We've got some options to consider. Obviously Caballero. If anyone would want to cause you any upsets, it would be Caballero."

"Mmm. What are the other options? Who else?"

"To be honest with you," he replied, "the list is endless. There were a lot of strong, political names on the list of clients we found in the Caballero files."

Katie pressed her lips together. "True. What a field day the press had."

"They did that."

"Who are the others?

"Could be Sharkey."

"Sharkey?" Katie's backbone straightened. "Why would he—?"

"You've got a man's wounded pride, Katie. I'm sure people in the business are talking about it."

"Oh, I don't know. . ."

"I'll look into that, too." He opened the pad and scribbled on it again.

"But you don't think Ben sent the necklace?"

Phil took a deep breath and sighed before answering. "Katie, why would Ben do something like that? Before we go on, let me see the necklace."

Katie frowned. "I can't. I lost it."

"You lost it?"

"It's a long story. I set it on the counter at Saks. When they told me my husband had purchased it, I became distraught, and they took me upstairs to the employee lounge. The necklace was left on the counter. When I realized it, the clerk went back for it, but it was gone."

"I see. This is not the season for leaving things like that lying around in department stores."

"I suppose not."

"Well! All this hasn't actually gotten me to why I'm here."

Katie's eyes widened. "Why are you here?"

"Katie, as far as I'm concerned, my job isn't completely done until I find Caballero. That's on a professional note. On a personal note, my job isn't done until I find William."

"Nor mine."

"I went over the case files again last night. Did a little more digging. Before Andi Daniels worked for Caballero, a woman named Victoria worked at the boutique."

"Yes, I remember her. She married Jordan Whitney."

"The politician?" Phil was genuinely surprised.

"Yes. You look surprised."

"Well, I'm surprised Whitney got away with it, to tell you the truth."

"What do you mean?"

"Victoria, if I'm guessing correctly, did the same job as Andi. . ."

"You mean the escort service. . ."

"Yes."

"So you think she might have known Jordan Whitney. . ."

"Professionally. Why would Jordan Whitney come into a ladies' boutique in a Midtown hotel?"

"Are you sure that's how they met?"

"No. I can't be sure until I talk to her. Not that it matters, really. However, she may know more about Caballero and his habits than we've thought about before. In fact, the idea to talk to her didn't occur to me until last night when I was going over the files."

"What if she doesn't want to talk about her job at Jacqueline's?"

"I won't give her a choice." Phil stood, and Katie stood with him.

"Will you go see her soon?"

"Today if I can."

They walked across the office.

"Like I said, technically, Katie, no crime has been committed against you. There's no law against sending a necklace. Even the news about Caballero possibly being in the city is pure speculation. I'm following through on it because he's still wanted, but right now there's nothing to tie these two things together. Legally, I mean."

"I understand. Phil, I don't want this to get to the media."

"I'll see to it that it doesn't. Katie, can you think of anyone else who might send that necklace?" Phil asked as they reached the door.

"No. I truly thought it was sent by Ben."

"No one. . .anywhere. . .here at the office perhaps. . .that might have something against you?"

"No! Why would anyone here. . . ." Katie stopped short.

Phil tilted his head slightly. "What?"

"Maybe."

"Maybe?"

"Maybe one person."

"Like?"

"James Harrington."

"Who is he?"

"My GM. I think he feels his authority was somehow usurped when I stepped into Ben's shoes. I think he felt he should have taken over." Katie shook her head sadly.

Phil lightly touched her arm. "You're doing a good job, Katie. Especially after September. We all know what you did. William would be proud."

"Will be, Phil. Will be. If I don't hold onto that, I truly will go insane."

Phil nodded just as a light tap came to the door, and it cracked open. Vickey stuck her head around it. Her lips were pursed, and her eyes unreadable.

Katie's shoulders squared. "What is it, Vickey?"

Vickey stepped into the office, holding a small package. It was wrapped in silver foil paper and topped with a silver and gold bow. "A delivery boy just brought it in," she said, repeating her words from the day before.

Katie sighed deeply, started to reach for the package, but pulled back.

Phil took it, lightly bounced it up and down as he spoke. "Is this like the other one?"

"Exactly like the other one," Vickey answered.

Katie stepped away, returning to her desk where she sat heavily. "I can't open it again."

"Allow me," Phil said. "Let's see what we have here before we get upset." He moved toward the chairs in front of the desk, and Vickey followed him.

"What about fingerprints?" she asked.

Phil smiled at her as he removed a small pocketknife from his pants pocket and began to slice the tape holding the wrapping paper in place. "You've read too many spy novels. Besides, you've held it. The delivery boy handled it. My guess is the clerk at the store held it. No telling who else."

"Do you think it came from Saks? Like the other one?" Vickey sat in one of the chairs as Phil sat in the other. Katie leaned forward, resting her forearms against the top of the desk.

"Could be. The wrapping paper is fairly common for this time of year and not exclusive to Saks, I wouldn't think."

"No," Katie interjected. "It could be from anywhere." She watched as the wrapping paper fell from the same mid-sized black box she had held in her hands just days before. Phil removed the top, revealing a black velvet box.

"Open it," Katie whispered. "Hurry."

Phil complied. He frowned, then turned the box toward Katie. "Is this your necklace?"

Katie nodded. "May I?"

Phil pulled the velvet box from the outer box, then stopped short. "There's a note here," he said.

Vickey reached for the velvet box and handed it across the desk to Katie, who quietly set the opened case on her desk, keeping her eyes on Phil. "Read it."

He pulled a small piece of folded paper from the bottom of the box, unfolded it, read silently, and nodded. "That figures," he commented.

"What?" Vickey asked.

"It's written in block print. Someone has deliberately disguised their handwriting."

"Read it," Katie said again. "Out loud."

Phil looked up at her, straight into her eyes before he repeated the words he had read. "It says: 'You should be more careful.' "

Katie took in a breath while Vickey's hands came up to cover her own mouth, as if to keep from screaming.

"Does it say anything else?" Katie asked.

"Yeah. It says: 'You should be more careful. . .*my love*.' "

CHAPTER EIGHT

Candy Tso sighed heavily as she pushed the housekeeping cart down the tenth floor hallway of The Hamilton Place. She mentally counted the closed doors ahead of her. Four more rooms and she would be done with this wing. She rolled her eyes. *Yeah, well. . .what did that mean?* Still, there were more wings to go. Even though the housekeeping staff worked in pairs, and she liked the young Hispanic woman she worked with, it didn't make the job any less disgusting. Life had, Candy decided as she entered Suite 504, really dumped on her. Here she was, at age twenty-four, earning a living cleaning up after those who didn't know—would never know—she even existed.

"I'll make the bed if you'll do the bath in this one," she said to her work mate, Iris.

"Sure, but I get the bed in the next one," Iris countered with a smile.

Candy forced a smile, then released it as soon as Iris turned to enter the bathroom.

I'm only twenty-four years old, she mused. *Why is it that I feel so much older?*

The answer came almost too easy. *Because, girl, you've seen more tragedy and heartache in your short life span than most people do in a lifetime.* As a child, Candy—who had been born Xi Lan Tso—had played with paper dolls her father had purchased for her at a secondhand store.

When he died, and her mother remarried, Candy thought life had smiled on her. She was wrong. Life with Jim Cassidy and his son Clint had been anything but sweet.

As Candy pulled the heavy comforter and linens from the bed, she remembered the night Mr. Cassidy, as she had been forced to call him, retired to the family room to watch television from the comfort of his oversized, imitation leather recliner. As was his usual habit on a Friday evening, he had begun to drink beer immediately after dinner, tossing the cans into a nearby wastebasket, then calling out, "Woman! Get me another beer!"

Candy stood in the kitchen with her mother, who was feeding her infant son, a brother Candy loved more than any other person in the world, with the exception of her mother. "Quickly. Quickly," her mother said to her. "Get his beer." Candy rushed to the refrigerator for an ice-cold can.

"Here, Sir," she said, extending it to him, careful to hold it near the base so as not to warm the beverage.

"Why didn't you pop the top? You expect me to pop the top? Why are you so lazy?"

"Sorry, Sir." She retrieved the can and popped the top for him.

"That's better."

Later, he called for another beer, and Candy rushed to do his bidding, this time to perfection, or so she thought. "Did you pop this?"

"Yes, Sir."

"Do you care to explain why?"

"I. . .I. . ."

"I. . .I. . ." he mocked.

"The last time—"

"Did you drink any of this?" He set the can on the small table on the opposite side of his chair.

"No, Sir!"

Mr. Cassidy had grabbed her by the wrist and pulled her close

to him. "Let me smell your breath, Girl," he ordered, and like an
obedient dog, she opened her mouth for him.

Candy's eyes narrowed at the memory. She jerked the bottom sheet from around the mattress and added it to the small pile at the base of her cart. Then, reaching for the freshly pressed sheets, she began the monotonous task of remaking the bed.

"This is for the birds," she whispered.

"Did you say something?" Iris called from the bath.

Candy swung around. "No. I was just talking to myself." She heard Iris chuckle, then returned to her work. *That's okay. Strip a bed. Make a bed. Same ole same ole. I thought I'd have it so easy here. Not that Katie hasn't been nice; she has. But I deserve more. . .I deserve. . .something. . .what? Something. At least I have my fun at night. . .and it's not like it's even work. There's just something about it. . .something that fills an empty place deep inside. . .*a place carved into her soul by the unwanted and unspeakable attentions of her stepbrother when she'd been a young girl.

She jerked the blanket and comforter back over the smooth crisp linens tucked neatly around the bed then walked over to the window and pulled the heavy drapes with the tug of a cord. Walking to the center of the window, she reached for the two wands for the sheers and, with a quick pull, opened them just enough to reveal the gray of the city beyond.

Candy turned her head to the right, looking through the buildings toward the southern tip of the island, to the place where Mist Goddess waited for her tonight.

"Candy, are you done with the bed in here?" Iris asked from the door to the suite's bathroom.

Candy swung around. "Yes."

"What's the matter with you today, *Chica?*" Iris walked toward her. "I don't believe I've ever seen you look so tired."

Candy forced a smiled. "I had a late night last night."

Iris rested a hand on her full hip. "Did you now? Tell! I need some excitement in my life. My life? My life is so unbelievably boring. I come to work, I go home, I deal with the kids, I fall into bed, and I get up the next morning and do it all over again."

Candy shook her head. "No. Not now. Let's get finished up here so I can get back to my room and take a nap." She raised her hand to adjust a nearby lampshade that had been knocked askew. In doing so the short sleeve of her uniform rode up her arm, exposing a bruise on the tender flesh there.

"Mother Mary, is that a bruise on you?"

Candy quickly jerked her hand down and brushed her hands against the front of her skirt. "Yeah. Trying to get around last night in the dark. I tripped over my shoes and hit the night stand."

"You should be more careful." Iris moved toward the door.

"Yeah, I should," Candy noted, remembering the patron at Mist Goddess from the night before who had grabbed her arm in an effort to force her to dance with him. She hated that man. He was a thorn in the flesh of humanity.

"Come on, Girl," Iris said. "You get the dusting, and I'll vac."

Marcy Waters stared blankly at the computer monitor. It sat atop her home office desk where she wrote her weekly Sunday column for the *Savannah Morning News*. Periodically she chewed her bottom lip, as if doing so would make the words she wanted to type. . .*needed* to type. . . come easier or perhaps even faster. What she was experiencing was what some might call writer's block, but she knew better. Actually, the problem was the sensitivity of the topic itself. Her chosen topic, "The Unlikely Union of Schools and Guns," was a difficult assignment to write about.

"From Where I Sit," the observations of a straightforward wife and mother on some of the day's hottest topics, had become one of the newspaper's most popular columns. Marcy had written about everything from local heroes to national controversies. She had inspired people to get involved and she had made a few people angry. She reckoned that the column she was now writing would anger a few people as well, which was why the words weren't coming so easily. She knew this column should *inspire*, not anger. However, something deep inside her—that sixth sense many writers tap into on a daily basis—told her that just the opposite would happen. Still, she had to write what was in her heart and on her mind, not only as a parent but as a human being.

Marcy leaned back in her standard secretary's chair, the one she'd purchased on sale at Target for $69.95. The back had a tendency to pop off, which was why she didn't lean back too far, but other than that, it served its purpose. Her purpose was to write, not become overly comfortable, she reminded herself. "Come on, Marce," she spoke aloud. "It's time to get crackin'."

She leaned toward the computer keyboard, cupped her hand over the mouse, clicked into a search engine and began to look for more information from the Internet. Ten minutes later, bile rose into her stomach, which was now positioned somewhere closer to her throat than it should have been. She decided to step away from the statistics on school violence and make another pot of coffee in the French press she received on her birthday from her childhood best friend, Katie Webster.

As she stepped out of the upstairs bedroom she'd converted into her office, her eyes glanced over the bookcase. Rows of her favorite books, her old collection of Archie comics, various resource periodicals and editions, and framed photographs were gathering dust. One of the photos in particular always made her smile: the yellowed, color photo of two young girls, dressed in two-piece bathing suits, their arms draped over one another's shoulders. In the background was their hometown's recreation center swimming pool; its crystal blue water shimmered with shards of glinting sunlight darting off the ripples. The girls were grinning, their prepubescent bodies slick and glistening wet. One child was tall and slightly overweight. The other was petite.

Katie and me, Marcy thought as she made her way down the stairs of the old, "haunted" house she shared with her husband and three children. She smiled at the memory. She missed those days, simple days when mothers dropped off their children at the local recreation center, then went home and had quiet time. Days when students weren't afraid to go to school and parents weren't afraid to let them go there. Days when getting a paddling during school hours was nothing compared to the spanking one was sure to get at home when Father found out. Days when summer break lasted a whole three months—from the first of June to the day after Labor Day. Summer days meant sleeping as late as eight or nine o'clock in the morning, waking to a gentle breeze billowing the curtain through the opened windows, and the smell of sweet flowers wafting through. On lazy summer mornings, children could lie around in their cotton pajamas watching game shows until eleven o'clock when their mothers said, "You need some fresh air," and the children knew that meant it was time to go play. And they did. They played and played and played until evening when it was time for best friends to catch fireflies in jars and watch them light in dark closets. These were the days of chasing after the ice cream man with a dime clutched in a sweaty palm, and hula-hoop contests in Katie's mother's backyard garden.

"Don't you break my flowers!" Miss Carolyn would yell from the opened kitchen window where the screen kept the mosquitoes out and allowed the fresh air in.

"We won't!" Katie would yell back.

"I'm watching you!" Miss Carolyn returned. Miss Carolyn had a thing about her flowers. "If you break one of my flowers, I'm going to break your fannies!"

Marcy grinned at Katie. "It's already cracked," she now recalled whispering to her on one occasion.

"Shh!" Katie warned. "Mama hears everything."

"I certainly do, Marcy Sue Anderson," Miss Carolyn said firmly. "I'll tear you up and call your mother, and she will do the same when you get home."

Marcy remembered blushing. "Yes, Ma'am," she said respectfully, if not fearfully. Then she gave a pixie-like smile. "I'll be careful, and I'll make sure Katie is, too."

Katie turned toward the back fence. "Oh, for crying out loud, Marcy. You're gonna get it."

That day, Marcy Sue Anderson giggled. Today, as she poured hot water over the freshly ground coffee in her French press, Marcy Anderson Waters smiled.

She snapped her fingers. "Brilliant!" she exclaimed out loud. "Why didn't I think of that sooner?"

Hurriedly, she placed the top of the coffeemaker over the steeping, dark liquid, then ran back up the narrow staircase that led from the pantry to the upstairs and into her office. She all but slid into her chair, scooted up to the cluttered, faux-oak computer desk and began to type furiously on the keyboard.

When I was a child, she began, and then proceeded to tell what life had been like in the tiny, homespun town of Brooksboro, Georgia. She told of escapades with Katie Morgan, who today was a beautiful, gifted executive in Manhattan. Not that anyone in a hundred-mile radius needed to be reminded as to who Katie was. Those who didn't know her. . .hadn't known her. . .had at least read the story Marcy had written about her over a year ago, a story of intrigue and danger. A story of survival and coming home. A story of love and love lost and believing in love's saving grace.

Marcy now wrote:

When we were children, Katie lived two houses down from the home I share with my husband and children today. In those days my home was owned by Mr. Grayson Cheevers. . .Old Man Cheevers, we called him. Mr. Cheevers lived here with his wife until he killed her, then hung himself, in what they say was a jealous rage over his wife's lover. Katie and I used to stand in front of the house for what seemed to be hours because legend had it that the house was haunted with the ghost of Old Man Cheevers, and we were hoping to catch a glimpse of an honest-to-goodness ghost. There was an evening. . . just one, mind you. . .when Katie swore she saw his evil, green eyes peering down at us. We ran up the street faster than jackrabbits, running for the safety of her home, where her mother and father laughed at us until tears spilled down their cheeks. We were indignant! How dare they laugh at our fear? Didn't they know that Old Man Cheever's ghost was real?

Today, children live with another fear. . .another ghost staring down at them with evil, green eyes. However, it's not haunted houses that we are concerned with; it's our schools. And parents aren't laughing anymore. Unlike the imaginings of two little girls, guns in schools are as real today as the chalkboards and pep rallies from days gone by.

I mention my old friend Katie for another reason. After each new report of school violence, there seems to be the inevitable follow-up story of the perpetrator's troubled childhood: "He was teased. . .he was ridiculed. . .he wasn't very popular. . .the kids made fun of his glasses. . .diminutive stature. . .his clothes. . . ."

This brings me back to Katie. Katie was born six feet tall. Not really, but it certainly seemed that way. From as far back as I can remember, she had legs to her throat. . .and I knew her from the first week of her life when her mother and father brought her home from the hospital to the little apartment across the street from my parent's home. In school she was teased mercilessly. No one was as tall as she was, boys included. When she came home from school with tears streaming down her face, I remember, her father used to tell her that models were tall. . .in fact that they had to be tall. . .and that she was as beautiful as a model. Psychologists call this "reframing." I call it "putting a positive spin on things."

I don't think I fully understood, though, how deeply the pain of the teasing went until we were adults, and she shared her thoughts and feelings openly and from the perspective of maturity and logic. And so while I certainly do not support the actions of the young men who have taken the lives of others (and in some cases their own) without regard to the outcome, I am also appalled at the lack of education about the feelings of others. It's no longer enough to instruct them not to play with guns. We must first teach them that each and every individual is a precious child of God. . .a piece of

His artwork. . .the crafting of His hands. Who are we to laugh or ridicule that work?

I remember the day I collected my eldest son from high school for a doctor's appointment. I stopped the car at the student crosswalk waiting for a procession of students to cross. They passed in three clusters, four girls walking shoulder to shoulder, a young fellow and his sweetheart walking hand in hand, two young men with sagging backpacks hooked over their shoulders and carrying baseball paraphernalia, and one lone boy whose pants were just a tad too short and whose shirt tail hung out of one side of his pants while the other half was tucked in.

"Look at that doofus," my son smirked from the passenger seat.

I turned sharply and pointed at his nose. "Don't you ever let me hear you say that again," I told him firmly. "That young man deserves to be treated with respect, the same as you and me and anybody else in this world."

"But, Mom, he's so. . ."

"So what?" I asked, almost daring him to answer.

"So weird."

"How do you know? Do you know him? Do you ever talk to him? Ever spend any significant amount of time at all with him?"

"No," he answered meekly.

"Then how do you know what he's like? He may just be a very nice young man who never had the chances you had. How can you possibly fault him for that?"

Next year, that young man and my son will be sharing a dorm room at Georgia Southern University.

Like Katie's father, it is up to us parents to teach our children about gun safety—yes!—but also about diversity and acceptance of others, and about opportunity for new friendships and relationships. Because today, unlike when we were children, access to violence and evil is available on television, at the movies, and in games. Musical lyrics that used to lament over "wanting to hold your hand" or that

made absolutely no sense are now teaching them how to rape, murder,
and seek ultimate revenge. Whatever that entails. As parents we
must educate our children as to the diversifications in people and how
God has placed His fingerprint on each and every one of us. Instead
of pointing out the differences, we should be looking for that print.
And that's my opinion on the subject; that's the way I see it,
from where I sit.

Marcy sat back in her secretary's chair and smiled. She felt good about what she'd written. It was quick and to the point. She saved it to disk, then attached it in an email to her editor at the paper. Then she stood, stretched out the eternal kink in her lower back, and turned off the computer before leaving the room to go back down the stairs and drink the coffee she was certain—by now—would be tepid at best.

"Oh, well, I'll heat it in the microwave," she said to no one as she skipped down the stairs in her stockinged feet, holding onto the banister for support. Marcy stepped into the kitchen, poured a mug full of coffee from the French press, then set it in the microwave. As it heated, she opened the back door and stuck her head out. "Brr," she said by way of comment, then quickly shut the door. She retrieved her coffee, prepared it to her liking, then walked into the formal living room in the front of the house. She lit the gas logs in the fireplace, curled up on the black leather sofa, wrapped herself in a white chenille throw and enjoyed the silence of the moment.

Charlie and I should take the kids out to the farm to cut down a tree soon, she thought. Christmas was just around the corner. Hard to believe. What had happened to the past year, and why did each year seem to go by a little faster than the one before?

Their children were no longer babies—hers and Charlie's—and she wondered how much longer they would even want to go with their parents to cut down a tree. Their oldest son, Michael, would be graduating from high school in a matter of months. Melissa, had just celebrated her fifteenth birthday and was letting *everyone* know she was quite grown up now and needed her own space. Marcy frowned, then reminded herself of what life had been like when she was her daughter's age. "She'll grow out of it," Marcy's mother reminded her when she had shared her frustrations over a lunch of tuna sandwiches and handfuls of bite-size pretzels.

"Are you sure?"

"You did, didn't you?"

Marcy smiled then, and she smiled now. Yes, she had grown out of the daily frustrations and aggravations that come from being a fifteen-year-old girl. Her face had finally stopped breaking out at all the wrong times, her body had ceased growing and stretching and reshaping and had finally found a stopping point, and the hormones finally ceased screaming and settled down to a mild roar.

At what age had that been? Eighteen? Nineteen? That meant she and Charlie only had four more years to endure year-round PMS and it would be over. *Oh, joy!*

Last but not least was twelve-year-old Mark, her precious baby who wasn't a baby any longer and the one who would rather be with his father than any other human being on the face of the whole wide earth, including his mother. Marcy didn't worry about Mark *not* wanting to go to the farm and cut down the tree. He would be the first to suggest it, the first to shove his short, stocky frame into his coat, the first to pull on his steel-toe Wellingtons. In fact, it would be Mark who would announce to the others as they drove along the unpaved road that led from the highway to the farm in their white Ford Explorer exactly which tree would be the one to grace their living room this year.

"I checked it out the other day when Dad and I were down here working," Marcy imagined he would announce to his older siblings. "It's a really cool tree."

Melissa would pop her gum and roll her eyes. Michael would lock his arm around Mark's thick neck and say, "Sport, you're always looking out for the family, and I want you to know how much I appreciate it."

Michael had absolutely no interest in the farm, but he dearly loved Christmas.

Marcy's phone rang. She jumped, pulled the throw away from her legs, set the mug on the coffee table, and walked into the hallway to the old 1950s phone table she had refinished and placed near the French doors off the living room.

"Hello?"

"Marcy?"

"Katie!" Marcy locked an arm across her waist and rested the elbow of her right arm on it.

"Busy?" Katie's voice was soft and trembling.

"What's wrong?"

"What makes you think something is wrong?"

"Who ya talkin' to here?"

"Marcy, can you come up?"

"To New York?"

"Yes."

"When?" She looked at her watch as though Katie meant "at any given moment."

"Tomorrow?"

"Tomorrow!"

"Please, Marcy."

Marcy sat in the seat of the phone table. "What's going on, Katie?"

"I'm not sure. But I sure could use your reporter's intuition. Not to mention, I just need you right now. I don't want to talk about it over the phone. . .and please don't tell Mama anything. . .just. . .can you come?"

"I'd. . .um. . .I'd have to talk to Charlie."

"Of course."

"And I have to think about the kids. They're still in school." Marcy reached for the legal pad and pen she kept inside the crescent-shaped opening of the table and began to jot notes. *New York. . .tomorrow. . . Charlie. . .kids. . .*

"Oh, of course. I'm sorry. I wasn't thinking."

"No, no! Katie, I'd be glad to come; I just need to get some things in order. For one thing, how long are we talking about here?" *Call Mama. . .*

"I don't know for sure."

"You're being awfully evasive." *Call Angela: cancel lunch tomorrow. . .*

"I know. I'd rather talk to you in person. You're the one who helped me find the missing files after Ben. . .disappeared. . .and I need you to help me again."

"Can't you give me a hint?" *What is going on here?*

There was beat of silence before Katie answered. "I suppose so. Just promise you won't think I'm losing my mind."

"Of course not."

"Okay. Here it is: either Ben has returned to the city. . .or. . ."

"Or?" The pen slipped from her fingers and rested on the pad below.

"Or someone is trying to cause me to lose my mind."

CHAPTER NINE
Tuesday, December 4, 2001
Early Afternoon

As soon as Phil left The Hamilton Place, he headed over to Saks Fifth Avenue. He identified himself, then showed Nora Taylor his credentials and asked if he could speak to Cassie.

Nora Taylor narrowed her eyes. "May I ask what this is in reference to?"

"I've been hired by Katharine Webster—"

Nora brightened a bit. "Does this concern the necklace?"

"Yes."

Mrs. Taylor sighed heavily, then came around from the glass jewelry case and waggled a finger at him. "Follow me," she instructed. When Phil fell in line beside her, she continued. "Cassie's not scheduled until Thursday. I'll take you up to my office and call her home, if you'd like."

Phil nodded in appreciation. "That'd be nice. Yes."

They stopped in front of the elevators, and Nora pushed the up button. "Young man, in case you need to speak with me, I was here the other day when Mrs. Webster came in to inquire about the necklace. Pity about her losing it."

"Yes."

The doors opened; Phil allowed the department head to enter first, then followed behind her. The doors closed, and they rode in silence, staring straight ahead, until the doors opened. "After you," he said.

Nora Taylor led the way to a small, tastefully decorated office where she kept personnel information in a locked filing cabinet. She invited Phil to have a seat, but he declined. Instead, he shoved his hands deep into his pockets and waited as she unlocked the filing cabinet and brought out a manila folder.

"Naturally the employees' main files are kept in HR."

"Naturally."

"But I like to keep information on my team." She laid the folder on her desk and began to go through its contents.

"I can see you are very proficient."

Nora Taylor stopped in her search and looked up. She smiled briefly. "Thank you, Mr. Silver. I'd like to think so." She retrieved a small piece of paper from the file, then dialed the phone number, handing the receiver to Phil. "I'll wait for you in the hallway."

Phil took the phone. "Thank you, Mrs. Taylor."

As Nora Taylor had closed the door behind her, Phil waited. A woman answered on the third ring.

"Is Cassie in, please?"

"Cassie? No. Cassie is gone until later tomorrow." The voice was stern and authoritative.

"Gone?"

"May I ask who is calling?"

"Is this Cassie's mother?"

"Her aunt. Cassie's parents are dead."

"I see. I'm calling from Saks—"

"I thought Cassie wasn't due to work again until Thursday."

"That's correct, but I was hoping to talk to her—"

"That girl!"

"Ma'am," Phil interjected. "I'm calling from Nora Taylor's office. If Cassie comes home early or calls in, will you have her call Mrs. Taylor?"

"Is Cassie in some sort of trouble?"

Phil smiled in an effort to sound reassuring. "No. Cassie isn't in trouble. She's doing a fine job at Saks." Phil was sure he was telling the truth. "Just have her call Mrs. Taylor."

When he joined Nora Taylor in the hallway, he told her Cassie was out of town until Thursday, but she might be hearing from Cassie. "If she does call," he said, extending his card, "please have her contact me as soon as possible. And please, stress to her she's not in any trouble."

Nora smiled. "Bless Cassie. She works hard for us here. She's just young and, from what I hear, under a lot of pressure at home."

Phil nodded. He could vouch for that much. "Mrs. Taylor, you said you were here the day Mrs. Webster was here."

Nora Taylor crossed her arms. "I was."

"Can you tell me what you saw? If you heard anything unusual?"

Nora shook her head. "Have you seen that crowd out there? I was helping one of our newest sales clerks ring up a purchase when I heard Mrs. Webster. She was in an absolute panic. I thought it best not to make a scene, so Cassie and I brought her up to the break room. She sent Cassie for her driver, and that's when she realized the necklace was not in her possession. Poor dear. You just can't leave things like that around in the city."

"Did you see anyone suspicious either immediately before or after Mrs. Webster left?"

Nora pursed her lips. "No. Then again, during the season, we've all we can do to keep ourselves above water, if you know what I mean."

Phil did. "I understand. If you think of anything. . .anything at all. . . call me." Phil left the third floor alone. He walked purposefully through the lobby of the first floor, then into the cold December air and toward his car. He slipped into the driver's seat, turned the ignition, cranked up the heat, and drove to John Jay where he intended to spend some time at the computer, looking into the career of one Jordan Whitney.

Tuesday
Late Afternoon

As far as Phil was concerned, the Upper East Side was another world, another universe for that matter. Well-heeled, conservative, family-centered professionals lived superabundantly with all the typical trappings of wealth. There were the luxury high-rise apartment buildings, the posh boutiques, the exclusive private schools like Dalton, the fine dining establishments and fashionable coffee houses, and, of course, the cigar bars catering to the chic-elite professionals.

Driving along the city streets, Phil passed by the windows and doors of some of the most famous businesses in the world. The red canopy over the doors of Christie's Auction House, various famous insignias, signs, and logos of stores such as Chanel, DKNY, Emporio Armani, Louis Vuitton, Bergdorf Goodman, Christian Dior, Dolce & Gabanna, Gucci, Prada, & Valentino were as commonplace as the sole proprietorships in some of the other neighborhoods that surrounded it. But what did it matter to a class of people who wore Polo and Donna Karan every day? To a people whose children grew up taking FAO Schwartz for granted. Toyland, in its grandest theme, would one day give way to shopping at Barneys and dining in establishments such as Heidelberg Restaurant, where Phil was now heading.

"I'll meet you at Heidelberg at five," Victoria Whitney had announced earlier over the phone. Phil had just completed about an hour's research on Victoria's husband, Jordan, one of the city's Assemblymen.

According to Phil's research, Assemblyman Whitney graduated from Oxford University with a degree in Modern History and Economics, then returned to the United States to further his education with a Juris Doctorate. Shortly after moving to the city that never sleeps, he married his first wife, the former Patricia Valmont. Twelve years later, Patricia—known as Patsy—was diagnosed with uterine cancer and died within six months, leaving three children. Shortly thereafter, Whitney threw himself into the political fray, working tirelessly for various causes: health care reform, breast and uterine cancer research, and nursing shortages in the city. He was an active father in his children's lives and was often seen at sporting events and piano recitals. With the exception of the occasional unknown female escort who attended social and political functions with him, his only regular companion was his adolescent daughter, Tina. Whitney was well heeled, well loved, and well respected. With the exception of being the lonely, available widower, he seemed to have his life on track. Then, in an act that surprised the Upper East-enders, he married a woman no one seemed to have ever heard of, the present Victoria Thomas Whitney.

Eighteen months ago, when the Caballero/Webster case opened, no one had known exactly what had happened to Victoria Thomas, the original manager of Jacqueline's. During the early days after Webster and Caballero disappeared, it had never occurred to him to ask Katie. This angered him. Usually he was more thorough. Now he tried to reason that, having lost one of his best friends, the grief might have clouded his judgment. Perhaps, when his supervisor suggested he be removed from the case, he should have listened. Either way, he knew where Victoria was now; she was waiting for him at Heidelberg, a restaurant located in the traditionally German section of the Upper East Side.

Phil gazed out the window at serene, tree-lined streets of august brownstones and distinguished townhouses. The few people walking on the sidewalks were bundled in stylish coats, their chins tucked into their chests as they bustled along. He swung around a corner and began to look for a parking space. Finding one, Phil parked, opened the car door, automatically locked it, and shut the door. A gust of cold wind licked at his exposed face and pushed against his body as he made his way to the front door of the establishment, jerked it open, and went inside. Warm air and the enticing aroma of *wiener schnitzel* and *sauerbraten* met him as he entered. He momentarily glanced around the place, trying to get his bearings. A variety of German flags hung on the walls between the occasional advertisements for Dinckelacker or Becks beer. Traditional Bavarian decorative pieces of bric-a-brac were strategically placed around the large room. The sound of a German polka piped through an overhead sound system.

Phil looked beyond a trellis-style screen dividing the bar and smoking area of the restaurant from the non-smoking dining area. He spotted Victoria Whitney easily. She sat in the back of the bar area at a small round table in the far right corner. Her blond hair was pulled back into a tight chignon and a multicolored, silk scarf draped over the shoulders of a gray wool suit jacket. He watched her for a few moments before approaching the table. Her long, graceful fingers fluttered along the linen tablecloth, sometimes stopping to brush against a gold lamé cigarette case. He thought her rings, which he could plainly see from where he stood, were almost too large for such slender hands. The parts of her wrists exposed below the cuffs of her jacket were laden with gold and gemstone bracelets. She sat ramrod straight, one leg crossing the other, the toe of her foot popping up and down in a rhythm only she could detect. It was the barely perceptible movement of nervousness. Perhaps even fear. Phil frowned. This wasn't going to be easy.

"Mrs. Whitney?" he inquired as he reached the table.

She started, then turned only slightly to look at him. "You are Mr. Silver," she said almost inaudibly.

"Yes, Ma'am." He reached into his pocket for his credentials, but she raised her left hand slightly and stopped him.

"Please, don't," she said, returning her gaze to the back wall. "The last thing I need is for someone to see you showing me your badge." Phil looked around the back portion of the restaurant. There was a thirty-ish couple sitting to the far left and an elderly gentleman nursing a drink near the bar. It was early still. Victoria followed his gaze at first, then rested her penetrating eyes deep into his as he looked back at her. "Sit down, please," she said politely.

Phil moved to the chair opposite her and, for the first time, looked into the face of the one person who had managed to escape his investigation from the previous year. She was pretty, but not glamorous as Andi Daniels had been. In fact, the African-American/Asian Andi Daniels had been nothing short of exotic. Victoria Whitney was, if he was any judge of ethnic background, of Scandinavian descent. Her eyes were vibrant blue, her complexion golden, and her cheekbones were high and somewhat regal. Her makeup was tastefully understated, giving her a more youthful and refined appearance. She had class, exuded it, though it was difficult to tell whether it was inherited or carefully developed. *Soignée*, he could hear his mother calling it.

Victoria Whitney took a deep breath and sighed heavily. "I wondered how long it would take you people to locate me," she opened.

A male server approached the table. "Would you care for something to drink?"

Phil looked at the pilsner of beer sitting on the table before Victoria. "I'll have whatever the lady is having. Would you like another one?"

"No, thank you," Victoria said, her voice still low and feathery soft.

"Will you be ordering?" the server asked.

"Ah—"

"Their *suppe* is delicious," Victoria informed him.

"Will you join me in eating something?"

She shook her head, almost imperceptibly.

"Are you sure?"

"Yes. But, please. Go ahead. It's really good."

"It's made with chunks of potatoes," the server offered by way of advertisement. "With a tasty base of bacon goulash."

"You talked me into it."

"I'll be right back with your *suppe* and beer."

Phil leaned his forearms on the table and looked intently at Victoria as the server walked away. "How long did you work for Bucky Caballero?"

Victoria picked up the beer directly in front of her and took a small sip. She swallowed hard before answering. "You get right to the point. Now allow me to do the same. Do I need to call an attorney, Mr. Silver? Aren't you supposed to read me some rights or something?"

"I'm not here to arrest you, Mrs. Whitney. In fact, I'd like to keep this as quiet as possible."

He thought he saw her shoulders sag, as though an incredible weight had been lifted. "If my husband knew. . . ." She didn't go on.

"Knew what? About your work with Caballero?"

"Oh, no. If he knew you'd called, he'd be very upset."

"I see."

"He knew about my work. He was a client."

"I assumed he was. I couldn't see him in a hotel boutique buying an overpriced dress."

Victoria Whitney smiled. "The prices are a bit exorbitant. Then again, have you ever shopped in this area of the city?"

"Yes, as a matter of fact, I have."

"I don't want you to think poorly of my husband," she said, ignoring his answer. "He's a good man, Mr. Silver. A wonderful, devoted husband and father."

"Who frequented escort services for sex."

Victoria looked horrified. "Is that what you think it was all about?" Her voice rose slightly.

"Isn't it?"

"No, I assure you it is not."

The server returned with a bowl of hot soup and a pilsner of beer, set it in front of Phil, then retreated to the table where the couple sat. Phil could hear him asking, "How are we doing over here?"

"What is it about, then?" he asked, removing his utensils from a tightly wrapped, crisp, white linen napkin.

"Mr. Silver, when prominent men and women come to the city, they often need dinner dates. Escorts for business functions. Most are single men and women. Yes, some of them are married. But they are all alone. And they don't like to be alone, Mr. Silver."

Phil took a sip of the *suppe*. "This is good. Thank you for suggesting it."

"You're welcome."

He shook his head. "I don't think we're really talking about dinner dates, Mrs. Whitney. Do you? Who would pay three- to five hundred dollars for a warm body to merely sit across the table or slip her arm into his?"

"That's personal between client and escort." She leaned over slightly.

A light waft of her expensive perfume reached his nostrils, blending with the smell of the soup. "Do you have any idea what it's like to be so terribly lonely? To just want to hold another human being in your arms for a short while. To feel the warmth of someone's skin? To want to feel the breath of someone and know—truly know—that you're alive? Even if you have to pay for it?"

Phil placed his soupspoon on the plate underneath the soup bowl. "No. I can't say that I do."

"You have a wife, yes?"

"Yes."

"Ever been unfaithful?"

"No."

"Has she?"

"Of course not."

"Of course not?" There was a brief pause. "Always there for each other?"

"Yes."

"Children?"

"Two."

"Happy? Healthy?"

"Yes."

"Now, then. What if—let's say—your wife suddenly died and you were left to take care of your children and work and do all the things your wife used to do."

"I don't even like to think about that."

"But let's just say. Humor me."

"All right."

"You know you aren't in the market for a permanent relationship. You're affluent. Handsome. A pretty good catch in any market. Suddenly the women of your social status are standing on your doorstep with dinner invitations, or words of advice like, 'Do you know what you need? You need an evening out with a friend. I just happen to have some theater tickets for this Friday night. . . . '"

"What's so wrong with that?" Phil reached for the nearby beer, blew at the small amount of foam left at the top, and took a hearty swallow.

"Nothing if you're in the market for wife number two." Victoria laced her fingers together and rested her elbows on the table. She leaned closer to Phil, as though she were now comfortable with what she had to say or had, perhaps, gained control of their conversation. "But let's say you aren't. Let's say you just want someone to attend the functions with you and then go home."

Phil imitated her actions. His fingers laced, his elbows propped on either side of the soup bowl, and he leaned forward before speaking. "Whose home?"

Victoria sat back abruptly. "Does that really matter? No strings, Mr. Silver."

"If it were always that simple. There are laws, Mrs. Whitney."

"We're talking about human beings with human emotions." She tilted her chin slightly. "And needs."

"Is that what happened with your husband?" Phil resumed eating the soup and watched as the woman sitting across the table from him blushed properly.

"My husband is a good man, Mr. Silver."

"You've indicated that. I know his public record is impressive. I don't know a lot about his private life, other than his wife died from cancer, leaving him with three children."

Victoria's eyelids lowered slightly. "Yes. But we aren't really here to talk about my husband, are we?"

"Not really. Though I will have to tell you that I find this interesting; why a man would go into a ladies' boutique for the purpose of finding a date."

"The business behind the business—the escort service—was very exclusive, Mr. Silver. And very expensive. Not just anyone could walk in there. We catered to a very impressive clientele."

"Yes. I have the records. At least from when it was managed by Andi."

At that Victoria laughed lightly as she reached for the gold lamé cigarette case lying next to her drink. "Do you mind?" she asked.

He shook his head. "Not at all." He watched her fingertips flip open the case. She used her manicured nails to pull a cigarette from inside, switched it to her index and second fingers of her left hand, then pulled a gold, monogrammed lighter from the case. "Allow me," he said, reaching for it.

Victoria handed him the lighter, placed the cigarette between her painted red lips, and leaned forward as he flicked the lighter. His eyes focused on the tip of the cigarette, watched the singeing of it, and heard the crackling of the paper and tobacco. Victoria withdrew the cigarette from her lips, blew a thin line of gray smoke over her right shoulder, and then leaned back in her chair. Phil returned the lighter to the top of her cigarette case.

"I still can't believe Andi ratted on Bucky and Mattie. If there's anyone out there you should be trying to locate, it would be her. I really don't have a lot to tell you about the business. I had been gone a very long time, as I'm sure you know."

"It's not so much the business I'm interested in, Mrs. Whitney."

"Then what?" She drew on her cigarette, repeating the actions of a moment before.

"I need to know more about Bucky Caballero."

She blinked slowly. "He was a wonderful man."

"Was?"

"Was. Is. He was wonderful when I knew him."

"When was the last time you saw him? Heard from him?"

She took another draw, this one deeper than the one before. As she exhaled, she rested the cigarette against the nondescript glass ashtray near the center of the table and thumped the ashes into it. "The night before he left the country. He called me before he left."

"Did he say where he was going?"

Victoria laughed again. "Do you honestly believe I would tell you if I knew?"

"Do you know?"

"No. Bucky is too smart for that. Not to mention, he would not have wanted to place me in that position."

"Were you in love with him?" Phil wasn't sure where the question had come from. It slipped out of his mouth before he had a moment to think about it.

She smiled then. A smile that came from only one side of her mouth, resembling something of a smirk. She pursed her lips before answering. "Every woman who ever meets Bucky falls in love with him, Mr. Silver. But no woman gets him."

"What does that mean?"

"It means," she began, then took another draw of her cigarette before exhaling and grinding out the butt, "that Bucky can't be had. He's too smart for that." She laughed again. "Sometimes he would call for one of the girls. Oh, my goodness. Those women would honestly think they were going to be the next queen. You could almost see it in their eyes. Ever hear of Esther?"

"From the story of Purim?"

"Yes."

"I'm Jewish. Of course, I have."

"Remember how the young virgins were called up to the king's chambers?"

"Yes. Of course. Esther won the king's heart when she was called."

"Bucky used to call it the Esther Syndrome. They all thought they would be the next queen because surely no one had ever treated him as good or been as attentive to his needs." She chuckled again. "Like I said, Bucky can't be had."

"I find it fascinating that you and Bucky talk about scriptural characters."

She smirked again. "Fine Christian upbringing."

"You really didn't answer my question. Were you in love with him?"

"I might have been infatuated at first. But I was too smart for that. I learned to appreciate my friendship with him and his sister."

"What about Andi? Was she in love with him?"

"Like no one I've ever known. She would have done anything for him. That's why it really shocked me that she ratted on him like she did."

"How did he feel about her?"

"She was an employee. A good employee, but nothing more. He and Mattie and Jordan and I used to have dinner together quite a bit. He would tell me about it—privately, of course. He bought her plenty of toys to keep her occupied, but it was never enough because she wanted him so badly. It must have killed her when he'd call for the other girls."

"I'm sure."

"What is it you want to know, Mr. Silver?" Victoria leaned forward again, resting her arms across her lap.

"Anything. Everything. Did he have any close friends? Any hobbies?"

"Art."

"Art?"

"French, to be more precise."

"French art."

"Daumier, Millet, Renoir, Maillol."

"Fouquet?"

"He dearly loved the work of Fouquet. How did you know?"

"There was a copy of *Les Heures E'tienne Chevalier* over his desk."

"How is it a man in law enforcement knows so much about French art?"

"This agent studied it when he was abroad."

"Really? Do tell."

"I think not. Is there anything else you can tell me about Bucky Caballero?"

"I can't think of anything I'd *want* to tell you about him, actually. Other than he's gone and won't be back. So why don't you leave this case alone? What brings you around after all these months to want to meet me here?"

"I have reason to believe he's been in town. . .is playing games with Katie Webster." Phil watched for changes in the woman's face, but she only laughed again.

"Please. If Bucky had been in town, I'd be the first one he'd call. Besides, he doesn't have time to mess with her. And why would he want to?"

"To make her think her husband is still alive."

Victoria leaned closer to the table. "Mr. Silver, I guarantee you that if Bucky had anything to do with Mr. Webster's unfortunate and untimely demise, it would be a done deal. *If* Bucky set a bomb in Mr. Webster's car, then William Webster is indeed dead."

Phil flinched. He hadn't meant to, but he did.

Victoria tilted her head slightly. "Surely that can't bother a seasoned investigator such as yourself."

He looked her directly in the eye. "William Webster was my best friend."

Victoria sat back. "I'm sorry. I had no idea."

"Why would you?"

She answered with silence.

"Anyway," Phil reached into his pocket and pulled out a card. As he slid it across the table, he said, "If you hear from him, would you call me? I know I'm talking to the air here, but I'd at least like to give you an opportunity to help with this case."

Victoria picked up the card, looked at it, then slipped it into her cigarette case along with the lighter. "I think you are looking for the wrong man, Mr. Silver. But if I hear anything, I'll call."

Phil stood and looked around the room, wondering when the newly arrived patrons had entered and how this woman whom he'd just met could have intrigued him so. He reached into his pocket for his money clip, pulled out a twenty-dollar bill and laid it on the table. "It was a pleasure meeting you. Thank you for the tip on the *suppe*."

Victoria Whitney looked up at him and smiled. "The pleasure was all mine. Sorry I couldn't have been of more help."

"Me, too."

She watched him walk toward the front of the restaurant and out the door. She waited a few moments before taking a sip of her warm beer, then reached toward the seat of the chair to her right where her purse had been safely hidden. She opened it slowly and retrieved her cell phone. She pressed the "one" with her thumbnail, then "talk." Bringing the phone up to her ear, she reached for her cigarette case again and, with the fingertips of one hand, pulled another cigarette from the case.

"Yes, my love," she heard the voice on the other end greet her.

"He's gone."

"What did he want?"

"To know more about you."

"Me? Why me?"

"Apparently someone is hounding Mrs. Webster."

A light chuckle came from the other end of the phone.

"Is it you? Are you messing with her mind?"

"Now, Darling. If I were, would I involve you?"

Victoria lit her cigarette.

"Are you smoking, Darling? Is that what I hear on the other end?"

"I always smoke when I'm nervous, Bucky. You know that."

"Why are you nervous?"

"I don't want anything to happen to you. Go back to Canada, Bucky. Leave today. Call your pilot and tell him you want out within the hour."

"I want to see you again before I go."

"No, Bucky. It's too dangerous. They may be following me."

"Don't be ridiculous."

"No."

"Meet me at The Plaza."

"You're staying at *The Plaza?* You didn't tell me that when we had dinner the other night. Bucky, that's dangerous!" she hunched her shoulders so that the patrons near her wouldn't overhear.

He chuckled again. "My pet, haven't I told you how very smart I am? Don't you know that it is harder to find the Easter egg in plain view than the one securely hidden?"

She took several deep breaths before answering. "Don't you think I should tell Jordan?"

"I would not involve him. He has his career to think of."

"*I* have his career to think of."

"Meet me at ten o'clock in the morning. I'm on the ninth floor. . . Room—"

"You're not in the Presidential Suite?"

"That would attract attention, *ma cherie.*"

She sighed heavily. "I suppose so, but at the very least, I'd expect the Fifth Avenue Suite."

He chuckled at her dry—albeit snobbish—sense of humor, then gave her his room number. "Ten o'clock. Don't let me down."

"Have I ever?"

"No. Never. With the exception, that is, of the day you married Jordan." There was a teasing lilt in his voice.

She smiled warmly. "You know how I feel, Bucky. The way I have always felt about you."

"Shh," he whispered. "That has always been our little secret. I will see you tomorrow. Until then, stay safe. *Mis-en-garde.*"

CHAPTER TEN

Katie returned the handset of her office phone to its cradle. Marcy had returned her call within two hours. In the interim, Katie busied herself in her office, trying to make the time go faster. She tried to focus on the tasks at hand, but found it difficult not thinking about the necklace and the inscrutable note that accompanied it. She wondered, now, what Phil might have discovered about Victoria Whitney, and she thought about calling him. She only had a vague recollection of Victoria, who was replaced by Andi Daniels before Katie had started dating Ben.

Instead, Katie called on the resolve she'd developed over the past months and busied herself with her work. The call from Marcy came as Katie was, once again, trying to review the information Ashley had given her on the spa in France. She had made several operational notes to take to the board and, although she was becoming more and more excited about the possibilities of an exclusive mountain spa, she was happily diverted by the call.

"Katie, I've just talked to Charlie. He says he thinks I should go to New York. He's a little nervous about me flying. . .with what happened in September and all. . .but says he feels strongly that I should go. Just tell me what you want me to do."

Katie's head dropped, and she sighed deeply. She immediately envisioned Marcy stepping off the plane. They would have dinner, and Katie would tell her old friend of the incidents of the past few days. Marcy, logical Marcy, would help figure all this out. If Ben was trying to let her know that he was near, Marcy would be able to deduce it. "Thank you, Marcy," she began, pulling her reading glasses from the bridge of her nose. "And thank Charlie for me. I'll have Vickey call my travel agent and have everything set up for you. I honestly can't thank you enough."

"No problem." The voice from her childhood friend seemed confident. "I don't know what's going on, but, like I told Charlie, I've always wanted to see New York City in December."

Katie smiled. "I'm already feeling better, just knowing you're on your way." She laid the gold-rimmed glasses atop the small pile of papers before her.

"Well. I'm a little anxious to hear what's going on up there. So, what do you think? Tomorrow?"

"Yes. I'll have Vickey call the travel agency now. She'll call you shortly, okay?"

"Sounds good. I'll start getting things together here." Katie imagined Marcy packing her clothes, dashing out to the grocery store for easy to prepare foods for her family, returning to a clean home only to clean a little bit deeper. Every garment in the dirty clothes hamper would be washed, dried, and folded. Projects for each child would be penned with a felt marker on a dry erase magnetic board stuck to the front of her refrigerator. Marcy lived in "Homemakersville." She paused and smiled. Except for Ben's absence—and this nagging business with the necklace—she was very happy with herself and her life, though too enfolded in those two things to think about them with a clear head. That's why she needed Marcy.

"Thanks again."

"You okay for now?"

"Yes." She was. For now.

"I won't say anything to Miss Carolyn."

"Thank you, again, Marcy. I don't think Mama needs this right now."

"I think mothers are always supposed to be there for you. That is, of course, just my maternal opinion."

"Mama would be frustrated that she couldn't solve this problem for me. Mama was always in control, or at least she wanted to be. She can't control this. Besides, there's no need to worry her at this point. I don't see where she can help me anyway."

"But I can?"

"Yes. Let me have Vickey make that call. Will you be near a phone?"

"Yes. I'll wait right here until I hear something."

"I'll have Vickey call you. See you tomorrow."

Katie returned the handset, took a deep breath, then picked it up again and called to the outer office. Instead of answering, Vickey tapped lightly on the door, entering before Katie could bid her to come in. Katie frowned imperceptibly and slipped her glasses back on. Was it just her imagination, or had Vickey managed to conceive every feasible excuse to keep interrupting her that afternoon? She looked at Vickey and said, "I'm about to make Shirley's day."

"Shirley?"

"At Admiral Travel Agency."

Vickey propped her forearms over the back of one of the chairs between her and Katie and frowned. "Going somewhere?"

"No. I'm having Marcy flown up here. I need you to call the agency and make the arrangements."

"Why?" Vickey moved around the chair and sat.

"I need her." Katie reached for a nearby pen and began to run her fingers along its gold shaft. "Could you do that now? Marcy is waiting." She peered at Vickey from over the rim of the glasses.

Vickey straightened properly. "I'll be right back," she said turning, then made her way into her office. Katie resumed the work she'd been reviewing before Marcy had called, listening absentmindedly to the hum of Vickey's voice from just beyond the door she'd left ajar. Within moments, Vickey returned.

"I called. Shirley is looking into the best deals and will call back shortly."

Katie looked up and smiled. "Thank you."

"You're welcome," Vickey returned primly. Katie could sense her displeasure.

"Okay. What?" she asked, again removing her glasses.

"You *need* your friend?"

"Yes."

"For?"

"Support."

"What am I?" Vickey looked something between hurt and surprised.

Katie dropped the pen and stood. "My dear friend. And my assistant. But Marcy is. . ."

"Your oldest friend."

"Yes. You're too close to this, Vickey. Sometimes it's better not to be. Marcy never knew Ben. She only knows what I've told her. Phil knew Ben well. She's a columnist; he's an FBI agent. It's perspective. Perhaps the two of them can come up with something that makes sense." Katie dropped the pen, stood, and walked to the window overlooking the skyline. "The more I think about it, the more I know this doesn't make logical sense. On one hand I want to believe that Ben is sending me the necklace. Perhaps slowly letting me know he is here. On the other hand, I ask myself why he doesn't just call. Then again, he may figure it could be too much of a shock. He was always so concerned about my emotions. He doesn't know what's happened to me in the last year. . .doesn't know to what degree I'm running this company." She paused. "My gosh, it's getting so dark out there. What time is it?"

"Nearly six."

Katie crossed her arms across her abdomen and drummed her fingers. "What a crazy day." She heard Vickey stand and walk up beside her.

"Crazy week."

"So far."

Vickey nodded silently. Katie looked over and smiled. Vickey turned slightly and looked at her employer with a slight toss of her head. "You know, it doesn't seem to matter what you are going through. You still manage to look like a million dollars."

"Ha!" Katie laughed out loud.

"You do!"

Katie turned and propped against the sill. "I feel old."

"You look wonderful."

"What brought that on? Are you looking for a raise?" Katie teased.

"No, of course not. Well. . ." she smiled, crossing her arms in like fashion and also leaned against the sill. "Perhaps a nice Christmas bonus."

The women laughed, then sobered.

"I need to pick up something for Marcy."

"Pick up something? A gift?"

"Yes."

"Like what?"

"I don't know. Something for coming up here on such short notice. Leaving her family."

"She has children, doesn't she?"

"Three. Oldest is Michael. I think I've told you about him."

"Yes. Plans to major in French when he goes off to college?"

"That's him. Quite a young man."

"Marcy is married, I take it."

"Yes. To Charlie Waters. We went to school together, though to my knowledge she never really paid any attention to him. When we were in school, she dated the same guy for three years until just before Christmas holidays of our senior year." Katie laughed and moved toward the sofas. Vickey followed her. "Marcy was so funny. She swore up and down that Wade—the guy she dated—broke up with her just before Christmas, so he wouldn't have to buy her a gift. I said, 'Marce, he's bought you a gift the past two Christmases; what is so different about this year?' She said she didn't know, but she thought that had to be it. Turns out he was madly in love with a sophomore."

"The glories of teenage love," Vickey said as she sat. The leather of the sofa sighed under her.

"Leather should sigh," Ben had once told Katie. "It sighs and then you sigh. Welcome to the world of style and relaxation."

"What about you, Vickey? Who did you date in high school?"

Vickey turned her face toward the desk and smiled. "It's getting cold in here. Don't you think it's getting cold in here?"

"I'll light the gas logs," Katie said, smiling. "Tell."

Vickey gave her best look of resignation. "All right, if you insist. His name was Andrew. Andrew Richard Bennett."

"You remember his full name?" Katie wasn't so surprised. Most women would remember the full names of their childhood sweethearts. Of all women, Vickey definitely would. She was one of the most capable executive assistants any businessperson could ask for.

Vickey nodded, her blond hair shimmering in the glow of the city's lights that now shone through the wide window behind them. "Other than my husband, he was the absolute love of my life. We dated our junior and senior years. Said we were going to get married when we graduated from college."

"What happened?"

"We went to separate colleges. He met someone else—"

"Just like Wade. . ."

"—I met someone else."

"Ah-ha." Katie pointed a finger at her secretary and winked.

"It was bound to happen. We were young."

"Weren't we all." It wasn't a question. Momentarily, Katie was transported to her own high school days, to her forbidden love-relationship with Chad "Buddy" Adkins. Her mother had disapproved of Buddy; he was from the "wrong side of the tracks." But Katie had loved him and had been loved in return. Loved so much, he had been willing to let her go to be the success he knew she was destined to become. Neither one of them could have known the downward spiral that would temporarily enmesh her.

"You know," Vickey leaned back into the richness of the sofa. "I don't think you ever told me how you met William."

Katie took a deep breath and lay back against the leather as Vickey had. She crossed her arms and legs simultaneously. "You know Cynthia."

"His cousin?"

"Yes. I was her secretary."

"That much I knew. But you know William. He was never one to divulge."

Katie closed her eyes and smiled. "Oh, yes. He certainly was discreet."

A moment of silence passed before Katie opened her eyes and darted a glance at Vickey, who frowned. "Is. I mean, is. He certainly *is* discreet."

"I knew what you meant." The words were barely audible.

Katie pressed her lips together and willed herself not to cry. "He came to the office to get Cynthia for lunch."

"William did?"

"Mmm-hmm. He arrived while we were going over something or another in her office. We were introduced and, according to what he told me later, he drilled Cynthia all during lunch."

Vickey smiled. " 'Who is she? Where did she come from? Who is she dating?' "

"Yes, more or less. When he returned to the office, he came to my cubicle, sat next to my desk, and asked me out for that Saturday night."

"And you said yes."

"After I picked up my pencils."

"Your pencils?"

Katie laughed. "I kept dropping my pencils. I had one tucked behind my ear, one in my hand. . . ." Katie shook her head. "I was a mess." Katie could easily bring the scene to mind. Ben, sitting next to her desk with his hands shoved deep in his coat pockets, wrapping the front of the coat tightly around him. Ben, who gave a new meaning to the words style and finesse.

"But he was impressed."

"Yes."

"How long before you knew you were in love?"

"Not long."

The phone on Katie's desk rang. Vickey stood quickly and walked over to it. Katie listened to Vickey's one-sided conversation. "Mrs. Webster's office. . .yes. . .yes." She reached for the gold pen and a sticky pad and began to scribble. "Got it. Thank you. Merry Christmas to you, too."

Katie stood. "Shirley?"

"Yes. Your friend will fly into LaGuardia tomorrow afternoon at 2:47. Delta, flight 6798 from Savannah."

"Good. Can you call Bonaparte's and reserve my table for tomorrow night?" She moved gracefully across the room, leaving past memories at the sofas and returning to her authoritative position.

"Certainly. You asked earlier about a gift."

"Yes. What do you think?"

"Why don't you run down to Jacqueline's in the morning and check out their new stock."

Katie brought her hands together in a gentle, ah-ha clap. "Oh! I was supposed to go down there. Didn't James say something about new management?"

"Yes. Zandra McKenzie and her brother Zane."

"Zandra and Zane? What names."

"Word has it they're twins."

"Oh."

"And gorgeous. Gorgeous and exotic."

"Gorgeous *and* exotic? My, my. They sound yummy. I can't wait to meet them." Katie moved toward the door while adding, "I can't do any more damage here today. I'm going upstairs to a hot bath. Wait a minute, though. What did you do with the necklace?"

"Mr. Silver took it."

"Oh, that's right."

Vickey switched off the overhead lights, and the two women stepped into the outer office.

"Unbelievably," Vickey interjected. "Wait for me while I shut down my computer."

"Unbelievably?" Katie stood near Vickey's L-shaped desk and waited for her assistant to close down for the evening.

"The twins. Unbelievably gorgeous." Done, Vickey stepped around the desk and toward the door leading to the hallway. Katie opened the door and nodded for Vickey to precede her.

"Have you seen them?" When Katie had closed the door firmly behind her, Vickey turned—keys in hand—and locked the door.

"Oh, yeah." The words were said with spunk and in jest. The women moved toward the centrally located elevators.

Katie pressed the up button for herself and the down for Vickey. "That good?"

Vickey grinned. "You can't even begin to imagine. Go down there tomorrow. You'll see."

CHAPTER ELEVEN
Tuesday, Late Night

Sharkey Garone's luck was changing. Especially from where he stood at the raised DJ's booth dominating the back left corner of his club. From there Sharkey had a view of his world. His girls. His patrons. His employees, his tables, and his chairs. This was *his* Mist Goddess.

He pressed the palms of his hands against the countertop and leaned over, straining his neck to get a better look at Candy, who stood atop a table, dancing for one of his best customers. Candy despised the man—said he made her feel creepy—but this was her punishment for having left him for the past few months. Besides that, the man was a big spender, probably one of the biggest he'd ever had in his club. Other than that, though, Sharkey knew very little about him. According to Jimmy, his bouncer, at one time the man had been an enforcer with one of the smaller arms of organized crime.

"He was a leg breaker," Jimmy had told him earlier.

"No kidding?"

"No kidding."

"He's built for it. What is he doing now?"

"Owns his own business, I'm told. Guess he made enough money breaking legs to do what he really wanted when he grew up."

"What kinda business?"

"I dunno, Boss. What do I look like, the Encyclopedia Britannica?"

Sharkey gave his bouncer a look that dared him to keep up with his sarcastic tone. It worked. The next line was a subdued, "I hear he's mean as a trapped snake. You don't want to make him mad."

"Yeah, yeah. As long as he's a paying customer, I won't."

"Well, I'd be wary of doing business with him, if you know what I mean."

"I don't do that kinda business."

Jimmy nodded. "Yeah, right."

Okay, so he did do that kind of business. Businessmen in the city had to in order to survive. It wasn't a morality choice. It was work ethics. It was survival. But he didn't get involved. He just did his job, paid his dues, and whatever else he had to do, all the while looking the other way.

What made him angry, what made his blood boil, were people like Katie Webster and all her do-good ways. *Well, ha-ha, Katie Webster. Everything you think you're doing for Candy isn't working. She's home where she belongs. With me.*

"Hey, Boss. There's someone here to see you." Sharkey looked over his shoulder to see Jimmy standing behind him.

"Yeah, yeah. Someone like who?"

Jimmy shrugged his beefy shoulders.

Sharkey cranked his neck to the right a bit, held his hands palms up and curled his lip. "Well, did you ask?"

" 'Course."

"And?"

"And he said it was none of my business. He didn't want to talk to me. He wants to talk to you. Something tells me you might want to."

"Yeah, yeah. Where is he now?"

"Table eleven."

"Does he want me to come out there?"

Jimmy shrugged again.

"Ah, all right."

"Maybe I'd better stay with you, huh?" Jimmy asked as Sharkey passed by him.

Sharkey stopped briefly and looked up at the brute. "Yeah, yeah. Maybe."

Sharkey clamped his stogie between his teeth, and the Mutt and Jeff duo headed toward table eleven. Even through the haze of smoke, Sharkey knew exactly which guest the bouncer had meant. The guest stood out. This was no ordinary Chinatown visitor. This man was class with a capital C. He didn't look like a very big man—in fact not much taller than Sharkey—but he wore power as casually as his extravagantly expensive suit. The dim lighting of the room shadowed his features; his beard added to the brooding nature of his face. Though Sharkey was the owner of the establishment, he suddenly felt inferior by comparison. For a moment he didn't know what to do once he arrived at the table. . .what to do with his hands even. He chose to stuff them in his pants pockets.

"I'm Sharkey," he announced, clenching his teeth to keep his cigar from falling to the floor.

The man, who was running a finger around the rim of an empty Tom Collins glass, looked up casually. "Hello, Mr. Sharkey."

Sharkey pulled one hand out of his pocket and removed the cigar. "Uh, no. It's Garone. Sharkey Garone."

The man smiled, but only enough to humor the establishment's owner. "I know."

Sharkey took a step back in order to pull out a chair and bumped into Jimmy. He turned, looked up, and scowled. "Whaddaya hanging around here for?"

Jimmy narrowed his eyes at the man sitting at the table. "You need me, Boss?"

"Nah, I think you can go do. . .whatever."

Jimmy kept his eyes on the man, nodded, then stepped away before Sharkey turned back to the guest. He started to sit but stopped when the man said, "Mr. Sharkey, may we adjourn to your office? It's a little busy out here."

Frozen halfway to sitting, Sharkey looked up without lifting his head. "Yeah." He stood. "You wanna follow me?"

The man stood as well and smiled. "How else would I know where to go?"

Sharkey pointed to the finished drink on the table. "Shall I have another one brought to you?"

"Would you?"

"I think I can arrange that." He glanced around briefly before spotting one of his waitresses. "Bonnie!" he barked. The thin, large-toothed brunette jumped. Seeing who had called her name she hurried over, eyes all large and glassy. "Bring the gentleman here a Tom Collins to my office." Sharkey suddenly wished he had a better-looking office. "On second thought, we'll be in one of the lounges."

"Which one?"

Sharkey gave her a look that read "figure it out" but answered, "I'll leave the door open until you get there."

"Am I staying?"

"No, you ain't staying! The gentleman and I have some things to discuss."

Bonnie looked from her boss to the guest and back. "What about you? Do you need anything from the bar?"

Sharkey paused. He rarely drank while at work. Still, he wanted to feel as though he were one with the man standing just a few feet behind him. "Yeah," he finally answered. "Make mine a Tom Collins, too."

"But Sharkey, you don't drink Tom—"

"Did I ask you any questions? I don't remember asking you any questions. I said, 'Make mine a Tom Collins.' That doesn't require a comment."

"Sure, Sharkey. Sure."

Sharkey turned to the man. "We're gonna go upstairs."

The man smiled knowingly. "One of your lounges?"

"I thought we'd be more comfortable. Unless you have another preference."

"No, that's fine."

"Ah, okay. Follow me then."

Sharkey made his way through the maze of tables and oblong stages and up a flight of wrought iron stairs to the second floor with the man keeping a steady pace about six steps behind him. Several times Sharkey turned his head slightly to make certain he was being followed. He was.

The second floor was mainly small rooms, or lounges, for private dances. Sharkey had begun to sweat on the way up, wondering if they would all be occupied, leaving him to look foolish and out of control in his own business. He breathed a sigh of relief when he saw that the very first one was unoccupied. He stepped aside and allowed the man to enter before him. The man nodded as he walked into the dimly lit room. The scent of cheap cologne and sweat permeated the air and seemed to almost cling to the pink and purple moiré wallpaper.

"Make yourself comfortable," Sharkey said, entering the room. He motioned to a pink and beige striped sofa. "Have a seat. Bonnie oughta be here any—"

Bonnie walked in just at that moment, carrying a small tray of four drinks. She paused momentarily, glancing from one man to the next before asking, "Where should I put these, Sharkey?"

"On the end table there," Sharkey said nervously. *Who was this man standing a few feet from him?*

The man reached into his pocket and drew out a money clip stuffed with bills. He pulled a twenty out from the top as Starkey said, "On the house."

The man cut his eyes over to Sharkey, then stepped over to the young waitress. "For you," he said in a low voice, holding the bill up to her face and caressing her cheek with it.

Bonnie smiled. "Thanks."

"Close the door on your way out, please," he said, keeping his voice low and commanding.

Bonnie looked at Sharkey, who nodded. The door closed, and the men retrieved two of the drinks, then sat—one on the sofa and the other in a nearby matching chair.

The dark stranger took a sip of his drink and pressed his lips together as though he was contemplating what he was about to say. Sharkey took several swallows of his drink, then cleared his throat. "Yeah, well. What can I do for you?" he asked.

The man looked at him. "Do you know who I am?"

"Should I?"

"I don't know. Do you?"

Sharkey took another swallow and shifted in his seat. "Look here. . ."

"Ever hear of Bucky Caballero?" the man suddenly interjected.

Sharkey's eyes became hooded. "Is that who you are?"

The man smiled. "Then you have heard the name?"

"Of course. Who hasn't? You don't look so much like the photos the feds were flashing around about two years ago."

"I understand you and I have a mutual thorn in the flesh."

Sharkey had to think for a moment, to assimilate the news from eighteen months ago with what was happening in his life. Why hadn't he thought of it before? William Webster had brought down the Caballero house of cards. Sharkey mentally kicked himself in the rear. Why hadn't he remembered that. . .used that. . .to his own advantage? "Webster's wife?" he finally answered. "That tall woman?"

Bucky answered with silence.

"Yeah, yeah. She came in and took three of my girls. But one of 'em's back."

"Is that so?"

"Yeah, the Asian girl you saw out there."

"Which one?"

Sharkey barked in laughter. "Oh, yeah. Forgot. I have more than one. Yeah, yeah. But only one Candy. She's a sweet one. Get it? Candy? Sweet?"

Bucky Caballero took another sip of his drink and forced another smile. "Yeah. I get it."

"So how'd you find me? How'd you know about me and Webster's widow?"

"I have sources."

"What kinda sources?"

"Let's just say I know everything that woman does."

The air in the room seemed to grow thick and stale, and Sharkey stood to help dissipate his uneasiness.

"Sit down, Mr. Sharkmeat."

Sharkey sat. "It's Sharkey. Sharkey Garone."

"I think," Bucky began slowly, sitting forward slightly and resting his elbows on his knees, "that you and I should come to some sort of a working relationship."

Sharkey shook his head back and forth. "Look here. I'm already doing business. I don't want trouble, you hear? I just do my job and pay my fees to the wise guys, and everybody else can leave me alone."

"I'm not talking about that kind of arrangement."

Sharkey took another swallow, draining his glass. He leaned over and took hold of another drink glass from the tray on the small table between the chair and sofa. "Just what then?"

"You say one of the girls is back?"

"Yeah."

"Candy, is it?"

"Yeah. Yeah. But she's still at the hotel during the day. Comes back here some nights."

"Why's that, do you suppose?"

"She came begging for her old job back recently. Literally got down on her knees and begged like a dog. Told her she could come back, you know, but I wanted her to stay at the hotel, too. That Webster woman is going to pay, and until I figure out how, Candy can work two jobs. She needs to be taught a lesson for walking out anyway."

Bucky smiled. "So she's your spy?"

"You could say that."

"Good deal, Mr. Sharkey." Bucky stood and Sharkey followed.

"That's it?"

Bucky placed his half-empty glass on the table. "For now."

Sharkey could feel himself getting anxious and excited. *Bucky Caballero wanted to do business with him, and that business included making Katie Webster sweat. Okay, that might not be so bad. He liked it. He liked it a lot. Maybe he could fill Caballero in on a little information. . .make him think he was valuable.* "You know," Sharkey began slowly, "I've known Katie Webster since I was a boy."

Bucky took a step toward the door, then paused and looked at Sharkey. "What do you mean by that?"

"She was a dancer at my old man's club over in Hell's Kitchen back in the seventies."

Bucky appeared genuinely shocked. "You don't say?"

"Yeah, yeah. Used to be a favorite among the customers. I remember how my old man cussed and swore when she left."

"Why do you suppose she left?"

"Went over to another club. . .better club. Uptown kinda place."

Bucky pursed his lips and nodded briefly. "That may prove to be valuable information."

Sharkey smiled. "Yeah, yeah. You let me know what you want me to do. I'm nearly always here."

Bucky smiled again. "I know."

Sharkey's smile faded. "So I'll hear from you soon?"

"Soon."

CHAPTER TWELVE
Wednesday, December 5, 2001

Late the following morning Katie opened the etched glass door leading into Jacqueline's. The new owner had made some dramatic changes. The boutique seemed warm and inviting in contrast to how she remembered it under Bucky Caballero's proprietorship. The post-Caballero owners had replaced the less up-market classic apparel with more trendy fashions. Then the store was taken over again, and the latest owners seemed to build upon the changes already made. Strategically placed overstuffed chairs added to the elegant yet homey atmosphere. Each chair was flanked by its own low table, topped with a teacup and saucer or demitasse for espresso. The room was expertly decorated with ornate terra cotta stands boasting oriental vases filled with silk floral arrangements.

Katie noticed several customers admiring the new line of clothes and accessories, which were an assortment of business, casual, and formal wear. The colors were as vivid as the fabrics were luxuriant.

Another new feature in the boutique was a jewelry counter, located in the direct center of the store. Katie made her way to it and peered into the glass case. The merchandise was separated by types of stone: diamonds, sapphires, emeralds, rubies, garnets, pearls, then combinations thereof. The tops of the counters were decorated with magnificent jewelry boxes, overflowing with costume jewelry, scarves, scarf accessories,

145

and the like. Interspersed among the boxes were statues of various sizes, all of angels. Adding to the magical feel of the room was the harp music overhead playing "O Holy Night."

"May I help you?" Katie looked up to see a petite woman of incredible beauty walking toward her from the back of the shop.

"You must be Zandra."

The woman didn't answer until she was nearly a foot away from Katie. She paused in front of the jewelry counter, placed her small hand gently against the glass surface while her other hand rested on her slim hip. She wore an olive-green, three-piece flutter cardigan ensemble that fell in soft folds to her small ankles. Her chestnut-colored hair was wound in a rope braid down the back of her head and over her left shoulder. Her lips were pouty, and her eyes and skin were Mediterranean in appearance. Katie found herself quite captivated by this striking young woman, who she guessed was perhaps in her early thirties.

"I am Zandra, yes. May I help you?" she repeated.

Katie smiled warmly. "I'm Katharine Webster," she answered, wondering what had moved her to use her formal name.

It was then that the woman smiled, "Mrs. Webster, I was hoping you'd come down to see us."

Katie looked around the store. "You have done wonders with this. I love it."

"Thank you. Please, wait right here. I want you to meet my brother. First, let me see if these ladies need anything," she said, indicating two customers who had approached the faux-antique cash register in the back of the store.

"I'm just going to look around," Katie said as Zandra walked away.

"Oh, please do. Let me know if you'd like to see anything in the case."

Katie returned her attention to a simple sapphire and diamond necklace displayed and draped over the neck of a crystal cat. She heard Zandra's question to the customers, "Would you like to make a purchase?" followed by the bells of the register. Moments later Zandra reappeared, this time on the other side of the glass cubicle of jewelry.

"You like the necklace?"

Katie looked up. "I do. I also like the way you displayed it on the cat. Is he for sale as well?"

"Everything is for sale," Zandra said with a chuckle. "I told my brother to come up front as soon as he can. He's putting new merchandise into the computer in the back office."

Katie nodded. "My GM told me you and I know some of the same people?"

Zandra nodded. "Yes, we do. Well, at least one mutual acquaintance. Mrs. Derrick Joyner is my godmother."

Katie tilted her head slightly. "I'm sorry, I don't believe I know her."

Zandra's eyes widened. "Are you certain? Annette Joyner? She lives in East Hampton. She's a widow. . .about seventy years old?"

Katie shook her head slowly. "No. I'm sorry. You say she's your godmother."

"Yes. My goodness, I could have sworn she said she knew you and your husband."

Katie shook her head again. "Perhaps she knows my husband. But I'm afraid I haven't had the pleasure of meeting her."

Zandra nodded. "Maybe that's it. Maybe she knows Mr. Webster." Zandra's voice trailed off, leaving her and Katie in an uncomfortable moment until Katie said, "May I see the necklace?"

"Oh! Certainly," Zandra answered.

"I'll get the key for you."

Both Zandra and Katie started, then looked over to where the voice had come from. Standing between them and the back of the store was a man Katie assumed was Zandra's twin brother, Zane. He was every bit as gorgeous as Vickey had described, though, having seen Zandra, she had not doubted he would be.

"Thank you, Zane," Zandra called back, then turned back to Katie as Zane stepped over to the cash register. "My brother."

Katie smiled again. "I assumed so."

"He should be a model, don't you think?"

Katie watched the man walking toward them. "I can see you're proud."

When Zane arrived at the jewelry counter, he flashed a golden smile and slanted his eyes down to his much shorter sister. "Is she giving you the model line?"

Katie laughed. "Yes, she is." She extended her hand. "Hello, I'm Katharine—Katie Webster."

"Mrs. Webster," Zane answered, taking her hand firmly in his. "It's a pleasure to meet you."

Zandra discreetly cleared her throat. "She wants to see the necklace draped around the cat."

Zane moved to the center of the glass cubicle. "Let me get that for you." He opened the case from the back, pushed the slider to one side, and reached into the case, bringing both the cat and the necklace out and placing them on the counter. "I thought you might like to see them both."

Katie nodded. "Yes, as a matter of fact, I'm quite taken with that cat."

"It's Swarovski."

"I thought it might be."

"Is this for yourself?" Zane slipped the necklace from around the cat and gingerly handed him to Katie.

Katie looked from the cat cupped in the palm of her hand to the dark, teasing brown eyes.

"No, a gift."

"Christmas?"

"More friendship than Christmas."

Katie heard the chiming of the store's door. Zandra and Zane both looked beyond her, and she resumed her inspection of the crystal cat as Zandra said, "I'll get this one. Mrs. Webster, it was a pleasure to meet you. I hope you will return soon."

Katie looked up again. "My pleasure. And please, call me Katie."

"I will," Zandra said, stepping away from inside the jewelry counter.

Katie looked back at Zane, who was smiling at her. "I'll take the cat," she said.

"I thought you might. Shall I gift wrap it?"

Katie took note of his dazzling white teeth, fleetingly wondering why he *wasn't* a model. "Please."

"We have a selection of gift cards near the register if you'd like to sign one."

Katie nodded. "Yes, thank you." She followed Zane to the register. "I assume I can open a credit account with you?"

"I can begin an account for you if you'd like," Zane said. "That way you can pay once a month."

Katie stopped in her search. "That's how I make most of my purchases. I'm sure I'll be in here often, having seen your new merchandise."

Zane smiled again and raised his eyebrows. "I won't try to stop you."

As he finalized her purchase, Katie stepped over to lightly finger a black georgette duster that had a garnishing of sequins down one side.

"It's truly gorgeous on," Zane said. "You would be magnificent in it."

Katie turned her head and looked back at the man. "Oh, you're good. I'd be willing to bet you could talk me into everything in this store."

Zane set the cat down next to the cash register. "No, not really," he said, walking out on the floor and directly to a pair of white leather pants. "I would never even think about trying to convince you to buy these. You're too refined." As he moved toward Katie and the duster, he continued. "But this," he said, removing it from its hanger with one finger, "is most definitely you. Try it on," he coaxed.

Katie's eyes danced as she took the duster from him and slipped into it. A quick look in a nearby floor mirror confirmed what he had told her. Even in her business suit, it looked stunning and she said so.

"No, Katie. It doesn't look stunning. *You* look stunning."

Zandra approached the two of them carrying a Dooney and Bourke purse obviously being purchased by the woman walking behind her. "Gorgeous," she mouthed at Katie, and Katie laughed.

"Okay. I'll take it, too. Just add it to the cat. When you're done wrapping the cat, could you send my packages up to my suite?" Katie looked down at her watch. "I'm meeting a friend at the airport, so I'd better hurry."

"What floor is your suite on?"

"Fourteenth floor. If you contact Mr. Harrington, he'll be happy to tell you exactly where it is."

Zane smiled. "I hope we'll see you again, soon."

Katie laughed lightly. "Oh, you will! You will!"

CHAPTER THIRTEEN

Phil caught a glimpse of Katie's limo pulling away from The Hamilton Place as he parked his car. He jumped out, closed the door, and headed toward the front door of the hotel, turning his neck a little to the right in hopes of seeing what direction the stretch white was going in. He looked back at Miguel, the doorman, who nodded professionally at him.

"Mr. Silver."

"Miguel, do you know where Mrs. Webster is heading?"

"No, Sir. She doesn't inform me of her comings and goings."

Phil buttoned the top button of his overcoat and pulled the wool scarf his wife had given him last year for Hanukkah a little closer to his chin. "Could it get any colder? Why are you standing out here?"

Miguel stayed as rigid as a soldier. "I just saw Mrs. Webster to her limo," he said matter-of-factly. "Otherwise, I'd be in my warm cubicle here." He motioned to the left with a jerk of his capped head.

"Well, get back inside. I wouldn't want you to freeze to death out here."

Miguel chuckled. "Yes, Sir," he said.

Phil pushed through the revolving door of the hotel, then paused as he often did upon stepping onto the pale green marble floor of the grand and opulent foyer in the hundred-year-old hotel. Even someone not typically moved by décor was forced to stop and absorb the luxury of muted tones, furnishings, Baroque mirrors, and hand-painted murals depicting English gardens. Phil knew it had cost William a small fortune when he had renovated it years before, but it had been well worth it.

After a moment, he slipped off his outer coat and headed for the central elevators, which he rode up to the floor of executive offices where James Harrington spent part of his working day.

"Mr. Silver," Harrington's secretary greeted him. Having seen him around the hotel many times since William's disappearance, she easily recognized him.

"Good afternoon, Deirdre," Phil replied with a nod of his head. "Harrington in?"

"No, Sir. May I have him paged for you? I'm sure he's around here somewhere."

"Would you mind?"

"Not at all." The secretary—Phil guessed her to be in her early thirties—turned to her desk phone and began to dial a series of numbers. He watched her long fingers dancing over the number pads as though she were using a calculator rather than a phone.

"I'm sure he'll be right here," she said, jarring Phil back to reality. His eyes widened and he nodded. "Would you like me to hang your coat in the closet for you?"

Phil looked down at the coat. "Certainly." He extended the coat just as Deirdre stood and the door to the office opened.

James Harrington stopped in mid-stride. "Mr. Silver."

Phil could read the general manager's mind. After the "Mr. Silver" was a question. "What are you doing here?"

"Mr. Harrington. May I see you in your office for a few minutes?" he asked, getting right to the point.

James twitched a bit, pulling his neck out slightly from the stiff collar of his white starched shirt. "Certainly. I was just returning from lunch with my wife. Were you on the schedule?"

Deirdre had, by this time, reached Phil. He handed his coat to her without comment, turning instead to the door leading to Harrington's plush office.

"No. I only need a few minutes of your time."

James nodded. "Then let's go into my office."

James led and Phil followed. As they entered the office, which was paneled in fine, polished cherry, Phil moved toward a sitting area and James closed the door, soon following him to a masculine blue, red, and green plaid sofa and matching chair. "May I offer you something to drink?" James asked.

"No. No, thank you. I only need a moment of your time. May we sit here?"

"Please do."

The two men sat, and James narrowed his steel-blue eyes. "Is this about William?"

Phil nodded. "Somewhat."

"Have you found him?"

"No. I'm afraid not. Mr. Harrington, let me cut to the chase."

"I wish you would."

"How do you feel about Katharine Webster?"

The blue eyes narrowed again. "Personally?"

"Personally. Professionally."

"I have no problems with her."

Phil rested against the back of the sofa, encouraging James to lower his guard.

"Is that personally or professionally?"

James stood. "What is this about, Mr. Silver?"

Phil remained where he was seated. "It's just a question."

James walked over to his desk and stood behind it, looking over to Phil as he unbuttoned his suit coat and placed his hands on his hips. "No, Sir."

"You have no problems with her."

"No. That's not what I mean. I mean no, Sir. You aren't here to ask me about that. What's going on here?"

Phil smiled. "You think something's going on?"

"There's been a buzz around here the last few days. I know Katie had a shock the other night, though no one seems to want to tell me what about."

"You think you should know?"

"I do."

Phil stood and walked over to the other side of the desk. "You don't know?"

"Would I be asking if I did?"

Phil nodded. "Maybe. Maybe not." He reached into his coat pocket and brought out the boxed necklace. Opening it, he asked. "Mr. Harrington, ever see this necklace?"

James leaned over for a better look. "May I?" he asked, reaching for it.

"By all means."

James took the necklace from its box, fingered it slightly before returning it. "They're real."

"I know. You've never seen it before?"

"No, of course not. Why would you think I had?"

Phil closed the box and returned it to his pocket. "Let me ask you again, Mr. Harrington. How do you feel about Katie Webster?"

James sat in the executive chair behind him and indicated with a wave of his hand that Phil should sit down as well. Phil glanced behind him, then sat in the nearby office chair. "I'll be honest with you. I didn't like her at first. Professionally, I mean. I always liked her personally. Never had any problems with her. Not to mention how William Webster felt about her. He was so in love he couldn't see straight." James smiled. "You know, the way we'd all like to be. . .or at least the way we'd all like to remain. Don't get me wrong. I have a good marriage. Good wife. Great family. But there was something very special about what William and Katie had." James grew pensive. "Tragedy. Dear God, what a loss."

"For whom, Mr. Harrington? You or Katie?"

James genuinely looked shocked. "For everyone, Mr. Silver. You two were childhood friends. Don't you feel a loss?"

Phil nodded. "William and I had grown apart somewhat over the last few years. I was somewhat surprised when he called me and told me about what was going on in the boutique. But it was good to see him again. We didn't have long before. . ."

"Do you think he's dead, Mr. Silver? Or, do you—like Katie—believe he's sequestered somewhere?"

Phil leaned forward, resting his elbows on his knees. "I only wish I knew."

James leaned back in his chair. "Doesn't make a lot of sense, does it? William Webster was crazy about that woman. Where would he be hiding if he were alive? Why wouldn't he come running back to her? Is he out there," he jerked his head toward the window behind him, "Watching her? Watching us? Makes no sense."

Phil nodded. "I have to agree with you. Logically, that is."

"So what's with the necklace?"

"Someone claiming to be William sent it to Katie a few days ago."

James narrowed his eyes again. "The shock."

"Yes."

There was momentary silence before James added, "I sent her flowers, you know."

Phil didn't answer.

"My wife says I should try to get along," James supplied.

"You don't get along?" Phil straightened. "You and Katie?"

"I'll admit I've given her a bit of a hard time."

"You have a reason for that?"

James chuckled. "Pride."

"Pride?"

"Yeah," James answered definitively. "Masculine, professional pride."

"You thought you should inherit the position."

"Yes, I did. Still do. But I'm not about to try anything stupid. The other day my wife suggested that I try to get along—as I said—so when I heard Katie was sick, I sent the flowers. I was planning to go up to her office later and offer my heartfelt assistance." He over-dramatized the words by placing his hand over his heart.

"Looks like you've got a ways to go before you really mean it."

James nodded in acknowledgement. "Most likely, you're correct."

Phil stood. "I'll show myself out. Thank you for your time."

James stood as well. "You're welcome. Keep me posted, if need be."

Phil nodded, patted the box in his pocket, then turned and walked out the door, leaving James to watch the door close behind him.

CHAPTER FOURTEEN

Bucky looked handsome in his pressed black Chinos, black turtleneck, and sweater when Victoria Thomas Whitney saw him at the doorway of his hotel room. She even said so. It had slipped from her painted lips as smoothly as the scotch she was craving.

"Sharp look," she said.

He smiled, almost sardonically. "Hello, Darling." He greeted her with a kiss to her left cheek. "Might I add how lovely you look this morning?"

Victoria swept into the magnificent room of pastel colors, resplendent in the glow from the chandelier overhead. "Takes your breath away, doesn't it?" she asked.

"Yes, you do," Bucky returned, closing the door.

Victoria turned and smiled playfully. "I meant the room."

"I know you did." He frowned. "You're late."

Victoria turned back to the large window across the room, sheathed by wispy sheers and framed with heavy draperies of material that matched the custom fretted bed. She made her way over to the chair between the window and the bed, sat and crossed one leg over the other in a fluid movement. "You're lucky I came at all." They stared at one another for a moment, and she added a whispered, "Bucky."

Bucky stepped to the room's desk, leaned against it and said, "Yes?"

"Don't act so. . .so. . ."

"So?"

"Cocky."

"Cocky?" Bucky chuckled.

"Glad I amuse you. Bucky, I'm worried about you. You shouldn't be here."

"Of course I should. The Plaza has a wonderful art gallery. Did you know that?"

Victoria turned slightly and began to lightly finger the draperies at her side. "I'm not talking about The Plaza. I'm talking about the city. For pity's sake, Bucky, I'm talking about the country. You shouldn't even be in this country."

"It's my home. I love it here. Especially this time of the year." He reached behind him and brought out his gold cigarette case.

"Light one for me, will you?" Victoria said, rising.

"You know I hate it when you smoke, Darling."

"And you know I hate it when you play stupid, frivolous games. Light one for me," she repeated.

They looked into each other's eyes, neither one blinking; a sort of contest to see who would break first. Finally, Bucky smiled, looked down to his case, and brought out two cigarettes. Placing them between his lips he lit them both, then handed one to his former lover. Victoria drew on it deeply, savoring it for a moment before turning her head to blow the gray smoke from her red lips. "I bought you a little something," Bucky said.

Victoria turned back to look at him. She smiled. "You did?"

"Ah, my dear. I could always make you happy, couldn't I, Victoria?"

It was a rhetorical question, but she lowered her lashes and answered it anyway.

"Yes, you could. Where's my present?"

Bucky glanced over to the top of the dresser. Victoria followed his eyes to see a small package, wrapped in silver foil and topped with a blue bow. "Looks like jewelry," she purred.

"Open it."

158

She did, all the while shaking her head. "Bucky, please tell me you didn't go out to purchase this. . .in public."

Bucky drew on his cigarette, pushed himself away from the desk and walked over to the window where he turned to look back at Victoria. She allowed the wrapping paper to fall to the floor and was now taking the lid off the small outer box. "The Plaza has Roxanne Jewelers, my love. The Plaza has everything. Bellissima Lingerie, a flower shop. . ."

Victoria cut a teasing glance his way. "I take it there are no roses or negligees in this tiny box."

"You are a wise woman, Victoria."

Victoria pulled the black velvet case from the outer box, setting it on the dresser before opening it to see a stunning gold and pavé diamond necklace. "Good heavens," she whispered. "This must have cost you a fortune."

Bucky moved stealthily toward her, gently took the box from her hand and pulled the necklace away from the safety clasps and placed it around her neck. "What is money if not to spend it on those who mean the most to us?"

Victoria stepped close to him, as he clipped the necklace into place. She could smell his strong, distinctive masculine scent and feel the heat from his body. "Bucky." The name fell softly into the room. "Why do you do this to me?"

When the necklace was secured, Bucky stepped away from the only woman he had ever been in love with, the only woman who—other than Mattie and their mother—ever meant anything at all to him. He had never told her, of course. He had never let any woman know how he had truly felt, whether love, affection, or disdain. However, his silence to Victoria had been his private regret. Victoria had thought she was but his lover—not his life—and in an unfortunate and impulsive move had chosen to marry Jordan Whitney. Bucky had given her away, literally walked her down the aisle, with his blessings. It was the best he could do for her, to let her go and find whatever happiness might be out there for her. "Jordan Whitney is a lucky man."

There was a pregnant silence between them. "I love Jordan, Bucky."

"I know you do."

More silence. "Bucky, please," she began, touching the marquee-shaped necklace cradled in the hollow of her throat. "Please leave the country. Go back to Canada."

Bucky took a final draw on his cigarette before grinding it out in a nearby crystal ashtray. "I will soon. As soon as my work here is complete."

"And what is your work?"

Bucky swung around and smiled. "Art. I'm buying art."

"Is that it?"

"What do you mean, Darling?"

"Don't *darling* me, Bucky. You know exactly what I mean. Are you in any way involved with whatever is going on with Katie Webster?"

"What did that agent tell you yesterday? Silver, isn't it?"

Victoria walked back to the chair and again sat down. "Phil Silver." She took a deep breath and exhaled.

"Ah, yes. Phil Silver."

"Is it you he is looking for?"

Bucky laughed heartily then. "He has been looking for me for some time."

"Bucky! Please. Please. I am begging you. If you are in any way involved in this. . ."

Bucky sobered. "Come here, my love."

Victoria rose dutifully and walked to where Bucky stood. He put his hands firmly on her shoulders, turned her to face the door, and guided her toward it. "Time for you to go home, my sweet."

"What?"

"I will call you soon." He opened the door as Victoria turned to him in protest. "Take special care of my girl," he said gently, then kissed her lightly on the lips, then more firmly on the cheek. "*Ciao.*"

Victoria returned home from her meeting with Bucky in a curious state of mind. Springing lightly up the staircase and into the master bedroom, she stripped off the exquisite and costly suit she had chosen for the tryst, tossing it onto the brass bed. Shuffling into the spacious walk-in closet, she grabbed an old, blue velour sweat suit kept for moments of distraction such as this. She draped herself onto the fainting couch in front of the French doors overlooking the balcony and stared at a fragment of the city visible beyond the wrought iron railing. Her mind wandered, first to her encounter with Bucky, to the idea of buying new furniture for the balcony, then to what she might have her cook prepare for dinner that evening, and back to Bucky. "Strange changes coming over me," she mentally sang. Her thoughts shifted and for awhile she considered what she would buy Jordan for Christmas, what Jordan would give her, how much to give her assistant, Gina, as a holiday bonus. She reached for the chenille throw at the foot of the couch and burrowed herself under it, bringing her hand up to lightly touch the necklace she still wore. She would take it off before Jordan came home, of course. There wasn't any need to upset him. Deceive him, yes. Upset him, no.

She closed her eyes and wished that by sheer virtue of her will, she could force Bucky back to Canada. She didn't want anything bad to happen to him, certainly not the same fate as David Franscella. Yet she knew that for Bucky time spent in prison would be worse than death. She sighed deeply, jolted back to reality when the door to her bedroom opened and her assistant, Gina, walked through.

"Are you going to lie there all day?"

"I might." Victoria gazed lazily at the petite woman standing over her. Gina wore her dark blond, shoulder-length hair in a blunt cut, curled under. Short bangs served to make her look ten years younger than her forty-seven years. Her eyes were a sparkling lucid shade of brown, but when she was serious, they turned amber. At this moment, they were amber.

"I am completely caught up on your correspondence."

"Good." Victoria closed her eyes again.

"I have your Christmas list prepared."

"Wonderful."

"Today's mail included two holiday party invitations."

"Where?"

"The Castles and the Langdons."

Victoria nodded.

"Both on nights you and Jordan are free. Shall I RSVP with a yes?"

"Yes."

Victoria listened as Gina moved about the room. She smelled the strong aroma of Scotch, opened her eyes and reached for the drink being extended to her. "It's a little early, isn't it?"

Gina sat on the couch next to her, near her knees. "Scoot over."

Victoria did, but only a fraction of an inch.

"You've seen him, haven't you?"

Victoria took a sip of her drink, avoiding Gina's eyes. "Who?"

"You know who."

"Drink your Scotch, Gina."

"How long has he been back in the city?" she asked, ignoring the order.

"Not long."

Gina sighed heavily. "Oh, Victoria."

Victoria swung her legs off the opposite side of the couch and stood. "No lectures."

"Did he give you that necklace?"

Victoria raised her hand and caressed the diamonds at her throat. "Yes."

"What is he doing here?" Gina also stood and walked over to Victoria so as to face her head-on.

"Buying art."

"Buying art?"

Victoria drained her glass of its contents. "That's right. That's what he does for a living now, you know."

Gina shook her head. "Victoria, you and I both know better than that."

Victoria's eyes were hooded. She walked over to the wet bar and set her glass firmly on the marble top. "What do you know? Why can't he simply be buying art now?"

"Come on, Vic. You and I were both his employees at one time; you his manager and me an escort. We know the man pretty well, don't we? Bucky Caballero doesn't just buy art. He always has a plan."

Victoria turned and looked at Gina. "I don't think he's involved. . ."

Gina's amber eyes narrowed. "Involved? Involved with what?"

"Katie Webster."

"Katie Webster?" Gina sat heavily on the fainting couch. "What are you talking about?"

"Someone is sending gifts to Katie Webster."

"And?"

"They think. . .thought. . .are suspicious. . ."

"Oh, no."

"I don't think so, Gina. Bucky isn't stupid."

"No, but he is vindictive."

Victoria nodded. That he was. "Still, it doesn't sound like Bucky." She stared at the room around her, a room she had recently redecorated with a circa-1800 Irish bed, draped in various shades of Irish linen in blues and reds, in contrasting florals and stripes. The walls had been painted pale blue and clusters of various sizes of prints and framed Irish lace doilies decorated them. Victoria liked this room. It was cool, yet inviting. In fact, she liked her entire home. Jordan had given her decorating *carte blanche* after they married. Their home had become her hobby; those who moved in their circles were always keen to attend their parties, in hopes of seeing what new piece had been added. She also loved her husband, and the prestige of being his wife. She *especially* loved the prestige of being his wife. She could have gotten the same being Bucky's wife, she thought wistfully, but Bucky wasn't having any talk of marriage, and Victoria wasn't willing to be just his lover and employee.

"I can't think of a living soul who knows Bucky better than I do, except Mattie."

"That's true."

Victoria looked at her watch. "I think I'll put a fresh face on."

"That's it? That's where we're going to leave this?"

Victoria made her way toward the master bath. "Yes," she said firmly. "That's where we leave it."

CHAPTER FIFTEEN
Wednesday, Late Afternoon

"I'm so sorry, I'm so sorry!" Marcy nearly sprinted from the crowd that had spilled out of the gate area and into baggage claim where Katie and Simon stood waiting for her. The flight had been nearly two hours late.

Katie wrapped Marcy in a tight hug and smiled. "Why? Were you flying the plane? Where did you go?" she laughed lightly. "Were you contemplating a trip to Barbados instead of the Big Apple?"

Marcy placed her hand on her cropped, wavy hair as if to hold herself to the ground. "Katie, don't give me a hard time here." She looked over to the large man standing next to Katie. "Hello," she said to him, then back to Katie with a whisper, "Who is that?"

"That is my chauffeur. Let's go get your luggage."

They turned to move toward the conveyor belts transporting various sizes of luggage. "I don't remember you," Marcy said to him. She looked back to Katie. "I don't remember him. And quite frankly I feel a little intimidated by the two of you. What are you?" she said to Simon. "Six-five?"

"Six-six," Simon answered stoically, moving and staring straight ahead.

"Two-twenty-five?"

"Two-fifty."

Katie looked at Marcy. "You're already making me laugh. Bringing

165

you here was a good thing."

"And just why am I here?" Marcy asked with a frown.

Katie returned her stare to straight ahead. "To be my best friend."

Marcy nodded. "I can be your best friend in Georgia. Which baggage thingy are we supposed to be at?"

Simon pointed to the baggage area just ahead. "Right here, Mrs. Waters."

Marcy looked from Simon to the conveyor belt and back to Simon. "Thank you." Then, back to Katie. "Just why do you need me here?"

Katie shook her head lightly. "We'll talk in the limo."

"Oh. The limo. . ."

Once inside the spacious luxury of the white stretch, Katie offered Marcy a ginger ale, which she accepted.

"Now, tell me why I'm here."

Katie handed Marcy her drink, then leaned back against the leather of the seat. "I received a necklace the other day," she began, then told her the story as best she could. When she was finished, they had arrived at the hotel, and Simon was stepping from the driver's side of the car and opening the curbside door.

"I'll have the luggage sent up, Mrs. Webster," he told Katie.

"Thank you, Simon."

Marcy stepped from the car, wrapped her coat closer to her body and shivered. "Oh my goodness. . .what *is* the temperature here?"

"We're at seventeen degrees, Mrs. Waters," Simon answered dutifully.

Marcy stopped and looked up at him again, then back to Katie with a smile. "I like him. He's handy."

Katie smiled, looking at Simon as he opened the trunk to the limo. "In many ways." She looped her arm through Marcy's and began to walk her up the steps to the lobby of the hotel. Miguel had come from the warmth of the glassed-in cubbyhole and was preparing to open the door for them.

"Miguel, you remember Mrs. Waters," Katie said to him.

"Happy Holidays, Mrs. Waters. We're happy to see you again."

"Thank you, Miguel," Marcy returned. "It's a pleasure to see you, too."

"Come on," Katie tugged lightly. "Let's get inside. We'll get you settled then go to Bonaparte's for a late dinner."

Marcy nodded, looking around the lobby as they stepped through it. "How in the world do you ever get used to this?"

Katie smiled. "There's only one other like it in the city, and that's The Plaza. Totally different feel, but glorious. We'll go there one day for lunch or dinner. How does that sound?"

"Wonderful. It sounds wonderful."

"Does Silver know I'm here?" Marcy asked Katie from across the dimly lit table at Bonaparte's. They had enjoyed a fine meal and were now sipping coffee and savoring the *crème brûlée* Katie had chosen for their dessert.

Katie shook her head. "I'll call him tomorrow and tell him."

Marcy smiled devilishly. "Won't that just make his day?"

"Phil has become a good friend."

"Oh, I'm sure he just loves you to death. But he's still not going to be thrilled with my arrival. He thinks I stick my nose where it doesn't belong."

Katie spooned more of her dessert and said, "That's what reporters are supposed to do."

"And that's why you need me here? To be a friend and a reporter?"

Katie nestled her spoon between the serving dish and the bowl of dessert before answering. "I just don't know what to do, Marcy. If it is Ben. . ."

"Do you honestly believe it is?"

Katie shook her head. "I don't know."

"Let's say it isn't. That means someone—"

Katie lowered her lashes. "I know."

"You and Ben made a lot of people mad two years ago. A lot of people. How many politicians lost their status when Caballero's client list was publicized?"

Katie looked back to Marcy's face. "A lot."

"That's what I said."

Katie smiled a half smile. "Yes, you did."

There was a moment of silence before Marcy went on. "The three of us will get through this, Katie. We got through the last incident—"

"Three of us?" Katie's eyes met Marcy's.

"Me, you, and God." Marcy smiled.

"Oh, I like that. I like that a lot," she whispered. "I can't imagine my life without Him, especially since Ben disappeared."

"I can't imagine my life without Him period."

Katie smiled again, this time a brighter, happier smile. "Ready for bed? You must be exhausted."

Marcy's shoulders sagged, as though by Katie mentioning her fatigue, they were now permitted to do so. "Unbelievably."

The friends rose from their places and walked quietly to the outer hall toward the central elevators. They passed Jacqueline's, and Katie was reminded of the purchase she had made for her friend earlier in the day.

"I bought you a little present today," she said matter-of-factly.

Marcy looked up at Katie. "You did? What for?"

"Just 'cause."

"I don't remember seeing it on that massive thing you call my bed."

"It's in my room. I'll give it to you tomorrow. If you're a good girl."

Marcy laughed and shook her head. "Oh, the pressure. The pressure."

CHAPTER SIXTEEN
Wednesday Evening

"How about if we cuddle up with some chilled wine and maybe watch an old movie?" Gail spoke evenly but with expectancy.

Phil Silver looked up from his place on the family room sofa to see his wife standing in the doorway. He had been transferring notes from his pocket-sized notepad to a yellow legal pad. His scribble, which resembled more a series of disconnected, vertical lines rather than the alphabet, was written in black ink. He had just squinted against the vision of black on yellow, wondering how much longer he could go without using the reading glasses his eye doctor had prescribed for him. *Vanity, Silver,* he had chastised himself a few times along the way. *Pure vanity. Why can't you just admit you're getting on up there in age?*

"Sounds good." Phil smiled at his wife.

Gail walked over and sat near her husband. "Are you working?"

Phil answered with a nod.

"You're sure you want to just sit with me? Sit and cuddle?" She smiled a faux-coy smile, which caused Phil to smile back at her.

"I thought you said something about an old movie."

"I did." Gail straightened, raised her arms, and grasped her black hair with her hands. She twisted it in a knot, pulled it up onto the top of her head, then let it fall. She had recently showered, and her hair was still a little damp, so the twisting of it left it in loose ringlets about her face. She had scrubbed her face of the small amount of daytime make-up she typically wore and applied a sweet-smelling night cream. She donned a gold sweat suit and wore black socks, looking like a twenty-one year old.

"You are beautiful, you know." Phil was beaming with genuine adoration. Dropping his pen, he reached over to kiss her lovingly on her forehead while caressing her long neck.

"So I've been told."

"Oh, have you now? By anyone but me? Recently, that is?"

Gail narrowed her eyes playfully. "Let me think. . ."

Phil kissed her lightly on a mouth that tasted like berries. He licked his lips. "Raspberry? Strawberry?"

"Strawberry," Gail nodded. "The great thing about lip gloss is that it tastes so good. The bad thing is that it tastes so good. I tend to want to eat my own lips."

Phil raised his brow. "Sounds wonderful to me."

Gail wrinkled her nose. "I'll be back with the wine. You finish up there so we can cuddle."

Phil watched his wife rise from the sofa. "You won't have to twist my arm. I promise."

Walking out of the room, she glanced over her shoulder. "I'd better not."

When she disappeared, Phil resumed his note transference. *What did he know so far about the latest chain of events in this case?*

He knew that on Monday, Katie Webster had received a pearl and diamond necklace, which sold for about $4500. Phil had scribbled *Saks* on the following line, followed by "purchased by husband?" The gift had arrived wrapped in silver foil with a gold and silver bow.

Under that he wrote:

Caballero seen at Maxwell Griffin's gallery.

Phil studied the line for several moments before adding:

Who is the curator there?

"Here you go," Gail said as she reentered the room. Phil looked up, watched her gliding toward him with a glass of wine in each hand, extending one to him. He reached for it. As Gail sat next to him, she glanced at the legal pad in his lap. "Katie Webster? What's going on with Katie?"

Phil took a sip of wine. "I wish I knew."

"Can you talk about it?"

"Not really."

"Not even to me?"

"Not even to you." Phil took another sip of his wine, then dropped the legal pad, pen, and his notepad on the floor at his feet. "What are we going to watch?" he asked.

"There's a Danielle Steel movie marathon," Gail informed with a wink.

"No, no, no."

She laughed out loud. "In about ten minutes *An Affair to Remember* will be on."

"The one with Grant and Kerr or you and me?"

Gail leaned back slightly. "Oh, I like that!"

"I can be quite cute from time to time, you know."

"Oh, I know."

Phil sighed deeply, happily. "Turn on the television, why don't you?"

Gail reached for the remote control on the round, glass coffee table and turned on the television. With her thumb, she punched in the right combination of numbers until the movie credits filled the screen. Phil stretched his legs and propped his stocking feet on the coffee table, while Gail curled up in a little ball and laid her head in his lap. He touched her hair lightly, rolling a damp strand between his thumb and index finger.

"That feels good," she mumbled.

"Don't talk during the movie," he said softly.

"It's not on yet."

"Shh. . . ."

"Phil?"

"You're not going to shush, are you?"

"I just wanted to ask. . .Phil, are you sorry you left the Bureau?"

Phil leaned over and looked at his wife's profile. "Where'd that come from?"

Gail turned slightly and looked up at her husband. "Just wondering. I know you left for me and the kids. . .to spend more time with us. . . I just wanted to know if you were ever sorry."

Phil leaned back slowly, nodded, and said, "Sometimes. Sometimes. But I like my job at John Jay. And the occasional work as an investigator quenches my thirst for detective work. It's good, Gail. I love my life. I do."

Gail settled her head back toward the television as the movie began. "I love you, Phil Silver."

"I love you, too, Sweetheart."

He watched Gail's lips curl in a smile. "You should," she said slyly, then shushed him. "Quiet. The movie is starting."

As Cary Grant and Deborah Kerr began their famous rendezvous in Europe, Phil's mind returned to Katie and the necklace. He tried to concentrate on the present, but his mind kept asking questions like: *Could Sharkey be the one sending the necklace? I need to talk to him. . .and to the girls Katie brought out of the club. What was she thinking? Why would she do something like bring exotic dancers into THP? The little sales clerk will be back on duty in the morning. I need to go by there and see her, too. Victoria Whitney. Now there's a piece of work. Says she hasn't heard from Caballero since the night he left. Is she lying? Says she doesn't know where he went. Is she lying about that, too? What was it she said about him? "Bucky can't be had." Can't be had. No man is an island, Mrs. Whitney. What about Harrington? He seemed to admire William, but he was upset about Katie taking his place. Still, he was believable enough when he said that he was attempting to bridge the gap.*

Tomorrow I'm off from John Jay. Go see Sharkey. Go see Cassie.

CHAPTER SEVENTEEN
Thursday, December 6, 2001

The floral arrangements began to arrive at precisely ten o'clock.

Katie, who had decided to take the morning off from work, and Marcy were enjoying their breakfast in the sunroom. A fresh dusting of snow enveloped the cityscape outside their window, which was framed by the oversized Scalamandre silk damask curtains. They were drawn clear across the "wall of windows" as Katie called it. The two friends, curled under cashmere throws, sat on cream and gold matching armchairs. They talked about everything from their days in kindergarten to the latest Brooksboro buzz as they sipped on a strong brew of Kenyan coffee.

At some point, Katie gathered the courage to ask about her high school flame, Buddy, and his wife Sarah.

"They're fine," Marcy said, with a nod. "I see Sarah more than Buddy, of course, every time I go to the drug store for one thing or another." For more than twenty years, Sarah had worked at the one and only drug store in Brooksboro, Georgia.

"I think of them often."

Marcy took a sip of her coffee and looked behind her, out the window to the snowy city beyond. "This is an incredible view."

Katie smiled. "It is, isn't it? It reminds me of one of those glass things. . .you know. . .with the snow in them. You shake them up and watch the snow fall. Didn't you have one of those when we were kids? A big one."

Marcy smiled. "Yeah. I'd forgotten about it. My grandmother sent it to me from Niagara Falls when she and my granddad went up there for what they called a second honeymoon. That's not a thought I'd like to entertain for long. Wow, they must have been in their fifties!"

They laughed. "Doesn't seem so old now, does it?"

"No. It sure doesn't." Marcy grew quiet again before adding, "This city makes the rest of the world seem so small. I'm a little over-whelmed here."

"I was, too, the first time I saw it."

"Did Ben live in this same apartment before you married?" Marcy asked, quickly changing the subject. She was sensitive not to revisit the days when Katie had disappeared from Brooksboro, seemingly to have disappeared off the face of the earth only to resurface in Hell's Kitchen. Since Marcy had learned the truth about her best friend's earlier days in New York City, she had researched Hell's Kitchen and what it had been like in 1975 when Katie would have lived there. Even now the thought made her shudder.

Katie took the last sip of her coffee, then leaned forward and placed the empty cup and saucer on the polished surface of the oval, walnut coffee table. "He did. Though he told me to redecorate it after we married. Not that he didn't have excellent style and taste, but he said he wanted me to bring a feminine touch to it."

"You certainly did that." Marcy looked around the sunroom, paint-ed in warm cream. Katie had used muted tones of sand, gold, cream, olive, and rose throughout the opened common area that broke off into a sunroom, living room, dining room, and foyer. It was almost impos-sible to determine where one room stopped and the other began, the décor had been so well blended. The parquet floors were covered in silk and Oushak carpets; something Marcy wouldn't have known had Katie not told her so. All she knew was that they were exquisite.

"Ben brought me here on our fifth date."

"To show you his etchings?" Marcy wiggled her eyebrows.

Katie laughed. "Sure. With Maggie standing guard every minute."

Marcy took her last sip of coffee and placed the cup and saucer next to Katie's. "I like Maggie."

"So do I," Katie said quietly. "I love her, in fact."

"She was good to us the last time I was here. . .back when. . ."

"When she killed David Franscella."

Marcy grew quiet. "I'd prefer not to even say his name."

"Me neither."

Marcy tucked the throw under her legs a little more securely.

"Cold?" Katie asked.

"Not really. So, tell me about your date with Ben?"

Katie glowed in the memory. "He brought me up here for dinner actually. Maggie cooked, of course."

"Do you ever cook?" Marcy interrupted.

Katie narrowed her eyes playfully. "Not a bit. Maybe a sandwich when I'm desperate."

"So unfair. So completely unfair."

"Ha." Christmas music began to play on the house sound system. "Maggie," Katie commented, as Marcy looked heavenward. "She knows how much I love Christmas music."

"So do I," Marcy agreed. "Back to Ben."

"Mm. Ben. We had dinner in the dining room that evening, then he brought me into the living room and served champagne in fluted glasses, which we sipped on while dancing to the most romantic music."

Marcy's jaw slackened ever so slightly. "You're kidding me, right?"

Katie merely shook her head; no, she wasn't kidding. Ben had been the most romantic and loving husband a girl could ever wish to have. "I lived the fairy tale."

"At least at that point." Marcy was honest.

"Yes. At that point. Up until then it had been a nightmare and then. . ." Katie drifted.

"Then?"

Katie opened her mouth to speak, and for the first few moments, nothing came out. Finally, she said, "Marcy, I love Ben."

Marcy's eyes grew wide. "I know you do."

"I want him back more than anything I've ever wanted in my life."

Marcy reached over and touched Katie's hand. "Where are you going with this, Katie?"

She licked her lips. "Would you think me horrid if I said I both anticipate and fear Ben's return?"

Marcy drew back a bit. "I don't understand."

"I loved my life before. . .before Ben disappeared. I truly did. Ben treated me wonderfully and after everything I'd been through, I felt I deserved a little Cinderella liberty. But, since he's been gone and I've been running THP. . .I. . ." Katie frowned at her own words.

"You also like the independence?" Marcy finished for her.

Katie nodded. "Do you think me horrid?"

Again Marcy touched her hand. "Not one single bit. I love Charlie Waters with my whole heart and my children, too. But I also enjoy my writing and my friends and hobbies. I have an independent streak, too, you know."

Katie smiled just as the buzzing of the intercom interrupted their conversation. Maggie bustled in from the kitchen, heading straight for the double front doors. She pressed the talk button, and in her brisk English accent announced, "Webster Residence."

Katie smiled at Marcy. "I keep telling her she only has to say 'yes,' but she insists on announcing who lives here," she said with a whisper.

"There's a floral arrangement for Mrs. Webster in the lobby."

Maggie looked over to where Marcy and Katie were relaxing. Katie's heart skipped a beat.

"What shall I do, Child?" Maggie asked.

Katie found herself unable to answer.

"Have them sent up," Marcy said, rising from where she sat. She picked up the cups and saucers and began to walk toward the kitchen as Maggie okayed the delivery.

"Where are you going?" Katie asked, her voice strained.

"To get us another cup of coffee." She returned within a matter of minutes, just as Maggie was opening one of the doors to a uniformed employee carrying a small floral arrangement of red and white carnations. "Is there a card?" Marcy asked, not stopping until she reached the sunroom. She placed one cup and saucer on the walnut table, the other in her friend's hand. "Take this," she said. Katie obeyed; the jingling of the porcelain pieces against one another betrayed how nervous she had become.

Maggie walked toward the two women. "Yes, Lamb. It has a card." She pulled the small white envelope from its holder and handed it to Katie, who shook her head, no.

"You read it, Maggie," she said.

Maggie placed the arrangement on the table, next to a set of ornate walnut candlestick holders, and opened the envelope.

"What does it say on the outside?" Marcy asked.

"Katie," Maggie answered. "It says 'Katie.' "

Marcy looked down at her friend, who was chewing on the inside of her mouth, something Marcy hadn't seen her do since they were in high school.

Maggie pulled the small card from the envelope and read silently.

"What does it say?" Marcy asked.

"What does it say, Maggie?" Katie repeated in a whisper.

Maggie handed the card to Katie. "It says, 'I love you.' "

CHAPTER EIGHTEEN

"Was there a card?" Phil Silver held the phone to his ear with his right shoulder pressed firmly against it while balancing himself on one foot, tying the laces of his sneaker on the other. He had been in the middle of getting ready for a run when Katie called.

"Yes." Katie stood in the office of her apartment with one arm crossed over her chest, the other holding the phone to her ear. She kept her shoulders hunched and her head bowed, studying the grain of the walnut desk, as if to keep from being heard.

"Was Maggie with you when they arrived?"

"Yes. Maggie and Marcy."

Phil dropped his foot. "Marcy? That woman from Georgia?"

Katie straightened. "She's my best friend, Phil."

Phil rubbed his forehead. "She interfered with an ongoing investigation," he reminded her, referring to the private search she and Marcy had performed when everyone was looking for the file containing Bucky Caballero's illegal business records.

Katie sat in the Louis XVI-style chair behind her desk. "Phil." His name was spoken like a sentence. "Had she not recognized the clues in the book Ben sent me as to the whereabouts of the file, you might still be looking."

"She could have told someone in authority what she suspected instead of the two of you handling it on your own."

"Well, she didn't. Neither did I."

"Did you call her? To come up here, I mean?"

"Yes. She's my best friend."

There was a momentary pause. "So you've said."

"And I want you to be as open with her as you are with me."

"Katie—" Phil walked into the master bath, retrieved his toothbrush from the porcelain cup next to the sink, then opened the vanity drawer in search of the toothpaste his wife managed to relocate every other day or so.

"I'm serious, Phil. I need her right now. If Ben is the one sending. . . ." Katie's voice trailed at the sound of the front door intercom.

"What is it?" Phil asked. "What's wrong?" He found the toothpaste, but rather than taking it out of the drawer, dropped his toothbrush back into the cup.

"The intercom just buzzed. Hold on." Katie set the phone on the desk and walked over to the opened door, where she had a clear view of Maggie and Marcy standing near the intercom in the foyer. Maggie's hand reached up and pressed the button, and Katie listened intently. Overhead, Perry Como crooned *God Rest Ye Merry Gentlemen*.

Again, it was the front desk. "There's another arrangement here for Mrs. Webster," the voice announced.

Both Marcy and Maggie looked back to where Katie had leaned against the doorframe for support. "Tell them to send it up, please," she said, though barely in a whisper.

Marcy walked past her. Katie watched as she picked up the phone and spoke into it. "Silver?"

Marcy heard an audible sigh at the other end.

"I take it this is Mrs. Waters."

Marcy didn't feel like sparring with the man. "Another flower arrangement has just arrived."

"Is this one signed, too?"

"It's not here yet." Marcy looked over to Katie, who had paled noticeably. "Katie, come over here and sit down," she ordered, pointing to a small sofa near the windows.

Phil didn't need to hear any more. "I'll be over as soon as I can get there."

Marcy nodded, hung up the phone, and looked back at Katie, who had closed her eyes.

"Are you okay?"

God rest ye merry gentlemen, let nothing you dismay. . .

Katie nodded. "I'm concentrating on the music," she whispered.

Marcy cocked her head slightly to the left and listened to the soft melody, playing overhead.

To save us all from Satan's power when we were gone astray. . .

"Perry Como."

Katie only nodded. Marcy reached for her hand, squeezing it as the doorbell rang. She heard Katie swallow, then looked toward the front door, watching Maggie open it and receive the new floral arrangement, this one larger and more extravagant than the one before.

Oh, tidings of comfort and joy. . .comfort and joy. . .

Katie opened her eyes. "Is there a card?"

Maggie entered the office, set the flowers on the desk and nodded. "Shall I read it to you?"

Katie took a deep breath and stood. "No. I'll read it myself." She took the few steps necessary to reach the desk and pulled the card from its holder.

"What does this one say?" Marcy asked, still seated.

"The same as the other."

"Just 'I love you'?"

Katie moaned a yes while replacing the card. She turned quickly and looked at Marcy.

"Marce, who would do this to me?"

"Not Master William, that's for sure," Maggie interjected.

"Why do you say that?" Marcy asked. She stood and walked over to the desk, lightly touching the petals of one of the flowers.

180

"Master William might have sent one gift, but he would never do anything like this."

Katie nodded in agreement. "I've been a fool."

Marcy put both hands on Katie's arms. "No, Katie. Don't say that. Anyone in your shoes would have thought—"

Quiet tears slipped down Katie's cheeks. "Why would anyone do this to me? Who would want to. . ."

Linking her arm into Katie's, Marcy began to lead her away from the office and back to the sunroom where they had been enjoying their morning. "I'd say when Phil Silver gets here, we ask him that very same question."

Katie paused and looked back at her housekeeper. "Maggie, take the flowers into the kitchen, will you? I don't want to see them. Either one of them."

"Yes, little dove."

"Come on, Katie," Marcy said. "We'll wait for Phil in the sunroom. Come on."

Two things had happened by the time Phil Silver arrived at the hotel; three more arrangements of flowers had arrived, each one grander than the last, and Katie had stopped shaking and had become fighting mad.

"I'm not putting up with this, Phil," Katie informed him as she crossed from the sunroom to the front door where Phil was handing Maggie his coat. Marcy stood up, but chose to stay where she was.

"Where are the flowers?" Phil asked, looking around the expansive apartment. He spotted Marcy. "Mrs. Waters."

Marcy crossed her arms resolutely. "You can call me Marcy."

Phil made a sound in his throat that sounded somewhat like an affirmative moan. "The flowers?"

Katie turned toward the kitchen. "This way."

Phil followed Katie into the kitchen with Marcy just behind him. He turned slightly when he noticed her, sighed deeply, then continued on. When Katie pushed open the swinging door that led from the dining room into the kitchen, Phil was met with a room that looked more like a funeral parlor. He stopped short, and Marcy nearly bumped into him.

"Good gosh."

Marcy wasn't sure if he was responding to the flowers or her near miss with his back.

"They're from The Little Flower Shoppe," Marcy noted.

Phil looked back at her and furrowed his brow.

Marcy's eyes widened. "I read the cards. Here's the strange thing. One of them has an envelope with the name of the shop on the front, but no address under the name. The others have plain white envelopes with no name whatsoever."

"Look, girls. Let's get one thing straight," Phil said, bracing himself by standing with his feet about twelve inches apart. "This is not a game."

"Of course not," Katie said.

"Who said it was?" Marcy asked.

Maggie bustled in. "Maggie, call downstairs," Katie instructed. "Have them come get these flowers and take them to some of our guests. I don't want to see them."

"Yes, of course," Maggie said.

"Hold on a minute." Phil's voice rose slightly. He took a deep breath and sighed, then turned to the flowers and began to take the cards from each one, placing them into his shirt pocket. "This is just what I'm talking about. You can't run the show here. If I'm supposed to be investigating this for you, Katie, then you need to allow me to do just that."

"Someone is trying to drive me crazy," Katie countered. "I'm not just going to sit idly by, not like last time. . ."

"Idly by? You call running around the house in the middle of the night looking for a file 'idly by'?"

Maggie pointed a finger at him. "Don't raise your voice to Miss Katie, young man."

Phil opened his mouth to say something, his hands coming up in defense, but then he closed his mouth deciding it was better to choose his battles wisely. "Can we go sit somewhere?"

Katie nodded, all the while repeating to Maggie, "Don't forget to make that call. I want these things out of here."

Katie, Phil, and Marcy settled in the sunroom, with Phil sitting next to Katie on the cream-colored sofa and Marcy sitting in one of the matching chairs.

"The snow has stopped," Marcy noted. Katie and Phil turned their heads slightly to look out the window.

"What are you going to do?" Katie asked forwardly.

"I say you should go down to The Little Flower Shoppe," Marcy said with a tone of determination.

Phil and Katie looked at Marcy, Phil's gaze all the more disenchanted. "Do you know how many flower shops there are in this city?" he asked

"No. But I'll bet not too many of them are called The Little Flower Shoppe."

"Would you two please stop?" Katie interjected, though her words fell on deaf ears.

"For your information they're everywhere. Midtown, Upper East, Upper West, Brooklyn, Queens, Chelsea. They're even found in hotels. They're a chain." Phil leaned forward. "A chain. That means more than one."

"I know what a chain is. Why do people from up here think that people from the South are stupid?"

Katie placed her fingertips to her temples and pressed. "He didn't say that."

Phil turned his face momentarily to gaze at Katie. "I can speak for myself." Then back to Marcy. "I didn't say that."

Marcy's brow raised in mock surprise. "I say you should begin with The Little Flower Shoppe located closest to the hotel."

Katie discretely cleared her throat. "That would be here."

"What?" Both Phil and Marcy asked at the same time.

"The Little Flower Shoppe has a small franchise here in this hotel."

Phil ran his fingers along his sharp jaw. "That means—"

"Someone right here in *this* hotel," Marcy finished for him.

Phil leaned back and stared ahead.

"What are you thinking?" Katie asked.

"Nothing. Nothing yet." He stood. "Look, I want you two to promise me you'll stay right here until I call you. I'll stop downstairs at the floral shop. Then I've got to go down to Saks to talk to the clerk who sold the necklace. I'll call you after that."

Marcy leaned over and placed her elbows on her knees. She squinted as she looked up at Phil and said, "When will you go to the other flower shops?"

"One thing at a time."

Katie stood. "Thank you for coming, Phil. I'll wait for your call." She extended her hand in a gesture of showing him to the door. With a nod to Marcy, he turned and walked out of the sunroom with Katie just behind him.

"Thank you again," she said, opening the front door for him.

Phil leaned over and kissed her cheek. "Katie," he said softly. "I'll call you shortly."

Katie nodded.

When he had stepped into the hallway, and she had closed the door, Marcy stood and walked over.

"We're not just going to sit here are we?"

Katie looked straight ahead for a few moments before cutting her eyes to Marcy. "What do you think?"

Marcy smiled. "That's my girl. I'll go get ready."

CHAPTER NINETEEN

Phil immediately went to The Little Flower Shoppe on the second floor of The Hamilton Place. The manager wasn't in, the sales clerk informed him, and wouldn't be back until after lunch.

Phil showed him his credentials. "Did you have an order for flowers for Mrs. Webster today?"

"Katharine Webster?"

"Yes."

"No, Sir. Not today."

"Did you work yesterday?" Phil asked.

"No, Sir."

Phil turned slowly, said "Thank you," and began walking out of the store. "Tell the manager I'll be back after two o'clock," he said as he reached the door.

Phil decided to head over to Saks Fifth Avenue where he would talk to the young sales clerk and could then return to the hotel's floral shop. It was almost noon when he arrived. He jostled amongst the holiday shoppers as they squeezed through the doors of the famous store in search of the perfect gift. Once inside the warmth of the store, he removed his gloves and scarf, stuffed them into his coat pocket and headed for the fine jewelry counter where he immediately spotted Nora Taylor positioning a pair of sapphire earrings inside the display cabinet.

She spotted him, too. "Mr. Silver," she greeted.

"Mrs. Taylor," he returned, looking down at the earrings. "Pretty," he said.

"Yes, they are."

"I like the color. Dark. Good quality."

"You know jewelry, Mr. Silver?"

Phil smiled warmly. "Enough to know what to spend my money on. Not enough to call myself an expert."

"You're married?"

"Yes, I am." Phil smiled.

"These would make a lovely holiday gift for your wife," she hinted with a smile.

Phil laughed lightly. "I was thinking that, actually."

"Shall I take them out for you?"

"I'd like to see Cassie first, if you don't mind."

Nora Taylor closed the sliding door to the jewelry case with a frown. "She's over on the other side. Follow me."

Phil walked around the long, glass cases to where a young woman with short, curly blond hair stood with a customer, showing a pearl necklace. Coming up behind Cassie, Nora Taylor nodded to Phil that "this was the clerk he wanted to see." Phil shoved his hands into his coat pockets and nodded his willingness to wait until she had finished with her customer. He turned slightly and panned the store. Holiday garlands and overhead music swept across the large establishment, enticing customers toward making a purchase. Phil thought the excess of silver and gold items scattered throughout were a sure indication of the season.

"Mr. Silver." Phil turned at hearing Nora Taylor say his name.

"Yes?"

"Cassie is ready to talk with you now."

Phil looked from Nora to Cassie and noted a genuine look of apprehension. He smiled to assure her and watched her shoulders visibly relax. "Cassie?"

"Yes."

"My name is Phil Silver," he said, showing her the credentials he'd pulled out of his inside coat pocket. Cassie looked at the badge, then back up to Phil as he replaced them. "I'd like to ask you a few questions."

"Am I in some sort of trouble?"

"Oh, no. I just need to ask you about the man who came in the other day saying he was Katie Webster's husband. Do you think you could remember what he looked like if I—"

"Dark hair," she answered before he could finish. She smiled then. Phil got the impression that Cassie. . .Langer, according to her name tag. . .was anxious to help.

He smiled. "Okay. If I show you a couple of photographs, do you think you could tell me if one of the men was him?"

Cassie looked to Nora Taylor, who stood just behind her right shoulder, then back to Phil. "I think so."

Phil reached into the same inside pocket where he kept his credentials, and pulled out the drawing of a bearded Bucky Caballero. "Cassie, this is a composite drawing—not a photograph—so I realize this may put you at a bit of a disadvantage—"

"No, that's not him," Cassie answered quickly.

"Cassie, please allow Agent Silver to finish before you answer him," Nora Taylor instructed.

Cassie looked back. "But that's not him."

Nora Taylor sighed. "Are you sure?"

"Yes."

"How do you know?" Phil asked, bringing Cassie's attention back to him.

"The man who was here didn't have such a broad face."

"Broad face?"

"Yeah. This man's face is square. The man who came in had an oval face. And he was much younger."

"Hmm," Phil said by way of comment.

"I'm an art student," Cassie added. "So I look for things like that. I do portraits. First thing I look at when I see a person is the shape of their face. . .shape of their eyes. . .nose. . ."

"I see." Phil placed the picture back into his pocket and withdrew a small photo of William Webster. "What about this man?" He held his breath, waiting for the answer.

This time Cassie paused and studied the photo more carefully before looking back to Phil and shaking her head, no. "Closer, but no."

"No? You're sure."

Cassie returned her gaze to the photo, then back to Phil. "Yes, I'm sure. Like I said, the man who came in here was young. Not that this guy in the photo here isn't good looking, but the guy who came in was younger. They have the same shape of face, but not the same eyes. Not the same eyes at all. Even behind the glasses, his eyes stood out."

"He wore glasses?"

"Yeah, little fashion glasses with blue lenses."

Phil nodded. "I see. Cassie," Phil said, placing the photo of William into his pocket, "Can you give me a little more information?"

"Sure."

"What did the man look like? As best as you can remember."

"Like I said, he was younger than the photos you just showed me."

"Can you estimate the age?"

Cassie pursed her lips as she thought. "Thirties?"

"Early? Mid? Late?"

The lips pursed again. "That's difficult to say. I'd guess middle. That way, I'm safe all the way around."

Phil nodded. "What else?"

"He was tall. Thin, but not skinny. Dark hair and eyes. Gorgeous eyes, actually. Very full lips, you know. . .kissable lips."

"Cassie, really," Nora Taylor interjected.

"I'm nineteen so I notice things like that."

"I understand from Mrs. Webster that he had long, dark hair."

"Long, but fashionable. Pulled back into a ponytail. Very sharp look. Sharp dresser, too. He even wore a black wool hat."

"Did he have facial hair?"

"Mustache and a bit of a five o'clock shadow. It looked nice though."

"You said he was well dressed?"

"Very. Pleated black pants, white turtleneck sweater and dark wool overcoat. Coat matched the hat. And I'm talking quality stuff here. Before I worked here I was at. . ." Cassie lowered her voice to a whisper, ". . .Lord and Taylor. I worked in men's wear, so I know quality."

Nora Taylor's lips thinned.

"I see," Phil said. "Cassie, I'm going to give you my card. Would you be willing to meet with a composite artist tomorrow afternoon?"

"Oh, sure, but I can bring my own drawing if you'd like."

Phil smiled as he handed her his business card. "Why don't you do that? I'll be back in the afternoon to pick it up from you. If necessary, we'll call in the composite artist. Okay?"

Cassie nodded. "Sure."

Phil touched his lips with his index finger. Removing it, he added, "One other thing. Would you be willing to look at some more photographs when I come in?"

Cassie raised her eyebrows. "Sure," she repeated. "Of what?"

"Dethroned politicians."

"Okay." Cassie laughed lightly at the thought.

"I appreciate your help with this."

"No problem at all, Mr. Silver."

"Now then," Phil winked at Nora Taylor. "Cassie, would you like to tell me more about those pear-shaped sapphire earrings I saw on the other side of the showcase?"

"Has anyone besides me noticed the new clothes in the window of Jacqueline's?" Brittany asked as she entered Katie's office in the hotel suite. She looked from Katie, who was sitting at the desk, to Marcy, who was sitting next to Ashley on the nearby sofa. There was a plate of untouched finger sandwiches and glasses of cold drinks on the coffee table before them.

Katie smiled wearily. "You like?"

Brittany laid her jacket across the back of a chair before sitting. "I like very much. I've always been a clothes hound, but not those kind of clothes. I couldn't afford to even pay attention in places like that." Ashley reached for her glass before answering. "I went in there the other day." She smiled brightly. "I acted like I belonged, but the woman who runs it—Zandra, I think her name is—she wasn't one bit fooled."

Katie smiled again, but remained silent.

Brittany shifted her gaze to the sofa. "By the way, I'm Brittany."

Marcy nodded. "My name is Marcy Waters. I'm a friend of Katie's."

"Best friend," Katie said. "Best friend since day one of my life."

"No kidding?" Brittany commented.

Maggie appeared at the door, and everyone turned to look at her. "May I bring anything else?"

"Something to drink for Brittany," Katie answered. "Coke, Brittany?" she asked. Brittany was wearing skintight jeans, a knee-length sweater and ankle boots. Katie thought, sitting in the chair with her legs crossed, she looked somewhat like a model.

Brittany turned back to Katie. "Sure." She looked at Maggie. "Sure. Thank you, Maggie."

Maggie didn't answer. She simply turned and walked out of the room.

"Where's Candy?"

"She's coming," Ashley answered.

"What's going on here?" Brittany asked. "Why'd you have us pulled out of work and why did you ask us to change into street clothes?"

"Katie received flowers today," Ashley answered. "Lots of flowers."

Brittany uncrossed her long legs. "From the anonymous gift-giver?" Brittany asked.

"Yes," Katie answered.

"What do you need us to do?" Brittany asked Katie.

Katie looked at Marcy, who answered instead. "The flowers came from The Little Flower Shoppe. A quick look in the phone book indicates there are quite a few in the city, but if we divide the city up into sections, we can each go out and see if we can find out which floral shop

190

they actually came from."

Brittany looked at Katie with a frown. "Girl, have you called the police about this?"

"I called my friend, Mr. Silver. He's a private detective."

"Private detective? Don't you think you should call the police or somebody?"

Katie reached for the rose-shaped crystal paperweight decorating her desk and began to fondle it. "Agent Silver worked the case when Ben disappeared. Besides, legally a crime hasn't been committed."

"Oh. I see."

"He's on the case," Ashley added. "He's trying to link the flowers to the necklace."

Maggie returned to the room with Brittany's drink. Candy, looking tired and sullen, was at her heels. Her blue-black hair was pulled back into a ponytail at the nape of her neck, and she was wearing a pair of black leggings, a man's white oxford shirt, and a red vest.

"Looking like the holidays there, Candy," Brittany said with a smile. "Worn out but sharp."

"Where were you last night, Candy?" Ashley asked.

"What do you mean?" Candy plopped into the chair nearest Brittany.

"I called your room to see if you wanted to do something with me, but you weren't there."

"I just went out," Candy answered with a shrug. She looked at Maggie, "May I have a cup of hot tea, please?"

Maggie frowned. "Certainly." Then to Katie, "Anything else, Miss Katie?"

"No, thank you, Maggie."

"What are we doing here?" Candy asked.

"Waiting, basically," Marcy answered. "By the way, I'm Marcy, Katie's friend from Georgia."

"Okay," Candy answered.

"What *are* we waiting for exactly?" Brittany asked.

"A call from Mr. Silver. As soon as he's done talking to the sales clerk at Saks where the necklace was purchased, he'll begin with the flower shops."

"What's going on here?" Candy asked.

Marcy explained the flowers and the wait for Silver's call. Moments later the phone rang. Katie answered it.

"Hello?"

"Katie. Phil."

"Anything?" she asked, setting the paperweight back on the desk. She could hear traffic in the background, an indication that Phil was calling from his car.

"Interesting turn of events. I showed Cassie—the sales clerk—a drawing of Bucky."

"And?"

"She says it wasn't him."

"It *wasn't?*"

"No."

"What does that mean? Do you think it was Ben?" Katie felt four pairs of eyes looking at her.

There was a pause of silence. "No."

"Why not?"

"I showed her a photo of William, too."

"And?"

"She said no."

Katie sighed deeply. "If it's not Bucky and it's not Ben, then who?"

"I don't know. Next stop is the back to the hotel to talk to the manager of the flower shop. Then I'll be up to talk with you about what he says."

"*Me?*"

Another pause. "Katie. . .tell me you weren't planning anything."

"No! I'm tired, that's all. I was thinking of having a light lunch and lying down for a while." Katie grimaced as she said these words. Now she would be forced to do exactly that.

"Good. I'll see you shortly."

"I'll be here. I'll tell Maggie to wake me when you arrive."

"Fine."

Katie hung up the phone and looked at Marcy. "It's not Bucky and it's not Ben."

"No?" Marcy asked. "What does Silver think?"

"He's not sure. He'll be here soon enough. He's coming back to the hotel's flower shop to see if they came from here. Then he'll be up to see me. That means—"

"You'll need to man this battle station and leave the rest to us. Okay, girls," Marcy said, looking from Brittany to Candy to Ashley. "I'm giving each of you a section of the city. We'll go to The Little Flower Shoppe in those areas and ask if someone has ordered flowers to be delivered to Katie." Marcy reached for a small stack of photographs of Ben she had gathered from Katie's photo albums earlier and placed on the edge of Katie's desk. "Take these with you. We don't really think it's Mr. Webster sending the flowers, but just to be on the safe side. And," she reached for a stack of index cards she'd prepared as well, "these are the addresses of the shops."

"What time should we be back?" Brittany asked, taking a card.

Marcy looked at her watch. "It's one-fifteen now. Be back no later than five. Sound good?"

Everyone agreed. Katie remained seated at the desk and looked at the four women heading out the door of her home office. "Marcy," she said quietly.

Marcy turned to look back at her.

"I'll have Simon drive you. You don't know the city well enough to try to go alone."

"I was going to have my first experience in the subway."

"It'd take me all day just to explain it to you."

Marcy shrugged. "Then I'll take a cab."

"I'd prefer if Simon was with you."

Marcy nodded. "Sure." She turned to leave.

"And Marcy?"

The soft voice stopped her again. Marcy placed her hand on the doorframe, but didn't answer.

"Thank you."

"You're welcome."

CHAPTER TWENTY

Marcy and Simon had casual conversation through the open partition of the limo as they drove from The Hamilton Place to the nearest The Little Flower Shoppe in the Upper West Side. Occasionally Simon would point out places of interest to Marcy, telling her the history of the city and why she really should go there before she left. She asked him about the World Trade Center disaster. . .where he was when it happened.

His face grew dark. "I was at the hotel. It was early still."

"Yes."

"I lost my brother," he said. "He was a firefighter. Got called when the first plane hit. He was in Tower Two when it collapsed."

Marcy placed her fingertips over her mouth. "Oh, Simon. I am so sorry."

Simon nodded and pursed his lips. Marcy could tell he was fighting back raw emotion, so she chattered a bit about her own family. Simon relaxed, then she asked him about the rest of his kinfolks, a word that made him smile. After that, Marcy sat back in the leather seat of the limo, stared at the passing rows of garland and wreath-graced buildings and thought about the possible suspects who could be Katie's stalker.

From the very beginning it hadn't seemed logical that Katie's husband would be sending the flowers. . .or the necklace. She was somewhat concerned about Sharkey, though. She understood Katie wanting to help the three young women, but at what cost had she done so? Just what type of man was Sharkey?

She leaned forward in her seat. "Simon?"

"Yes, Mrs. Waters." Simon leaned his head back slightly.

"What do you know about Sharkey?"

"The owner of the club where the girls came from?" He turned to look at her briefly before staring back into traffic.

"Yes."

"There's not much to know about him. Mrs. Webster hasn't really discussed it, and my research on him hasn't pulled up a whole lot."

"Your research?"

"Yes, Ma'am. Part of my job is to take care of Mrs. Webster. That means I check out everything. The first day Mrs. Webster went into his club, I waited in the limo, booted up my trusty laptop—"

"You have a laptop up there?" Marcy adjusted her seating so as to get a better look. "Son of a gun, you sure do," she said, peering over the seat.

"Yes, Ma'am. I plug her up here," he said, pointing to the power adapter, "then connect to the Internet using the car's phone line."

"I'll be dog."

"Excuse me?" Simon jerked his head to momentarily look at her.

Marcy laughed lightly. "It's a southern saying."

"Oh."

"Short for I'll be doggoned."

Simon's brow furrowed. "You know, that doesn't make a lot of sense either."

Marcy frowned. "I suppose not. At any rate. . ."

"Yes, Ma'am."

"You were saying that when Katie went into—"

"Yes, Ma'am. When Mrs. Webster went into the club the first time, I did some research. Mist Goddess certainly isn't the best club out there—they don't even have a website—but city records show Sharkey Garone owns and manages it. He's a two-bit kind of greasy weasel. Petty crime. A couple of domestic violence charges—"

"Domestic violence?"

"Yes, Ma'am."

Marcy sighed. "Wife?"

"Oh, no, Ma'am. Some of his girls who've lived with him."

Marcy's shoulders slumped and she sighed again. "There's probably a whole other life out there I'm not even aware of."

"Yes, Ma'am. I'd say there is."

"What about involvement with the Mafia?"

Simon shook his head. "Nothing in the files. But I'm sure there's some involvement. You can't do business in that part of town—not that kind of business anyway—without owing the man."

"You mean the Mafia."

"Yes, Ma'am."

"I understand."

The car slowed to a stop. "Here you go, Mrs. Waters. The Little Flower Shoppe."

He stepped out of the car to open the door for her. "I'll wait right here," he told her.

Marcy shivered from the car to the door of the shop. When she opened it, the strong scent of cinnamon and sweet smell of apples met her. She breathed deeply and smiled as she looked around at the quaint Victorian shop. Perched along rows, atop glass shelves and inside antique sideboards and china cabinets, arrangements of silk flowers were clustered and displayed. China teacups and saucers had been transformed into unique gifts. Bears and bunnies were dressed in their frilly Sunday best, sitting amongst petite wrought iron patio sets as though gathered for tea. Clusters of dark brown branches speckled with red berries sprung from porcelain vases. Dried wild flowers hung from hooks in the far corners of the ceiling. Marcy spun around, her head tilted back in childlike wonder before a woman said to her, "Happy holidays. May I help you today?"

Marcy turned to a woman, about sixty years of age with snowy white hair and crystal blue eyes that peered over half glasses, smiling at her.

"Happy holidays," Marcy returned. "You have a charming place here."

"Thank you. I think so." The woman gave the shop a quick look of pride.

"Are you the manager?"

"Owner."

"Oh. Well, actually I'm on a bit of a mission." Marcy pulled the photo of Ben out of her purse, but held it down by her side. The woman's gaze followed her movement, then came back up to her face. "My friend, Mrs. William Webster, received some flowers today—a lot of flowers, as a matter of fact—from one of The Little Flower Shoppes."

"Yes, an arrangement came from here." The woman nodded.

"Just one?" Marcy took a step closer to the woman. This was easier than she had anticipated.

"Yes. The gentleman came in yesterday and ordered it."

"Yesterday. Was it this man?" Marcy held out the photograph.

The shop's owner took the photo and studied it through her half-glasses, then shook her head. "No. No, that's not him. Nice looking man, though."

Marcy frowned as she took the photo back from the woman. "When did the man come in?"

The owner took a step toward the back, then turned and looked at Marcy. "Is there a problem? We don't usually give out that information, you know."

Marcy came up short. "Mrs. Webster received several arrangements of flowers today from an anonymous giver—"

"Yes, he asked to be kept anonymous, but there was only one arrangement."

"He asked?"

"Yes. Said it was to be a surprise when he finally revealed himself as her secret admirer." The woman smiled sweetly as though she was privy to a magical confidence.

Marcy took a moment to think before she went on. "Mrs—"

"Gramm."

"Mrs. Gramm, my best friend's husband has been missing for near-ly two years. . ."

"Oh, how tragic!" Mrs. Gramm's brow furrowed. "How tragic indeed." She stepped over to a pair of bunnies having tea in the garden and adjusted them in their seats.

Marcy stepped closer to her. "Yes, it is tragic. And we think the per-son who sent her the flowers may be trying to pass himself off as her husband."

"This man most definitely wasn't her husband."

"How do you know?"

Mrs. Gramm straightened. "Because, my dear. He had that *madly in love* look about him. You know, the one men get when they are courting a young woman."

"What else did he look like?"

"Well," Mrs. Gramm thought carefully for a moment. "Tall. Trim. Very nice looking. Dark eyes."

"Hair color?"

"Dark." She touched the nape of her neck. "Ponytail. I never under-stood why a man would want to wear his hair. . .well, I suppose our very first president did. . ."

"I think that was a wig."

Mrs. Gramm thought a second. "Oh, yes."

"Dark hair, pulled back in a ponytail. . ."

"Yes."

"How old was this man?"

"Young. Early thirties, I'd say."

"Can you tell me anything else? Like, what he said?"

Mrs. Gramm frowned. "I don't know about all this—"

"Please, Mrs. Gramm. My best friend is very concerned and upset about this attention."

Mrs. Gramm pulled the half-glasses from her nose. "He came in—like I said, very nice looking man, very polite—and said he needed to order an arrangement to be sent—"

"One?"

"Yes."

"Not five?"

"No. Just one."

"Hmm."

"Were there five?" The half-glasses were placed back on her nose.

"Yes." Marcy started to place the photo of Ben back into her purse, then stopped and held it up for Mrs. Gramm to see one final time. "And you are sure it wasn't this man? Maybe disguising himself?"

Mrs. Gramm looked again. "Is that the man who is missing?"

"Yes."

She shook her head. "No, it wasn't him. Definitely wasn't him."

Marcy took a step back and was about to thank the businesswoman for her help, but suddenly stopped. "How did he pay?"

"Cash."

Marcy frowned. "Rats."

Mrs. Gramm's eyebrows rose. "I'll tell you this much. . ."

"Yes?"

"I'm surprised you found me."

"What do you mean?"

"The man insisted that we not use our usual little envelopes. You know, the ones that have our address printed on the front."

"Really?"

"Yes." Mrs. Gramm crossed her arms over her abdomen. "I thought that was odd. He handed me a generic white envelope with the card already inside. In fact, he had already written his message on the card."

"Did he say why he didn't want to use the store's envelopes?"

"Yes. When I asked him why he didn't want me to use our envelopes, he said that if Miss Webster—and *he* said Miss, not Mrs.— knew which area of town the flowers had come from, she would know they were from him. When he had paid and gone, I remembered we had envelopes in the back, printed only with our name across the front, but not our address. I thought, after all, this is about business, isn't it? Surely it won't hurt to at least advertise the name of the flower shop. Especially since there are so many of us in the city. Several in each borough, actually. That's why I said I'm surprised you found me. You were *lucky* to have found me."

Marcy was suddenly struck with the notion that she'd have to tell Silver the news she had just gathered. "Yeah, lucky me."

"Besides," Mrs. Gramm added. "He tipped very, very well. You don't argue with a man who can tip like that."

Katie greeted Phil at the door with a smile. He shrugged out of his coat, placed it in Maggie's outstretched hands, then turned to Katie. "You look better than when I left. Good nap?"

"Very good nap," she lied. She had lain down, that much was true. But she hadn't slept at all. Still, she thought, the rest had done her good. "What did you find out?"

"Let's sit down, shall we?"

Katie frowned. "Would you like a cup of hot tea? From the looks of things, it's gotten even colder out there."

"I would and it has." Phil looked around the foyer of the apartment. "Where's your friend?"

"She went out." Katie turned to walk toward the kitchen. "Why don't you have a seat in the living room? I'll be back in a moment."

Phil cocked an eyebrow. "Oh, no. Where'd she go?"

Katie looked over her shoulder and smiled. "She just went out, Phil. My goodness, she's in the Big Apple. It's the holidays. Simon is driving her around."

Phil followed Katie into the kitchen. "Uh-huh."

Katie grinned sweetly. "There's nothing to worry about, Phil. Let's just have a cup of tea, and you can tell me what happened when you went to the floral shop."

Maggie bustled in. "Would you like some hot tea?" she asked. Her accent seemed stronger than usual.

Katie laughed lightly. "Maggie's accent always intensifies when she mentions the word 'tea.' " Phil seemed to relax. Noticing the change in him, Katie eased back in her chair. "Yes, Maggie. Hot tea with milk. We'll be in the living room. Would you bring it in there, please?"

"Of course, Miss Katie," she said, then gave Phil a look that dared him to upset her mistress.

When they had gotten comfortable in the living room, Phil commented, "You know, sometimes I'm not sure who's the hired help and who's the guest around here. That woman can make me feel as though I were a child."

Katie stretched and curled her feet up under her. "She's a piece of work, isn't she?"

Maggie entered, pushing a serving cart with a silver tea service and a plate of pastries, announcing "Peppermint tea this afternoon." She frowned at Katie. "Never figured how you drink it, though. We Brits stick to *real* tea."

"Yes, Maggie, I know. But this is perfect for today, don't you think?" Katie finished with a nod. "Absolutely perfect. I'll take care of everything from here. You run along and take a nap. If you are going to take care of me, you must be well rested."

Maggie responded with a "humph," then left the room.

Katie stood and began to pour the hot, aromatic brew into china cups. "Tell me what you found out."

Phil nodded as Katie handed him the cup and saucer. "Well, for starters, one of the arrangements did come from here in the hotel."

Katie paused. "Just one of them?"

"Yes."

Katie picked up the sugar bowl, filled with cubes, and extended it to Phil. Holding the silver prongs with his fingers, he took a cube and dropped it into the cup. "Right here." Katie asked in a near whisper.

"Yes."

In silence she handed Phil the creamer, which he declined, then set about the preparation of her tea. When she had returned to her seat, and once again curled her feet up under her, she took a sip, stared out the window for a moment, and then said, "You're being awfully quiet."

"I'm thinking. I haven't really had time to process all the information."

"What are you thinking exactly?"

Phil took a sip of hot tea and swallowed. "I asked the flower shop manager downstairs if he could describe the man who ordered the flowers."

"And?"

"This is the strange part. He said a woman ordered the flowers."

"A woman?" Katie sat upright, placing her cup and saucer on the coffee table. "That's odd. . ."

"Not really." Phil took another sip of his tea, set the cup and saucer near Katie's, then stood and walked over to the cart where he placed a pastry on a china plate. "Anything for you?"

"No. No, thank you. I couldn't eat. Phil, what do you mean, not really?"

"Let's explore all the options."

"Okay."

"Let's begin by supposing that it is Sharkey."

"Is that what you think?"

Phil sat on the sofa, took a bite of the pastry, and shook his head. "Let's just look at the possibilities. You've taken three of his girls, a fact I'd like to take a moment to talk to you about."

Katie lowered her lashes. "Do we have to?"

"Katie, if I'm going to get to the bottom of this, we have to be straight with one another."

Katie returned her gaze to meet his. "I suppose so."

"Why in the world would you take three girls out of a place like Mist Goddess and bring them to the hotel to work? I know you're a good person. . .have a good heart. . .but that makes no sense to me."

Katie looked out the window and was quiet for a long moment. So long, Phil worried she might have forgotten the question or that he was even in the room. "Katie?" he spoke softly.

She merely nodded. "Phil, did Ben ever tell you about my past? I mean, when I first came to New York?"

"No."

Katie paused again, as though seeking the right words. She blinked, then whispered, "I was one of them."

"I don't understand. One of whom?"

She returned her eyes to his again. "One of *them*. I was a dancer, Phil. It was 1975, I was broke, living in Hell's Kitchen and there were few options."

Phil took a moment to digest it all. "I see." It was all he could think of to say.

"Do you judge me harshly for that?"

"No, of course not," he came back suddenly. "I just find it hard to believe. You say William knew."

"Mmm. I didn't know that he knew until after. . .you know. . .but he did."

"So now you want to offer young ladies a chance. . .young ladies who work in the business." It wasn't a question. Phil knew the size of Katie's heart. It made perfect sense.

"Yes. I'm attempting to teach their *souls* to dance."

Phil didn't respond for several moments. "Which leads us back to Sharkey. As a businessman in that part of the city. . .and in that line of work. . .he's sure to have connections with *La Cosa Nostra*. . .thus, the money to do these extravagant things." The conversation as far as it dealt with Katie's past was over.

Katie frowned. She knew all about men who owned or managed men's clubs and the types of businessmen who came there for their pleasures. It was how she had met David Franscella. David was a patron, and Leo had ordered Katie to meet David. Back then she thought nothing of using men like David. . .or being used by them. She didn't worry about the risks. But that was then. This was now. "Have you spoken to Sharkey?"

"I will as soon as I leave here. I'll go by the club and then home."

"Be careful." It was all Katie knew to say.

"What makes you say that?"

"Don't *you* think he's dangerous?"

"I don't know. My gut tells me he's not. My gut tells me that if it's him, he just wants to scare you a little."

"If it's him, he's spent an awful lot of money to scare me a little."

"Hmm. That's the part that doesn't quite fit here."

"Well, if it doesn't quite fit. . ."

Phil reached for his tea, took a final sip, then placed the china back on the coffee table. "I've got to have some time to think about this. We know Caballero didn't purchase the necklace. Unless, of course, Caballero has paid someone to purchase the necklace and say he's your husband. . ."

"But what about the woman?"

Phil shrugged. "Could easily be Victoria Thomas Whitney. Description fits."

"What description?"

"I asked the manager of the floral shop what the woman who purchased the flowers—cash by the way—looked like. He described a woman who looked a lot like Victoria Thomas Whitney. With the exception of. . ."

"Of?"

"The age. The woman described was in her late twenties, early thirties. There's a slight chance, I suppose, that Mrs. Whitney could pass herself off. . ."

Katie shook her head. "I don't honestly think so, Phil."

"She's an attractive enough woman."

"All the Estee Lauder in the *world* couldn't make a woman of Victoria's age look like a woman in her late twenties, early thirties."

Phil nodded with a frown. "Okay, so Thomas-Whitney is out."

"Phil, is Bucky Caballero involved with the Mafia?"

The lines of Phil's lips grew thin. "Bucky Caballero is his own Mafia. I've often wondered what he's doing when it comes to all this. There's evidence that *La Cosa Nostra* took out his father—"

"Bucky's?"

"Yes. If that's so, why would he join a group whose actions forever changed his world? Or even want to imitate their ways?"

Katie raised an eyebrow. "To somehow get an upper hand and bring about his own justice?"

"That's possible. That's something I've thought about, actually."

They were silent for a moment before Katie asked, "What are the other possibilities in my case?"

"I've already talked to James Harrington, and I thought he was clear on this, but the thought has crossed my mind that perhaps he and his secretary—"

Katie held her hands palm up. "But why, Phil? I know why *James* might want me out of the way, but his secretary?"

Phil looked straight ahead as if something had just come to mind.

Katie tilted her head slightly. "What?"

Phil slid up on the sofa, braced his elbows on his knees, and flexed his shoulders, as he looked Katie in the eyes. "She doesn't fit the description anyway." Phil paused. "Katie, how well do you know Vickey?"

"Vickey?" Katie exploded, coming to her feet. "Don't even think about it, Phil!"

Phil stood. "Let's just think about the possibilities. As an investigator, I have to do that."

Katie began to pace. "Maybe *you* do. I don't."

Phil walked to where Katie had come to a rest. "Let's just talk about it."

"I won't listen."

"You don't have to. I'll just talk and ask you a few questions."

Katie pursed her lips. "What questions?"

"Who brought the necklace to you the first time?"

Katie didn't answer right away.

"Katie—"

"Vickey, but—"

Phil raised a hand to stop her protests. "Okay. Who brought the necklace to you the second time?"

Katie crossed her arms across her abdomen. "That's no proof."

"Have you seen the receipts from the courier?"

"No, but I'm sure she can produce them."

"Okay, then. Now, I'm done playing devil's advocate. She fits the woman's description. She's in her mid-thirties. She's a little older, but Vickey is a nice looking woman. . .she could pass. . ."

Katie's eyes pleaded with Phil to stop. "Phil, don't be ridiculous. What possible reason would she have to do that? She's my assistant and my friend."

"I'm playing devil's advocate again. What if she were secretly in love with William. . ."

"Phil!" Katie stomped her foot.

Phil returned to his place on the sofa. "Sit down, Katie. Or what if she thought she should have gotten a higher position when you took over the presidency."

"Don't be ludicrous." Katie sat near the end of the sofa but looked straight ahead.

"You *have* to consider all the possibilities, Katie. Have you ever played the game of Clue?"

"The child's game?" She looked at him.

"Not so childish. It's a game of skill and deduction."

"What does that have to do with Vickey?"

Phil shifted to look at her. "The object of the game is to answer *who, where, and how.* In the center of the playing board is an envelope and inside the envelope is the answer to those three questions. *Who, where, and how.* Determining the answer—and subsequently winning the game—depends on deduction. As a player moves from one room to the next, he or she makes suggestions as to the answers. Suggestions, Katie."

Katie grimaced. "I understand."

"Deduction and common sense."

Katie sighed. "All right. So, you're looking at three possibilities. Bucky Caballero and Victoria Thomas Whitney, who we've ruled out, James Harrington and Deirdre Randall, who we've ruled out, or Vickey, who I've ruled out. And here's a question for you: Vickey and who else?"

"Here's a question for *you:* Are we *only* looking at three possibilities? And. . .what's the motive?"

"Motive. . ."

"We know what we've got so far. Sharkey is unhappy with your taking the girls out of his club. James Harrington was or is unhappy with you taking over here."

"Was or is?"

"He indicates that his attitudes have changed and, quite frankly, I believe him."

"I see."

"Any motives from Vickey would be purely speculative."

Katie frowned. "And I won't even consider it."

"Then, of course, there's Caballero. Motive is easy. Revenge pure and simple."

Katie was silent for a moment. Her eyes were downcast and her gaze faraway. When she finally spoke, she said, "If he killed Ben, he's had his revenge. He couldn't take anything else from me."

CHAPTER TWENTY-ONE

By luck of the draw—or at least, that was how Candy saw it—she was sent to the part of the city where Mist Goddess was located. On the way there, she stopped at a pay phone. She called Sharkey at the club. He hadn't come in yet, so she tried his cell phone. A groggy voice answered on the first ring.

"Sharkey," Candy said anxiously. "Sharkey, I have to talk to you."

"Who is this?" he demanded.

"It's Candy," she hissed, drawing closer to the stainless steel encasing around the phone.

"Candy, whaddaya calling me for? Whaddaya want?"

Candy placed her gloved hand near her cheek in an attempt to both warm her face and keep herself from being heard. "I'm near the club." She rubbed her booted foot up and down the back of her leg. "Dang, Sharkey. It's cold out here. I need to talk to you, and I need to talk to you now. It's about Katie Webster."

There was a moment of silence before a slightly more alert Sharkey asked, "Yeah, yeah. Why didn't you say so? What is it?"

"I'm not going to stand out here and freeze myself to death to tell you this, Sharkey. I can meet you at the club or I can—"

"Hold your horses. Call me back in about five minutes."

"Sharkey, no. It's cold—" He had already hung up. Candy held the

earpiece away from her face and looked at it dumbfounded. "Son of a—"
She slammed the earpiece back onto the receiver. It fell off. She picked
it up and slammed it down again. Spinning around, she spotted a small
coffee shop and ran inside to warm herself.

"How many?" the hostess asked her.

Candy looked around briefly. The café was narrow, with just enough
space for the row of small four-chair tables placed along a mirrored wall
in the front. With the exception of the first table, they were all filled. She
saw two doors at the back wall near the service bar. The door with the
round glass pane in it was obviously the kitchen door. The other had a
black and gold "restroom" sign stuck on it.

"What?" she asked.

"How many?"

"How many do I look like?" The words spewed out of Candy's
mouth before she had time to think about them. When she saw a look
of irritation on the hostess's face, she stepped back and whispered,
"Sorry. It's cold out there and I—"

"Yeah, I saw you out there on the phone. You want a cup of coffee
or not?"

"Sure." Candy sat at the empty table. Minutes later, the hostess returned with a thick mug of black coffee and a handful of creamer tubs.

"Do you want to see a menu?"

"No."

"I'll leave you to your coffee then," the hostess said, then walked away.

Candy turned her attention to preparing the coffee to her liking,
then took a sip of it and looked down at her coat, which Katie had
bought for her. She felt a momentary pang of guilt. Katie had been good
to her. Why was she calling Sharkey to let him in on what was happening at the hotel? Because he had told her if she didn't keep him informed
of Katie's business, he would beat her 'til she begged for death. She had
no reason not to believe he'd do it. The first night she'd gone back to
Mist Goddess he had made her work a table occupied by a man who
frightened her. It was her punishment for having left in the first place.

In fact, every night the man came in, Candy was told to dance for him. Sharkey knew the man was capable of violence. Knew he had slapped her once during a private dance. He just didn't care.

"You probably deserved it," Sharkey had said. "I know I'd like to slap you every so often myself."

"You wouldn't—" Candy had said, narrowing her eyes.

He slapped her just to prove that he would. . .that he could. The pop across the face had stung, but it hadn't broken anything. It hadn't even bruised. Sharkey knew just how to hit and where. When she swung back to face him, her eyes brimming with tears, he had grabbed her chin and squeezed. "Don't tempt me, Little China. You hear me?" There was no compassion in his voice.

Sharkey was a little man, not like her brutish stepfather, so he had more to prove. Jim Cassidy was just plain-old mean. Sharkey was trying to live up to an image created by his father, who had died with a repu-tation of being one of the best managers in the business. In this case "best" meant "able to keep his girls in line and turn a good profit."

Candy had nodded her head, yes.

"What was that? I don't think I heard you?" He squeezed harder.

"I said yes, Sharkey. Yes."

He pushed her back slightly. "Good girl. Now get away from me."

Now Candy took the last sip of her coffee. Pulling a few bills out of her purse, she set them next to the mug. On her way out, she brushed by the hostess, giving her a curt nod. Then, as she stepped outside once again, the bitter cold enshrouded her vengefully.

The snowfall had picked up. Candy tightened the coat around her and crossed the sidewalk to the pay phone to call Sharkey again. He answered on the first ring, as before, though this time his voice was clear and forceful.

"Yeah."

"Sharkey, it's me."

"Where are you?" he bellowed.

"Dang, Sharkey. Don't yell."

"I told you to call back in five minutes."

"How long has it been?"

"At least seven."

"Sharkey, do you want to talk to me or not? I gotta go to some flower shop and get back to the hotel by five."

"You gotta do more than that. Get yourself over to The Plaza."

"The Plaza?"

"Is there an echo in the room or are you just hard of hearing?"

"Why am I going to The Plaza?" Candy took a step back, leaving the semi-privacy of the stainless steel with an advertisement displayed on the side—Brooke Shields starring in Cabaret. She had to raise her voice above the city traffic.

"Are you yelling at me?"

Candy sighed deeply, took a step closer to the phone. "No. No, of course not, Sharkey."

"I don't believe I heard an apology."

"I'm sorry," she said, stepping even closer to the phone and lowering her voice.

Sharkey laughed. "I'm picturing you there, on your knees, begging me again."

Candy didn't respond to his digs. She waited until he had had his moment then asked. "Why am I going to The Plaza?"

"It's the best you've ever seen, even compared to Hotel Webster." He waited for her response, but when she said nothing, he gave her the room number instead. "That's on the ninth floor, in case you weren't smart enough to figure it out."

"Sharkey—"

"There's a man there who needs a little of your time."

"Sharkey, I don't think you understand what I'm trying to tell you—"

"Not that kind of time, Stupid. He needs to talk to you about Katie Webster. You be nice to this man, you hear? This man could make or break me. And if you mess anything up for me, I'll break you, you understand?"

Candy nodded. "I'll go right now."

"You didn't answer me."

"Yes, Sharkey. I understand. I'll go right now."

She hung up the phone, then took a few steps down the street. She hailed the first vacant cab. It screeched to a halt and swerved toward the sidewalk. As she slid gracefully into the back seat, she couldn't help thinking about the noxious thrall that seemed—once again—to be gripping her life. "You are morally enslaved," an intellectual derelict had told her once in an all-night coffee shop where he regularly handed out sage advice for free. "Have you ever tried escaping from your servitude? I bet you feel out of place trying to lead a normal life, don't you? Your abusive childhood is always casting its ugly shadow over your thoughts, your feelings, your goals, and hence. . ." he paused for effect, "your actions. You routinely spurn others' noble attempts at liberating you from your turpitude."

Candy frowned at the memory. Maybe it was true, but she didn't have time to think about it now.

"The Plaza," she said to the cab driver. "And please step on it."

Living at The Hamilton Place for the past several months, Candy had become accustomed to opulence. If not, the stately grandeur of The Plaza might have overwhelmed her to the point of anxiety. Her apprehension about the mysterious meeting was enough to deal with right now, and she very much wanted to be able to exude confidence in this type of setting. There had been something in Sharkey's tone of voice that intimidated her though. *There's a man who needs a little of your time*, he had said.

Typically, as a dancer, those words meant only one thing. But Sharkey had said, "Not that kind of time, Stupid." Remembering his words, Candy frowned. He had called her stupid. Now, standing in front of The Plaza's first floor elevators and pushing the up button, she raised her square chin slightly. She was *not* stupid. She was just a girl who had gotten mixed up in something larger than herself. A girl who couldn't seem to get out, even when she had the key handed to her on a silver platter. For the life of her, she couldn't figure out why it wasn't enough.

The elevator door opened, and Candy stepped in. The brass doors closed, doors so highly polished Candy could see her reflection in them. She removed a hand from her coat pocket and, beginning at the crown of her head, ran it along the inky black hair until it caught the fashionable elastic band holding it back. She pulled gently and her hair released. She tossed her head and watched it shimmer as though moving in slow motion about her. The elevator came to a smooth stop, the doors glided open, and she stepped out and into the hallway. As soon as the doors closed behind her, she looked straight ahead and began to follow the signs toward the room number she had scribbled on a forgotten envelope found in the back of the cab. Along the way she stopped at a gilded, beveled mirror hanging over an ornate bombe chest, took a tube of red lipstick out of her purse, and reapplied a thin moist layer. She replaced the lipstick, set her purse on the chest, ran her fingers through her hair, and secured it once more. She stared at her reflection for only a moment before she pulled her hair free again, wrapping the band around her wrist like a bracelet. Satisfied with her appearance, she continued down the corridor.

Finding the room, she took a deep breath and knocked. Within seconds it opened, revealing a handsome older man, bearded and dark.

"You must be Candy," he said smoothly. "Come in, Puppet."

Candy stepped into the room and past the man who had summoned her. When he had closed the door, he added, "May I take your jacket?"

Candy swung around to face him. "Yes," she said, barely above a whisper as she slipped it off. He stepped over to help her, then hung the jacket in a nearby closet.

"Would you like to have a seat?" he asked.

"I can stand," she said proudly, which made him chuckle. Her face turned an appealing shade of pink.

"I think you should sit down, Puppet." He moved past her then as though it really didn't matter to him whether she did or she didn't. Her eyes followed as he made his way over to the bar where he began to prepare a drink for himself. "I'd offer you a drink but you look to be under age."

"I'm old enough," she said simply.

He turned his head as he took a sip of his drink and smiled. "I wonder, Puppet."

Candy narrowed her Asian eyes, watching him like a hyper-vigilant cat as he sat in a nearby chair, crossing his legs and flexing his shoulders at the same time. "Why do you keep calling me 'puppet'?" she asked.

He chuckled again. "It must be a Freudian slip. You remind me of a beautiful young girl I once thought I knew."

Candy continued to frown at him. "In what way do I remind you of her?"

He took another sip before answering. "She, too, was Asian. Asian and African-American actually. The most exotic creature I'd ever laid eyes on."

Candy didn't respond.

The man cocked an eyebrow. "I often called her 'Puppet.'"

"Why? Was she your slave?"

The man laughed out loud then. "No. Perhaps I was hers."

Again, Candy didn't respond.

"You're a tough nut to crack, aren't you, Candy?" he asked her.

"I don't know why I'm here."

"What did Mr. Sharkey tell you?"

Mister Sharkey? The name made her smile, but only for a moment. "Nothing. Just to come here."

"And so you have." He took another sip of his drink, then with a nod of his head indicated a nearby chair. "Sit down, Candy." When she still did not move, he fixed his eyes. "That's not a request, young lady."

Candy moved then, slowly, without taking her eyes off him. Once she had sat down, she asked, "Am I here for a private dance? Is that it?"

"No. I'm not into that sort of thing." He drained his glass, then stood and walked past her, over to the bar to refresh his drink.

Candy raised her chin and looked straight ahead, sensing his movements behind her, then flinched when a crystal whiskey-filled glass was placed under her nose. "Drink, my dear. It will warm you. Bitter cold out there today."

She took the glass, but refused to drink.

Bucky returned to his seat. "So let's get down to business."

"Yes, let's," she agreed, still without looking at him.

"I understand you know my good friend Katie Webster."

Candy turned her head to look directly at him. "Is that what this is all about? Katie?"

"I'm afraid that's all it is. Are you comfortable, Candy?"

"Comfortable?"

"Yes. Comfortable. Is the chair to your liking?"

"Yes."

He nodded. "Good. I'm going to tell you a little story, and I want you to be comfortable."

Candy licked her lips. "I'm fine."

The man visibly relaxed in his chair. "Have you ever wanted something so bad you could taste it—By the way, what's your real name, Candy? I know you girls like to change your names."

Candy would typically not give her real name, but something about this man told her she should. "Xi Lan," she answered assuredly.

The man breathed deeply, seemingly drinking her in with his eyes. "Beautiful. Why in the name of all that's good and decent would you want to change it?"

They were silent for a moment before Xi Lan answered, "Yes."

The man gave a half-smile. "Yes, what?"

"Yes, I have wanted something so bad I could taste it."

"Do you still?"

Xi Lan kept her gaze steady on his eyes. "Yes."

"I thought so. I had a business here in the city. . .a very prosperous business. . .did you know that?"

"No." Candy took a sip of her nearly forgotten drink.

The man smiled. "It was. Then, one evening without warning, my world came to an end. Mrs. Webster's husband decided that what I was doing was wrong—"

Xi Lan narrowed her eyes. "What were you doing?"

"I was a real estate broker."

"What's so wrong with that?" Candy brushed her fingers through her hair again.

"One would wonder."

"So Katie's husband brought your business down, or something like that."

The man's eyes darkened. He fingered round the top of his glass.

"I'll take that as a yes."

He didn't answer her right away. Instead, he nursed his drink thoughtfully. Finally he said, "Tell me *your* dream, Xi Lan. Then I'll finish with mine."

Xi Lan took another sip of her drink before answering. If she were to tell the dream, would it mean the dream couldn't come true? Would this man be able to help her see her dream become a reality? Was he her savior? She felt as though he had been playing a game of cat and mouse with her, but. . .maybe. . .maybe this time. . .maybe this man. . . . "I want my mother and brother to be able to live with me. I want my mother to be free of her husband."

"He's not your father?"

Xi Lan's words were cold. "My father is dead."

"And your stepfather, he's a cruel man?"

"You could say that."

"I *did* say that. Did he ever hurt you?" The man tilted his head slightly and narrowed his eyes, as though the very thought of it would anger him beyond words.

"No. But he. . . ." Xi Lan stopped, remembering briefly the night she had bent over him, mouth open, allowing him to smell her breath for traces of alcohol.

"Was not very kind," the man finished for her.

"No." Xi Lan looked around the room. "What time is it? I should be getting back to the hotel soon. Katie is expecting. . ."

"Not yet." The man crooked a finger at her. "Come here, Xi Lan."

The old subservient nature rose up within her. She set her drink on a nearby table, and when she had come to stand in front of him, he grabbed her wrist and pulled her down to her knees before him. "Sit at my feet, Xi Lan."

She did. She turned her face away from him and, with the insistence of his hand, laid her head against his knee. As he began to stroke her hair, he whispered, "What is stopping you from your dream?"

"Money."

"But isn't that why you went to live with Katie Webster?"

"She promised a better life for us."

"She didn't keep that promise?"

"Yes. I suppose she did." She felt a momentary sting of regret, then let it slide down her spine as she pulled herself upright. If this man was to be her savior, she'd have to play him. . .play him like all the other men she had played as she regained the control her stepbrother had stolen. She furrowed her brow at the thought. She had played them, hadn't she? Maybe they had played her, were still playing her. Not that it mattered. Either way, everyone got what they wanted in the end. Didn't they? "We work in housekeeping, but she says it's only for a short time. Soon we will move up, but I don't know to what. Or when. I don't know when I will make enough to bring my mother and brother here."

"So you went back to the club." His strong hand began to rub the muscles in the back of her neck.

She sighed deeply and closed her eyes. Life was so complicated and she was so tired. "Yes."

"Why is that?" his voice lowered.

She shrugged her shoulders. "I'm not sure."

He tugged lightly at her hair. "For the money? Is the money so good in a place like that?"

She swung around to look at him, fire shone in her eyes. "It's fair. Not as good as some places I've been."

"Why did you leave those places?"

"Sometimes you just get washed up, I guess. Time to move on. You hear about a better deal in another place. You get on the bad side of the boss's girl. You make her angry and moving on is in your best interest."

Bucky smiled a crooked smile. "I think I know more about you than you do. You like the attention, Xi Lan. You like having men look at you. You like the control of knowing they can look but not touch."

Xi Lan's jaw became rigid at hearing the words he spoke, words she had thought only moments earlier. "I don't know—"

"Yes, you do."

"No, I. . ."

"Yes, you do."

She sat silently for a moment then, dipping her head slightly, but keeping her eyes fixed on his.

"What if I could give you your dream, Xi Lan? Would you give me mine?"

"I don't know," she answered. "I don't know your dream."

"I want Katie Webster to pay for what she and her husband did to me. I'm a very powerful man, Xi Lan. And unforgiving. I don't take things like this lightly." Xi Lan listened to the hypnotic power of his voice, drank in the words. "If you help me bring her down, I'll make certain your mother and brother come to live with you. In fact, I will take you back to Canada with me. All three of you. Canada is a beautiful country, Xi Lan. Have you ever been there?"

"I went to the Canadian side of Niagara once."

He leaned close. She could smell cologne and whiskey. She tilted her head back, and he touched the tip of her nose with his finger. "Are you with me, then?"

"Yes," she whispered. The word was firm and clear. "Tell me what you want me to do."

The man smiled. "Very good, Puppet. Very, very good."

A half hour later, having been given exact instructions as to what she was to do next, Xi Lan left The Plaza. She rushed out of the hotel lobby and hailed a cab from the circular curb, suddenly struck with an interesting thought. She didn't know the man's name.

The man had never told her his name.

CHAPTER TWENTY-TWO

"One of them came from The Little Flower Shoppe located in the Upper West Side," Marcy announced ceremoniously from the foyer of Katie's apartment as she slipped out of her coat and handed it to Maggie. From the door, she had a straight view of Katie and Phil.

"I should have known—" Phil moaned from the living room.

"Now, Phil—" Katie spoke lightly, touching his arm with her fingertips as though to console him for what was about to happen next.

Marcy made her way to where Phil and Katie were sitting. "Now don't get yourself all bent out of shape there, Silver. And don't blame Katie—"

Phil turned to Katie. "You lied to me, Katie."

"I never said *specifically. . .*"

"Argue about it later, Silver. Let me see those envelopes," Marcy sat next to him on the sofa. He shifted away from her.

"I most assuredly will not. Let me say this again—"

"Silver, you have to listen to me on this. I've already done some of the legwork for you—"

"Legwork?" Phil stood in exasperation. "This isn't a movie, Mrs. Waters!"

"You can call me Marcy," Marcy said emphatically.

"And this isn't some suspense novel, either."

Marcy stood as Katie buried her face in her hands. "I'm not saying it is, Silver. But if you'll just let me see those envelopes—"

Phil looked heavenward, opening his hands. "Why am I fighting this?" He took the five small florist envelopes out of his pocket and handed them to Marcy. She returned to her seat on the sofa and began to shuffle through them like a deck of cards.

"Here. Look at this, Silver. Katie, look at this."

Phil returned to sitting and Katie leaned over for a better view of the rows of envelopes Marcy had placed on the coffee table. "Notice that the four over here are not marked as having come from The Little Flower Shoppe. Even the cards on the inside are no indication of where they come from. They're generic. In fact. . ." Marcy continued as she opened all five envelopes, removing the cards. "Look. None of the cards have the name of the shop either. They just have pretty little flowers. And, like the note with the necklace, they have the same block-style handwriting."

"I'd already noticed that," Phil said with a slight hint of sarcasm.

Marcy ignored it. "Mrs. Gramm—the woman from the floral shop— said that the man who came in insisted this type of envelope. . ." she pointed to the blank envelopes, ". . .be used rather than the ones they typically use with their store name and address on the front. She said the man didn't want Katie to know where they had come from, then try to figure out who sent them. She said he wanted it to be a surprise, like a man would do if he were dating a woman and was madly in love. But! Mrs. Gramm remembered that they had some with *only* the name on the front and not the address. So she used one of them instead, thinking it was better for business."

Marcy sat back as though her work for the day had been done. Phil and Katie sat silently looking from one stack to another until Katie said, "Phil?"

"*What?*"

"What what?" Marcy asked. "What did I just say or what to Katie's question?"

Phil shook his head. "A little of both."

Katie could hear the terseness in his voice. She swallowed hard.

221

"Phil, what about the one that came from inside the hotel?"

Marcy started to say something, but Katie shot her a warning glance and she closed her mouth.

"What about it?"

"Did you ask about the generic envelope?"

Phil picked up one of the envelopes and began to fondle it. "The manager made the same statement. The woman who came in—"

"Woman?" Marcy asked, sitting straight up.

Katie waved at her to be quiet and she sat back again.

"Yes," Phil said, turning his head slightly to glance back at her. "Woman. A woman came into the shop downstairs and ordered the flowers. *And* she gave her the generic card, insisting that she use it rather than one with the name across it."

"Did the manager ask why?" Katie responded.

"She said she didn't. She said why should she care what the woman wanted when she was tipping as generously as she did."

"Mrs. Gramm said that, too. I mean, about the tip," Marcy interjected. "She said the man tipped really well."

The three sat silently for a moment before Katie added: "We still don't know where the other arrangements came from."

"I'm sure we will shortly," Marcy answered.

Phil jerked his head around. "What does that mean?"

Marcy looked beyond him to Katie. "You may as well tell him, Katie-girl."

Katie rolled her eyes.

Phil looked back at Katie. "Tell me what?"

Katie stood and walked around to the other side of the coffee table. "Ashley, Brittany, and Candy are out there—"

"*What?*" Phil stood. "Katie!"

Katie nodded. "I know, Phil, but we really thought we were helping. Besides, look at the information Marcy brought back. She saved you some time, didn't she?"

Phil didn't answer, which caused Marcy to smile. She looked at her watch. "It's nearly five now. The girls are supposed to be back shortly."

Phil stole a glance at his watch, then walked around the coffee table and gave Katie a quick kiss on the cheek. "Call me when they return and let me know what they say. I want to go home to spend the rest of the evening with my family. Before I do that, I'll stop by the club to see what's what there."

Katie stood and walked him to the door, leaving Marcy alone on the sofa. "Phil, I promise you—cross my heart—we won't do anything else without talking to you." Katie etched an imaginary X over her heart with her finger.

Phil stopped short and turned to Katie. "You won't do anything period, Katie. Look here, I'm taking off my investigator's cap and putting on the cap of William's friend. I'm telling you as *his* friend, do *not* take another step without me. And that goes for Professor Plum in the parlor over there, too," he said with a quick jerk of his head toward Marcy.

Katie smiled. "I promise."

"I have a full day tomorrow at John Jay, but Saturday I'm going to see the curator where Bucky Caballero was spotted."

"Okay."

"I'm supposed to go back to see Cassie. . .to get her drawing of the man who came in. I'm going to show her some photos of Caballero's clients when he was in the escort business."

Katie looked down at her feet. "Dear Lord, Phil. It could be so many people."

"It could. It could. We'll get to the bottom of it, I promise."

Katie placed her hands on her hips, nodded, but remained silent.

"I'm also going to go back and interview some of the people we talked about earlier."

Katie nodded again. "Okay."

Phil placed his hand on Katie's upper arm and squeezed gently. "I mean it, Katie. Stay put. You've come a long way in the last year. Don't let this short circuit you."

"I know. I promise."

Phil rolled his eyes a little and Katie smiled. "Thanks, Phil."

"You're welcome."

Sharkey didn't like this. He didn't like it one bit. Not one bit. A private investigator in his office. . .talking to him. . .*what did he know already?*

"This will only take a minute." Silver stood on the other side of his desk, refusing to sit when Sharkey had offered him a chair. Sharkey stood, too; behind his desk, the one from the old club his father had operated, arms crossed over his middle, and chomping on an old, thin cigar.

"Yeah, yeah. Well, what can I do for you, Sir? I'm keeping my nose clean. I'm running a legit business here."

Silver stared at him in disbelief. "I'm not here about your business, Mr. Garone. I'm here to tell you to back off from Mrs. Webster."

Sharkey extended his arms, palms up. "What? What? All I've done is go down there a time or two and make a little noise in the lobby. She stole three of my best girls, you know. I can't let her just get away with that. I gotta show my resentment a little. Otherwise, I'll be laughed out of the business."

"What else are you doing, Mr. Garone? What other messages are you sending her?"

Sharkey knew exactly where the investigator was going, but he wasn't about to let on any. Years in this business taught a man how to wear a poker face when necessary. "Whadaya talking about there?"

"Sent any gifts?"

Sharkey crossed his arms again. "Gifts? What kinda gifts?"

Silver narrowed his eyes. He was looking for any telltale signs and Sharkey knew it. "Expensive gifts."

Sharkey laughed. "Look around you, Mr. Silver. Do I look like a man who could afford expensive gifts? I got a girl, you know, a personal friend, let's call her. She wouldn't mind a few expensive gifts now and then. A nice dinner every so often is about all I can do for her. This business is a tough one. Competition is fierce, not to mention the time I had to close down after the terrorists struck. Everything around here shut down, but bills kept piling in. And have you taken a look around lately? Businesses like mine springing up all over the place. A man's doing the best he can to keep mind and body together these days."

"Well, I'm going to tell you how I see it. According to what Mrs. Webster has shared with me, she brought gifts to your girls here, and some of them left with her. . ."

"And your point?"

"Gifts for gifts? She brought gifts so in return. . ."

Sharkey merely stared at him without answering.

"When was the last time you were at her hotel?"

Sharkey took a moment to feign thought. "I think about a week or so ago. I haven't been back since. What's the point, you know?"

Silver didn't respond. "Mr. Garone, do you know a Bucky Caballero?"

"Know of him," Sharkey answered quickly.

"Know him personally?"

"What would a man like Caballero want with someone like me?"

"You're not answering my question."

"No. I don't know him." *Technically, that's not a lie,* Sharkey thought. *Yeah, yeah. He's come into the club, but who can really know a man like Bucky Caballero?*

Silver pulled a card out of his credentials holder and flipped it onto the desk. He sighed deeply. "All right, Mr. Garone. You'll call me if you hear of anything, correct?"

Sharkey picked up the card and looked at it. "Sure, sure. This is a great business for hearing stuff."

"I'm sure it is."

Silver turned for the door. "Mr. Silver," Sharkey said, stopping him. He turned back. "Yes, Mr. Garone?"

Sharkey Garone smiled devilishly. "You know, I've known Mrs. Webster near about my whole life. I'm upset with her, but I wouldn't want to see anything happen to her. My old man would come back from his grave. . ." Sharkey paused to make the sign of the cross over himself, ". . .to haunt me if I did."

Silver's brow furrowed. Just the reaction Sharkey hoped for. "What do you mean, you've known her most of your life?"

Sharkey faked a look of shock and near-remorse. "Oh, man! I shouldn't have said that. I mean, she's a lady and all now, right? But, yeah, yeah. She used to dance at my old man's place down in Hell's Kitchen." Sharkey watched Silver's face grow dark, almost angry. "You knew that, right?" he asked innocently.

"As a matter-of-fact, I did. But I didn't think it was something gentlemen should discuss."

He turned then and walked out of the door. Sharkey crooked his neck to watch him slip into the shadows of the hallway, then gave a little laugh. "You knew, my eye," he said to himself. He sat in his office chair with a thud, pulled the old cigar out of his mouth and threw it into the nearby trash can. "This calls for a new cigar, boy," he said to himself. "Katie Webster's feathers are ruffled, her secret is out, God's in His heaven," Sharkey again made the sign of the cross, "and all is right with the world."

Katie called Phil later to tell him that Ashley had returned with news that one of the arrangements had come from Chelsea. As in the hotel shop, a woman had made the purchase. And, like the others, the manager of the shop had been instructed to use a generic envelope provided by the woman. That left the origin of two arrangements unaccounted for.

"Maybe they didn't come from The Little Flower Shoppe," Phil interjected aloud.

"What are your plans for tomorrow?" he added suspiciously.

"I'm taking Marcy to Saint Thomas' for eight o'clock morning prayer and the Holy Eucharist."

"As I said before, I have a full day at John Jay, but during lunch I'll run up to Saks and see Cassie."

"Okay."

"I went to see Sharkey tonight."

"And?"

"He's a liar and a snake. That's really all I can say at this time."

"I could have told you that and saved you the trip."

Phil was silent for a moment. "Katie?"

"Yes?"

"Stay out of trouble," he ordered.

CHAPTER TWENTY-THREE
Friday, December 7, 2001

Katie and Marcy stood on Fifth Avenue, looking up at the impressive structure of Saint Thomas Church. Marcy took in a deep breath. "This is it, huh?"

Katie nodded, barely able to speak. "This place means a lot to me, Marce. I don't know if I could have made it without what I found here."

Katie had discovered Saint Thomas Church on September 11, 2001. She had risen earlier than usual that morning, slipped into the kitchen—without Maggie hearing—and prepared a pot of coffee. When it was ready, she poured a mug of the aromatic brew, which she took into her office, and began to read her morning devotions. As the sun crept through the buildings of the New York City skyline, changing them from inky midnight to silvery gray, the Spirit of God wrapped around her in a way she'd never felt Him before. But her prayers were emotionally draining; instead of feeling spiritually energized, she'd felt burdened by a heaviness she'd not experienced before. Even when she mourned over Ben's absence, she hadn't felt quite like this. It was almost as if she were bearing the responsibilities of the world in her heart.

She went downstairs to work at eight-thirty. Vickey met her with a smile and another cup of coffee, this one served in her personal Noritake Edwardian Rose set. "Good morning, Lady Boss," she greeted cheerfully.

"Something wonderful happen I have yet to be notified about?" Katie asked, stepping into her office.

Vickey followed her with the cup of coffee. "Why do you ask?"

"You seem awfully chipper." Katie slid gracefully into the leather office chair behind her desk.

Vickey placed the cup and saucer on the desk. "What? Can't I be happy?"

Katie closed one eye for a teasing moment and studied her assistant. "Sure," she said smiling. "Go get a cup of coffee for yourself and join me. I want to go over a few things before we get started with all the other things we have on our schedules for today."

Vickey turned toward the door. "I'll be right back."

Moments later she returned to the office, carrying an ornate silver tray holding another cup and saucer and a silver and crystal carafe filled with coffee. A silver creamer and sugar bowl sat cozily in one of the corners, and Katie could see a small plate filled with pastries in the center.

"Yummy," Katie smiled.

"I thought we'd treat ourselves."

Katie closed the file she had been looking at and blinked her eyes a few times. "You know, I'm going to have to think seriously about getting reading glasses. My eyes literally burn after trying to read anything." The semi-constant background music of emergency sirens wailed as they passed the hotel in the streets below.

Vickey placed the tray on the wet bar and prepared her coffee and plates of pastries for Katie and herself. "Vanity, thy name is Katie."

Katie frowned. "I know. Do me a huge favor: Call my eye doctor as soon as you get back to your office. Make an appointment and then force me to go."

Vickey sipped her coffee, raised her right hand, and gave a curt nod of her head. "I promise." She leaned forward a bit, as though to look out the window behind Katie. "My goodness, have you ever heard so many sirens?"

Katie turned her face toward the side windows. "Wonder what—"

The door to the office swung open and an unannounced James Harrington barged in. "Turn on the television."

"*What?*" Katie stood.

"Turn on the television. Quick." He made his way over to the built-in entertainment center near the leather sofas, opened it, grabbed the remote control, and turned on the set himself.

"Mr. Harrington, what is—" Katie's hand flew to her mouth. "Oh, dear Lord, what *is* that?" She came around her desk and followed Vickey to where James stood transfixed in front of the entertainment center.

"One World Trade."

Within the next few minutes, even though the world seemed to have come to a complete halt, an alarm sounded within Katie. *This is far from over,* she thought, her sense of responsibility to her customers—and her hotel—taking over. Everything she had learned the past year, grinding through her grief as she learned Ben's job, now kicked into gear. More than that, people around her were going to need help. "Mr. Harrington, we need to gather our security personnel together. I want to rope off the front of this hotel. No one enters who is not a paying guest."

James pulled his cell phone from his pocket and attempted a call, punching the numbers on the keypad with his thumb. He placed the phone to his ear, then flipped the earpiece back and said, "No good. Must be jammed from all the calls about this."

Katie grabbed the hand piece of her desk phone and extended it to her general manager. "Use this phone."

While James made the call to Security, Katie turned her attention to Vickey. "I need to call my mother. She'll be worried. . .thinking we're closer than we really are."

"I'll try to reach her from my phone," Vickey said, then turned and headed toward her desk in the outer office, leaving the door between the two offices open. From where Katie stood, she could see Vickey's vain attempts at reaching an outside line. She continued to listen to James calling the various departments. Vickey returned to the office. "Getting a line out right now will be difficult. . . ."

"Keep trying," Katie remarked. "I'll go back to my apartment and check on Maggie."

At the door, she turned back to James. "Mr. Harrington, I'll return shortly. I'll page you so you can keep me apprised. Until then, if you need me—"

"I'll contact your assistant." The seriousness of the situation could be heard in his voice; a level of professionalism added to the strength with which he had always handled emergencies.

"Thank you, Mr. Harrington."

"Certainly." He nodded, then continued with his business.

The rest of the morning was spent dealing with the effects of the national crisis as they directly pertained to the hotel. Katie and James Harrington joined a team of staff members who helped guests scheduled for check out that morning but were now looking at an indefinite stay in the city. Their concerns and questions seemed endless.

"We won't be thrown out, will we?" a nervous tourist asked Katie from across the marble reservations counter.

"Certainly not, Ma'am," Katie answered calmly. One of her reservation clerks stood next to her, busily re-typing the woman's information into a computer system that had shut down earlier and was now—blessedly—back up and running.

"Do you have any idea how long before we can get back out?" another guest—an elderly man—asked.

"No, Sir. I'm sorry. I don't. But we will make you as comfortable and as safe as we can while you are here." Katie smiled a smile she hoped was reassuring.

"Is it safe to leave the hotel?" he asked. The man's head quivered as he asked the question.

"I wouldn't go far," Katie advised honestly. "We haven't received any word from outside security, so if you feel you must go outside, I'd advise against leaving the Midtown area. And I wouldn't go anywhere near the towers." *Where the towers had been*, she thought. The enormity of it was hard for everyone to comprehend.

She watched the man walk toward a woman, obviously his wife, who had waited near a grouping of sofas and tables just beyond the lobby. From the corner of her eye she caught a young deliveryman carrying an arrangement of flowers toward the elevators. She turned to the staff member beside her. "I'll be right back," she informed, then slipped quickly from behind the counter and toward the elevators. "Excuse me?" she called out to the boy. He turned. "How did you get in?" she asked upon catching up to him.

The young man seemed perplexed. "Front door?"

"Where are these going?" She pointed to the flowers.

He reached between the stems for the secured card. "Uh—says Mrs. Weiss, third floor—"

"Yes, I know Mrs. Weiss. What I mean to say is: How did you get past security?"

He shrugged his shoulders. "I guess they saw me getting out of the van, Lady. What's the deal?"

Katie didn't like the implications. "My name is Katharine Webster. I am the president of this hotel, and I ordered that no one—except guests and personnel—be allowed in. *That's* the deal. Furthermore, while I *am* a lady, it is impertinent of you to say it in such a way. Now, hand me the flowers and leave the hotel in the same way as you entered." She exhaled. "I can hardly believe you're delivering at this time anyway," she added under her breath.

The boy shoved the flowers into her outstretched hands. "Yeah, well. . .my boss said to at least get these out before we closed down. No telling how long before we'll be doing business again." He read the shock on her face. "Hey, those were his words, not mine." He turned on his heel and stomped away.

Katie stood ramrod straight for a moment, trying to collect herself. . . trying to remember when she had ever been so hard on anyone. One of her employees walked by. "Mrs. Webster," she said. "Can I help you with something?"

"Yes, you can take these up to Mrs. Weiss on the third floor. Her office number is on the card," she said, handing the flowers over. When the woman had entered the elevators and the doors had closed behind her, Katie called James Harrington and ordered additional security to stand guard at the front of the hotel. "Mr. Harrington, I want more than our standard number of security guards at the front."

"We have three out front now."

"Then I want six. No one enters this hotel without a guest key," she told him. "Under *no* circumstances." She explained to him what had just happened.

"I'll call Security." His voice was terse.

"Thank you. I appreciate it more than you can know."

With everything else to deal with, the most difficult task for Katie was assisting personnel who had family and friends in South Manhattan or who were residents there and were dealing with evacuations. Frequent phone calls were made or received. At one point, she exhaustedly looked at James and said, "It seems that once the phone lines are back up, everyone and his brother is calling."

"This city is filled with panic," James noted, then looked down at his hands. "But not like anything I've ever seen." His eyes met hers again. "It's panic mixed with shock. You don't see that too often. Not here anyway. The phone calls are a reflection of that."

Some calls were personal. Others were business. All were grim. All the while, Katie stayed tuned to the news coverage and instructed the hotel's lounge to keep the wide screen television tuned to CNN. She also ordered several small sets to be brought down to the reception area. It went against the grain of the décor, but now was not the time to worry about propriety. Lastly, she contacted her attorney, Cynthia, about sending a donation from The Hamilton Corporation to the Red Cross. It was the least she could do. . .at the moment, it was the *most* she could do.

A little after noon, when Katie had taken all of four bites of the salad Maggie had prepared for her, she decided to take a walk outside.

"I don't think it's safe," Maggie told her, stepping lightly behind her mistress as she made her way to the door.

"I won't go too close to South Manhattan, Maggie."

"But Miss Katie, what if this isn't the end of it?"

Katie's mouth drew a firm line, and her eyes looked downward. "Oh, Maggie. I'm afraid this is definitely not the end of it. My heart tells me that life as we knew it before this morning has ceased to exist." She touched Maggie lightly on her sweatered arm. "This morning, during my prayer time, my heart was so heavy."

Maggie nodded firmly, all the while patting Katie's hand. "God's Spirit calls to us to intercede. You were in intercession."

Katie looked away, tears brimming the corners of her eyes. "I can't say that's ever happened before." She sighed deeply, clutching at Maggie's hand. "I need to walk, Maggie. I need to clear my head a little. I won't go far, I promise. And I assure you, I'll be all right."

But when Katie stood facing south at the corner of Fifth and Fifty-seventh, she was astounded by what she saw and heard on the streets of New York. Though above and behind her, the sky was a brilliant azure, before her it was ashy gray, the billowing remnant of the collapsed center of international trade and finance. Traffic had nearly ceased, and what was there was almost silent. People moved quietly, spoke only about the atrocity before them. As she continued to walk slowly southward, she listened as "suits" talked on their cell phones about what they had seen and heard. Ironically, she heard the same conversation between two men donned in worn out jeans, thin cotton shirts, filthy baseball caps and tattered sneakers; men who sat on the edge of the curb, resting their arms across their knees, trying to gain some understanding of the day's events. They were, as Ben often put it, the working poor.

"Joe works down there, right?" one was saying to the other.

"No, man. Not Joe. Joe quit down there, remember? But Sammy does. Sammy's been down there since—oh, about '89 or '90."

"We need to go over to Sammy's house, man. Make sure he's okay."

Katie kept walking, her gaze straight ahead. She took deep breaths. . . when she remembered to breathe at all. Sporadic emergency vehicles continued southbound, reminding Katie of the men and women who—

that very day—had lost their lives trying to save others. Because of them, thousands had been spared. . .because of their dedication; life—for so many—would go forward. *But not for them.*

Occasionally she noted a computer-made sign in the storefront windows.

Due To Today's Tragedy, Our Store Will Be Closed Indefinitely

Some were given the addendum: *God Bless America.*

Already, gift shops had pulled their postcards depicting the Towers in better days, selling them at higher prices than just the day before. Katie frowned, then slipped into the cool air of one of the shops, drawn by something primitive inside her. Her eyes scanned the merchandise and studied the dozen or so visitors who perused the aisles. "Do you have anything with the Towers on it?" a woman was asking the sales clerk.

"We have these T-shirts." The older man pointed to a rack of shirts.

Katie stopped at the costume jewelry counter, wrapped her arms around herself, and peered into the glass case of silver trinkets. She noted a small charm, oval, surrounded by filigree and shaped into the skyline of New York as it had been just hours before. The Twin Towers stood high above the rest.

"May I help you?"

Katie looked up. A sales clerk, tall and lanky, with long, slicked black hair pulled tightly back in a ponytail, was standing on the other side of the case. He held a small cigarette between the index and middle finger of his right hand.

"May I see the charm there?"

"The one of the skyline?" He took a drag from the cigarette, blowing the smoke upward.

"Yes."

Katie watched as he methodically placed the cigarette between his thin lips, reached into the back of the case and drew out the charm. He laid it on a piece of black velvet cloth as though they were standing in the middle of Tiffany's. Katie touched it with the tip of her fingernail, then picked it up. It was light. Fragile.

"Heck of a time to be a visitor here," the clerk commented. "When did you arrive?"

Katie raised sad eyes to his. "1975. Thank you for showing the charm to me."

"No problem." He stabbed the butt of his cigarette into a nearby tin ashtray, and she walked out of the shop, more confused than she had been earlier.

Moments later, as she approached Fifth and Fifty-third, she noticed a stream of men and women ascending the steps of Saint Thomas Church. She paused briefly, wondering why she had never taken the time to tour the landmark before. A notice posted on the doors invited everyone to join the church in prayer for the country. Suddenly, she knew she had to go in. . .to be with the others. Somehow, being on her knees seemed to be the thing she wanted to do most.

Inside, the reverence of the church took hold of her heart and she began to weep quietly. The French High Gothic architecture, brilliant stained-glass windows, and the various monuments to war and peace wooed her. As she stepped down the center aisle, she listened to the hushed prayers around her. She took a seat in one of the old pews; its patina was slick and glossy. She closed her eyes, felt hot tears slip from between her lashes and along her cheeks, stopping briefly on the line of her jaw, then cascading down her throat and pooling in its hollow. She listened to the liturgy as it was being recited, not knowing it herself. She just listened. Allowed God to touch her heart, her brokenness. At times her shoulders shook. She reached into the small clutch purse she had brought with her and pulled out a tissue.

She mustn't fall apart, she told herself. She was the president of The Hamilton Place. She mustn't fall apart. Her staff would need her. Her husband would expect her to be strong. . .but this time of prayerful solace helped to resuscitate her, and get her to the place she needed to be to go on.

She pushed her broken thoughts aside and returned her attention to the priest. "As our Lord and Savior taught us to pray. . ."

The congregation began praying in unison. "Our Father, who art in heaven. . ."

Katie lifted her eyes heavenward, suddenly struck by the magnificent, stone Great Reredos. As she recited the ancient prayer, her eyes beheld the carvings of Jesus, standing in the center, high above the empty cross, flanked by His mother, Mary, and by Saint John.

"Forgive us our trespasses, as we forgive those who trespass against us. . ." she prayed quietly, though a little bolder than she had ever prayed the prayer before.

Forgive us, Father. . .forgive us. . . .

Her eyes scaled downward the Great Reredos, noting Saint Thomas kneeling before Christ, no longer in doubt. No longer questioning the Messiah.

"For Thine is the kingdom, and the power, and the glory. . ."

Oh, Lord God. Protect Your children. . . .

"Amen."

Afterward, when Katie had walked out of the church, she had turned north, away from the disaster and toward Central Park South. Arriving tired and a bit weary, she sat on one of the benches and began to watch the people; amazed at the ordinary things they were doing on such an out-of-the-ordinary day. In spite of it all, joggers, bikers, and skaters continued with their daily exercise. Perhaps, Katie thought, it was what they needed to get through. Perhaps, like her, grasping at some element of normalcy was paramount to survival.

Seemingly, out of nowhere, an elderly man approached the bench where she sat and joined her. He wore nice pants and a nice shirt, though a little too large for his frail and aging frame. He wore large glasses with thick lenses. Dark, watery eyes stared out of them, though Katie couldn't tell just what it was he was looking at.

"Are you all right?" she asked.

"What?" he asked, continuing to stare straight ahead.

"Are you all right?"

"I work here," he answered.

Katie looked about the small section of the immense park.

"Here in the city?"

"I work here," he repeated.

Katie understood, then, that the man was in shock.

"Where do you live?" she asked.

"I have nowhere to go," he answered.

"Do you have friends you can call? Family in the city?"

"I have friends." Still, the man focused on some unseen object in front of him.

"Have you called them?" Katie reached a tentative hand toward the elderly gentleman.

"No one is home."

Katie shifted to look ahead, like her new comrade beside her.

"What can I do for you, Sir?"

"I don't know." He hung his head, tired chin touching heaving chest.

"May I pray for you?"

For the first time, he turned to gaze at her. "Pray? Yes. Yes." And then he stood and shuffled away from the bench. Katie sat, stunned, and watched him go.

Dear Lord, what am I doing here? What would you have me do?

For the first time in a long time, Katie felt purposeless. Since the day Ben had disappeared, she was driven to do what must be done. Every morning she rose, read her morning devotions, went to work, ran an empire. Each evening, when she physically and mentally was unable to put another foot in front of the other, she made her way back to her apartment within the hotel. Most weekends she and Maggie went to the house in the Hamptons. Somehow, she had placed herself in a tunnel and simply managed to keep moving forward. Now. . .she wasn't sure anymore. Deep down, she knew that when the sun rose over the scarred skyline tomorrow, she would continue as she always had. It had somehow become a way of life for her. She was a survivor. She was a New Yorker.

The following Sunday, Katie had taken Maggie back to the church for services. The priest began his sermon by speaking of two parables, the Parable of the Lost Sheep and the Parable of the Lost Coin. He posed the question on the hearts and minds of everyone: *Why does God allow evil to happen?* He reminded the congregation that this was the same question found in the Book of Job, that Billy Graham himself had asked the question two days earlier at the National Cathedral.

And then he gave the answer. "I don't know."

But, he reminded everyone; no one ever asks why good happens. Only why evil happens. Good, he said, is as much a mystery as evil.

There was so much good to be found since September 11. The heroism of the men and women on the doomed flight that went down in Pennsylvania, the comfort that came from the phone calls from men and women who would die atop the Towers—to say "I love you" one last time, to remind each of us of the importance of those words and uncertainty of time. He spoke of the countless volunteers and the outpouring of love from other countries. He told the congregation that during Friday's noon Eucharist, the church had welcomed thousands of people, rather than the typical few.

The difference between the sheep and the goats—he said—were the acts of goodness.

"Amen," Maggie, who sat to Katie's left, whispered.

Katie turned to look at the kind, older woman, then felt a warm hand take hers. Maybe all wasn't right with the world, but right here, right now, things were good.

They *are* good, she thought, raising her head to look again at the artwork filling the room. *I have been given such incredible gifts.* Remembering the words of Mr. Mosley's widow, Katie knew it was time to act on that and she knew where she had to start. Hell's Kitchen. She had to give something back. *But what?*

Shaky ground. But the world had changed. *Her* world had changed. She wanted to pass on the favor and grace that had been given to her, first by Mr. Mosley and then by Ben. She felt her heart lift with a confidence she'd not felt all week. The only thing missing now. . .*still.* . .was Ben.

Ben. . .

Marcy said softly, "Katie?"

Katie took a deep breath and snapped out of her reverie. "Yes?"

"You just whispered Ben's name. Are you okay?"

Katie squared her shoulders and smiled, then took her best friend by the arm. "Let's go in. There's something I need to share with you. . ."

CHAPTER TWENTY-FOUR

"Thank you for meeting me for breakfast," Phil said to Agent John Weaver as they slipped into a booth near the back of a small café.

"Not a problem," John said. When two orders of coffee and "Today's Special Number Two" had been ordered and the waitress had sashayed away, he leaned over the old Formica table and listened intently as Phil went over the details of the Webster case. He didn't look directly at Phil, rather at the tabletop, as though concentrating on every detail.

"I'm going to go with the least likely of our known couples first," Phil was saying, analyzing as he was speaking. "James Harrington and Deirdre Randall. I've run their profiles through the computer, and neither one of them has come up for anything so much as a traffic ticket. Both married, dedicated to their families. . .in fact, Mrs. Randall has been married less than a year. I've tossed them out as a possibility, but I don't really think we should be spending a lot of time there." The waitress returned to the booth with two white ceramic mugs filled with hot coffee.

"Anything else, gentlemen?" she asked.

"I think that will be it for now," Phil answered, looking into her eyes. "Thank you."

"I'll be back shortly with your food, then," she said, then stepped to the booth just beyond them.

"Let's move on," John said quietly.

"Let's say it is Caballero," Phil continued. "Even though Cassie, at Saks, said the man in the drawing is not the man who made the purchase—"

"He could have someone working with him."

"That's what I'm thinking. We know the man is in town. Question is, how do we proceed from here so as not to scare him back out of the country?"

"Move quietly. Contact various precincts. Question to answer is, where do you think he's staying?"

"My gut tells me Mrs. Jordan Whitney knows more than she originally let on, though I doubt he's staying with her. She wouldn't put her husband's career on the line like that. And a man like Caballero won't stay in some flea infested dump. My thoughts are to look in classier hotels, most likely near Mrs. Whitney's home."

"Why don't I check out some of our better known establishments?"

"What about your own work? The Griffin girl. . ."

"I'm running a few things right now but basically have some time to myself."

Phil smiled, pulled a notepad out from his inside coat pocket, and made some notes. After all, if someone was missing—or in this case, hiding—Weaver was the man to call on. "I'm supposed to go back to Saks to pick up a drawing of the man who purchased the necklace—"

"A drawing?"

Phil nodded. "The sales clerk—Cassie—just happens to be an art student. She said she'd have no problem drawing the man for me."

"Is she any good?"

"I don't know. Must be. She's studying. I'm also going to take her some photographs of our fine, upstanding politicians who were named in Caballero's escort records. . .see if the man was one of them."

"Good thinking."

"Anyway, I'll call Victoria Whitney, which should be interesting to say the least. I'll tell you this; she's a good actress. She's a very good actress. I also need to go by the art gallery to see the curator."

"Want me to handle that?"

Phil thought for a moment. "Perhaps you should."

"I'll go in and talk about the kid's disappearance. . ."

"Good. Good." Phil made more notes, then dropped his pen just as the waitress returned with two plates of piping hot flapjacks, sausage, and eggs resting on her left forearm, and a pot of coffee. She set the plates in front of each of them, then took a moment to refill their coffee cups, and moved on.

"Let's talk logistics. Where did the flowers come from?"

Phil reached on the seat beside him for a small but detailed map of the city he had posted on a sheet of cardboard and brought with him. Having placed it flat on his table between him and Weaver, he opened the tightly wrapped utensils at his elbow and used the handle of the fork as a pointer. "Here we go," he said by way of commentary. "Here," he pointed to the Midtown area of town where The Hamilton Place was located. "Right in the hotel. Then here," he added, his finger tracing downward to the location in Chelsea where Ashley had gone."

"A bit of a stretch."

Phil moaned in agreement.

"And the others?"

"Here," Phil moved his finger up and to the left. "Upper West Side. We only know for sure about three of them."

"Isn't that where Mrs. Whitney lives?"

"Yes."

"Distance from her home?"

"Just around the corner."

"Next question: What possible tie would Victoria Whitney have to Chelsea? Is she from that area originally? Does she have family there? Friends?"

"I know one way to find out, but I'll have to call you later."

"That works for me." Weaver unwrapped his utensils and stabbed at his sausage with the fork. "Pass the syrup, will you?" he asked. "The sooner we eat, the sooner we can get on this."

Katie sat at her desk, sipping on a second cup of coffee as she listened to Byron Spooner giving her details of the holiday mother-daughter tea. James Harrington sat next to him, nervously tapping a tune on the arms of his chair with his fingers, and Vickey sat in a third chair brought in from her office, busily taking notes.

"It looks as though we are set," Katie said proudly, raising herself slightly in her seat and squaring her shoulders. "I knew we could do it!"

James discreetly cleared his throat and added, "We've sent out nearly a hundred invitations and have received about half that many in RSVPs by phone."

"We probably won't hear from all of them—*if* we hear from all of them—until later in the week. What about the menu?"

"I talked to Mrs. Marshall who handles our afternoon teas. She said that on such short notice she can serve the same menu as the one served in the lobby, but will have her staff make certain the floral arrangements are a little more special and, of course, that the room is nicely decorated."

"Perfect. Mr. Spooner, have you been able to keep close tabs on the cost of all this?"

Byron Spooner pulled a sheet of paper from a leather folder he had opened across his lap. "These are the figures so far. There will be other costs, to be sure, but for now I think we are well within budget for something like this."

"Oh, good." Katie placed her hands flat on her desk and splayed her fingers. "I want this to become an annual event. Something that mothers and daughters and grandmothers and granddaughters will cherish as a precious memory. Something that will set us apart from the other hotels."

"Speaking of the other hotels," Vickey commented. "You have a luncheon meeting at The Plaza in about two hours," she said.

Katie looked at her watch. "Oh, yes. Vickey, call upstairs and see if Marcy would like to go with me. She will be a little bored with all the shop talk, but I'd like for her to see a little of what I do." Katie turned her attention back to Byron and James. "Gentlemen, I suppose we'll meet again on Monday morning, but thank you, again, for coming in for this special meeting. You have no idea how much this means to me." Katie stood, then walked around her desk to escort the men to the door while Vickey stepped over to Katie's desk to call Marcy. Byron reached the door first and opened it. Turning, he said cordially, "Mrs. Webster," then departed.

Katie placed her hand on James's back. "Mr. Harrington?"

James Harrington turned to look inquisitively at Katie, who smiled at him.

"I wanted to take a moment to thank you for the lovely flowers."

James smiled back. "I'm glad you liked them. I'm very sorry, Katie, for all that's happened."

"You mean the anonymously sent gifts?"

James shook his head, no. "No. Certainly, I am a bit concerned as to what this might mean—these gifts—but I am apologizing for my behavior over the past eighteen months. I've taken some time for self-reflection and realized I should have been supporting you all along. William would expect that, and if for no other reason, I should honor what he would require of me as the GM of this hotel."

Katie's eyes filled with tears, and she dabbed at them lightly with her fingertips. "How unbecoming of a hotel president; crying at the end of a business meeting."

James pulled a clean, white handkerchief from inside his coat pocket and handed it to Katie, who took it and used it to catch the tears. "Indeed. But how *becoming* of a lady."

"I don't know if I buy that or not," Vickey said from Katie's desk when Katie had shut the door behind James Harrington.

Katie looked down at the handkerchief she still held in her hands. "People can change, Vickey."

"Not snakes. Snakes are snakes."

Katie walked over to the bar and poured herself a glass of water.

"Maybe we only thought he was a snake."

Vickey joined Katie at the bar and poured herself a glass of water. Together the two women leaned against the edge of the counter, sipping their drinks. "What if he wasn't ever really a snake? What if he is just a kind, old bear who felt cornered?"

Vickey looked at Katie in exasperation. "You're kidding me, right?"

Katie shook her head. "No, I'm not. I mean, do you ever remember him being difficult with Ben?"

Vickey shifted her weight to set the glass down on the counter of the bar. "No, but you're talking about the difference in levels of superiority. James Harrington knew he could never hold a candle to William Webster. He was blessed to even stand in his presence. Or crawl on his belly. . ."

Katie took another sip of water. "But not so with me."

Vickey smiled warmly. "I don't mean to hurt your feelings."

Katie thought for a moment before adding, "Vickey, tell me something. How did you *really* feel about me taking the presidency after Ben disappeared?"

Vickey laughed nervously and placed her empty glass on the bar. "What? Why would you ask that? You and I are friends, Katie."

Katie nodded. "I know we are friends, Vickey. I'm your friend. You're my friend. I trust you, but I wouldn't hand you a scalpel and ask you to do surgery on me."

Vickey walked over to the chair where she had previously been sitting and gripped its back with tight fists, her back to Katie. "I know you wouldn't. That's preposterous! Katie, what is this about?" she asked, turning to face her employer. Her expression was something between irritation and confusion.

Katie blushed slightly. "Nothing, Vickey. I'm sorry. I was feeling a bit sorry for myself. . .just wondering what other people thought of my taking over Ben's position."

Vickey sighed. "All right, I'll tell you then. At first I thought you were insane. Katie, I knew more about the business than you. A lot more. But no one came running into my office asking me to sit behind that massive desk over there," she said, pointing to the desk that had, at one time, belonged to her employer, William Webster. "Dear God, sometimes I can still see him sitting there," she added with a whisper.

Katie set her glass on the counter, walked over to Vickey and placed her hands on her shoulders. "I know," she whispered. "Sometimes I can, too. Sometimes I can feel him in here. Smell him, even."

Vickey smiled. "He always smelled good, didn't he?"

Katie breathed in deeply. "Yes. Yes, he did."

"What was the name of that cologne he liked so much?"

"Aigner Essence."

"Oh, yes. For awhile there, it was—"

"Kouros Fraicheur."

A light tap at the door startled the two women. They swung around to see it open ever so slightly, followed by Candy's dainty Eastern face slipping around to look at them. "Katie?" she asked shyly.

Vickey stepped away from Katie. "I called Marcy. She'll be down in about a half hour," she informed Katie, suddenly taking a more professional tone as she moved toward the door where Candy stood.

"Vickey?" Katie asked, stopping her.

"Yes?"

"I'm sorry if I sounded—"

"Think nothing of it," Vickey said with a smile. "We're friends. Remember that."

"I'll remember."

When Candy had stepped into the office and Vickey had closed the door, Katie walked over to the sitting area. "Candy, you are just the girl I've wanted to see! Can you join me for a moment?"

Candy, dressed in her housekeeping uniform, nodded as she followed Katie to the other side of the room. "You wanted to see me?" She sounded nervous.

Katie sat and patted the sofa's cushion beside her. "Yes. I've been worried about you. Ashley and Brittany have, too." Candy sat next to Katie, clutched her hands together, and slowly raised her eyes to meet Katie's.

"I know. They've told me."

"Look, Candy. I'm going to come right out and ask you a question. If the answer is yes, I won't be angry, but I will want to talk to you. . .to help you if I can. . ."

"Okay."

Katie took a deep breath before going forward. "Candy, have you returned to the club at night?"

Candy stared at Katie for a moment before blinking. . .once. . . twice. . .and then answering, "No. I've been going out, yes. But not to the club."

Katie seemed visibly relieved. "Oh, good. I was so worried."

"Why would I go back there? Sharkey would eat me for lunch."

Katie reached over and took Candy's hand. "Yes, he would. Candy, I want you to know. . .I understand that it would be easy to go back. . ."

"How would you know, Katie? Really, I mean? What do you know about the kind of life I've led?"

Katie smiled sadly. "More than you know, Candy." She took Candy by the chin and gently forced her to look into her eyes. "One day I will tell you just how much I know about that life. For now, I hope you can trust me. . .believe in what I'm trying to do for you."

Candy pulled her chin away from the touch of Katie's hand. "Sometimes it's hard to remember. I don't like housekeeping so much. I want—"

"Is that why you came to see me? Do you want another position?"

Candy had been about to say that she wanted her mother and brother to be able to come to live with her at the hotel, but decided to go with the direction Katie was taking the conversation. "I think I would do better somewhere else. It's not that I think I'm above it, but—"

Katie stood and walked toward her desk. "Not everyone is good at housekeeping. Besides, I had no intention of you staying there. What are you good at, Candy?"

Candy stood. "I'm pretty good at math. When I was in school, I was pretty good."

Katie picked up the phone and dialed a few numbers, waited, and then said, "Mrs. Beal? This is Katharine Webster. I'm going to send Xi Lan Tso down to personnel. I would appreciate it greatly if you would set her up in accounting as an assistant. . . . thank you, Mrs. Beal. She'll be down in about half an hour."

As Katie hung up the phone, Marcy entered. "Hi!" she said, looking fashionable in a pink wool slacks and sweater set. "Am I dressed okay for this?"

"You look wonderful," Katie said admiringly. "I'm almost ready to go."

"Hi, Candy," Marcy greeted the young woman standing nearby before adding, "I'll just be out here with Vickey."

Katie smiled. "Thanks, Marce."

Marcy left the room as Katie scribbled on a notepad then handed the paper to Candy. "Go down to human resources. Mrs. Beal is expecting you. Before you do, though, run upstairs and change into something a little more suited for an office job."

Candy took the paper and nodded as Katie patted her shoulder. "I'll talk to you tonight, okay? You'll come upstairs and let me know how it went?"

"Sure." Candy kept her gaze on the paper in her tiny hands.

"Good. I'll have to move Ashley and Brittany up, too, you understand."

"Yes."

"All right. We'll talk tonight."

CHAPTER TWENTY-FIVE

John Weaver stepped into the warmth of the Upper West Side art gallery owned by Maxwell Griffin. He nodded at the security guard, and the guard nodded in return, recognizing the agent from his numerous visits over the past three weeks. Agent Weaver walked self-assuredly across the Italian marble floor to a wide marble staircase that rose majestically with flanks to the right and left, leading to the second floor of the gallery. Disregarding the occasional employee, he slipped from room to room until he came upon the narrow hallway located just off the Art Nouveau display. As he stepped down the narrow hall, he could hear the sound of his footsteps echoing against the confining walls. He thought of the numerous morgues he had visited as part of his job. It was true; he was good at finding missing people. Unfortunately, not all of them were found alive.

When he came to the door of Mr. Kabakjian's office, he opened it, greeted the secretary, and told her that he would like to see Kabakjian for a moment. The secretary nodded, said, "Yes, Mr. Weaver," then picked up the phone and announced his arrival. He placed his hands in his pants pockets and swung around, pretending to admire the artwork that adorned the walls. He had never understood man's fascination with art, but he felt it was incumbent upon him to feign appreciation while he was investigating the disappearance of Maxwell's daughter. He knew that when people think you are interested in what they are interested in, they begin to feel as though you are their friend. They begin to relax. Talk.

"Yes, Sir," the secretary concluded, then remarked to John, "You can go in."

"Thank you," he said, already halfway through the door.

Maury Kabakjian stood on the right side of the brightly lit room. He was holding a framed painting in both hands, arms extended to full length, tilting the piece of artwork slightly away from him. "Come in, come in," he said, allowing the frame to slip from his grip. He grabbed the top of the frame as though he had been doing this sort of thing all his life, then propped the painting against a dark blue leather sofa. "I take it you have good news, Agent Weaver."

"I have leads," John acknowledged.

"Have you spoken to Mr. Griffin?" Mr. Kabakjian remained near the sofa. He was wearing a dark suit, and John thought that it made the cold and sinister-looking man look all the more menacing.

"I did, last night at his home. May we sit down, Mr. Kabakjian?"

Kabakjian seemed ill at ease, but motioned toward the chairs across from his desk as he stepped toward them. "By all means. I'd offer you a drink, but I know you're on duty."

"A little early in the day anyway."

Kabakjian smiled wryly, his crystal blue eyes looked narrowly suspicious, somewhat threatening, especially against his tanned complexion. "Never too early for me."

John sat in the nearest chair. "Mr. Kabakjian. . ." he waited for the curator to sit behind his desk before continuing. "Mr. Kabakjian, when was the last time you saw Miss Griffin?"

Maury Kabakjian leaned back in his chair, placing his elbows on the armrests and lacing his fingers together. "I thought we had gone over that."

John crossed one lanky leg over the other. "We did, Mr. Kabakjian, but I need to ask you these questions one more time. We feel we know whom Miss Griffin left the state with—"

"You're saying she wasn't kidnapped. That she *did* leave with the man I saw her with."

"No, Sir. I'm not saying that. I'm not saying one way or the other. I'm simply saying we feel we know the particular individual she left the state with. But the time and place you saw her last is important here. I need to go over this one more time, if you don't mind."

Kabakjian nodded cordially, though it was obvious he was ill at ease. "I see. Yes, I saw her that Friday, November 30, I believe it was."

"The Friday she failed to return home."

"Yes."

"And she was here, at the gallery?"

"Yes," Kabakjian said with a nod. He laced his fingertips together. "I saw her leaving her father's office around noon."

"I've been wondering, Mr. Kabakjian. . .and perhaps you can answer this for me. . .at fifteen years of age, why wasn't Miss Griffin in school at noon?"

Kabakjian flexed his shoulders. "I would have no idea, Mr. Weaver, having no children of my own."

"I didn't realize that."

"I'm not married, Mr. Weaver."

"I see." John nodded, scratched an imaginary itch on his left cheek with his right hand and added, "Children are nice to have, but you'd certainly want to be married first, I suppose."

Kabakjian leaned forward. "I suppose."

"I have children and I'll have to tell you, I don't know what I'd do if my fifteen-year-old daughter was missing."

Kabakjian didn't answer.

"Now then, you said she was alone?"

"Yes."

"But you observed her looking around, as though—"

"As though she was looking for someone, yes. I told you all that before. Yes."

John nodded, scratched his itch again, and continued. "Let's talk again about the man you saw her with previously."

"Again, Mr. Weaver, I've told you before that I saw her with an older gentleman on a previous occasion. Found them in her father's office. . . kissing. . ."

"Kissing?"

"Passionately."

"At fifteen. . ."

"The girls start young these days, I suppose."

"And apparently the men finish old."

Kabakjian smiled slightly. "Apparently."

"And you said the man may have been around thirty."

"From what I could tell."

"And you said you told her father what you had seen."

Maury Kabakjian nodded. "Oh, yes. Brownie points, you know."

"What was Mr. Griffin's reaction?"

"He was angry, naturally. In a. . .cold sort of way. I can't say I blame him."

"And you said—at that time—that you couldn't identify the man. . . couldn't even give us a description."

"I told you what I know. As soon as I walked in, he swung around and looked the other way. Shari nearly attacked me with her accusations."

"About not knocking."

"Yes."

"If I showed you a lineup of photos, do you think you could possibly pinpoint the man?" John knew that he couldn't—or possibly wouldn't—but he hoped to confound him with his line of questioning, so that when he asked him about Caballero he might be caught off guard.

"I don't think so. As I said—"

"Because I was thinking," John interrupted him. "Sometimes you see someone, and it brings back a familiarity, if you know what I mean."

"The man never looked at me directly, Mr. Weaver." Maury Kabakjian stood, an indication that the meeting was over. "I really have nothing new to add and, quite frankly, I'd be more comfortable discussing this with Mr. Griffin."

John stood, walked toward the door, and then turned. "What about the security videotapes? We've gone over the ones you've given us. The man kept his head down. . .as though he knew better than to look at the camera."

"I'm sure Miss Griffin told him to do just that."

"But I'm thinking perhaps if we go back a few weeks. . .before he knew. . .perhaps he had been here before."

Kabakjian stared straight ahead. "I'll have my secretary round those up for you."

"Thank you, Mr. Kabakjian."

Kabakjian continued to stand behind his desk. "I'm sorry I wasn't of any more help."

"Yes." John placed his hand on the doorknob, then stopped and turned back. "A few days ago. . .when I was here speaking with you. . ." John watched the curator's face grow dark.

"Yes."

"The man you were with—"

"I have no idea what you're talking about."

John smiled. "I'm not talking about anything, Mr. Kabakjian. I was just going to say that he looked remarkably like someone I used to know. Can't quite put my finger on who it is though. You know how that sort of thing just plagues your mind." John painted a perplexed look on his face.

Kabakjian sat and began to shuffle papers on top of his desk. "Yes. Disturbing." His eyes stayed on his hands.

"Do you remember who the man was?"

"No." Maury slapped his hands on his desk and stood. "Mr. Weaver, I must be moving on to my work. I'm sure you'd understand."

John nodded. "Thank you, Mr. Kabakjian. I'm sure it will come to me sooner or later."

"Yes, I'm certain it will."

CHAPTER TWENTY-SIX

Candy inserted the plastic key into the door to the place she had called home for the last two seemingly drawn-out months. Katie had allowed each of the girls to decorate their rooms—bedspreads, linens, draperies, accessories, and pictures on the walls—to their personal liking. Candy had chosen a satin comforter set—black, with accented, bold brush-strokes of plum, mauve, and teal oriental blossoms. When the lights were out and the room was illuminated either by natural light or from the city lights, the bed appeared to have fairies dancing across it. The softness of texture was disrupted somewhat by this evocative activity. Candy liked the way it looked. . .the way it felt under her skin when she lay upon it. . .the sleek, lustrous sensation under her fingertips as her hands brushed against it in passing.

Standing in the doorway now, she smiled. As pretty as this room was, it would soon be only a stepping-stone to her ultimate goal. Soon—very soon—she would send for her mother and brother Jon. Soon the three of them would live with the handsome stranger in another country. She would be able to start over. The man would most likely give her a job—a good job, if the looks of him were any indication—and she would support her mother in a style she should have grown accustomed to.

She would have to convince her mother to move, of course. That would be nearly as difficult to do as was the task of deceiving Katie.

Candy closed the door behind her and frowned as she began pulling her housekeeping uniform away from her small frame. "Good riddance," she muttered into the silence of the room. She threw the light blue dress into a corner of the room, followed by her work shoes and socks. "I've never felt so ridiculous in all my life. I'd rather walk around naked than wear this lousy stuff."

She walked to the small closet in the room and began to scan over the few clothes she had purchased with Katie's credit card. A sudden thought made her smile briefly. No one could say she had abused Katie's generosity, now could they? Ashley and Brittany had purchased twice as much.

She hurriedly chose a red wool skirt, white oxford top and hunter green Lacoste pullover sweater. She had purchased a man's preppy necktie to go with the outfit. When she had finished dressing, she watched herself in the bathroom's vanity mirror as she fastened the top button of the oxford, knotted the tie, then pulled it loose slightly and decided to undo the top button after all.

After brushing her hair—somewhat brusquely—then clamping it into a ponytail with a black barrette, she brushed her teeth and freshened her lipstick. Switching off the light as she left the bathroom, she walked back into the bedroom and plopped down on the right side of the bed where she had a clear view of the snow-draped city through the windows. She looked around for a moment as though she wasn't quite sure of what to do next, then stood and slipped her hand between the mattresses, reaching for the folded paper she kept hidden there. After pulling it out, she sat again on the side of the bed, picked up the bedside phone and dialed the number neatly inscribed on that small piece of paper.

"Yes," the nameless man answered.

"Hello."

"Xi Lan. Is that you, Puppet?"

Xi Lan pressed her lips together. "I don't. . ."

"You don't what?"

"I don't know your name."

Xi Lan waited through the next few moments of silence, holding her breath. Would he tell her? Would she know the name of her savior, the man who would take her away from this city. . .this country. . .this life she had so come to hate?

"I suppose you don't," he finally said. "You may call me Mr. Caballero."

Xi Lan nodded. "Mr. Caballero, I have information for you."

"Do you now? So soon?"

"I'm a fast worker."

"I'd say you are."

"I want to leave this country, Mr. Caballero. I want to leave with you and send for my mother and brother like you said."

"I'm certain you do. I'm very certain of it now. What do you have for me, Puppet?"

"I think Katie suspects that Vickey—Katie's assistant—is the one behind the gifts."

The man named Caballero let out a resounding peal of laughter. When the laughter subsided, he added, "Oh, my dear. You have made my day. What makes you say that?"

"Just the conversation I overheard today."

"What else did you overhear?"

Xi Lan shook her head lightly. "I'm not sure it's important."

"I'll decide that."

"Only that. . ." Xi Lan sighed deeply. "They were talking about Mr. Webster. . ."

"What about him?"

"The type of cologne he wore. That's all."

"You don't say? What type was that?"

Xi Lan looked down at her lap. "Oh. I—"

"Don't tell me you have forgotten? You wouldn't want to disappoint me, would you, Xi Lan?"

"No! I. . .I wrote it down. . . . hold on for a moment."

Xi Lan stood and ran over to the clothes she had thrown in the corner of the room, dug her hand into the uniform's pocket where she had kept pad and pen, and came back to the bed. "I didn't recognize one of them; Katie named two. The first one was Aigner Essence. I recognize that one because I knew a guy once who wore it. Not that you need to know that."

"No."

"Katie said that's what Webster wore when he died."

"He died?" The dark man sounded sarcastically astonished.

"Don't you know?"

"Should I?"

"I don't know. . ."

"Who does? What was the second one?"

"I didn't recognize it. But I can tell you what it sounded like."

"Go ahead."

"Curious Frack-something."

"Kouros Fraicheur?"

"Yes." Xi Lan wadded the paper then threw it toward a nearby black trash can where it bounced off the rim and into the can. She smiled. *Two points*, she thought. *Score*.

"Anything else?"

"No. That's really it."

"Tell me, Xi Lan, is Mrs. Webster continuing to receive gifts?"

Xi Lan was silent for a moment. "I thought you—"

"I, what?"

"I assumed that you—"

The dark stranger who was becoming stranger with every moment laughed again, then sobered. "Has she?" he asked with a new and serious tone in his voice.

"Not that I know of."

Again there was silence before the man finished with, "You're my girl."

Xi Lan smiled and sighed deeply. "Thank you. I have to go now. I have to go back to work."

"But not for long. Soon, you will be with my sister and me in Canada. We will send for your family. You'll like that, I know."

Xi Lan closed her eyes. "Yes."

258

"Will you go to the club tonight?"

Her eyes opened again. "Yes."

"I'll see you there. We'll have a little meeting—you and Mr. Sharkey and me. Tell Mr. Sharkey to be expecting me. Can you do that for me?"

"Anything for you, Mr. Caballero. I think. . .I think you may be my savior."

Xi Lan listened for a verbal reaction, but all she could hear was the steady breathing of the man who remained a stranger. "You flatter me, Xi Lan." Xi Lan heard a distinctive click over the phone line. "Puppet, I'm getting another call. I'll see you tonight."

CHAPTER TWENTY-SEVEN

Katie and Marcy left Katie's executive office shortly after Candy did. They said goodbye to Vickey, promised to stay warm, then rode the elevators down to the first floor with several of the hotel's guests.

"Good afternoon," Katie greeted them. "Are you enjoying your stay at The Hamilton Place?"

Marcy watched in fascination as the handful of people warmed to Katie, telling her what a wonderful holiday season they were having in the city. A gentleman stated he was here often on business, and that even though he was away from his family, THP always made the trip pleasant for him. The obvious satisfaction at hearing this made Katie smile appreciatively. An elderly couple explained that they had just arrived in celebration of their fiftieth wedding anniversary, at which Katie whipped her cell phone out from her purse, dialed her office number and—as she waited for Vickey to answer—asked the couple, "What room are you in?"

"The honeymoon suite," the wife declared proudly. "A gift from our four children."

Katie smiled. "How lovely—Vickey! Katie. Do me a favor, will you?" She turned back to the couple, and, raising her eyebrows, asked, "Plans for dinner tonight?"

They looked at one another as the elevator came to a stop. The doors opened, the operator called out "Lobby," and everyone hesitated to get out, wanting to know what the hotel's president was about to do for the elderly couple. When Katie stepped out, however, everyone followed, each going his own way, with the exception of the couple. They stayed close to Katie and Marcy, explaining that they had thought to go to Bonaparte's, but had also heard of an Italian restaurant close by that several of their friends insisted they try before leaving the city. Katie nodded, then spoke again into the phone, "Vickey, call down to the front desk for me. Tell them that Mr. and Mrs.—"

"O'Connor."

"—O'Connor will be having dinner on the house tonight." Katie turned her attention back to the couple. "How about a romantic candlelit dinner in your room?"

Marcy watched the couple as they beamed with excitement.

"I'll take that as a yes," Katie said with a smile. "Vickey, anything they order is on the house. Oh, and Vickey. . .make a note and leave it on my desk. We should do something like this for our anniversary couples staying in the honeymoon suite. Dinner tickets or theater tickets or something. . . . thank you, Vickey."

Katie turned back to the couple. "Order anything you want. It's on the house." She extended her hand for a handshake, which both of them took in turn. "My name is Katharine Webster. If you need anything while you're here, please feel free to call my office. I'm the president of The Hamilton Place." She began to take a step. "Enjoy your stay with us."

"We will!" the couple said in unison as Marcy and Katie walked away.

"I love watching you work!" Marcy declared with a laugh. "Did you see the looks on their faces?"

"They've made it fifty years. They deserve it."

Marcy thought for a moment. "They must have been children when they married. They didn't look to be that old, did they?"

Katie smiled and then pointed to the door of Jacqueline's. "Let's stop in here for a minute, okay?"

Marcy grinned. "Are you gonna get me another crystal kitty cat?"

Katie opened the door and frowned at her friend. "No, you spoiled little child, I am not."

Marcy feigned disappointment. "I'm heartbroken."

"You'll survive." Katie winked at her.

As they entered the boutique Zane McKenzie met them immediately. "Mrs. Webster!"

"Please," Katie said emphatically. "Call me Katie."

"Katie. You are just the person we wanted to see." Zane took a few steps to the rear of the shop and called for his sister, who soon emerged from the office area.

"Katie," she said sweetly. "You brought a friend."

Katie took a moment to introduce Marcy to Zane and Zandra.

"Twins?" Marcy asked, as she shook their hands.

"Yes," Zandra replied curtly, then turned her attention back to Katie.

"So, you wanted to see me?" Katie asked. "That's good, because I wanted to talk to you, too."

"You go first," Zane said with a brilliant smile.

"I have a young woman who is on staff that I think would be an asset to you during the holidays. . . ."

Zane and Zandra looked at one another pensively. "Well, we—" Zandra began.

Katie reached out and touched her forearm. "Oh, no! I'm not asking you to hire her. I understand what it's like to just be getting started in a business. She'll stay on my payroll, but would work here for you."

Marcy stood silently nearby, looking disinterestedly at the merchandise, thinking it sounded like a great deal to her. Hired help and you don't have to pay them. When she looked back to the brother and sister, she was a little surprised to see them struggling with a response.

Katie saw it, too. "Please," she said. "It won't cost you a penny. I promise. And I think you'll like Brittany. She's an absolutely stunning African-American woman. Tall, willowy. Chic haircut. She could model anything in this store and sell it, I promise you!"

Zane took a deep breath and sighed. "You're right, Katie. We were going to try to make it on our own this season. Possibly bring my wife in. But if she is to stay on your payroll—"

"You're married?" Katie asked. "I didn't realize that."

Marcy looked intently as Zandra frowned and Zane smiled. "Yes. For about two years now. We're expecting our first child in about six months as a matter of fact."

Zandra interrupted with, "Why don't you send the girl down to us later this afternoon. Her name is Brittany you said?"

"Yes," Katie nodded, taking her attention from Zane to his sister, and then back. "Thank you! Thank you so much. Now, you said you wanted to see me?"

Zane started a bit. "Oh, yes! We've been asked to take part in a holiday fashion show next Wednesday at Rockefeller Center. *Good Morning, America* is going to be there; it'll truly be an event."

Katie beamed. "Really?"

"Yes, and we were thinking. . .if you felt that you could. . .that perhaps you would model one or two of our pieces. You know, to have the president of the hotel modeling for the boutique. . .we thought it'd be an angle."

"I could do that," Katie said. "Certainly, I could do that. Sounds like fun."

Marcy decided Zane and Zandra seemed pleased enough with Katie's agreement to help them. It was a kind of "I scratch your back, you scratch mine" arrangement, she thought.

Zandra looked from her brother to Katie and added, "Could you possibly come to our place Tuesday evening, then? We thought we'd meet together—and since I'm going to model, too," Zandra added, "we could try on the clothes. . .have a glass of wine. . .perhaps get to know one another a little better. . ."

Katie looked around briefly. "Why not just do that here?"

Zane and Zandra looked at one another again, then Zane answered, "Beginning this weekend the store will stay open until nine. . .for the holidays."

"Oh, I see."

"My wife is planning to be here that night so we can deal with the last minute preparations. She and Brittany could work together."

Zandra interjected, "We'd be honored to have you in our home, of course. Please, Katie, don't make this difficult." She blushed with a smile. "This is our way of getting you to come over."

Katie smiled. "Well, okay. If you insist." She looked over to Marcy. "Marcy may still be here—"

Marcy noted a look of apprehension cross between the siblings, and she quickly added, "No, no. I'm not really into all that. If I am still here, I'll want to stay in for the evening. . .call my family. . . ." Marcy raised her eyebrows and pursed her lips slightly as she witnessed the relief pass over their faces.

"Oh, but Marce. . ." Katie began.

"No, seriously, Katie. I can see that Zane and Zandra are thinking business here. I'll take my cue. . ."

Zandra moved one step closer to Marcy. "We didn't mean to—"

"It's okay, really. I truly don't mind."

Katie seemed ill at ease with Marcy's decision not to join her at the McKenzie's home. "Well, it shouldn't take more than what? An hour?"

Zane nodded. "Let's give it two hours." He walked to the back counter and pulled a business card from a cardholder. There was a nearby crystal bowl holding several pens, fanned out in all directions. He retrieved one, then neatly printed an address on the reverse side and handed it to Katie. "Here's our address. We'll see you about seven?"

Katie took the card and smiled. "Perfect," she said, placing the card in her purse without looking at it. "I can't thank you enough for allowing Brittany to work here." She began to move toward the door and Marcy followed. "I'll send her down when I get back from The Plaza."

Marcy decided to poke a little fun. "We have a meeting there," she said with a nod of her head and a smile, but neither Zane nor Zandra smiled back. On their way out, Katie stopped at an accessory table and fondled a silk scarf. "Nice. . ." she said absentmindedly.

When Marcy and Katie had settled into the comforts of the limo with Simon at the wheel, Marcy turned to Katie and burst out laughing.

Katie laughed, too, but it was obvious she didn't know at what. "You don't even know what I'm laughing at!" Marcy exclaimed.

Katie continued to laugh, admitting, "No, I don't. But it's so fun to see you so tickled."

"I was obviously the unwelcome guest. They instinctively knew I don't belong in all this." Marcy waved her hand around the limousine.

Katie shook her head. "No, no. It's not you, Marcy. It's me. In this town it's all about who you know. They want to say they know me. I know that sounds snobbish, and I don't mean it to. . .but it's one of the things Ben taught me. Everyone wants to be one of the 'beautiful' people. . .or at the very least be *with* them."

"I suppose so."

"I've been rich and I've been poor—" she quoted.

Marcy grinned. "And rich is better?"

Katie's features darkened. "Happy is better."

Marcy reached over and lightly touched her friend's arm. "But you said you were happy here."

Katie nodded. "I am. But real happiness is Ben back with me, and maybe the two of us managing that empire. But, the money has nothing to do with it. Not really. If he called me today and said that he was somewhere in the poorest section of America and asked if I would come join him, I'd say yes." Katie paused for a minute. "The thing is—when you are classified as one of society's finest, you're never really sure if people like you because of who you are or because of the number of zeros in your checkbook. Shakespeare wrote: *The very substance of the ambitious is merely the shadow of a dream.*" Katie touched her lips lightly with her fingertips. "One night, two years ago, when I had come home to Georgia, I had a dream that Bucky Caballero had me cornered in the old club where I used to dance. He quoted that very line to me. *The very substance of the ambitious is merely the shadow of a dream.* It's true, you know. A shadow can be the outline consisting of nothing or can be a sort of power that pulls us in and—in some ways—protects us."

"Like in the Psalms, when David writes 'the children of men put their trust under the shadow of Thy wings.' That would be a good shadow, I would have to say." Marcy grinned at the pleasure of quoting from the great Psalter.

"That's the kind of shadow I wouldn't mind calling out to," Katie said with a smile, then sobered. Her eyes grew dark for a moment as she said, "But who wants to summon the shadows that the dreams of unscrupulous men are made of?"

The limo came to a stop in front of The Plaza. As Simon slipped out of the driver's side of the car, shutting the door behind him, Katie looked out of the window to the grand entrance of The Plaza, the flags hanging high across the front. "He springs up like a flower and withers away; like a fleeting shadow, he does not endure." She turned a tender gaze back to Marcy, looking her directly in the eyes. "Job, chapter fourteen, verse two."

"Everyone wants to be Cary Grant. Even I want to be Cary Grant," Marcy quoted back to her, smiling broadly as Simon opened the door for the two friends.

"Cary Grant," Katie returned with a laugh as the two women stepped out into the cold and the snow. "I get it. Everyone wants the image; they just don't know what's really behind it all."

"What time shall I return, Mrs. Webster?" Simon asked dutifully, interrupting their play.

Katie looked at her wristwatch and said, "Give us two hours, I'd say."

"Yes, Ma'am." He tipped his cap. "And if I may add," he said with a grin. "You two are funny, you know that? You must have been a riot growing up together."

Marcy really laughed then, the sound dissipating as the city's snow began to fall harder. She looked up. "Hey, looks like we're really going to get the white stuff."

Katie rolled her eyes, looped an arm around Marcy's arm and began walking. "Let's go," she said emphatically. "You're a nut, you know that?"

"Yeah," Marcy replied lightly. "But ya love me!"

CHAPTER TWENTY-EIGHT

"Hello, my love." Bucky spoke into his cell phone, having ended his phone conversation with Xi Lan.

"Bucky," Victoria sighed from the other end. "Bucky, I have to talk to you."

"You know where I am."

"Yes, I know where you are, and I know where you're going to be."

Bucky walked over to the desk of his hotel room and sat heavily. "And where is that, Victoria?" His voice sounded weary.

"Jail. Do you know who just called me?"

"Let me guess. Mr. Silver."

"Yes," Victoria hissed. "And that can only mean one thing. They know you're in the city."

"They know all right."

There was a pause on the other end. "What do you mean?" Victoria's voice quivered. When Bucky didn't answer, she added, "Bucky?"

"I received a call earlier from Mr. Kabakjian."

"Who?"

"He's a curator at an art gallery."

"Why would a curator from an art gallery call you?"

"Because an agent had been to see him. . .asking about me. . . ." Bucky picked up his gold cigarette case, pulled a cigarette from it, and lit it with a small lighter lying nearby.

"I don't understand. . ."

Blowing gray smoke from his lips, Bucky answered, "You see, my dear, I really am here to buy art. The other day, while at the gallery, this particular agent came in. I'm afraid he may have recognized me."

"Oh, dear God. . . ." She began to cry.

Bucky listened to Victoria's tearful voice with disdain. "Stop it, Victoria. Enough of your theatrics."

"I can't help it. . ."

"You *can* help it and you will. If for no other reason, for Jordan."

Bucky waited a few moments for his former lover to calm herself, then went on. "I'm leaving the hotel now, if it makes you feel any better. My bags are packed; I just called the front desk to expedite my check-out. I'll be out of here within the hour."

"Thank God."

"God has nothing to do with it, Pet."

"You know what I'm saying. Bucky, for pity's sake, get on the next plane and go home to Canada."

Bucky drew on his cigarette, giving him time to think on what Victoria had just said. "Home? Home is New York. Home could never be Canada. But I've called my pilot. He'll pick me up later this evening."

"This evening? No, Bucky! Now!"

Bucky stood suddenly, thrust his cigarette into the crystal ashtray and ground it out. His jaw flexed and an angry vein popped out on his neck. "Victoria!" he said through clenched teeth. "You lose yourself. Do *not* presume to tell me what to do!" He heard Victoria gasp, and he went on. "Do you understand me?" When she didn't answer, he added, *"Do you?"*

"I suppose I just shouldn't care."

Bucky began to pace, calming himself. "Are you seeking an Oscar this afternoon, Darling? Stop your female theatrics." His voice—though firm—was smooth and gentle again. "I love you, still."

He could hear Victoria struggling between indignation and fear. "Then leave now." Her voice was barely a whisper.

"I have an important meeting tonight. I'll leave immediately after that. However, if it will make you happy, I promise you that I'll lay low until then. I have a few stops to make along the way, but this city is big enough to hide me, I think."

The strength returned to Victoria's voice. "The city may be large, but the circle is small."

Bucky stopped in his pacing and smiled. "Darling, I'll call you from Canada tomorrow. I promise."

Victoria paused before answering. "I love you, Bucky. Always remember that."

Bucky smiled. "It's kept me warm many a night, Victoria. Talk to you soon. . .and Darling. . ."

"Yes?"

"My best to Jordan."

CHAPTER TWENTY-NINE

"The crown jewel of Fifth Avenue," Katie whispered with a smile to Marcy as they walked purposefully through the highly polished, opulent Fifth Avenue lobby of The Plaza hotel.

Marcy tried not to gasp as she took in the palatial allure of the world's most famous hotel. "I am impressed." She placed special emphasis on the last syllable of the last word. "Tell me again why we're here. I seem to have forgotten."

Katie smiled warmly. "I have a luncheon meeting."

"With?"

"A very small group of business women within the hotel industry who get together once a month in various restaurants to talk about the things within the business that affect us as women."

Marcy nodded. "Oh."

"Today we'll be dining in the Palm Court."

"Sounds lovely." Their footsteps padded straight ahead, through a massive opening and across rich carpet until they reached the popular restaurant, highly decorated at the entrance with small palm trees wrapped in small white lights.

When they had been properly seated at a table—round and draped in linen—and had ordered their drinks, Katie opened her menu, slipped her reading glasses along the bridge of her nose and said, "The others should be along soon." She glanced around the room absentmindedly, noting it was already filling to capacity.

Marcy frowned. "I somehow wish it were to be just the two of us."

Katie laid her menu to the left side of her plate. "Why?" She peered over the tiny, gold-framed lenses. In the corner of the room, a pianist began a new medley of holiday songs on a grand piano.

Marcy shrugged her shoulders as she glanced around. "I'm a little out of place here, Kate."

"Don't be silly." Katie resumed studying her menu.

Marcy leaned over hers and whispered. "I'm not. I'm serious."

Katie smiled, removed her glasses, and whispered back. "You'll do fine. In fact, behave and I'll bring you back later for the Palm Court Tea."

"Oo-la-la. I take it that's a proper tea."

"It's *the* event here of the Season." She glanced over Marcy's shoulder. "Oh, Linda and Grace are here."

Marcy turned her head slightly, trying to glance over her right shoulder. Sensing the presence of the two newcomers, she turned back to face Katie, who greeted them. "Good afternoon, ladies."

"Good afternoon," they returned simultaneously. "Happy holidays," one added as they were seated on either side of Marcy and Katie.

"Linda, Grace, allow me to introduce my oldest and dearest friend, Marcy Waters. Marcy, this is Linda Desmond and Grace Emerson."

Marcy smiled warmly. "It's nice to meet you. Please call me Marcy."

Both women smiled. "Marcy, what brings you to New York? Holiday treasure hunting?" Linda asked. She was the shorter and heavier of the two women. Her features were soft and child-like, her blond hair perfectly styled and turned under just above her shoulders. She wore a large gold-knotted necklace with matching earrings, which brought out the gold thread weaving through the sharp but simple dark blue skirted-suit she wore. As she opened her menu, several bracelets around her wrists jangled against one another. Marcy's eyes noted them, and an impressive set of wedding rings, and when she glanced back to her pretty face, Marcy warmed to her contagious smile instantly.

"Something like that," Marcy returned, giving Katie a knowing look. It wasn't so much the treasure they were after, but the giver of the gifts.

"I see Kitty hasn't arrived yet," Grace interjected. Marcy switched her attention to the other woman. Unlike Linda, she was tall and slender, with porcelain fine features and short, dark hair that framed her face in soft waves. She wore very little makeup and—with the exception of a plain wedding band—no jewelry. Her clothes were just as simple; she wore a pinstripe suit cut like a man's. Marcy knew instinctively Grace was all business.

"Kitty is always late," Linda replied with a smile, though her eyes never left her menu. "Ladies, are we going for a nice salad today?"

Katie laughed lightly. "Don't we always? Unlike Grace, some of us count every calorie." She glanced briefly at Marcy and, noting her shoulders relax, added, "Should we go ahead and order for Kitty?"

Moments later, Kitty, an exquisite Norwegian blond with a perfectly straight nose and cat-like green eyes, arrived with a "Darlings, I'm sorry I'm late, but my son's school called and needed permission to give him an aspirin for a slight headache," and the conversation during the remainder of the lunch remained easy banter. No one really spoke about business. Instead, they chatted happily about planned holiday vacations—if they even dared leave their offices for any significant length of time—and what their children wanted from the mythical gift-giver from the North Pole.

"What about you, Marcy?" Linda asked at one point. "Do you have children?"

Marcy had just placed a fork-full of food into her mouth. She made a funny face—causing everyone to laugh—swallowed, and then said, "Three." She took a sip of water and added, "Two boys and a girl."

"They're wonderful children," Katie added proudly.

Kitty reached over and grabbed Katie's hand. "Katie-dear, I'm so sorry you don't have children, especially during the holidays."

Marcy swallowed hard, watched Katie's smile fade, then reappear. "Oh, but I do, Kitty. Marcy's children and Vickey's children. . . ."

Grace rested her fork on her plate. "Oh, Kitty. Sometimes you say the most inconsiderate things."

"It's okay." Katie soothed Kitty with a pat on her hand. "I don't regret not having children nearly as much as other people regret that I don't have children."

She cast her eyes to her plate, remembering the evening when Ben had told her she was made for raising children. He knew, of course, that she had lost one child—David Franscella's child—when he severely beat her after learning of their baby's conception. The miscarriage was met with complications, leaving her unable to conceive again.

"We can adopt," Ben had told her. "Whenever you're ready. We'll hire an adoption attorney. . .the best. . .whatever you want, Katie. A girl? A boy? One of each, it doesn't matter to me. But you were meant to raise children."

"Oh, Ben," she whispered, burying her face into his chest as they lay on their bed, talking. . .talking. . .the way they always did. . . . "Maybe one day. Not now." Before she could become a parent, she wanted to clear things with her own mother. But, as life would have it, she no sooner reconciled with Carolyn Mills Morgan than Ben had disappeared.

And now, here she sat, eighteen months later. . .still waiting.

"Who's for dessert?" she asked, hoping to break the tension she felt deep inside. "I, for one, don't need anything sweet to carry around on my hips," she added, looking at Marcy, "but the *crème brulée* is to die for."

Everyone ordered dessert, and as Marcy dreaded, conversation then turned to business. She had enjoyed herself up to this point and, although she took pleasure in watching Katie at work, listening to these women converse on some of the more boring details (this committee and that organization) was mind-numbing for her. When the last bite of the delectable *crème brulée* had melted in her mouth and she had sipped the last drop of coffee, she quietly excused herself on the pretense of needing "the little girl's room." What she really wanted was time to explore.

For several minutes she walked the vast expanse and grandeur of the registration lobby, craning her neck to study the architecture, touching things lightly with her fingers. She smiled often, thinking of Katie in the restaurant, so competent with the women who had joined them for lunch. The thought stayed with her as she returned to the Fifth Avenue lobby and stared out a window, looking onto the wintry holiday street beyond. Her eyes darted back and forth, noting the number of passing limousines in a single minute. She smiled again, remembering Katie as a child, sitting atop a pink and white bicycle, leaning over the handlebars, pedaling as hard as her long legs could pedal. "Come on, Marce!" she called back. The wind carried the lilt of laughter on carefree days, reaching Marcy, who rode her blue bicycle behind Katie, up and down the sidewalks of Main Street. Marcy was always behind Katie when they biked. It was a matter of physics; Katie's legs were almost twice as long as Marcy's.

"Slow down!"

"I can't slow down. You speed up!"

"I can't! Slow down, Katie! Slow down!"

And then Katie would come to a sudden halt, jumping from the padded white seat, planting her feet securely on the sidewalk, cracked and broken from years of erosion and oak tree roots that didn't go deep enough.

Marcy smiled at the memory, wishing she could somehow go back and visit those days again. . .even if only for an afternoon. She turned from the window, heading toward the center of the lobby, past the gilded stands and ornate candelabrum, decorative urns filled with poinsettias, and under the elaborate chandeliers when she was suddenly struck with an idea for a column, comparing the past to the present, the simplicity of Brooksboro's one and only motel to the magnificence of The Plaza, and the changes that come from moving from one time to another. . .one place to another.

She walked out of the lobby, past the Palm Court, and turned right, heading toward the registration lobby. Upon spotting the concierge desk, she approached it and asked the attractive woman standing on the other side if she might ask a few questions. She also put on a few airs, hoping it would garner assistance.

"I'm a columnist from Georgia," she began with a smile. "I'm visiting

The Plaza for the first time, and I was wondering if you could give me some information?" As she asked, she reached into her slim purse and pulled out a small notepad and pen she kept with her for times such as this.

The woman—Danielle, according to her name tag—looked up at her from the computer monitor atop the polished desk, glanced at her watch and, looking back at Marcy, smiled warmly. "I'd be more than happy to. For whom do you write?"

"The Savannah Morning News." Marcy rested the pad on the counter before her.

"I adore Savannah. My sister lives there, on Victory Drive."

Marcy was impressed. "That's a lovely area. An older, established area. Speaking of lovely and established, how old is The Plaza?"

"Built in 1907. It has served this city for nearly a century as one of the most desirable places to stay while in New York. The original construction took two years and twelve million dollars, which was unheard of in those days."

"I can imagine."

"Money was not an object. Henry Janeway Hardenbergh—well known for his work—was hired to design the hotel with all the pomp and opulence of a French chateau at whatever cost was necessary."

Marcy smiled. "He did a fine job."

"During the early years, The Plaza was used as a residence for the upper crust of New York society. Those who wished to rent a room for a short stay, however, could do so for $2.50 a night."

"You're kidding." Marcy stopped writing and allowed herself to think about that.

"No, I'm very serious. Today, people travel from all over the world to stay here, and movies have been filmed here. *North by Northwest* was the first, and I'm sure you remember *The Way We Were. . .*"

"Home Alone 2. . ."

The woman nearly glowed at Marcy's knowledge. "Yes!" she exclaimed.

Marcy shrugged. "I have children," she commented, just as the concierge phone rang. "Oh, excuse me, please," Danielle apologized, answering the phone with a professional, "Concierge, hold please." She turned back to Marcy. "If you'd like more information, you may want to visit our gift shop. There's a wonderful book which details the history of The Plaza." With that she turned her attention back to the caller. "Concierge, how may I help you?"

Marcy jotted a few more notes, then turned to take in more visuals for her column. It was then that she saw him; a well-built man in his late forties with thick dark hair combed straight back and handsomely chiseled features hidden only by a short beard and the sunglasses he wore over his eyes.

She wasn't sure at first. . .*she was almost positive.* She jumped just a bit, then slid around in hopes that he hadn't spotted her staring at him. "Bucky Caballero," she whispered, ducking her head and turning to look again, this time slowly and deliberately.

She squinted her eyes at the man who walked slowly and purposefully down the narrow double staircase, carrying two small cases of luggage in his hands.

He was leaving!

The concierge continued in her conversation, apparently a request for theater tickets. Marcy looked back at her, mouthed: *Thank you*, then darted toward the Palm Court as inconspicuously as she could.

When she approached the table, however, she found only Linda, Grace, and Kitty. "Where's Katie?" she asked, interrupting their conversation. She blushed. "I'm sorry. I didn't mean to interrupt. Where's Katie?"

"She went looking for you," Kitty answered, in a you-shouldn't-have-been-gone-so-long voice.

Marcy placed her hand lightly to her throat, then turned back toward the door. "I was talking to the concierge."

"Is something wrong?" This from Linda.

"No!"

Grace laughed. "Are you certain? You seem a little anxious."

Marcy placed her hands on the back of her empty chair. "I just need to find Katie."

"Find me for what?" Katie asked, walking up behind her. "Where did you run off to?"

Marcy swung around and grabbed Katie by the hands. "Don't leave this room," she nearly hissed.

"Marcy, what on earth?" Katie drew back slightly.

Marcy looked around as though she were casing the place, then pulled Katie a few feet from the table. "Don't panic, but Caballero is in the registration foyer."

The lovely features from Katie's face seemed to fall. "What?" she whispered, leaning over slightly. She crossed her arms protectively over her abdomen.

"Katie—"

"We need to call Phil." Katie moved toward the opening of the restaurant, reaching into her purse for her cell phone.

"Katie, what's going on?" Grace asked, elevating her voice slightly above the patrons and piano.

Katie turned her upper torso toward the table and extended a hand. "It's okay. I'll be right back."

"Katie, you don't need to go out there. I don't want him to see you," Marcy implored. "In fact, he'll probably be walking right past here any second. Please. Go sit down and keep your back to the entrance."

Katie sighed deeply. "What can he do to me out there? What else can he take from me?" she asked, moving toward the hallway leading to the registration foyer as she dialed Phil on her cell phone. Marcy was at her heels. When they reached the concierge desk, they stopped. "Where? Where did you see him?" Katie dropped her cell phone back into her purse. "Phil's not answering."

Marcy pointed behind them. "He was leaving, Kate. He had luggage."

"He *is* in the city, then."

"Apparently."

"Is anything wrong?" The woman behind the concierge desk stood, addressing Marcy.

Marcy started slightly. "Oh, no. When you answered the phone, I thought I saw an old friend. . . ."

The woman smiled, but Katie frowned down at the two of them. Marcy clarified, "I was asking this nice lady here a few questions about the hotel when I saw him."

Katie pressed her lips together, then turned toward Marcy and began walking slowly to the restaurant. "I'd better call Simon to come back for us. We should get in touch with Phil as soon as possible." She stopped briefly and looked down at Marcy. "Are you *certain* it was him?"

"Yes. Katie, when I returned to Georgia last year, I studied everything I could get my hands on about Caballero. I know him—with or without a beard. It was him. His walk, his manner. I'm talking his very essence of control infiltrated this room when he entered it. You have to believe me on this."

Katie nodded, breathing heavily through her nostrils. "Of course I believe you. Like you said, Bucky Caballero is in a league all his own." She paused for a moment. "All right. If he's gone, I think it's safe to call Simon."

Marcy looked back toward the lobby. "Yeah. I guess you'd better."

CHAPTER THIRTY

Late that afternoon Phil returned to Katie's office with John in tow. Katie, looking more tired than concerned or, for that matter, even frightened, sat on one of the leather sofas. She sipped delicately on a cup of hot tea Vickey had brought in on the silver service tray now sitting atop the coffee table. Vickey sat behind Katie's desk, shuffling through a manila file as though she were reorganizing it, and Marcy stood at the window, gazing at the flurry of snow as it fell in violent torrents from the sky. As Phil and John walked in unannounced, she turned from where she stood, smiled briefly, then became serious. "What'd you find out, Silver?" she asked, approaching the back of the sofa where she placed her hands on Katie's shoulders.

Phil jerked his head toward the door. "Katie, no one was out front—"

Katie smiled at him. "That's okay."

The two men walked to the sofas. "Katie, allow me to introduce Agent John Weaver," Phil said.

Katie extended her hand. "Agent Weaver."

"Call me John," he said, taking her hand in his.

Marcy leaned over the sofa. "He won't introduce me," she said with a quick nod to Phil, "so let me introduce myself. I'm Marcy Waters, Katie's best friend from Georgia." She extended her hand toward John.

"She's also a reporter," Phil said, taking a seat on the sofa opposite Katie.

John shook Marcy's hand, frowning. "A reporter? For whom?"

Marcy shook her head. "I'm not a reporter. I write a column for *The Savannah Morning News.*"

"Oh, I see," he responded as though that ended that and took a seat next to Phil.

"Weaver has agreed to work on your case with me, Katie. Unofficially, of course. Let me begin by apologizing for not getting your phone call earlier."

"That's okay."

Vickey walked over from the desk. "Katie, shall I bring in a fresh pot of tea? Coffee?"

Katie looked from Vickey to the men sitting in front of her. "Gentlemen, shall I have my assistant bring you anything?"

"Something cold, actually," John said. "Water is fine."

"Tea for me," Phil answered.

"Marcy?" Vickey asked, turning her attention to the woman who continued to stand behind Katie.

"Nothing, thank you."

"I'll be right back," Vickey said, reaching for the tray on the coffee table.

Phil waited until she had left the room before continuing. John looked up at Marcy uneasily, cleared his throat, then looked back at Phil.

"She's clear," Phil said. "May as well talk in front of her, she'll get it out of Katie later."

Marcy grimaced, made her way around the sofa and sat next to Katie. "That's why I'm here, Silver." The two women held hands. "Besides, I'm the one who saw Caballero first."

Phil nodded, almost in defeat. "Tell me what happened."

Marcy took a deep matter-of-fact breath. "I went with Katie to The Plaza for lunch—"

"What were you doing there?" John asked.

"I had a business luncheon," Katie supplied the answer.

"Oh, I see."

"Anyway—" Marcy continued, "I decided to walk around the lobby a bit while Katie and her friends had their shop talk. I was talking with the woman at the concierge desk, and she got a phone call. While she was talking, I turned and looked around—taking in the incredible architecture of that lobby—and that's when I spotted him."

"Are you sure it was him?"

"Absolutely. No doubt in my mind. He wore sunglasses and was sporting a beard, but it was Caballero all right. I'd be willing to place a bet."

"That won't be necessary," Phil said. He turned to look at Katie. "Katie, did you see him?"

She shook her head, no. "I was in the restaurant for the most part. I *had* gone out into the lobby at one point to look for Marcy, but we must have missed one another."

"Any chance he could have seen you while you were looking for your friend here?"

Katie thought for a moment. "I don't really think so."

Phil nodded. The office door opened just then. Vickey entered carrying the silver tray. Conversation came to a halt as she prepared the tea and handed Agent Weaver a glass of ice and Perrier. "I'll be at my desk if you need me," she said when done.

Katie looked down at her watch. "Why don't you call it a day? Surely you have things to do at home."

Vickey seemed at odds for a moment, then answered, "I'll wait until you're done here. . . . in case you need me for anything."

"Thank you, Vickey," Katie returned with a smile. "And thank you for the tea."

When Vickey had left the room again, Katie turned her attention back to John. "So. . .John. . .what is your role in this?"

Phil extended a hand slightly, as though to interrupt. "Before he answers, Katie, let me tell you that Agent Weaver is the best in the Bureau when it comes to finding people who are either kidnapped or hiding."

John blushed appropriately. "Sometimes it takes a while longer than others, but I do my best. At any rate, I went to see Maury Kabakjian earlier today while Phil headed over to Victoria Whitney's home."

Katie shook her head lightly. "I'm sorry, who is Maury. . ."

"Kabakjian. He's the curator at Maxwell Griffin's art gallery."

Katie's chin rose in recognition. "Oh, yes. You're the agent who saw Bucky Caballero there."

Weaver leaned forward, set his untouched glass of sparkling water on a coffee table coaster, and rested his elbows on his knees. "That's right. My intent was to talk to Mr. Kabakjian on the pretense of the Griffin girl's disappearance."

"I see."

"Kabakjian is a smart man, Mrs. Webster. He wasn't giving an inch when it came to my questioning him about the man I had seen in his office. No doubt, though, it was Caballero. Kabakjian was too quick to want to end the conversation when I mentioned his name. Now, with what your friend has witnessed. . . ."

"You still feel it's Caballero sending the gifts to me? Even though the sales clerk at Saks said it wasn't him. . .or Ben?"

"Yes, Ma'am, we do. Caballero could have any number of people working with him, you understand. He still has contacts in the city."

"Which brings me to our next point," Phil said, straightening a bit, and pulling a large piece of paper from a leather folder he was carrying. He had finished his tea while John and Katie were speaking and set the cup and saucer on the corner of the coffee table. "I went back to Saks today to see Cassie—"

"The sales clerk?"

"Yes. I took photos of the politicians who lost their position when the news came out about the escort service."

"And?"

"She said it that it wasn't any of them. I also took her a photo of Jordan Whitney, though he certainly didn't match the description."

"I take it that it wasn't him."

"No."

"Is that the sketch of the man who came in? The one in your hand?"

Phil nodded, "Cassie is a fine arts student. Quite the artist," he continued, looking at the impressive sketch. This is a copy I made for you." Phil extended the paper across the coffee table and Katie took it, studying it for a few moments. "Katie, do you recognize him?"

Katie looked up at the men and smiled a half-smile. "You're right. She is quite the artist."

"But do you recognize the man?" John asked.

Katie took a deep breath and sighed, studying the dark, handsome features of the mustachioed man in the drawing. "There's something vaguely familiar about him. . ."

Marcy leaned over and studied the drawing as well. "Hmm. . ."

Katie looked at her. "What is it, Marce?"

"I'm thinking the same thing. . .something familiar. . .*what is it?*" The two women looked back to the drawing. "Something about the mouth. . . ."

Phil placed his hands together as though he were about to pray. "Katie, I hate to ask this. . . ." He looked around the room uncomfortably. ". . .and it certainly wouldn't explain Marcy's sense of familiarity, but could this man be someone from before?"

"Before?" Katie seemed genuinely perplexed.

Phil bowed his head slightly. "Before William?"

Recognition fell on Katie's face, and she raised her chin slightly. "Oh." She looked down at the paper and studied it again, then shook her head, no. "I don't think so."

"Katie," John added quietly. "Are you sure?"

Katie blushed. Obviously Phil had to tell John about her past. She looked at the drawing again. *From before Ben.* It could have been any number of men. *Not* that she had been with a large number, that hadn't been her style, but there had been so many customers. Perhaps someone who knew her then. . .saw her picture in the paper when Ben disappeared. . . . She looked up at Phil, caught his expressions and knew he was thinking the same thing. She felt the hot flush burn her cheeks, and she answered, "No, I'm not sure. It's been too many years. But I think not."

Phil wanted to change the subject. "Okay, then. Let's move on. I also called Victoria Thomas Whitney today." He watched as Katie set the drawing next to her on the sofa, giving it a cursory glance. He went on. "I was left with little doubt that she knows a lot more than she originally let on."

"Which leads us back to Caballero," John interjected, grateful to note that the topic had been changed. "When Silver notified me today of your phone call, I had already planned to hit some of the better hotels in the city, to see if Caballero was possibly staying at one of them."

"And?"

"By the time I got the call, I had already gone to three in this general area, but with no success. In my way of looking at it, a man like Caballero isn't going to stay too far from what he loves. He loves this part of the city, and he loves fine things. You won't find him staying at a less-than-classy hotel."

"No, I would suppose not." Katie leaned over, lifted the delicate teacup from its saucer, took a sip of her tea, then sighed heavily. "After my call, did you go to The Plaza? Did you find out anything?" She returned cup to saucer.

"I met Silver there, and together we went to see the general manager. The GM is a good man."

"Yes, I know him," Katie said. "Ben always spoke highly of him."

"The three of us went downstairs to check the records. Bucky Caballero hadn't checked in, but a David Franscella had."

"David?" Katie said quickly.

"But Franscella's dead!" Marcy interrupted.

Phil frowned at her. "We know that. Caballero is simply using his ID, credit cards, etc."

Marcy nodded. "I see."

"We've notified all the charge accounts Franscella had," Phil continued. "When the reports come in we should at least have some idea as to where the bills are going. We can track Caballero down from there."

"So." Katie set her teacup and saucer on the coffee table. "You're not here to tell me you found Bucky and arrested him?"

Weaver shook his head, no. "As you know, he had already checked out. Calls to the airports, etc., came up with nothing as well."

"And chances are, he's using a private plane," Phil supplied.

"Have you contacted the private airports?" Katie asked.

"Of course. But. . .a man's silence can be bought, Katie. There's an entire network of—"

Katie raised her hand to silence him. "I know. It's okay."

"Hmm," Marcy said. "If I'm reading all this correctly, we're looking at so many possibilities, there's no way to really know where to begin. Even though you showed Cassie those photos, what's to keep a man from hiring someone to do his dirty work? We know it's not Katie's husband; we don't think Sharkey is smart enough to know how to pull something like this off; Caballero is a shot in the dark. . . ." She allowed herself to stop voicing her thoughts.

Katie didn't respond. "What now?" she asked the men sitting opposite her.

"Basically," Phil answered, "we wait."

"Wait?"

"To see what happens next. My guess is Caballero was checking out in order to leave the country again. If you continue to hear from your admirer, we'll have some idea that it may not be him."

"Is that what you think, Phil? I don't seem to be getting a clear answer as to what anyone thinks." Katie's voice rose a half-octave. "And what I need right now is to know *something.*"

"Katie," Phil said, reaching a hand toward her. "I'm fairly certain Caballero's our man. Even so, we're going keep our options open. In fact we're leaving here to take a little trip over to see Sharkey."

"I don't understand. . ."

"Leave no stone unturned," Marcy supplied.

"Exactly," Phil agreed, then frowned at the thought of having agreed with Marcy Waters. The irony was not lost on Marcy; she grinned at him. Phil continued, "Even though I went to see him and I think he's too much of an idiot to come up with anything this complex, I also think a little pressure might be good here. Just in case he knows more than he's saying."

"What more could he know?"

"It's just a feeling I have," Phil said dismissively.

"Will you let me know something soon?" Katie asked.

"First thing in the morning." He fidgeted a bit before going on. "Katie, have you considered. . .have you given any more thought to. . ."

"What?"

"Your assistant." His eyes met hers and held.

"Vickey?" Marcy asked, obviously astonished. "What in the world are you think—"

Katie reached over and touched Marcy on the arm. The desired affect was achieved. Marcy fell silent. "Absolutely not," Katie answered resolutely.

Phil nodded. "We have to keep all options open. Just a few minutes ago you offered to let her go home, and she refused. What's she staying for? To gather more information, perhaps?"

"I won't talk about this with you, Phil."

John looked from Phil to Katie. "Katie, it's imperative that you keep your options open. We see it all the time. . .the person closest to the victim. . ."

Katie laughed lightly, but it wasn't a laugh of humor. "Gentlemen, please," she implored them to stop with the direction of their thoughts. "Think it if you will, but don't discuss it with me until you have hard, cold evidence."

"Have it your way, then," Phil answered.

The two men stood, and Marcy and Katie followed.

"Thank you, gentlemen, for your help with this," Katie said, extending her hand toward John for a shake.

John accepted her gesture. As their hands released, he said, "If it's any consolation, Katie, you haven't received any death threats."

"No. No, I haven't."

"My guess is whoever is doing this just wants to shake you up a little.

286

If, however, it's tied to what happened last year. . .well, we'll take care of it. We'll bring this to an end as soon as we can."

Just then the door to Katie's office opened.

"Katie." Vickey stood in the opened door. Her face seemed devoid of color.

"What is it, Vickey?"

"Another—" Vickey looked behind her.

Katie's hand pressed against her breast. She took a deep breath, then squared her shoulders. "Another gift?"

"Yes."

"What is it?" Phil asked, as the foursome moved toward her.

Vickey reached to her right, bringing back a large, wrapped parcel.

"It looks like a painting or a picture of some sort," Marcy said. She leaned over slightly, crossing her arms over her waist.

"Let me see this," Phil said. "Katie? May I?"

"By all means."

Vickey continued to hold the package upright as Phil dipped into his pant's pocket and removed a small pocketknife, which he used to slice away the tape holding the thick brown paper in place. It fell away, revealing a rich, oil painting.

"Delaroche," Katie said.

"Who or what is a Delaroche?" Marcy asked.

"Paul Delaroche," Phil answered. "Nineteenth century French painter." Phil looked at the perplexed stares around him. "What? I studied art in college."

"Is the painting an original?" Marcy asked.

Katie bent down to touch it lightly with her fingertips. "Oh, I seriously doubt it. This one is called *The Martyr*." She noticed a small envelope lying amidst the rumpled brown wrapping paper. "What's this?" She picked it up, turning it over in her hands. The front of the envelope had her name written across it. "Another note," she clarified.

"Katie," Vickey said. "Are you sure you want to open that?"

"Of course, I am." Katie's eyes met the eyes of the others in the room as she tore open the sealed envelope. Inside was a greeting card. "To my dear friend," Katie read the printed quotation. Opening the card, she saw it was customizable blank.

The personal message therein was written in bold strokes. "You flatter me, Mrs. Webster," she read aloud. "I don't know who sent you such extravagant gifts, but I shan't be outdone." She looked up at Phil. "It's signed: B. Caballero."

CHAPTER THIRTY-ONE
Friday, Early Evening

"It makes no sense at all," Phil said to John during the drive to Mist Goddess. "Either he's telling the truth in the note—he hasn't been the one sending the gifts—or he's trying to throw us a curve ball."

"Which way do you vote?" John asked, leaning over from the restraint of the seat belt and looking out the front windshield. "We're going to be snowed under if this keeps up," he commented.

"Should make for very few people at the club."

John looked over at Phil and chuckled. "You think so, do you? What better place to stay warm than a gentleman's club?"

Phil slowed to a stop at a red light. "I wouldn't know. I've never gone into one. . .other than for business," he added with a jerk of his head.

John turned and looked at him head on. "Never?"

"Nope."

"Not even in college?"

"Not even in college."

John chuckled again. "Me neither, but if you tell that, I'll deny it."

Phil looked over at John and grinned, then turned his attention back to the traffic light as it turned green. "Back to your question. I don't know what Caballero is thinking. But I do tend to think that our little visit with Sharkey tonight will shed some light on the matter."

"You honestly don't think it's Sharkey?"

Phil slowly turned the steering wheel to the right. "I don't think Sharkey is smart enough to know a diamond from a CZ, but who knows. Maybe he is. Maybe he's got connections."

"Oh, you can bet he's got connections."

Phil remained silent until they had pulled into the parking garage near the club. As he switched off the ignition, he turned to John, "Let's go see what we can pull out of him."

Brittany tapped on the door of Jacqueline's precisely at six-fifteen, the time Katie had told her to arrive there. She heard the lock shift, and the door opened to reveal an exotic, petite woman with long dark hair pulled over one shoulder. "You must be Brittany."

Brittany nodded. "Zandra McKenzie?"

Zandra stepped back. "Won't you come in? My brother and I are in the office taking care of some end of the day business. Follow me."

Brittany thought the woman seemed very cool. Walking behind her, she attempted to imitate her gait, the way she held her back as though a broomstick was holding it into place, the gentle sway of her hips, the purposeful step of one foot directly in front of the other. Brittany frowned. Zandra McKenzie made it look simple, but it wasn't. At least, not for a woman who stood five-nine. Maybe when a woman was. . . what?. . .five-two if she were an inch. . .it was easier.

Brittany's eyes caught the expensive fabrics and designs around her. "You have beautiful things," she said politely.

"Thank you," Zandra said, without turning her head. When they reached the office, a room just off from where the cash register sat on a counter, Zandra fully opened a nearly shut door and announced, "Zane, she's here."

Brittany peered into the nondescript office to see a young man—a stunningly gorgeous young man, if she could be so bold to think it— sitting behind a large and modern black desk. He had a pencil wedged between his teeth and was using a small calculator. He looked up abruptly, pulled the pencil from between his teeth, jotted some figures onto the paper lying before him, then extended his hand for a handshake. "Brittany?"

Brittany took his hand. "Yes. You must be Zane."

"I am," he smiled. "Sit. . ." he looked around for a chair. "Somewhere," he ended with a laugh.

Brittany laughed with him, turned to Zandra, and noticed the lack of humor on her face.

"I'll get a chair from the front," Zandra said, then left the room, returning within a minute with an armed occasional chair. "Here we go," she said, placing the chair near the desk.

Brittany sat.

"So, Brittany, tell us something about yourself?" Zane asked. Zandra walked over to a disorganized shelf overflowing with boxes, wrapping paper, and ribbon and began to straighten.

Brittany clasped her hands in her lap to keep them steady. "What would you like to know?" she asked smiling, showing straight white teeth that seemed all the more white against her dark complexion.

"Have you worked in retail before?" Zane continued.

"Yes. When I was in high school. I worked in a small department store in my neighborhood. It wasn't much, but it was good experience."

"Where are you from?"

"Right here in the city. The Bronx actually."

"How long have you been working here at the hotel? Katie tells me you've been in housekeeping."

"Since October, yes." Brittany kept her voice calm. She didn't want to tell her new employers she had been a dancer. . .didn't want any reminders of her old lifestyle. Katie had taken her away from all that, and as far as she was concerned, it was history. Not just history, ancient history, and she hoped he wouldn't ask her where she had worked before meeting Katie.

Zane leaned back in his chair, held the pencil suspended between the fingers of both hands. "How'd you meet Katie? How do you know her?"

Brittany cocked her head to the left. "She's just a friend. I knew her before I came to work here."

"She seems like a nice lady."

"She's the best." Brittany smiled again.

Zandra turned from her work. "I can't make heads or tails out of all this, Zane. We need to get the Christmas paper off the shelves and onto these rolls."

Zane winked at Brittany, then looked back at Zandra. "Hold your horses, *Chica.*"

Brittany rested her elbows on the arms of the chair and leaned forward. "Where are you from? I detect a bit of an accent."

"Orlando originally. Our parents are from PR."

"Puerto Rico? Really?" Brittany asked. "I vacationed once in San Juan."

"What took you down there?" Zane asked, seemingly interested.

"My next door neighbor—from the old neighborhood—she and her family went back home one summer for a couple of weeks, and I got to go. It was nice. *Hot,* but very pretty, I remember."

Zandra made her way back to the desk and leaned against the side of Zane's chair, propping her weight against his shoulder. Her arm slid easily along his shoulders. Brittany smiled in understanding. These two were more than siblings. They were twins. They had known one another from their very moment of birth, perhaps even before, and the thought of that made her just a little awestruck at the work of God's hand. "We used to go every summer, too," Zandra said. "Zane loved it and I despised it. Remember, Zane?"

Zane looked up at her and smiled. "Oh, I remember. When Zandra doesn't get her way about something, she's pretty difficult to live with. Summer visits to Puerto Rico were miserable for her. . .and subsequently, the rest of us, too."

"So," Zandra said to Brittany, but with a pop of her hand against her brother's head, "You've known Katie for awhile?"

"No, not long really. But we've gotten to know one another fairly well in a short amount of time."

Zandra sat on the armrest of Zane's chair. "Is it true what they say about her husband?" The tone of the question sounded as though Zandra considered Brittany a confidant.

Brittany leaned back and crossed her legs. "I don't know what you've heard. . .he's been missing for nearly two years, if that's what you're talking about."

"I can't imagine how hard it must have been for her," Zane said.

"Well," Brittany interjected. "Yeah. I mean, surely. But she's doing a lot of good things. She's done real good with the business, I think."

"Speaking of business," Zane remarked, shifting his weight suddenly. "What do you know about the fashion business?"

"I've always loved nice clothes. I couldn't afford them, but when I was in high school, I would go down to the library and read the fashion books and magazines. I picked up a lot of knowledge there. I'm not totally fashion savvy, but I can learn." She looked from Zane to Zandra. "I can."

Zandra smiled a crooked smile. "When I was a little girl," she began, "I wore hand-me-downs."

"Me, too, girl," Brittany nodded. "I never owned a new thing in my life until I made my first dollar. Then I went out and bought a pair of new shoes." Brittany shook her head at the sadness of it all.

"I used to slip into the local grocery store and steal the latest copy of Cosmo," Zandra admitted. She squeezed Zane's shoulder. "Remember, Zane?"

"Oh, yes."

"I'd hide it between the mattresses of my bed, and when the house finally got quiet, Zane and I would pull it out, sneak out of the house with our father's flashlight and devour every page."

"I don't know how she talked me into that," Zane admitted. "But I used to whisper to her '*Chica*, one day we will wear fine clothes and live in pretty houses like the ones we see here in these pages.' Now we do."

Brittany nodded. "Dreams are nice."

"Dreams are everything," Zane agreed. "We all need them if we're going to succeed."

Zandra stood as though wanting to change the direction of the conversation. "I'll tell you what, Brittany. First thing tomorrow—nine o'clock—be here to start, okay?"

Brittany smiled. "Okay!"

"The first thing I want you to do is straighten out that gift wrap mess over there. Can you do that for me?"

"I can do it!"

Zane laughed. "When she's done with that, I want her to help me pick out the clothes for the fashion show."

Brittany raised her eyebrows, felt her heart pounding excitedly against the wall of her chest. "Fashion show?"

"We've been asked to take part in a holiday fashion show at Rockefeller Center. Katie has agreed to be a part of it."

"She'll be wonderful. I think she's the most beautiful woman in the world."

Zane stood and Brittany followed. He extended his hand, and she took it. "Welcome to Jacqueline's, Brittany. We'll start you out slowly, but soon enough you'll be selling top name fashion as though you've been doing it all your life."

Brittany smiled again and dipped her head to the right. "Thank you again. You won't be sorry you took me on. I promise."

CHAPTER THIRTY-TWO
Friday Night

Sharkey was nervous. Sweating bullets kind of nervous. He had two agents in the main section of his club; a shaking, Asian dancer hiding in one of the dressing rooms; and a powerful, determined man due to arrive at any moment.

It was Candy who came out of the nearly packed club to warn him of the agents' arrival.

"How do you know so much?"

"I recognize one of them as the man who comes to see Katie, that's why," she told him, narrowing her eyes in an I-dare-you-to-doubt-me attitude.

Sharkey looked from Candy to the office door and back to Candy again. "Wipe that look off your face, Little China. I believe you." He watched Candy flush in anger. She hated being called "Little China." Told him it was rude and prejudicial. He had showed her just what he thought of her opinion on the topic. He called her by that name for a week and swore to fire any of his other personnel who didn't do the same. Candy never complained about what he called her again, whether it be Little China or any other racial slur that might come to mind.

"He can't see me here."

"You say there's two of 'em this time?"

"What do you mean, this time?"

"Agent Silver came by the other night, but he was alone then." Sharkey paced from the door to where Candy stood.

"Well, this must be his partner or something."

Sharkey looked back at the door again and nodded. "Go sit in the dressing room. Do something with yourself while you're in there. You could use a little fixing up tonight anyway."

Candy crossed her arms. "What are you talking about, Sharkey? What the *heck* are you talking about?"

Sharkey sneered at her. "You! Look at you. Go fix up and quit thinking about what I gotta deal with out there, you hear me? Go." He jerked his head toward the door in dismissal. She didn't argue anymore; she ducked her head and walked out of the room and toward the dressing rooms farther down the hall.

Sharkey stood for a moment staring after her. She didn't need fixing up, he thought momentarily. Goodness knew she was one of the most beautiful creatures he'd ever seen, if she weren't so uppity all the time. One day, he thought, he'd break her like a filly, and she would really be his. Someone like that, loving someone like him. And, yeah, he knew he wasn't no Brad Pitt, but to the right woman, he could be. . .would be. . . a good provider.

For now, he had other concerns: more agents in his club. This could mean only one thing and that one thing connected Katie Webster to Bucky Caballero. He may as well find out what.

He walked out of his office and into the main area of the club where the cacophony of music, laughter, and idle chitchat nearly knocked him down. He smiled. They were nearly packed already, and it wasn't even eight o'clock. Cold weather was good for his business. Cold weather outside meant warm dancers inside. Men knew that, and so they came to the club in droves. Okay, so they weren't the best men society had to offer, but some were. Take Bucky Caballero, for example. If he—Sharkey—could strike up the right business arrangement with Mr. C (as he thought of him), then the upstanding Mr. C would bring in more of the right kind of people. This was just good business decision-making on his part, Sharkey concluded with a chomp of the short stogie clenched between his teeth.

Then, too, there was the man Candy despised, but the one Sharkey made her dance for regularly. Sharkey didn't know his name, but he knew—from what Jimmy told him—he had connections into the kind of business that could bring good money into his club. After all, that was the bottom line, wasn't it? It wasn't really about *who* so much as it was about *how much*. The better the clientele, the more money they had to spend. The more money, the sooner Sharkey could go uptown with his girls. Yeah, he liked that. He liked that a lot.

What he didn't like was having two federal agents in his club. This could be bad for business. He looked around for Jimmy and spotted him near the front door, then made his way over to him quickly. "You seen two men looking like 'the man' coming in just a bit ago?" he asked the brute, raising his voice to be heard over the noise.

"You mean the two fellas sitting over near the bar?" With a nod of his head, Jimmy indicated a table toward the bar.

Sharkey followed Jimmy's eyes. "Yeah, that's them. Gotta be them; Silver's one of 'em."

"Who are they, Boss? You need me? Need me to rough 'em up?"

Sharkey looked at Jimmy as though he had completely lost his mind. "You know, Jimmy, sometimes I think you're just itching for a fight."

Jimmy smiled at the thought.

"No, you idiot, I don't need you. Not that I don't appreciate the gesture," he added, because—if truth be told—he didn't want to make Jimmy mad enough to quit. "Just keep an eye on the door, if you don't mind." Sharkey took a step, then turned back. "And, Jimmy. . .if the man from the other night comes in. . .you know who I'm talking about?"

"Yeah, Boss. I know." Jimmy appeared excited, as though he were about to be let in on a big operation. Maybe he was, Sharkey thought. Maybe he was.

"The second. . .the absolute second. . .you see him step through that door, you spin him around and back outside, you hear me? Bring him in the back way to my office. Tell him Candy's in the dressing room. She can fill him in and take him up the back stairs to the private rooms. Got that?"

"Yeah, Boss." Jimmy nodded, folding his arms across his beefy chest and leaning over for a better look at Sharkey's face.

"Repeat it back to me."

"Stranger comes in, turn him around, take him to the back. Candy's in the dressing room. She'll explain and take him upstairs. Got it."

Sharkey sighed deeply. "Good boy." He reached up and patted Jimmy on the cheek. Jimmy sprang upright, embarrassed. Sharkey made his move toward the table where the agents sat. As soon as he approached, the men swung their attention from panning the room to focusing just on him.

"Gentlemen? Mr. Silver, I see you can't get enough of my girls," Sharkey said, making a stab at humor to hide his anxiety.

Silver did not seem pleased. "Mr. Garone, this is Agent Weaver," he said as both men stood. "We need to ask you a few questions. I thought perhaps we'd go somewhere a little. . .quieter. Your office?"

Sharkey looked back at Jimmy, then to the door leading to his office. "Yeah, yeah. Uh—sure."

Sharkey began to walk toward the back of the club, aware that the agents had noted his stalling tactics, his mind racing a hundred miles an hour. *What to do? Candy in the back. . .Caballero on his way. . .play it cool, Sharkey, my boy. Play it cool.* Sharkey glanced to the left and the right of him, wanting to note who of his regulars might be there. . .who might see him going to the back with these two men who obviously didn't belong there. He grimaced when he saw the man who always asked for Candy. He'd be asking for her tonight, too, but as it stood, Sharkey couldn't afford to have her come out. He also couldn't afford for her *not* to.

Sharkey opened the door to the back and stepped aside to allow the agents to go in ahead of him. Agent Silver stepped in first and assumed the role of leading the way. The hinged door closed behind them, and the sounds from the dance floor muted and eventually faded as they entered Sharkey's office. Sharkey closed the door, extended his hand to offer them a seat, and this time Silver accepted. Sharkey moved to sit behind his desk.

"Mr. Silver, I don't know why you've returned." Sharkey forced a smile, which faded immediately. "I told you everything there was to tell you the other night."

Silver crossed his legs comfortably. "Yes, I'm sure you did. But I thought we'd stop by on the off-chance that you might have remembered something and. . .I don't know. . .perhaps lost my card."

Sharkey opened the middle drawer of his desk and pulled the card from where he had placed it the day before. "Got it right here," he said, flashing it. "See?" He closed the drawer by pushing on it with his belly.

"Then should we take it you haven't remembered anything?" The other agent spoke.

"Agent—"

"Weaver."

"Agent Weaver. I have nothing to tell you. I haven't been to the hotel in a week. Haven't caused any ruckus recently, if you know what I mean." Sharkey bit a little harder on his cigar. "I don't think anyone would blame me for it, you understand." He shifted his focus from Weaver to Silver and back to Weaver again. "You know, I suppose, that Mrs. Webster took three of my girls."

"Yes, I've heard."

Sharkey noted how stoic this man's expression was. He didn't like it. He didn't like it at all. He reopened his desk drawer and threw the card back in, again closing the drawer with his belly. "I haven't heard from them in months. *Months*. Good girls, too. I mean, as far as dancers go." He laughed nervously, but the agents didn't join him. His smile faded again.

Agent Weaver looked down at his hands and massaged the top of one with the other, as though he were trying to rub out an imaginary pain. "Mr. Garone, let me be honest with you. I've got a bit of a problem with you." He looked up sharply.

Sharkey rested his forearms on the edge of his desk and flexed his shoulders. "Yeah, well, I got a problem with you, too."

Agent Weaver leaned forward. "I keep thinking: *Who* more than Garone has a reason to upset the apple cart over at THP?"

"THP—"

"The Hamilton Place," Agent Silver supplied.

"Not me!" Sharkey stood. "I don't know what you are trying to pin on me, but I'll tell you right now, I got rights!"

"Sit down, Mr. Garone. No one's pinning anything on you. We're just here to reason out why it's *not* you doing these things."

Sharkey sat. "Yeah, yeah."

"Because," Weaver continued, "if it's not you, then the question that lingers in my mind is *who?*"

"Don't know. Can't help you with that. Anything else? If not, I'll walk you to the door." Sharkey was ready to get these men out of his club. He looked down at his watch quickly. Caballero would be there any minute. Any minute.

"And," Agent Weaver continued, "we thought about you being able to send gifts such as the ones Mrs. Webster has received."

"I already told you. I can't afford it." He looked down at his watch again. Mere seconds had passed since the last time he looked, but it felt like hours.

"Gifts like necklaces."

"Necklaces?" Sharkey looked up.

"Diamonds. Pearls. You know."

"No, I don't know." He took the stogie out of his mouth, threw it in the trash and reached into a drawer for another.

"Flowers."

"What kind of flowers?" Sharkey began to light the cigar. His hands trembled, and he cursed them for doing so.

"Don't you know?"

"I told you I didn't."

"What do you know about art, Mr. Garone?"

"Art? What kind of art?" He shoved the cigar into his mouth and began to puff.

"Ever hear of Delaroche?"

"Dela-what?"

"He was a French painter."

Sharkey laughed nervously. *"Moi?* French art?" His smile faded again. He puffed harder on the cigar.

"Why not you? A man of your stature in the business. You said you've been around since you were a pup. . ."

"Yeah, yeah, but not me. I mean, maybe someone like Bucky Caba—" Sharkey cut his eyes to the office door and back to the agents.

Their eyes met his. He flexed his shoulders again. "Not me. I don't know nothing about art or flowers or necklaces." Sharkey stood. "Gentlemen, I got a club to run. I'm going to have to ask you to leave."

The two agents followed. "You'll call me if you think of anything?" Silver asked.

"Yeah, yeah," Sharkey sat. "You'll forgive me now if I don't walk you out."

Sharkey watched as Silver turned to Weaver. "I think you were right, Weaver. He doesn't know anything. This is a dead end."

"I said that, didn't I?" Sharkey asked, though neither man turned to him.

"I'm afraid so," Weaver responded to Silver.

Silver turned to Sharkey now and smiled. "Thank you for your time anyway."

"Yeah, yeah." Sharkey pretended to shift his attention to some papers near the telephone. He heard the door open and the muffled sounds from beyond slipped in again.

"Sounds like business is good, Mr. Garone," Weaver commented.

"Yeah, yeah," Sharkey said quietly. He sat, continuing to gaze at the papers for a few moments, then raised his eyes. The men were gone.

The men were gone, and he was in a lot of trouble.

Phil and John stopped outside the doors of Mist Goddess, pulled their coats a little tighter around their necks and looked at one another. "What are you thinking?" Phil asked as they turned toward the parking garage.

"That we might want to take advantage of the evening and check out some of the private airstrips."

"May as well. I need to call the wife and let her know this could take awhile."

"Yeah, me too." The two men walked in silence for several feet before Phil added, "So, what do you think about Mr. Garone?"

John looked up. "I think the snow has stopped." A puff of cold air lingered in the air around his mouth.

Phil looked up, too. "Wretched stuff." He understood John didn't want to express his thoughts just yet.

The men continued toward the parking garage in silence. As soon as they settled into the icy interior of Phil's Crown Victoria, Phil turned the ignition and began to fiddle with the heat.

"Your man Sharkey in there is a liar," John commented matter-of-factly.

Phil looked at him with a looked of bemusement. "Ya think?"

John laughed. "Let's think about this for a minute, shall we? Did you get the impression he was looking for someone to walk into the club any minute?"

"He looked at the front door. . .his watch. . .his office door. I wonder what instructions he gave to the big guy at the door before he walked over to our table."

"Exactly. What would make a man do that unless he's expecting company?"

"Could be. . .could be one of the girls from THP. Katie's having some doubts about one of them. Worried she's been going back to the club." Phil reached into his pocket for a stick of gum.

"This could be where information is being supplied. My other thought was—"

"You don't even have to tell me your other thought. Caballero." He tri-folded the gum and popped it into his mouth. "Gum?" he asked John.

"No. Thanks." John looked out the passenger's window and into the semidarkness of the garage. "What possible connection would Caballero have to Sharkey Garone?" he asked, turning back to Phil.

"You mean other than the obvious? Katie Webster?"

"Katie Webster may be enough. Then again, maybe not." John was silent for a moment. He looked out the window again and back to Phil. "Are you *really* ready to check out the airports? Might be a bit premature."

Phil grabbed the keys from the ignition and switched the car off. "Let's see what might be across the street from the club. Maybe there's a coffee shop or someplace warm where we can watch the front door."

Both men exited the car, shutting the doors behind them quietly. "What if our man Caballero doesn't walk in the front door? What if he walks in the back door?"

Phil grimaced as the two men headed back toward the city street. "All right. I'll take a post near the back. You take whatever warm spot you can find near the front."

John grinned at him devilishly. "After all, it's your case."

"Yeah." Phil agreed, ducking his head slightly against the intensity of cold air that rushed around him as they stepped out of the parking garage. "Yeah."

"They're gone?" Candy stood before Sharkey's desk, shivering.

"Yeah, yeah." Sharkey stood on the other side. "Those men know too much."

"Do you have a number for Mr. Caballero?"

Sharkey gave her a sharp look. "Worried about your new friend, Little China? Don't you think he's a little old for you?"

"Stop calling me that, Sharkey!" Candy flinched when Sharkey made a quick move toward her, then stopped just as abruptly. He snickered at her, and she stuck out her tongue at him. It was the only thing she knew to do. "It's not like that anyway," she said, smoothing her dress around her hips. "He's a nice man, and he's going to help me. . ."

"Help you what?" Sharkey narrowed his eyes. He moved around the desk so quickly Candy didn't have time to think of retreating. Grabbing her forearms, he squeezed tightly. She looked down, saw the tough, tanned flesh against her golden complexion, and she grit her teeth against the pain.

"You're hurting me, Sharkey."

"I'll do more than hurt you," he said, squeezing tighter, "if you even so much as think about leaving this city with Caballero."

Candy didn't say anything.

"Do you understand me?" he squeezed tighter still.

"Yes," Candy whispered through her teeth.

"Yes? Is that all you can say?"

Candy looked into the coldness of Sharkey's eyes. "What do you want me to say, Sharkey?" Her teeth were pressed so hard together she was afraid they would break. "Yes, *Sir*? Is that what you want? Do you want me on my knees to you again and again? Night after night? Ouch! Sharkey, let go of me!"

"Not until you tell me you aren't leaving."

"I'm not leaving." She looked down at her arms again.

He jerked her toward him. "Look me in the eyes, Little China."

She looked him in the eyes. "I'm not leaving," she spat out.

Sharkey jerked her toward him, closer still, pressed his thin, wet lips against hers as he wrapped his short arms around her small frame. She pressed against his shoulders with the palms of her hands, pushing hard to stop the kiss. She moaned in protest, but to no avail. When he finally released her, she spit at him, and he slapped her soundly across the face. She fell to the floor, covered her head with her arms, and curled into a fetal position. Sharkey reached down, grabbed her wrists, and pulled her to her feet so she was standing before him. He pushed her roughly, and she stumbled, but regained her balance. He pushed her again. This time she fell against the old sofa opposite Sharkey's desk, landing on her back.

"No!" she screamed, as Sharkey loomed over her. "No!" She pushed herself away from the sofa, but Sharkey pressed her back down.

"Too good for me? Is that it?" Sharkey held her against the rough fibers of the sofa with the palms of his hands against her chest and his knee and shin pressed firmly across her thighs.

Candy's eyes went wild. "Get off of me, Sharkey. Get off me!" She bucked her body as best she could, seeking escape from a man who had held her captive in more ways than one.

Sharkey's hands went around Candy's throat, and for a brief moment Candy thought he would kill her. The smell of hot, old tobacco faded, and her ears clogged. His face began to blur. She felt her eyes roll back and her body begin to shudder. A buzzing sound rang through her ears. Was this the sound a person hears before death, she wondered, as suddenly her captor released her, jerking himself toward the desk. Candy fell to the floor, gasping for air as she wrapped her hands around her throat.

"Yeah, yeah!" Sharkey was screaming into the phone. "Yeah, Mr. Caballero," he said loudly.

Candy scrambled to her feet, grabbing for one of the chairs in front of Sharkey's desk. *Bucky Caballero was on the other end of that phone call*, she thought. *Bucky Caballero. . .* "You were going to kill me, you pig!" she screamed, loudly enough to be heard by her new ally. Her throat burned from the assault.

Sharkey slammed the phone down on the desk, then just as quickly brought it back up to his ear. "Sorry, Mr. Caballero. I'm having problems with one of my girls. . .you know how it can be. . .yeah, yeah. . . yes, Sir. . . *Xi Lan?* You mean Candy?. . .Yeah, yeah." Sharkey extended the phone toward Candy. "Say one word of what just happened here, and I *will* kill you," he whispered. "I'll cut you into tiny little pieces and feed you to the pigeons."

Candy took a deep breath as she took the phone and exhaled. "Hello."

"Xi Lan, my love. Is that you?"

"Yes, Mr. Caballero," she answered meekly, wrapping her fingers around her bruised throat.

"Are you all right?"

"Yes."

"Has he hurt you?"

Xi Lan could hear concern in Mr. Caballero's voice. "Yes."

"I want you to listen to me." Xi Lan heard the sound of traffic in the background on the other end of the line. "I'm leaving now. I've got to get out now while I still can, but by the first of next week, I'll call you at the hotel. You'll be picked up and brought to me then. Don't say a word to anyone, do you understand?"

"Yes." Xi Lan looked down, then back up at Sharkey. "Yes, Sir, I understand. I'll do whatever Sharkey tells me to do."

There was a pause from the other end. "Good girl, Puppet. You're my girl. I'll take care of everything."

"I'm sure Sharkey will be happy to help you with whatever you want us to do," Xi Lan continued in her ruse.

Mr. Caballero laughed on the other end. "You're good, Precious. No wonder you and I get along so well."

Xi Lan smiled in spite of herself.

"Give the phone back to Mr. Sharkey now, will you? You'll hear from me soon."

Candy gave the phone back to Sharkey, looking him bravely in the eyes. "He wants to talk to you."

Candy took a few steps and then sat in the nearest chair. She pressed her face into her hands and allowed her thoughts to drown out the sound of Sharkey's voice. Mr. Caballero was going to send someone for her. Only a few more days of this hell she called life. Just a few more days and she was free. . .free to begin again. . .free to call her mother and brother. . . free to live like a real human being. . .with Mr. Caballero and his sister. . . in Canada. . .free. . .free. . .I've made a deal with the devil, she thought, but it beats the one I've made with his little demon over there.

She felt a sudden pop against her head, and she looked up.

"Sleeping?" Sharkey asked her, taking the seat next to her.

"No."

Sharkey scooted his chair closer to hers and touched her arm gently. "Look, Candy. I'm sorry, okay?"

Candy narrowed her eyes as she looked over at him. "What did you just say?"

"I said that I'm sorry."

Candy laughed. "Boy, Mr. Caballero must have some power over you." She watched Sharkey fight off his anger.

"Let me see your neck." He reached toward her, but she jerked back slightly.

"I'm okay."

"Let me see." His voice was unusually gentle but commanding. She'd never seen this side of him.

She tilted her head back slightly and allowed his fingertips to lightly brush across her sensitive flesh.

"You'll need to wear turtlenecks for a few days."

Candy lowered her chin. "What did Mr. Caballero say to you?"

"He's leaving now. He saw the detectives leaving a little while ago. But he's got one more thing for us to do. Are you up to it?"

"Would it matter if I weren't?"

Sharkey grinned. "No." He stood, walked over to his desk, and opened a drawer. He pulled out a large box containing small books of matches. He retrieved one and handed it to Candy.

"What's this?"

"Matches."

"I can see that. What's Private Dancer?" Candy asked, looking at the logo on the cover of the book of matches.

"It used to be my old man's club. . .and, it just so happens it's where I met Katie Webster for the first time."

"Katie?" Candy looked up sharply.

"That's right. She used to be a dancer there. . .way back when. . ."

Candy looked down at the matchbook. "You've got to be kidding." But then she paused. "So that's how she knows so much about the life."

"She was a good one, I'll tell you that. My old man used to say he'd never met anyone like her before she arrived or after she left."

Candy swallowed hard, watching Sharkey pace back and forth like a caged animal. "What happened? Why'd she leave the club?"

Sharkey stopped for a moment, long enough to take another book out of the box. "Found a better place. More uptown. What was it. . .yeah, yeah. West End Men's Club, or something like that."

"Is it still there?"

"No. But then, what is? All the good places are gone, replaced by newer ones. . .where girls like you join unions and such."

Candy smiled briefly. "You're the last in a long line of the way it used to be, huh, Sharkey?"

Sharkey smiled back at her. "You got that right."

Candy looked down at the matchbook again. "So what am I going to do with this? Burn down The Hamilton Place?"

Sharkey had picked up a pen from his desk, poised to write something on a nearby notepad. He pointed the tip of the pen toward Candy and smirked, "You got a pretty good idea there, little girl, but no. Not this week anyway. Give me a second here, and I'll tell you what you're gonna do." He resumed writing the note he had begun, and Candy licked her lips as she gripped the matchbook tighter in her hand. Sharkey chuckled, not seeing Candy's frown as he said, "She may have gotten away before, but not this time. Not *this* time."

CHAPTER THIRTY-THREE

"Where are you, Mrs. Webster?"

It was a lovely fall afternoon in the Hamptons. The leaves had begun to change color, setting the trees ablaze with tones of red, orange, and golden yellow. Katie and Ben decided to take a leisurely walk down a winding dirt path too narrow for most automobiles, but perfect for lovers who wished to stroll hand in hand. They had been walking for nearly a half hour, but for Katie it felt like only a moment in time. Why couldn't time stand still? Why couldn't she be with Ben like this forever?

"Hmm?"

Ben smiled at her. "I asked you where you were. . .walking along all starry eyed and dreamy."

Katie smiled back at him. "Oh," she said, then thought for a moment before answering. "Somewhere between reality and the place where dreams are made." She brought his hand up to her lips and kissed the knuckles.

Ben tilted his head back slightly, took in a deep breath and sighed. "Did you ever smell anything so crystal clear in your life?"

Katie did the same while shoving her free hand into the pocket of her light jacket. "No. Never. It's freeing."

Ben frowned at her a bit. "Are you cold?"

Katie shook her head, no. Her chestnut hair floated around her shoulders, a small strand of it caught on her lips. Ben stopped, pulled the hair gently from captivity, then replaced it with his lips, gently at first, then more arduously. Katie pulled her hands free, wrapping her arms around his broad shoulders, and gave in to the surge of emotion she always felt when her husband kissed her like this. When they finally broke for air, she leaned back and laughed lightly. A burst of sunlight winked at her from beyond the tree branches. "Where did you learn to kiss like that, Mr. Webster?"

He smiled back at her. "What was her name?" he teased.

Katie raised an eyebrow. "Ashley Silvia Trenton?" she toyed.

Ben laughed heartily, then turned his wife back toward the road and their walk. "Ashley Silvia Trenton. The biggest snob I've ever known."

"She sure had her eyes on you." Katie cut her eyes teasingly up at her husband.

Ben blushed appropriately. "She certainly did at that."

"Ah-ha!" Katie stopped and turned back to Ben and grinned. "I knew it! I knew it all along! You're in love with Ashley!" She pouted for effect.

Ben grabbed his wife's shoulders playfully. "Take it back."

"No." Katie's eyes danced in merriment.

"Take it back or else."

"Or else what?"

"Or else. . .or else. . .I won't tell you where I'm taking you for Christmas this year!"

Katie relaxed in his grip. "You're taking me somewhere for Christmas? Where? Tell me, Ben. Tell me."

Ben wrapped his arm around his wife's shoulder and drew her close as the walk continued. "Oh, no. First, you apologize for the Ashley remark."

"I apologize. Where are you taking me?"

Ben chuckled again. "You're like a kid in a candy store."

"I'm like a kid at FAO Schwartz during the holiday season," Katie corrected.

Ben nodded. "That's even better. I like that."

"But it would have been better if you'd said it."

"Of course."

"I agree. Now, where are you taking me?"

"As it turns out, a friend of mine has the most charming little chalet near the Lötschen Valley. . ."

"Where is that?"

"It's part of the Swiss Alps."

Katie felt as though she were about to burst. "Are you serious? You're taking me to the Swiss Alps for Christmas?"

"Don't forget about the little chalet."

Katie stopped in their walk again and turned to face her husband. "Ben, I know you. When you say 'little' it's big. But, I don't care about that. I've never seen the Alps." She clapped her hands for effect. "I'm going to the Alps! I'm going to the Alps!"

Ben laughed again. "Okay, hold my hand and walk with me. I'll tell you the truth."

Katie frowned. "The truth? You aren't taking me to the Alps?"

"Yes, Sweetheart, I'm taking you to the Alps. I want to tell you the truth about the little chalet."

"Oh."

They began to walk again and Katie listened to her husband as he described the place he would be taking her. "You'll be so impressed. It truly is perfect. Perfect for healing from emotional bruises and things like that."

"And Christmas holidays?"

"Most especially Christmas holidays. It's very French Country. Stone fireplaces and hearths and polished stone floors with scattered rugs. Louis Philippe furniture. Fantastic tapestries and a kitchen filled with lots of baskets hanging from the ceiling."

"I love it already."

"You will love it more when you see it. The countryside is breathtaking, Katie. In the morning, if we wake up early enough, we can sit outside and sip on hot French coffee and watch the sun rising over the lake behind my friend's place."

"A lake?"

"A fantastic lake. Mist on the water. . ."

"It sounds magical."

"It is. In the distance, you can hear the cow bells echoing up through the valley."

Katie stopped walking and turned to her husband again. "Take me there, Ben. Take me there, now."

She closed her eyes. Cupping her face in his hands, Ben kissed her again. Again and again and again until she was breathless from the sheer pleasure of it. His lips traced a line from her mouth to her eyes and finally to her ear where he whispered something to her in French. . .something she couldn't quite make out in the feathery softness of it.

She kept her eyes closed as she asked, "What?" Her voice was nearly inaudible.

He said it again.

"I don't understand," she whispered back.

"Yes, you do." He spoke into her ear, nibbling here and there as he made love to her with his words.

"No. No, I don't understand."

"Listen. Listen with your heart, not your ears."

He released her face, took a step back from her, said the words a third time, then fell silent. Katie's breathing was slow and steady as she tried to decipher the words. "I don't know," she whispered again, then became aware of the stillness and silence around her. She opened her eyes.

He was gone. He was gone, and she stood alone on a small country lane leading nowhere.

CHAPTER THIRTY-FOUR
Saturday, December 8, 2001
Early Morning

"What are you doing up?" Marcy, clad in red and green plaid flannel pajamas and dark socks, shuffled into the kitchen. Katie stood at the open refrigerator door, reaching for a pitcher of orange juice on the top shelf. She jumped slightly, then gave a heavy sigh.

"Did I wake you?" She whispered back to her friend, who had leaned over the kitchen island, which was graced by a bowl of fruit, topped by a cluster of white grapes. She plucked one with her finger and popped it into her mouth.

"No. I woke up a few minutes ago and had actually sat up to do some reading. I heard you when you came out of your bedroom. What's wrong?"

Katie closed the refrigerator door quietly, set the pitcher on the island near Marcy, then reached into a nearby cabinet for two glasses. "Juice?" she asked.

"Sure." Marcy straightened.

Katie poured cold orange juice into the glasses and offered one to Marcy. "I had a dream," she said, by way of answering Marcy's earlier question.

The two friends sat at the bar and sipped their juice.

"Nightmare?" Marcy asked.

Katie shook her head, no. "Not really." She placed her elbows on the black marble bar, brought her head down a bit, and tucked her hair behind her ears.

"Did you dream about Ben?" Marcy's question was quiet and understanding.

Katie nodded, then surprised herself as a torrent of tears streamed down her cheeks. "I'm sorry. I'm sorry," was all she could say.

Marcy slipped off the bar stool and walked across the room to the other side of the kitchen where she pulled a napkin from a retro chrome napkin holder, then brought it back over. "Here. Blow," she instructed maternally.

Katie obeyed, took a deep breath, and regained her composure. Marcy hiked herself back up on the stool and placed her hand on Katie's shoulder.

"Sorry," Katie said again.

"It's okay. I know how I'd be if it were Charlie."

Katie looked over at Marcy, with her eyes red-rimmed and glossy. She sniffled lightly. "I miss him so much."

"I know you do. Do you want to tell me about the dream?"

Katie's shoulders slumped a bit. "It was about the time. . .not too long after we married. . ."

"You dreamed about something that really happened?"

"Yes, but. . ."

"But?"

"Well, it. . .it didn't exactly happen as I dreamt it. In the dream, Ben and I were walking down this path that cuts through the woods near our country home. . ."

"Ah, yes."

Katie smiled briefly. She knew how much Marcy loved to tease her about her "weekend house."

"Sorry. Go ahead." Marcy took a sip of juice.

"We were just walking. The leaves had turned so it must have been in the fall of the year. And the weather was crisp and cool, but not too cold yet. We were talking. . .and talking. . .and he said he was going to

314

take me someplace wonderful for Christmas. He said he was going to take me to the Alps."

"The Alps?"

"Yes. Which he actually *did*. Our first Christmas together after we married, he took me there. But back then—in real life, so to speak—we stayed at this marvelous hotel owned by a friend of his father's." Katie narrowed her eyes. "In the dream, he said he was taking me to a quaint chalet that belonged to a friend of *his*."

"Okay," Marcy said sweetly. "What do you think that means? I mean, if you were into dream interpretation and stuff like that."

Katie drained her glass of juice. "I'm not. . .so I don't know. I just know what I dreamt." She tilted her head a bit. "It's the end of the dream that upsets me the most, I think."

"What happened?"

"One minute he was there, kissing me." Katie touched her lips with her fingertips. "He kissed my lips, my eyes, my ear." Her hand went to her eyes and ear. "Then he whispered something, but I couldn't understand it because it was in French."

"But you speak French."

"I know, I know. I do now, but back then I didn't, and it was as if I couldn't understand him in my dream because when we were first married, I couldn't understand it. Does that make any sense?"

Marcy smiled. "Sure."

Katie frowned. "No, it doesn't."

"Sure, it does."

Katie shook her head. "I'm insane."

"You most assuredly are not. Don't even go there. So, tell me. What did he say?"

"I don't know. I really don't know. He said, 'Listen with your heart, not your ears.' And then he said it again, and. . .my eyes were closed, you know, because he had been kissing me. When I opened them, he was gone. He had just vanished and, for the life of me, I can't figure out what he said to me. But—"

"But?"

"It's like, it's important that I figure it out." Katie's shoulders rose and fell with a heavy sigh.

Marcy raked her teeth over her bottom lip. "You know what?"

"What?"

"I'll bet that in the morning, when you wake up, you'll remember. It'll just come to you out of nowhere."

"You think?"

Marcy slid off the stool again, reaching for her glass and Katie's. "I say, we go back to my room, cuddle up under that warm comforter and talk like old times. When we wake up in the morning, it'll probably be the first thing to pop into your head."

Katie slid off her stool and followed Marcy to the sinks where she carefully set the glasses down. "I like that idea," Katie said. "But I can't talk too long." The two women began to walk out of the kitchen. "I have to work a little while tomorrow morning to wrap up some things that haven't received proper attention this week, and I'm having a phone conference with some people in Wyoming about the spa I want to build."

Marcy frowned. "Don't you people ever stop working around here?"

"Not here," Katie shook her head lightly. "This is New York. New Yorkers work hard, play hard. . ." she paused. "And we're survivors."

Marcy wrapped an arm around Katie and squeezed. "Glad you finally realized that."

CHAPTER THIRTY-FIVE

Phil and John hurried for the warmth of the car still secure in the parking garage near Mist Goddess. It was after three o'clock in the morning. The heat came on and began to warm them; still neither man appeared very happy. "Do you know how many cups of coffee I had in that coffee shop?" John asked.

Phil frowned. "Don't go there with me. I nearly froze back behind that club. And for what? Nothing. Not a single person came in or out that back door."

"You know, I always imagined the personnel walking out the back door of establishments like that, but it was obvious that most of the girls are picked up by their boyfriends or husbands through the front door. I didn't see a single one walk out alone."

Phil dismissed John's observation. "So now what have we got? Do you think it's been Caballero all along?"

"No. I take that back. One did," John continued his original thought. "An Asian girl. Hunkered down in her jacket, slipped into a cab and was out of there."

"Because his little gift yesterday would suggest not."

"Unless he wants us to believe he didn't send the other gifts. His way of throwing us off."

"That could be."

"Then again, a man like Caballero wants credit for his misdeeds."

"True, which is why he sent a signed note with the painting last night." Phil shoved the car into reverse and began to pull away from the parking space. "I don't suppose there's any hope that Kabakjian is keeping accurate records on who purchases his merchandise and where it's going."

John frowned. "Don't count on it. Okay, let me tell you what my instincts tell me here. He's still the man you're looking for in the disappearance of William Webster, but I don't think he's the one sending Katie Webster gifts. Which means what you basically have here is stalking. . .and mild stalking at that. And the fragments of information you have are not a lot to go on."

Phil slowed the car at the exit of the parking garage, lowered the window to pay the attendant. When he had pulled into the street he said, "What are you saying?"

John threw up his hands. "I'm saying until you've got a little more, you've got nothing."

CHAPTER THIRTY-SIX

Katie spent the remainder of the night restless in Marcy's bed. Her mind played the dream over and over again, pushing to determine what Ben had said to her. But the words wouldn't come.

When the alarm went off in her bedroom at 5:30, she wasn't there to hear it, but Maggie did. A few minutes later, the near-frantic British housekeeper opened the door to Marcy's room. "Oh, there you are, dear child!" Maggie exclaimed. "Whatever are you doing in here?"

Katie sat up, pushing the heavy cover away from her. She realized she had fallen asleep, though it couldn't have been for long because she felt as though a truck had run over her. "I had a nightmare and came in to sleep with Marcy."

Marcy remained supine and under the cover. "Just like old times, Maggie. Katie and I used to spend hours and hours in the same bed. . . chatting. . . giggling. . . ."

Maggie smiled. "Old chums are good for the soul. Miss Katie, I'll prepare breakfast for you now, unless you wish go into your office a little later."

Katie swung her legs over the side of the bed. "No, Maggie. I've worked on less sleep than this."

Marcy grinned at her. "But you were younger."

Katie frowned back at her best friend. "Ha. Ha."

Maggie stepped out into the hallway. "Hurry up now, Child."

Katie grinned obediently. "Yes, Ma'am. I'll take my shower and be right in." Her last thought as she left Marcy's room was that she still did not know what Ben had said to her in the dream.

Katie arrived at the office by eight-thirty and, as Katie had requested, Vickey was there to meet her. "Good morning, Vickey. Thank you for coming down for a few hours this morning."

Vickey, who sat at her desk and was already at work, looked up. "What happened to you?"

Katie stopped short and looked down at herself. "What do you mean?"

Vickey leaned over, resting her arms on the desk. "What are those? Circles under your eyes?"

Katie slumped just a bit. "I know. Bad night. Even Coco Chanel couldn't hide it."

"I'll get the coffee," Vickey stood, then walked around the desk.

Katie turned as she passed her, following her with her eyes. "Thank you, Vickey," she said, before turning to enter the closed door of her office. When she opened it, she stopped short and took a step backward. "Vickey?" she called out, her voice forceful. When Vickey didn't answer, she called out again. "Vickey?"

She heard Vickey's footsteps coming back down the hall. "You called?" she asked, peering around the door to her office. One look on her employer's face, however, and she came fully into the room. "What? What is it?"

"Have you been in my office this morning?"

Vickey took several steps toward where Katie stood in the open doorway. "No, why—*dear Lord in heaven!*" She pushed past Katie, who then followed behind her. "*Who* did this?"

The two women stood before Katie's desk, devoid of all desktop contents, which had been scattered about the room. Files were opened, the papers strewn hither and yon. The phone was lying on its side, the handset disconnected from it and the cord disconnected from the wall.

A crystal paperweight had been shattered; the fragments glistened in the carpet. Katie's chair had been turned to face the window behind it. Katie inhaled. The scent of Kouros Fraicheur permeated the room.

"Ben," Katie whispered.

Apparently her assistant also smelled the cologne. "Kouros Fraicheur."

Katie began to wrestle with her thoughts. "Was your office door locked last night?" she asked.

"Of course it was," Vickey answered quickly. "You know me better than that. I never walk out into that hallway at the end of the day without locking the door."

"Was it locked when you came in this morning?"

"Yes." Vickey bent down to pick up some papers at her feet.

"Don't, Vickey." *Was Vickey avoiding her line of questions?* She took a deep breath before continuing. "We need to call Phil first."

Vickey straightened. "You're right. I'll call him from my office." She turned and left the room. Katie moved toward the chair behind her desk, carefully stepping over and between the fragments of glass and scattered papers. When she came to it, she looked down at the seat inquisitively. What appeared to be a small piece of folded paper lay in its center. Assuming it to be from her desktop, Katie leaned over to retrieve it, flipping it over in the palm of her hand. What she saw startled her, and she gasped.

She was holding an old matchbook from Private Dancer.

She took a step backward, then another and another until she was able to turn and walk out her office door. She heard Vickey's voice explaining to Phil what they had found. When she reached her assistant, she extended her empty palm and said, "Give me the phone." Her voice was ominous and her expression stoic.

Vickey looked at her curiously. "Katie?" she asked, her voice laced with concern.

"What is it?" Katie could hear Phil's muffled voice from the handset of the phone. Vickey's hand had lowered the phone away from her ear.

"Give me the phone," Katie repeated.

Vickey complied. As Katie took it from her, and brought it to her own ear, she took in a deep breath and—almost without exhaling—said, "Phil, whatever you do, don't call the police." She could hear the sound of traffic behind him. He was on his car phone, no doubt on his way to work.

"Katie, this is breaking and—"

Katie squeezed the matchbook in her hand. "No, Phil. Don't. Just come yourself. No one else, you understand?"

There was a pause, a silence that began to fill with understanding. "I'll be right there," he said.

Katie told Vickey she wanted to be alone.

"Katie, what's wrong?" Vickey implored. "What are you holding in your hand?"

"You don't know?" Katie raised her eyebrows, hating herself for even thinking Vickey might be involved.

"Know what?"

Katie squeezed the matchbook again. "Nothing." She turned to reenter her office.

Vickey took a step toward her. "No. Katie, what is going on here?"

Katie turned, now standing just inside her office door. "It doesn't matter. Just stay in your office and work. Take all messages. I won't. . .I won't accept any calls while Phil is here."

Vickey dipped her chin. "Okay." There was a lilt of question in her voice.

Katie turned back toward her upturned office. She glanced over to the sofas, where apparently nothing had been touched. "I'll just sit over here until Phil arrives."

"Do you want me to bring you anything? Tea? Coffee?"

"Tea, but not until Phil arrives." Katie closed the door behind her, ending the conversation, then walked past the sofas to the window and looked out at the gray skyline. She peered upward. The snow had stopped, but the sun had yet to peek out that morning. When she looked down at the street below, she saw the shredded blanket of white, marred by street slush and booted feet on sidewalks. She looked up then, studied the building directly across from her, a seven-floor modular co-op with cookie-cutter apartments. Each floor from the second to the seventh looked identical. A single left-side window, a large picture window in the center, a single right-side window, and the pattern repeated itself. The apartments themselves appeared small, but when she looked through the pulled draperies and open blinds, she saw that the rooms were large and spacious.

This morning, as she studied the building intently, she saw a young woman—just one floor below her—opening the living room blinds of her apartment. She was petite, and wore black jeans and a red sweatshirt with some sort of Christmas emblem in the center. Her blond hair had been pulled back from her face, held in a high ponytail by a large red bow. Katie tilted her head and watched as the woman peered upward— just as she had earlier—then to the streets, and then abruptly from the window to something just behind her. When the woman turned, Katie saw the object of her attention; a small child, dressed in footed pink pajamas, holding a doll to her chest with one hand and rubbing her eyes with the other.

Katie smiled as the child's mother reached for her, gathering her to herself. She swung the child around once. . .twice. . .then bent over and kissed the child affectionately.

Katie's smile faded. She looked down at the hand clutching the matchbook. She opened it, allowing her fingers to uncurl in a manner devoid of emotion. She studied the emblem on the cover, then closed her eyes and remembered walking through the doors bearing the same emblem of a shadowy naked woman draped inside a martini glass.

She could almost hear the music, loud and sultry, and smell the air, sweltering and sweaty, smelling of something primal. She tilted her head back, took a deep breath, then exhaled, as though to rid her body of the stench of remembrance. Her brow furrowed at the memory of the hands that had touched her. . .caressed her possessively. She heard Leo, ordering her to a table to see a man who wanted to meet her. . .this one was important, he had told her. "Be nice to this one, you hear me?"

"When am I not nice?" Katie had stood before his desk, dressed in pink satin lingerie, sounding more like a New Yorker than she ever had.

Leo had looked up at her, pulled his stogie from his clenched teeth and said, "When *were* you? You're cocky; you know that? But you're the best thing that's ever walked in this club. That's why I keep you here. You're pretty in pink, and you bring in lots of the green stuff."

Katie had narrowed her eyes at him. "Shut up, Leo."

He didn't crack a smile, but his eyes had twinkled a bit as he shoved the stogie back between his teeth. "You listen to me, now. You'll go out there and be nice to the man, if you know what's good for you."

"What do you mean, 'If I know what's good for me?' You threatening me, Leo?"

"No, I ain't threat'nin' you," he had replied, again removing the short, fat stogie. "I'm telling you, this man can do things for you. He's a class act. He's got connections. If he likes you, you just may amount to somethin' someday."

Katie opened her eyes slowly in recollection. David Franscella had most assuredly done things for her. He had taken her back to her upper class roots, impregnated her, beat her to the point of miscarriage, and damaged her to the point of being unable to conceive. With that thought, her gaze moved back to the window across the street, where the mother and child cuddled in an overstuffed chair that diagonally faced the window. As the child sucked her thumb, Mother read to her from a small book. The scene gripped Katie's heart, and she fell to her knees and began to cry.

"Katie?" The soft voice came from Phil, who had entered without her noticing and knelt beside her slumped form beneath the window. She turned her tear-streaked face to his. Her eyelashes were drenched and clumped together. "What is it?" His voice was tender as he helped her to her feet.

She turned a bit, saw Vickey at the door, and shook her head. "Vickey, I'm sorry. Close the door behind you, please?"

Vickey raised an eyebrow. "Shall I bring the tea?"

"Oh. Yes. Then close the door behind you."

Disapproval and disappointment crossed Vickey's face, but she complied nonetheless. Phil walked Katie over to the nearest sofa, guiding her to sit. "What has happened here?"

"Oh, Phil," she said, wiping her eyes. Phil reached for the clean handkerchief he kept in his coat pocket (a habit taught him by his father) and extended it to the broken woman beside him. She took it, dabbed at the corners of her eyes, pressed it against each cheek, then discreetly blew her nose, all the while clutching something in her fist. "Why is it some sins are never atoned for?"

Phil touched the fist. "I don't believe that and neither do you."

Katie nodded. "Yes, I do." A fresh torrent of tears began to fall.

"What happened?"

She uncurled her fingers, revealing the matchbook. He took it from her, turned it over once. . .twice. "Where'd this come from?"

"I found it in my chair."

Phil looked beyond the clutter to the swivel executive chair, which had been turned to face the window, then back to the evidence resting in his palm. "What is Private Dancer?"

Katie's shoulders slumped a bit more. "It was a club in Hell's Kitchen back—" She stopped.

"What?"

She looked him in the eye. "I was going to say 'back in the day.' "

Phil understood. "Some habits die hard."

Her lips curled in disdain. "And some just won't die."

Vickey opened the outer door, bringing in the hot tea Katie had requested earlier. Phil stood and walked toward the desk, carrying the matchbook with him. "Thank you, Vickey," Katie said.

When Vickey had placed the silver tray on the coffee table, she stood erect. "Are you okay?"

Katie looked up. "I will be."

"Katie, I—" She shifted her weight, resting her fist on her hip.

"I want to help. What can I do?"

Katie forced a brief smile. "I know you do, but I just need time alone with Phil."

Vickey swung around to look at him. "What can I do?"

He stared at her for a moment before answering. "For now, make certain Katie is not disturbed."

Katie could sense Vickey's disapproval with his suggestion. When she had closed the door behind her, Phil returned to sit next to Katie. "Looks like Sharkey's our man."

"I know. But you'll have to be able to prove it with more than a matchbook. And. . ." she paused without breathing, ". . .don't you smell the cologne? It was one of Ben's favorites. How would Sharkey know about that?"

Phil sat silent for a moment. "Who *would* know about that?"

Katie hated herself for what she was about to say. "Phil, the other day. . .Vickey and I were talking about it."

"About William's cologne?"

"Yes."

"Are you telling me you're now ready to consider your assistant?"

"Yes." Katie set her jaw.

"What about the matchbook? Does she know about Private Dancer?"

"To my knowledge, no."

"To your knowledge." Phil rose and began to pace a bit. Where were his Clue pieces when he really needed them? "Could she have a connection to Sharkey?"

Katie shook her head. "Again, not that I know of." She paused briefly. "Phil, no matter what, I don't want an arrest."

"What are you saying?" Phil returned to the sofas, enabling a better look at the woman's face.

"I can't have this out, Phil. It's one thing to go in and get three of his girls. It's quite another to have the wife of William Benjamin Webster labeled as a stripper."

CHAPTER THIRTY-SEVEN
Saturday, Late Morning

Candy awoke Saturday morning feeling strangely energetic. She donned coat, gloves, and scarf and headed outside for a long walk and happy daydreaming along Fifty-seventh Street between Fifth and Park, where she could gaze into storefront windows of Chanel, Christian Dior, and (her all-time favorite) Victoria's Secret. As she moved along, shuffling between the crowds, she entertained satisfied thoughts of the previous evening's escapades.

Were there any regrets for what she'd done? Perhaps a few. After all, Katie had been good to her. . .for the most part. But Bucky Caballero was going to do even better by her. She stepped under a section of scaffolding where the wind cut around the corner and sliced through her coat. Her head ducked against the brutality of it as she wondered if Bucky had heard the news yet. Surely by now. . .

What would he think? Had she done enough damage for him? Or was the placing of the matchbook into Katie's chair enough? It was the whole point, really. Wasn't it?

She stopped at the corner of the street, waited with the other pedestrians for the WALK sign, bobbed up and down trying to shake off the cold, then proceeded across when the light changed. Her mind shifted to her bond with Bucky. . .wondering when he would send for her. . .

what their relationship would be like once she had moved to Canada with him and his sister. Would she literally live with them, or would Bucky get her an apartment of her own?

Yes, she decided. That's what she wanted. She'd tell him he owed her. Owed her for what she did last night. Owed her for going down the street in Chinatown, purchasing the pretender cologne from one of the shops and returning to do the deed. Yes, he definitely owed her an apartment. . .one with enough space for her mother and brother. Not that he couldn't come over any time he wanted; he could have his own key. Her mother would understand. Her mother was smart enough for that, at least. Even if she hadn't been smart enough to see what Clint had done to her. . .surely she would understand the relationship she would have with Bucky Caballero. Yeah, sure he may be old enough to be her father—*was* old enough in fact—but maybe this time the daddy would turn out all right. No more dying. No more abuse.

Phil pounded on Sharkey Garone's nondescript apartment door.

"Yeah, yeah. Who is it?" The voice of Sharkey barked from the other side.

"Phil Silver, Mr. Garone. I need to talk to you."

"I gave at the office."

"Open up, Garone. Now, or I'll call the nearest precinct to send a few of their finest down."

A disheveled Sharkey swung open the door, dressed in a faded gray tee and plaid flannel pajama bottoms. His unshod feet and bloodshot eyes belied the lateness of the morning. "Mr. Silver, this is my residence, don't you know? I'd prefer to keep our communications solely to my office."

Phil pushed his way past the man, into the shabby apartment living room. "Too bad."

"Hey!" Garone barked. "I can call the cops, too, you know!"

Phil swung around. "You do that, Garone." He reached into his coat pocket and pulled out the matchbook, displaying it between his index and middle fingers. "Wanna talk about this?"

Garone smirked, closing the door behind him. "Mr. Silver, whaddaya doing with that? Your old man been messing around at my old man's club back in the day?"

Phil narrowed his eyes at his last words, remembering what Katie had said earlier. "You son of a—

Garone raised a hand, palm out. "Ah-ah-ah," he cajoled. "Not nice to call a man names in his own dump."

"Tell me something, Garone," Phil calmed himself, placing the matchbook back into his pocket. "Exactly what is it you want from Mrs. Webster?"

Sharkey walked past him, toward the worn, blue velour sofa-loveseat-chair set near the large single window, the only window in the room. Phil followed him with his eyes, noting the dirty ashtrays and half-filled tumblers on the filthy glass end tables. Behind Garone the walls were bare except for a pin-up of the month calendar hanging over the loveseat. The view from the window was of another apartment building across the alley. Very little sunlight made its way through the blinds—broken and dilapidated as they were.

"It ain't much, is it?" Sharkey asked, reaching for a lighter and an old cigar resting among the gray ashes of one of the glass ashtrays. "Bet you got a nice place. A real nice place. Let me guess: Upper West?"

"What do you want with Mrs. Webster, Garone?" Phil repeated.

Phil waited as Garone lit the cheap stogie, repeatedly puffed on it, then blew a thin line of blue smoke from between his thin lips. The stench of it reached Phil's nostrils within seconds, and he frowned as Garone continued. "What makes you think I want anything from her?" he asked, sitting on the sofa behind him. "By the way, care to sit down?" He smiled.

Phil felt disgusted by the whole thing, momentarily realizing that at one time this had been Katie's world.

"Sharkey?" a sleepy female voice called out. Phil looked to see a young female, immodestly garbed in a man's tee, standing in the doorway of what was obviously the apartment's one bedroom. "What's going on?" The girl, pale and freckled, with shoulder-length, pillow-tossed red hair, leaned a shoulder against the doorframe, brought her hand up to her hip, and gripped her waist, drawing the too-short tee even shorter.

Phil turned his gaze back to Garone, who had turned an angry shade of red. "Get back to bed! No one called you out here!" he barked.

Phil could see the girl peripherally, noted that she straightened herself. He cautiously shifted his eyes back to her, keeping his jaw firm and breathing steadily. He did not want to be drawn into this sleazy mind game with Garone. . .a game he played all too well.

"But what's going on?"

"Misty!" Sharkey barked again. "Go back to bed. Didn't I tell ya?"

Phil wondered how old the girl might be. Eighteen? Nineteen? Certainly no more than twenty. No doubt a dancer from the club. The manager's favored girl, in fact. There was a term for it. . .but Phil almost made a deliberate effort not to think about it.

"I want to know what's going on, Sharkey!" the girl pouted, stomping a foot.

Phil returned his attention to the man on the sofa, who now jumped up, taking a quick leap toward the girl. Phil's eyes darted to the bedroom door again. The woman-child jumped, spinning around and closing the door behind her. "I'm going!" she yelled through the safety of the closed door, then followed up with a string of obscenities.

Sharkey returned to the sofa. "Women. Can't live with 'em. . . ."

"I'm not here for clichés, Garone. But since we're talking about her, am I to suppose that girl's legal?"

Sharkey grinned. "Now, Mr. Silver. You know I can get any woman I please just like that." He snapped his fingers.

Another set of obscenities came from beyond the bedroom door.

Sharkey stood and stomped toward the door. "You shut up, you hear? And don't you be listening in!"

"You shut up, Sharkey!" she called back, but the door didn't reopen.

Sharkey turned back to face his guest. "Sorry 'bout that, again."

"Mr. Garone, I'm going to ask you one more time; what do you want with Mrs. Webster."

Garone puffed on the cigar. "Want *with* her? Nothing. I want my girls back." He leaned forward. "You think you can get them back for me?"

Phil ignored his question. "What was your purpose last night? At The Hamilton Place?"

Sharkey opened his arms wide. "The Hamilton Place? *Moi?* I ain't been there in. . .what. . .a week or so?"

"Then how did the matchbook get there?"

"Is that how you came upon the old matchbook? I was wondering. . . ." He nodded victoriously.

"Mr. Garone, can you verify your whereabouts after hours last night?"

"Of course I can." Sharkey walked back to the bedroom door, opened it wide, revealing a sparsely furnished bedroom. In the center of the far wall was an unadorned mattress set, covered in several old quilts and blankets and no less than six narrow pillows. The supine lump in the middle sat erect, taking in a frightened breath as she rose. "Tell him, Misty!" Sharkey ordered the girl. "Who was your squeeze last night?"

Misty curled her lip contemptuously. "You were, Sharkey." She sounded as appalled as Phil felt.

"Were you with Mr. Garone all night?" Phil asked.

Misty looked from Phil to Sharkey and back to Phil. "At the club and then here, yeah."

"Mr. Garone didn't leave the apartment during the night at any time?" Phil challenged.

"No." The girl tucked a strand of wayward hair behind an ear.

"What time did you leave the club?"

"Three. . .three-thirty. Usual time."

"Did you see Mr. Garone at the club?" Phil looked over at Sharkey, who stood grinning beside him. He knew his alibi was solid. Whether it was the truth or not was another issue.

"Sure, I saw him. As soon as we closed and I got back into my street clothes, I went into his office and waited for him to finish up."

"As the manager it's imperative that I get my paperwork done," Sharkey smirked.

"Yeah." Phil turned back to the girl.

"We came home, had a drink or two and went to bed." She sounded almost incredulous. Like, *what else would we have done?*

"And at no time from the club until now have the two of you been apart?"

"No."

Phil's lips drew thin. Darn it all, he believed the girl. His eyes narrowed, and he began to smile. Looking at Sharkey he asked, "Then who did you send to THP with the matchbook, Garone?"

Sharkey made his way over to the front door of the apartment. "I assure you I don't know what you're talking about. Now, if you don't mind, it's nearly noon and I gotta get ready for the day, if you know what I mean."

Phil followed him, stopping at the door and looking down on the weasel. "Garone, let me make this perfectly clear. I'm on your heels, you got it? If you look ahead, I'll be waiting for you. If you look behind, I'll be watching you. If you so much as glance to the left or the right, I'll know about that, too. Am I making myself understood?"

Garone didn't flinch. "Yeah. Yeah. I got it. Have a nice day."

CHAPTER THIRTY-EIGHT
Sunday, December 9, 2001
Late Night

Sharkey looked down at his wristwatch, across his desk to where Candy sat with her legs crossed, swinging one up and down, while fidgeting with an earring she'd removed from her right lobe, and back to the phone.

"What time did he say he'd call?" Candy asked.

Sharkey looked at her sharply. "What? How many times you gonna ask me that? Do I look like a parrot; I gotta keep repeating myself?" When Candy didn't respond, he answered. "Eleven."

"Our time? He said eleven, our time? And he definitely said tonight? Sunday?"

"Yeah, yeah. Shut up, will you? He'll call."

Candy wiggled the earring back into the hole in her lobe. "I'm a little nervous, is all."

Sharkey was, too. Mr. C should be calling any minute now—any second, really. Just minutes before eleven Candy had slipped off the dance floor and into his office to await the anticipated call with him. He was glad for that; he liked having her to look at when he was distressed. And look, he did. From the tops of her bony knees, which were the first things he could see, to the tip of her blue-black hair she had pulled up into a frizzy ponytail. He glanced over her shoulder to the door leading to the hall, and for the first time noticed it had been left ajar. "You left the door—"

The ringing of the phone interrupted him. He grabbed at the receiver. "This is Sharkey," he bellowed.

Candy uncrossed her legs and slipped to the end of her seat. "Is it him?"

Sharkey nodded his head. Candy thought he looked all the more like the felt, bobbing-headed bulldog her stepfather used to keep on the dashboard of the family car. "Yeah, yeah. . .Mr. Caballero, she did it. She did it good, too, 'cause Mr. Silver came by my apartment yesterday." Candy watched as Sharkey listened to the distinctive voice on the other end of the line. "He had the matchbook with him. . .wasn't happy at all. Threatened me, if you want the truth of it." Then some indistinguishable talking from Bucky.

Candy reached for the edge of the desk and gripped it. "What's he saying?" Sharkey shushed her and she pouted, narrowing her eyes at him. "Let me talk to him, Sharkey."

Sharkey shushed her again, all the while continuing to talk to Bucky. "Yeah, yeah. I got the money. Came by courier this afternoon. . .yes, Sir. It was plenty good enough. Anytime you want to do business again, you let me know. . .anytime you want me to mess with Mrs. Webster, I'm your man."

"Sharkey, come on," Candy hissed again.

Sharkey looked at her and grinned. She was getting itchy to talk to the man, which put her at his mercy. "Mr. Caballero, there's a little miss who wants to talk to you. . .yeah, yeah. I've been good to her. She's a real asset, this one is." Sharkey extended the phone to her. "It's for you."

Sharkey watched the girl through eyes he'd narrowed to slits as she jumped to her feet and grabbed the phone out of his hand. "Mr. Caballero?" she asked meekly. Sharkey sniffed. He'd never seen Candy respond to him with this much respect and admiration. What was going on in that little pea-brain of hers? What was she thinking Caballero was going to do for her? What did she possibly imagine she would gain from her insignificant involvement with the man? "Yes, Sir, I did. I did it exactly as you told me to. . .yes, Sir. . .yes, Sir. . .no, Sir, I don't feel guilty. I mean, Katie Webster has been good to me and everything, but. . . ." She turned her back to Sharkey, leaned her narrow hips against the desk and hunkered her shoulders. "I will," she whispered. "I will. Yes, Sir. . . Wednesday night. . .Goodbye, Mr. Caballero."

When Candy turned to hang up the phone, she met Sharkey's glaring eyes. He had stood to his full five-feet-six-inch height and was looking miffed. She smiled to divert him, but it didn't work. "What was that little bit at the end about there?" he asked, coming around the desk.

Candy backed up a step. "Nothing." She kept her jaw firm. "I just turned to rest against the front of the desk."

Sharkey stood directly in front of her. "What are you talking about 'Wednesday night'? What's going on Wednesday night?"

Candy shifted nervously, took several deep breaths to steady herself. "Nothing, Sharkey. He just said to tell you he'd call you back Wednesday night." She reached out and touched the sleeve of Sharkey's silk shirt. "Nice shirt, Sharkey."

Sharkey looked down at the tiny hand that had graced his arm, then up to the beauty before him. "You like that?"

She gave him a tender smile, rubbed her hand up and down the sleeve. "Yeah, I do."

He took a step closer to her, extended a tentative hand to her waist. She didn't flinch from his touch; he became bolder, bringing the other hand to rest against her hip. She stepped into his embrace, wrapping her arms around his shoulders, leaning into his kiss. When they broke, she whispered, "I'm sorry about the other night."

"Yeah, yeah. Me, too, baby."

She inhaled, then sighed as though the moment had brought her great satisfaction and pleasure. "You've been good to me, Sharkey. I know Misty's your girl, and I'm okay with that—"

He shushed her, this time tenderly. "You're the one I've wanted, didn't you know that?"

She gave him a demure smile in answer. "I suppose I'd better get back out there." She indicated the lounge of the club with a jerk of her head.

He patted her on her backside. "Don't forget where we left off."

She kissed him quickly again. "I won't." She was about to step away, then leaned against him again. "Sharkey?"

"Mmm?"

"This week. . .can I move in with you?"

Misty Hamlin couldn't believe what she was hearing. Standing just outside the door of Sharkey's office, she'd witnessed the whole nasty incident. Hearing that in a few days she'd be out of Sharkey's apartment, she swung on her heel, ran down the hallway toward the dressing room, and slammed the door behind her. The only girl there was GiGi, who sat at one of the dressing tables, nursing a drink. She looked up abruptly at the intrusion. "What's the matter with you?"

Misty paced six steps forward, turned, and paced five steps back toward the door. Within the space of the saved step, she kicked the door soundly with her booted foot, expletives spilling from her painted lips. GiGi snickered into the glass she raised to her mouth. "Girl, let me guess. You just found your old man with another lady." She took a deep swallow of her drink.

Misty turned and glared at her. "How long have you known?"

"Known what, baby girl?" She set the drink down on the vanity. "That Sharkey is a weasel? Let me think; since about ten minutes after he hired me and made his first move on me. Why do you think men like Sharkey go into business like this?"

Misty stomped to a nearby vanity chair and plopped into it. Her arms folded around her petite middle; her shoulders slumped back into the chair and her knees stayed about four inches apart. "Piece of—"

GiGi leaned forward. "Who? Her or him?"

"Her and him!"

"And just who *is her*, baby girl?"

Misty glared. "Like you don't know."

GiGi reached for the glass again. "Pffft. I don't know. Don't really care. I just know it ain't me and it ain't gonna be me."

"Why? What's wrong with Sharkey? He's nice enough."

"Give me a royal break, girl. Listen to you, defending him. He's with another woman, right?"

"Candy."

"Candy? Well, sir. That one came out of nowhere. I would have never dreamed the little cream puff would. . ."

"What?" Misty grabbed a nearby hairbrush. She brushed her red hair briskly, almost violently. Just as suddenly, she slammed the brush back down on the vanity. "Look, I know what you girls think. You think I live with Sharkey just so I get special privileges. Well, it ain't like that."

"What is it like, baby girl?"

Misty pouted for a moment before her eyes fell. "I just need someone to hold onto."

GiGi stood and began to make her way toward the door. She wobbled a bit, paused and straightened herself at Misty's chair, leaned over and planted a kiss on top of her head before leaving. "Don't we all, baby girl. Don't we all."

CHAPTER THIRTY-NINE

Monday, December 10, 2001
Early Morning

Candy spit the toothpaste foam from her mouth and into the basin. She had returned to the hotel only moments before, and the first thing she wanted to do was brush her teeth and take a shower. She had to get the disgusting stench of Sharkey off her skin. . .her soul. . .or she'd die. She just knew she'd die.

The shower was already running, the temperature setting as hot as it would go. Steam filled the room in a wet cloud. Candy stripped out of her clothes, jerked back the shower curtain, and stepped into the hot spray. She allowed it to hit the top of her head, and pelt the rest of her body with stinging punishment for her deed.

Turning her face upward she shook her head, no. She had to do it, didn't she? She had to touch him, allow him to touch her, to kiss her. . . to tell him she wanted to move in with him. . .to buy her time. . . .

She opened her mouth, allowing the hot water to fill it, then spat toward the small gold drain at her feet. She coughed a few times for good measure, then took the bar of soap growing mushy in the tray and began to scrub her skin, beginning with circular motions on her flat stomach, moving up to her shoulders and down her arms.

Technically, today is Monday, she thought. *Only two more days. Only two more nights.* Heck, maybe she wouldn't even go in to the club tonight. Maybe she'd take a night off. . .make Sharkey a little crazy. He'd be all over her like bees on honey by tomorrow. She could get away with anything. . .she would, too. She'd get the good customers, make herself some spending cash for the trip up to Canada, and then be out of there.

Out of here. Out of this joke of a life. *Katie Webster, you did your best to help,* she thought. *You tried; God knows you tried. But I need more than a job and a roof over my head, albeit a nice roof. I need a man to take care of me, a man like Bucky Caballero.*

Candy placed a foot up on the tub's back corner, rubbed the soap up and down her leg, all the while acknowledging her need. It was about time, wasn't it? Her whole life had led up to this moment. Clint needed her to fulfill his boyish, twisted needs. Her stepfather needed her to prove his male superiority. She knew that now as well as she knew she'd been somehow forced into this business by virtue of what life had shoveled onto her path. Not that it mattered. How you get there doesn't matter. How you get *out* does. And how she was going to get out was flying to Canada on Wednesday.

She placed her foot back to the tub floor and began to wash the other leg in the same way as before. . .thinking of what Mr. Caballero had told her. All she had to do was get to Kennedy, walk up to the ticket counter, and claim her prize. By Wednesday night she'd be with Bucky— Mr. Caballero—and his sister. By Wednesday night, life would finally begin for her.

Phil Silver felt as though he'd received a break when Katie told him she suspected Vickey. Perhaps her suspicion was not as deep as his, but it was a start, and with that he could move forward. His thoughts had raced all through dinner the night before and had kept him from falling asleep quickly when he and Gail had gone to bed. Now, as he gazed at the digital clock beside his bed that told him it was only four-thirty in the morning, he realized he couldn't stay asleep either. He wanted to know more about Katie's assistant; any tidbit that might connect her to the gaslight treatment Katie was receiving. He slipped out of bed, trying not to disturb Gail, who moaned a bit in her sleep, then turned to her side and began to breathe evenly again. He reached for his robe and slipped his feet into slippers, then tiptoed his way out the bedroom door and to the small office he kept at home.

While he waited for the computer to boot up, he skimmed through Katie's file again. . .one last time. . .looking for anything he might have missed. When the computer came to life, he typed in his password and began his search. What he found was that Vickey McWhorter had been born Vickey Meredith Frederick on March 16, 1960, to Richard and Grace Frederick, of Wolcott, Connecticut. She had graduated from Wolcott High School with honors in 1978, graduated from the University of Connecticut four years later with a degree in Business Administration. According to county records, she married Sean McWhorter in late 1984; two years later she gave birth to a daughter, two years after that, a son. She was hired by THP just out of college to work in administration. A year later, she was promoted to then-president Donald Webster's assistant. When William Webster had taken over the presidency, she remained in her position. Now, Phil mentally noted, she worked with Katie.

There seemed to be nothing of consequence concerning the life of Vickey Frederick McWhorter. She paid her taxes on time, had never been arrested, didn't have so much as a parking ticket.

Phil leaned back in his chair, crossed his arms over his abdomen and gazed out the window and into the blackness of night. *Nothing. Nothing to connect Vickey to Sharkey.*

Nothing.

A thought crossed Phil's mind—the kind that comes from nowhere and tells you instinctively that it needs to be reckoned with. The kind that let's you know you've heard something—maybe two somethings— and those two unconnected somethings are related in some way. . .some form. . .some fashion.

It was something about Katie. *Something distinctive about her.* What? What? "Okay, Silver, what do you know?"

Katharine Webster was married to his best friend. Before that, she'd worked for William's cousin, Cynthia Ferguson, at Mosley, Carter, and Troup. Before that—according to what he now knew—she'd been an exotic dancer at a place called Private Dancer. It was her history that caused her to bring the three girls out of Sharkey's establishment.

*I was one of them. . .*she had told him. *One of them. . .*

What did he know about "them?"

He knew their names, Brittany, Ashley, and Candy. Brittany was a breathtaking African-American; Ashley, the epitome of the farmer's daughter; and Candy was an Asian beauty whom Katie wasn't too sure of. . .

Phil's head jerked at the thought.

And he wondered why. . .

He opened the middle drawer of the desk to reveal pieces of a Clue game nestled in a cubbyhole designed for gem clips and other oddments. He pulled out the white playing piece representing Mrs. White, rolled it around his fingers awhile, then set it on the desk.

Ashley.

Reaching back into the drawer, he pulled out the blue playing piece, repeated the same fondling with his fingers, then set Mrs. Peacock next to Mrs. White.

Brittany.

Finally, he retrieved Miss Scarlet—the red playing piece—and set it upright in the palm of his hand. He narrowed his eyes as the light from his desk lamp cast its illumination upon it. As he was about to set it next to the other playing pieces, his private business phone rang; the piece fell from his hand, bounced off the arm of his chair, and fell to the hardwood floor below, rolling aimlessly until it came to rest at his feet.

Misty woke up early. At least, for her it was early.

She disengaged herself from Sharkey's heavy, hairy arm he'd thrown possessively over her middle during the night. Before last night, she'd thought it was a protective arm he kept around her as they slept. Now she knew better. Sharkey Garone thought he owned her. She decided he wouldn't own her for long. If Candy wanted him, she could have him. Not that there was much to have; Sharkey was a two-bit businessman, a two-bit man, even, and a two-bit lover. Everything about him was second rate, and as long as she shadowed him home every morning after closing, she'd be second rate, too.

She padded into the bathroom in thick socks, quietly closed the door behind her, and bent over the laundry basket that served as a dirty clothes bin, digging around until she found a pair of wrinkled jeans. She quietly slipped them over her thin frame, zipping and buttoning them before turning to pull a dark blue sweatshirt from the hook on the back of the bathroom door. She tugged it over her head, then grasped her hair in her fingers and secured it with a barrette lying discarded on the back of the toilet in a small plastic basket filled with hair accessories and brushes. Her eye caught a tube of red lipstick and she smiled, reaching for it, twisting the bottom of it until the lipstick peeked from over the top of the tube. Leaning over the sink, she drew a picture for Sharkey with the lipstick. . .a message she was sure even he could understand. . . an impression of her hand, with only one finger exposed.

Done, she bent over the sink, turned on the cold water just enough to permit a stream, but not enough to cause the howling of the old pipes that occurred when the faucet was turned on too high. She brushed her teeth quickly, threw icy water on her face, then patted it dry with the hand towel that reeked of mildew. Done, she threw the towel on top of the heap of dirty clothes and slowly opened the door leading to her escape.

The bedroom floor creaked under her light step. She stopped abruptly, catching her breath in her throat and looking over at the sleeping hump in the bed. She frowned. Lying on his stomach, Sharkey looked like a beached baby whale. Or perhaps something worse than that. Baby whales could be a lovely sight. Nothing about Sharkey was.

He snorted, but slept on, and she continued to tiptoe out of the bedroom, into the living room where she gathered up her sneakers and coat, then out the front door. She sprinted down the hallway toward the stairs, stopped halfway down to jump into her shoes and don her coat. She shivered in the bitter cold of the stairwell, marked by old, chipped paint and the handprints of playing children or adults too drunk to walk up straight. When she finally made it to the front door, she nearly blew out of it, shoving her hands into the coat's pockets, and sprinting toward Midtown. She had no money for a cab. She didn't even have enough for the subway. Sharkey saw to that. He kept every penny she made. If she needed anything, she asked him. She didn't so much as have change for a pack of Juicy Fruit.

Tears began to slip down her cheeks, made red by the arctic weather slapping her as she jogged. How foolish she had been. She'd thought he was taking care of her. . .but he was, in fact, making her a prisoner to his whims. Well, she might be "some-dumb, but she wasn't plumb-dumb." From this day on, no man would own her. From this day on, she would belong to herself.

"Silver," Phil answered, talking into the phone quickly while looking down to the floor and turning his foot just so as the playing piece rolled beside it. He reached down and grasped it with his fingers, popping it into his hand, wrapping his fist around it.

"It's John," the voice from the other end said, broken by the static and sound of traffic beyond him. "I hope I didn't wake you. . . ."

"What's up?"

"I'm on my way to the airport. . .just wanted to let you know. . .got a break earlier in the Griffin case. Young lady was spotted in Los Angeles."

"Los Angeles? What's in Los Angeles?" Phil smiled. At least one of them was solving a case.

"Other than art galleries where she was trying to sell some of the stolen artwork from her father's gallery. . .and a few lawyers in an old television show. . .I don't know."

"I didn't realize she'd stolen any artwork."

"Neither did I. Kabakjian is a smooth operator. He reveals nothing, believe me. Which is why, when I get back, I'm hauling him in on charges of withholding."

"Hey—"

"I'm already one ahead of you. We'll run a deal. Perhaps some community service in exchange for information about Caballero."

Phil grinned. "I feel like I may be getting somewhere here. . . ."

"While I'm gone, think on this. Remember me telling you about the Asian girl who left the club alone the night we camped outside of Mist Goddess?"

"Yeah." Phil opened his fist and looked down at Miss Scarlet lying between the lines of his palm.

"Something about her is bothering me."

"Why? Sharkey must have a half-dozen Asian girls working for him."

"True, but remember I told you she left alone?"

"Yeah."

"She's the only one who did. Every girl left with a man. Someone to escort her back from the jowls of hell, if you know what I mean."

"I know."

"But not this girl. Sits as strange with me. . ."

Phil paused for several moments, remembering what Katie had said to him. . .that she thought Candy was slipping back to the club at night. . .

Candy. . .access to Sharkey. . .access to Katie. . .

He placed the red playing piece next to the other two. *Miss Scarlet,* he thought, *are you holding the knife? Are you the one in the library?* He had a full day at John Jay but first thing in the morning, he'd go by and see Katie. She wouldn't want to hear anything against one of her girls; that much was for sure. But, by then he'd have information about Candy. By then, he may have just solved this case.

CHAPTER FORTY

An hour later, Misty reached The Hamilton Place, and when she did, she wasn't quite ready for what lay inside. She didn't even know the word for what she was looking at. . .except. . .maybe "pretty." But "pretty" didn't seem to say everything. . .it didn't even begin to say enough.

She halted just inside the door, standing on the polished marble floor of the lobby. She dug her fists deeper into the torn lining of her coat pockets, realizing how shabby she looked. She wrapped the opening of the coat tighter around her slender frame, lifted her chin just so, and took several tentative steps toward the central elevators.

Where to go from there, she had no idea.

"May I help you?"

Misty turned abruptly, sniffing back a trickle of mucus dripping from her nostrils, to find herself face-to-face with a woman best described as hoity-toity. An arched eyebrow, perfectly shaped and filled in, looked as though it would break from right off her forehead. The thin red lips pursed as the arms crossed with defiant indignation.

"I'm. . .I'm looking for a friend of mine."

"Here? I'm sure you're mistaken."

Misty wiped her nose with her palm, and then—lacking a handkerchief—rubbed it against the outside of her coat near her thigh. If Hoity-toity was displeased before, she was doubly unhappy now.

"No, she lives here."

"Young lady, this isn't the set of *Pretty Woman*."

Misty sighed heavily, ducking her chin. "What? Look, Lady. My friend lives here. . .with a woman named Katie."

"With a woman named Katie. . ."

"Yes." Misty felt herself growing uncomfortable. "Katie Webster."

Hoity seemed taken aback and Misty gloated, but only for a moment. Not even a moment. A milli-moment. "Katharine Webster?"

"I guess."

A man approached just then. "What's going on here, Mrs. Willis?"

Misty turned to look at him. For an older man, he wasn't bad. Silver hair against tanned skin. Fine looking character lines around his eyes and across his brow. She felt herself relaxing; good-looking men she could deal with. Snobby women, she could not. "I'm looking for Katie Webster."

"Mr. Harrington, I just found this young woman walking about the lobby. . ." Mrs. Willis began in explanation.

Harrington raised his hand to stop her. "It's okay. I'm certain I know what's going on here." He grabbed the sleeve of Misty's coat near her elbow and tugged. "Young lady, won't you come with me?" They took several steps away from Mrs. Willis.

"I'd love to," she answered. Her tone was coy and practiced.

He stopped short and looked down his nose at her. "Let me make this perfectly clear. I'm aware of who and what you are. I do not approve, and I am here neither to be entertained by you nor to entertain you. If you need to see Mrs. Webster, I will see to it that you do. When you are done, I will see to it that you are escorted out. . . ." He lowered his voice and tugged her into walking with him again, ". . .if I have my way about it."

Misty snorted. "I know your type."

Mr. Harrington ignored her until he had pulled her into the semi-privacy of the elevator. Other than the elevator operator, they were alone. With her free hand she reached behind her head and unclasped her hair, tossing it lightly, allowing the curls to dance about her face and head.

"Ignore me if you will, but I've seen you plenty of times."

Harrington continued to stare straight ahead.

"Maybe not you, exactly. But men like you. You come down to China-town for kicks, and then pretend we don't exist." She leaned closer to him. "But our scent lingers and you know you like it. Better than your old lady's perfume, huh?"

Harrington narrowed his eyes, and the elevator came to a stop; the doors opened. He tugged hard on the sleeve, jerking her out of the eleva-tor and down a hallway of closed office doors. Misty sniffed again. "You got a snot-rag, Honey?" she toyed.

He pulled a handkerchief from his pocket and handed it to her. She halted slightly. "Care if I blow my nose?"

"Wait until I get you inside Mrs. Webster's office. I'm sure you can manage."

They reached the door near the end of the hallway, and he opened it, releasing her sleeve, and extending an invitation for her to enter. "After you."

She walked in, honking into the handkerchief, looking up at the pretty blond woman sitting behind the desk to their left.

"Vickey, is Mrs. Webster in?"

Vickey seemed perplexed at first, but then a semblance of under-standing crossed her face. "Another one of the girls?"

"I'm afraid so," Harrington answered.

Vickey stood. "She's here." She looked at Misty. "Why don't you have a seat? I'll let her know you're here."

Harrington grabbed Misty's sleeve again, drug her over to a seating area where he released her and followed Vickey into the inner office. Misty rolled her eyes from the left to the right, taking in the plush office, listening to the muffled voices from beyond the door. Momentarily, the door opened and the woman from that past summer strolled through, looking more like class in black pumps than Misty remembered.

Katie Webster came to a stop halfway between her office door and the place where Misty sat. "Misty?" she asked, tilting her head. "Is that you?"

Misty stood. "Hi." She sniffed one more time.

"Oh, dear," Katie crossed the steps between them, reaching for her—not in the way Mr. Harrington had, but in a tender, maternal sort of way. Misty dropped her chin and began to cry. She hadn't intended on it; it just happened. "Vickey," Katie continued, wrapping her arm around Misty's frail shoulders, "bring in some hot chocolate, please." She moved Misty toward the door and the frowning man who blocked the way into the inner office.

"Mrs. Webster," he began, his tone low and professional.

Katie Webster pushed past her general manager. "Not now, Mr. Harrington. We'll discuss this later."

Misty found herself ushered into another room. . .another world, actually. So, this was where Brittany, Ashley, and that backstabbing Candy had been hiding out. . . . Misty found herself all the more confused as to why Candy would leave all this and run back to Sharkey. She shuddered at the thought.

"Are you cold?" Katie asked her, showing her to the sofas to the right.

"No," Misty whispered. "Not anymore."

Sharkey Garone threw himself on the rumpled covers of the bed, waiting for an answer from the other end of the phone line. How many rings did Candy have her cell phone set for? Three? Four? Five. . .

"Hi, Baby," Candy's recorded message was sultry and inviting. "You've reached Candy, and Candy loves to hear from you. Leave a message, and you'll see how sweet I can be. . .here's the beep. . ." *Beep.*

Sharkey frowned; disturbed at the way her voice and words affected him. Just a few more days, and she would be here. . .and she would be his. . .all his. . .he couldn't believe his luck. "Hey, Baby backatcha," he cooed. "Look here. I think Misty knows about us, Baby, 'cause she's flown the coop, if you get my drift. Left me a nice message on the bathroom mirror this morning. If I know Misty. . .and I do. . .she's not so stupid we're gonna have to throw her out. What I'm saying, love of my life, is you can move in tomorrow if you'd like. . .I'd say tonight, but I got a little job for you. . .just got the call. . .and you're the only one right for the job. Don't give me a hard time, you hear? It's a lot of the green stuff. . .and I do mean a *lot*. . .we'll be able to get some new furniture and stuff with this much dough. Skies the limit for you, Baby. Call me. . ." A beep and the line disconnected.

Sharkey jerked himself up from the bed, grinned and began to sing.

"You'd better not pout, you'd better not cry. . .Santa Claus is coming to town. . ."

Candy didn't like the sound of the message Sharkey had left her. . .but she didn't know any other way around it. Then again, he did say she'd make a lot of money. She could use a lot of money. It would be great to fly into Canada with enough cash to impress Mr. Caballero and his sister. A job like what Sharkey was talking about could easily bring in a grand. The client would pay Sharkey, then tomorrow she could go to the club and get the money. . .tell Sharkey she was going to get new things for their new life together. He'd buy it, too. Hook, line, and sinker.

It was with a smile that she called him back. He answered his office number right away and, with a cross of her eyes, she said hello back to him. "I got your message."

"Where are you?"

"In my room."

"Packing?"

Candy could hear the glee in his voice and she sneered, then gained composure. "Of course, I am. Tell me about the job tonight."

"Just a private party. That's all I'm going to tell you 'cause that's all you need to know."

"How much?"

"What difference does it make?"

Candy sat on the edge of her bed. "I'm hoping to take the money out tomorrow while the stores are having such good sales. I want new sheets, Sharkey. And new towels. I want everything in that apartment new for me. I don't want even a hint that the redhead was ever there."

"You're sounding a little uppity, if you ask me. You stay in your place."

Candy frowned. Sharkey sounded like her stepfather and stepbrother. "In your place. . .in your place," she mocked, then stopped and swallowed. "Sharkey, let's not fight." Her tone changed and she knew he'd like it. He'd like it a lot.

"That's better."

See. . .

"You'll get the money, Baby. You do a good job tonight, and I'll give you anything you want, you hear? Big client. Important client. Got it?"

"Aren't I your best girl?"

"Always have been. . .always will be."

Candy bit her lower lip. "Better than Katie Webster was to your old man?"

There was a pause on the other end. "Nobody could ever compare to Katie, Little China. Don't even try. You just do your best. Now, then. . . want the address for the job or not? It's in SoHo."

Candy stood and walked over to the desk against the wall. "Yeah. Give it to me."

"I can't believe we're doing this again," James Harrington frowned over Katie's desk.

"Mr. Harrington, lower your voice please. I'm still the president of this establishment."

"And perhaps you've forgotten what it is we do here," he commented, pacing back and forth in front of Katie's desk. "This is a five-star hotel, Mrs. Webster. Five-star. This is not a home for wayward prostitutes."

Katie stood. "Mr. Harrington, for the hundredth time, they are not prostitutes."

At those words James stopped his pacing, placing his hands on his hips. The glare in his eyes seemed to cut Katie in half. "Whatever it is that they are," he said in a low voice, "they are a distraction to this hotel. I have tried to help you. . .I have. . .but you and I see things from different viewpoints."

Katie crossed her arms. "What are you saying, Mr. Harrington? Is this your resignation?"

James Harrington licked his lower lip, slowly. . .seemingly to study the woman before him and the situation at hand. "You'd like that wouldn't you?"

"No. No, I would not. You are an asset to this company. But I cannot have you dictate to me who I can and cannot allow entrance into a building my husband's family owns."

The air between them settled into something heavy and ugly. He pointed a finger at her, but said nothing. His hand went back to his hip, and then came back up again, pointing one last time. "When this place falls, I won't be here to help you pick up the pieces."

"What makes you think it will fall?"

"You are allowing the lowest of people—people with no class whatsoever—into a business that it took over a hundred years to build. Do you understand that? Do you even care what that means? We cannot have The Hamilton Place associated with these kinds of women."

Katie lifted her chin. The irony of his statement was lost on him, but not on her. How would he feel if he knew she had been "one of these kinds of women?" "When I'm done with them, they won't be 'these kinds of women.' They deserve a chance, Mr. Harrington. They deserve to know a better life and to have the love of God shared with them. Don't *you* understand that there are people out there who have never felt the hand of love except when it fondles them inappropriately?"

James shook his head. "This is *not* a ministry center. This is a hotel. If you're looking for a ministry center, there's that church at Times Square. . .that 'Cross and the Switchblade' church."

"As long as I'm here, THP will be a *place* of ministry. That much I will not relinquish." Katie sat, as though that were that.

James turned, headed toward the door, and then turned back before reaching it. "And if it costs you everything?"

Katie Webster leaned her forearms against the desk and looked the man directly in the eyes. "God's unfailing message of love cost Him the life of His Son. If my helping these girls costs me this hotel, then so be it."

James lowered his eyes, but he did not answer. He could not. God alone knew how right she was about that. . .but God also knew what it could mean in the end. He shook his head sadly. A hundred years, down the drain. A hundred years. . . "Where is the girl now?"

"She's resting in Ashley's room. She didn't want anyone to know she was here just yet. So, please. . .keep this morning's events quiet."

James looked up. "Oh, believe me, no one will hear it from these lips."

CHAPTER FORTY-ONE
Monday, Late Night

Candy slipped out of The Hamilton Place unnoticed. She hailed a cab. When one in the sea of yellow taxis pulled over to the curb down the street from the hotel, she jumped into it, throwing her small sports bag in ahead of her.

"Where to?" the cabdriver asked.

She gave him the Prince Street address in SoHo, pulling the sports bag into her lap and unzipping it. She peered in, hoping she had everything she needed. She had chosen the perfect costume for her farewell dance. . .the right shoes. . .silk stockings with seams up the back. She had already applied makeup, but she put her case in the bag on the off chance she needed to make herself look a little more exotic for the client. Some liked her that way. Asian women. . .looking like Geisha girls.

The drive to the address was quick and uneventful. When the driver slowed next to the curb beyond the cobblestone street, she passed him a ten over the back of the seat, said, "Keep it," opened the door and stepped out onto the sidewalk. She shut the door, and the taxi cruised away.

Candy looked up at the dark structure before her. Like most buildings in this ancient section of the city, it had once been a factory warehouse, renovated into one of many art galleries and museums. This one, according to the sign at the door, was a gallery of displayed holograms.

Candy's upper lip curled. She'd never liked holograms. Not since, as a child, she'd seen a traveling exhibit at the mall back home. As far as she was concerned, it wasn't natural. It wasn't natural at all.

Then again, SoHo was a little out of the ordinary, but she'd always liked walking up from Chinatown to experience some of the local events. The area was trendy and kinky because mostly artists and artsy types dwelt it in. One never knew what one would see while walking up and down the sidewalks and between the buildings with their cast-iron facades and large, open windows.

Candy looked down at the sports bag in her hand. Unfortunately, she didn't know what she was going to see tonight either. Her client obviously owned or worked at this gallery. Either that, or she'd been given the wrong address. She dug through the bag, searching for the paper she'd scribbled the address on. It was, naturally, at the very bottom—crumpled and wrinkled.

She pulled it from its corner, studied the address, and looked back to the number over the door before her. Yes, she was in the right place. She took tentative steps, approaching the entrance between the occasional pedestrian. She rang the bell beside it, waited for the briefest of moments, and heard the buzzing beyond the wood of the door and the metal of the lock, allowing her access.

Candy opened the door, stepped into the dimly lit first floor of the gallery, then turned and closed the door firmly behind her. She shivered. The heat had obviously been turned off hours earlier. The room smelled of paint and wood. She slipped the strap of the bag over her shoulder, took a step—maybe two—and called out a faint "Hello?"

"I'm over here," a voice returned.

Candy could feel her heart pounding within the small cavity of her chest. "Where? I can't see anything."

"Yes, you can. Follow the sound of my voice." It was an ominous, masculine voice.

Candy took a step. Then another. "Keep talking."

"See the direct line of facing holograms?"

"Yes."

"Walk through them."

Candy did as she was told, keeping her focus straight ahead. "I'm not overly fond of holograms," she said, hoping to break the tension. "Do you own this place?"

"Yes."

Silence. . .other than the sound of her small feet shuffling across the wooden floor. "Say something else," she coaxed. The scent of a man's cologne and exotic traces of incense reached her nostrils, burning them.

"Why don't you like holograms?"

Candy licked her lower lip. "They frighten me."

"Why is that?"

She swallowed. Hard. "I'm not sure. They just do." She was beginning to see the form of the man—a tall, powerfully built man—at the back of the gallery. "I think I see you." She stopped walking.

"I'm studying my most recent purchase."

"Oh, yeah?"

"Why did you stop walking?"

She resumed her steps toward the shadow.

"That's better. I like the sound of your feet on my floor."

Candy's breath caught in her throat. "That's an unusual thing to say."

"You're getting closer to me."

"Yes."

"Stop."

Candy stopped. "Why? What do you want me to do?" She was beginning to sweat, even in the chill of the unheated room. The shadow stepped to the left, revealing a large hologram of an angel's face, the classic kind of modern popularity. . .an angel with tussled blond ringlets and eyes that met their observer from every corner of the room.

"What do you think? Are you afraid of this work? Would you be afraid of an angel?"

There was something sinister about the face, and she said so. "It's evil."

"An angel? Evil?"

Candy's eyes fixed on those belonging to the artwork overhead. They looked down on her as though they owned her. . .directed her steps. She narrowed her eyes, hoping to break the spell she felt pinning her to this place.

"Step to the right. Just a bit, now," the voice commanded.

She did, gasping. The eyes of the angel stayed the same, but the face changed into that of Satan. A force of horror pushed into her chest and her hands flew to her face, covering her eyes.

"Now, now," the voice said soothingly. She felt masculine arms wrap around her tiny frame. He shushed her while rubbing his hands up and down her spine. "It's only art. It can't hurt you."

"Who are you?" she hissed into the steeliness of his chest.

"I am the one who loves you."

She looked up, but the shadow and light from the holograms were not enough to reveal the face of the man who looked down at her. "I recognize your voice, but. . ." She felt his hand wrap around her wrist. He tugged gently—an invitation to follow him—and she did. Past the face of Satan to a flight of steps she had not seen before. "Where are you taking me?"

He shushed her again, saying, "Do you know how much I love you?" They began the ascent, taking each darkened step slowly. . .carefully.

She took a deep, broken breath. "Sure." She could play this game. She wanted to look up—to try to determine the identity of the man— but was forced to keep her eyes on her feet, lest she fall.

"I don't believe you really do. I've paid quite a bit of money for you this evening, did you know that?"

"Yes."

"Oh, you do?"

"Yes." She could see the outline of the top of the stairs from midway there.

"Then you'll be sure to be a good girl."

"I'm always a good girl." They neared the top of the stairs.

"It is my birthday, after all."

"Oh, I see."

"Do you?" They reached the landing, where the light was a shade better. He turned then, and she looked up with a quick intake of breath. It was the man from the club. . .the man she despised. "Happy birthday to me," he cooed.

Candy jerked her hand out of his grip, but he grabbed her wrist again, wrapping his fingers like a vice. She felt the sports bag slip from her shoulder and onto the floor near her feet. "Let go of me!" She jerked her hand again, but he held tight.

"Now, now. I'm not so bad."

He took a step forward. She bent her knees and dug her feet into the flooring. "Let go of me!" she screamed again. "Let . . .me. . .go!" She bent at the waist, sinking her teeth into the flesh of his hand, and heard his scream before she felt him release her. She tried to move quickly, but she wasn't fast enough. Before she could turn to flee down the dark staircase, his uninjured hand flew up, slapping her firmly under her chin. She felt herself toppling. . .strained to gain control. . .but lost to his second blow.

Candy tumbled down the staircase, feet-over-head until she came to rest on the first floor landing. The last thing she remembered was the vile sound of bone snapping and the fragmented thoughts of her mother and brother and that this was a pathetic way to end a life.

CHAPTER FORTY-TWO

Tuesday, December 11, 2001
Early Morning

Phil arrived at Katie's office early Tuesday morning.

"I'm so glad you're here," she greeted him, closing her office door behind them.

They began to move toward the sofas. "Why? Has something else happened?"

"No," Katie answered, sitting on the farthest sofa. Phil took a seat directly opposite from her. "I just hate myself for my thoughts and concerns about Vickey. I want you to tell me—one way or the other—whether or not my assistant is involved in this."

"I don't think so."

Katie breathed a sigh of relief. "So, then what do you think?"

Phil gave a just-go-with-me-on-this-one look.

"What?"

"I think we may be looking at a continuing relationship between Sharkey and one of your girls."

Katie was quiet for a moment, allowing reality to set in. "Candy," she finally said.

Phil answered with a nod.

"What kind of proof do you have?"

Phil shared with her what John Weaver had witnessed. "I've done some background check. If you want I'll show you the file I'm building on her. And, the rest is intuition. Until we talk to her, we won't know anything for certain, at least as far as how she is tied to Caballero."

Katie stood and walked over to her desk where she picked up the phone and dialed a number. "This is Katharine Webster. Is Xi Lan where she can come to my office for a moment?. . .What do you mean?. . .I see. . .I see. . .yes, thank you." Katie returned the handset to the phone and turned to Phil behind her. "She's not at work. . ."

"You want to check her room?"

"Yes. Yes, I think we'd better."

Candy's room gave no indication as to where she was, only that she had not slept in her bed the night before. . .or perhaps she'd made her bed before leaving for the day. Neither assumption told Katie or Phil of her current whereabouts.

"Care if I look around a little?" Phil asked.

Katie shook her head. "No. Go ahead."

Phil strolled about the room, went through trash cans, opened and closed drawers, peeked into the bathroom. Katie continued to stand near the bed, arms folded across her abdomen, lips pressed firmly together, looking from one corner to the other. When Phil returned to her, she asked, "Anything?"

He shook his head. "Nothing out of the ordinary. If we don't find someone who's seen her recently, I'll dig a little deeper."

"Can you call someone? Missing persons?"

Phil moved toward the door and Katie followed him. "We'll need forty-eight hours to file a missing persons report."

"Forty-eight?" Katie and Phil exited the room and moved purposefully down the corridor.

"I'm afraid so."

Katie stopped, touched Phil lightly on the sleeve of his coat. "There's someone who might know something."

"Who?"

"A new girl came from the club yesterday. Misty. . ."

"Sharkey's girl? The redhead?"

Katie nodded. "Yes. How do you know about her?"

"She's Sharkey's. . .girl. . ."

Understanding fell over Katie's face. "Ah. Well, not anymore. She's here. If you think Candy has been at the club recently. . .or even in contact with Sharkey. . .she's the one to ask."

The two moved toward the elevators.

"What has she told you so far?" Phil asked. Reaching the elevators, he pushed the down button, then stood back and waited for the doors to open.

"Nothing. I put her in Ashley's room for the night last night. During the holidays we don't have rooms to spare, so—" The brass doors of the elevator slid open. Three patrons of the hotel got out and Phil and Katie got in.

The elevator operator smiled at them. "What floor, Mrs. Webster?"

Katie gave the floor of the girls' rooms. Moments later she and Phil were in front of Ashley's room, knocking lightly. "Misty? It's me. Katie Webster."

The door opened almost instantly. Misty's smile toward Katie was faint, but when she saw Phil standing beside her, it turned cold. "What's he doing here?"

"He's my friend. Misty, we need to talk to you."

Misty stepped back into the room. "I ain't talking about Sharkey. I don't ever want to talk about him again."

Phil extended a hand. "Misty, my name is Phil Silver. I'm not here to talk to you about Sharkey—though it may come to that. We need information about Candy."

Misty turned and climbed back into the unmade bed. She sat cross-legged in the middle and brought the coverings around her. "I don't want to talk about her either."

Katie walked over to the bed and sat on its edge, gracefully crossing one leg over the other. "Why not?"

Misty looked at her with piercing eyes. "Because she's trash, is why!"

Katie took in a quick breath. "I see. When was the last time you saw her?"

Misty snorted. "Night before last. Tramp was making plans with my old—my *ex*-old man."

Katie's eyes narrowed as though she were trying to understand. "Sharkey?"

"Yeah, who else?"

Phil moved toward a nearby chair, sat down and propped his elbows on his knees, leaning over slightly. "Let me see if I've got this straight. Candy was making plans with *Sharkey?*"

Misty looked at him. "Yeah. Talking about moving in with him this week." She looked back at Katie. "Why do you think I'd had enough? Like he's all that. . ."

"She was at the club?" Katie asked.

"Yeah."

"Has she been dancing there again?" Phil asked.

Misty gave her best boy-are-you-an-idiot look. "No, she was selling Girl Scout cookies."

Katie looked at Phil with a hint of compassion in her eyes. "Let's go back to her room and see. . ."

"They were up to no good, too." Misty's interruption brought both heads to a jerk.

"What kind of no good?" Phil asked.

"I heard them talking about this man who called them."

"What man?"

"Someone named Caba-something."

Katie and Phil looked from Misty to one another. "Bucky Caballero?" Phil asked.

"I guess." Misty shrugged.

Phil stood and Katie followed. "Let's go back to her room. The pieces are finally beginning to fit."

Phil and Katie returned to Candy's room, this time determined to dig a little deeper.

"What are you thinking?" Katie asked as they made their way back upstairs.

"That somehow Sharkey and Bucky connected with one another—hard to believe, but possible—and that Candy has been used as a pawn."

"Do you think the gifts came from them?"

"Yes."

"I suppose it makes sense."

"The matches and destruction from the other night was most likely their finale. Candy has made her choices and now that the deed is done, she's moving in with Sharkey."

Katie frowned. "That's a little hard to imagine."

Phil nodded. "I didn't want to say anything in front of Misty, but why in the world would a woman who looks like Candy want to sleep with a man like Sharkey?"

"Why indeed?"

The two stood before the door to Candy's room. "My professional opinion?"

"Sure."

"Candy was the victim of an early sexual encounter against her will. Some sort of molestation or rape. . .perhaps incest. . ."

"She never talks about her family, other than to say she has a mother and baby brother. I asked her once about her father, and she said he was dead, but her personnel sheet shows that her mother has a different last name."

"So she has a stepfather?"

"I assume so."

"There you have it."

Katie opened the door to Candy's room and they stepped in. "So what then?" Katie inquired.

"So Candy needs to know that she is being accepted. The only way for her to feel accepted is to use her sexuality. Your efforts were good, Katie, and I commend you for them, but someone like Candy needs deep counseling." Phil walked over to the nearest bedside table and began to plunder through it.

Katie frowned. "I should have remembered that. Some girls dance because it's good money. Others dance because they don't know any other way to make a living than with their bodies. They think what they are doing is somehow acceptable because they aren't prostitutes and because the exotic dance business is legitimate."

Phil walked over to the desk where a pad and pencil lay forgotten next to the phone. He picked it up and began to study it. "Sounds about right. May I advise that if you want to keep this help line open, you employ the aid of a professional counselor?"

Katie looked down. "I will." Glancing back up, she commented, "What are you looking at on that piece of paper?"

Phil picked up the pencil and began to sketch across the top piece of paper. "Looks like we have an address written here."

Katie stepped over. "Where?"

Phil returned the pencil to the desk. "SoHo."

"SoHo?"

Phil tore the top sheet off the pad, folded it, and placed it in his coat top pocket. "Tell you what we're going to do," he said, patting his chest over the pocket. "You're going to go back to work, and I'm going to head over to One Police Plaza to have a little chat with some old friends there."

They moved toward the door of Candy's room. "From there?" Katie asked.

"I'm going to see about having some warrants issued. From there, I'll take part in a little chat with Mr. Garone, then follow up on the address on this paper."

Katie and Phil exited the room and began—again—down the corridor. "You'll keep me apprised?" Katie asked.

"Of course."

They continued toward the elevators in silence. Upon reaching them, Phil cut teasing eyes at Katie and smiled. "I believe our case is coming to a close. Merry Christmas, Katie."

Katie placed Ashley and Brittany on prayer alert for Candy, explaining to them as best she could what had occurred since any of them had last seen Candy.

"I can't say I'm surprised," Brittany responded from across Katie's office desk.

"Me neither," Ashley added.

"Why do you say that?" Katie asked.

"That girl always went along with whatever she thought would get her ahead the quickest. I tried to like her—really I did—and I thought you'd be the one to help her. But she's got issues."

Ashley nodded. "I think she was raped or something when she was young."

"That's no excuse," Katie answered. "We've all had difficult times, but we have to come to a point where we stop looking at excuses or reasons or whatever you want to call them and begin fresh. It's not wise to allow past mistakes—whether ours or those brought upon us—to dictate what we do in the future."

"Easier said than done, Katie," Brittany commented.

Katie paused for a moment. . .looked over her left shoulder, beyond the sofas and the window to the buildings beyond. She remembered the mother and child she had seen together, and her eyes filled with tears. Looking back to the girls, she said, "Ladies, I think it's time I told you the story of my life. . . ."

CHAPTER FORTY-THREE
Tuesday, Early Evening

Katie tugged black gloves over her slender hands with a frown. "Phil called late this afternoon. They've taken Sharkey in for questioning and went to the address on Prince Street."

"And?" Marcy stood with Katie in the foyer of her apartment, watching her prepare to go out for the evening.

"By the time he got there, the gallery was shut up tight. I guess they closed early."

"Odd for the holiday season."

"Phil thought so, too."

"Are they running some background on who owns the place?"

Katie placed her hands on her hips. "You know too much, you know that? And the answer is yes. Yes, they are. He'll call as soon as he knows something. Now, then. Are you sure you won't go with me to the McKenzie's tonight?"

Marcy shook her head, no. "Not on your life. Those *sweet* people," she said with a grin, "don't want me there and you know it."

Katie's frown increased. "Marcy, didn't we talk about this before? The reason why? Please tell me you understand."

Maggie approached with Katie's coat, which Marcy took from her. "Allow me, Mags."

Maggie handed the coat to Marcy with an opinion of her own. "Doesn't do a body any good to go out on such a night as this, Miss Katie. I think you should cancel the whole thing."

Katie smiled. "Sweet Maggie," she began, turning so Marcy could slip the coat sleeves over her arms, "I won't be gone long. I promise." She turned back to face the elderly woman, buttoning the wool coat around her. "You worry too much."

Maggie shook her finger at her. "And you don't worry enough." With that, she walked away.

Katie grimaced. "That's one sweet woman."

Marcy nodded. "That's one tough bird."

Katie reached for the door handle. "All right then. What are you going to do this evening?"

"Call Charlie. . .you know, I'm going to have to set a time to go home. . ."

Katie's shoulders sank. "I know. We're days away from Christmas; you should be with your family."

Marcy touched the sleeve of Katie's coat. "Why not come with me? You and Maggie? To Georgia for the remainder of the season?"

Katie shook her head. "Oh, I can't do that. I have too many responsibilities. The tea. . .the hotel in general. . .and I may have to stick around if Phil tells me there's a case against Sharkey." Katie opened the front door of her apartment.

"What would you like me to do if we hear from Candy?"

Katie took a step out into the hallway, then turned a sad face to her childhood friend. "Call my cell phone if you hear anything."

Marcy reached out her arms for a hug.

The friends embraced one another, and Katie added, "Ashley is keeping tabs on Misty tonight, and Brittany is working downstairs at Jacqueline's. I instructed them to come to you if *they* heard anything."

When they separated, Marcy responded, "I'll see you later, then."

"Okay." Katie moved toward the elevators.

"Have fun with your new friends," Marcy mocked.

The elevator doors slid open. "Ha-ha," Katie said smiling, then stepped into the elevators. "See you when I return," she called out.

The elevator doors closed, and Marcy returned to the apartment.

CHAPTER FORTY-FOUR

Katie pulled the address of Zane and Zandra McKenzie out of her purse where she had stashed it several days earlier. "Here you go," she said to Simon, who had opened the door of the limo for her. "I haven't even had time to look at it."

Simon looked down at the card in his hand. "No problem. We'll be there in no time."

"Oh, good," Katie replied, slipping into the warmth of the car.

Simon closed the door behind her, ran around to the other side of the car, opened the front door and slid behind the wheel. He slowly pulled away from the curb in front of The Hamilton Place, then lowered the partition between them. "I'm going to run an address scan on my navigator up here at the red light, Mrs. Webster."

"That's fine, Simon."

"I think I know where this is, but I'm not a hundred percent."

Katie nodded. The partition returned to its original position and Katie sat back and closed her eyes. She was so tired. She hoped this dress rehearsal didn't last the two hours Zane and Zandra expected it to. As soon as they were done, she'd excuse herself—explain that she'd been under a lot of stress lately...explain about Candy's disappearance and the need to get home in case Phil called. She needed sleep, she'd tell them. After all, tomorrow was the fashion show, and they would want her to look her best. To make up for her leaving early, she'd invite them to dinner after the first of the year. She'd tell them about Maggie and what a wonderful cook she was. . .

She felt the car come to a stop. They were at the red light, so Simon would be checking for an exact location of the address. She admonished herself for not having done it earlier. Her eyes opened, knowing her chauffeur would inform her of their destination momentarily.

The glass of the partition lowered. "I've got a location, Mrs. Webster," Simon said, turning his head to look over his right shoulder.

"Okay."

"It's not too far. Right down the road in Chelsea. They live in the Chelsea Mercantile."

Brittany loved her new job. She thought herself the luckiest of girls, too, to be working for people like Zane and Zandra McKenzie. They were distant sometimes, but mostly kind and willing to teach her what she needed to know to succeed in a fashion career. One thing was for sure; they were extremely interested in Katie—always asking questions about her. If it made them happy, she didn't mind answering them. . .as long as they didn't get *too* personal.

"Brittany," a voice from behind her spoke. She turned from where she had been unboxing a new shipment of purses and setting them on a counter in the back room, to see Zane's wife, Miller. Brittany called her "Miller, the chick with the unusual name," but not to her face. To her face she called her Miller. So far she enjoyed working with the wife of her employer immensely. They had talked about everything from their favorite designer to their favorite rock group. They'd even talked about catching a movie before Christmas because they both loved George Clooney and his new movie was due out any day.

"Yes, Miller."

"I'm going to go out for a little while. . .to get something to eat. The baby is hungry. . . ." She patted a tummy not yet showing.

Brittany leaned against the counter. "How far along?"

"Three months. Nearly four."

"Girl, I remember when I was pregnant. I couldn't have worked, I'll tell you that much."

Miller smiled, showing small and even teeth. Miller McKenzie was a lovely though somewhat plain and unadorned blond in her late twenties. "It's not easy!" she said with a laugh. "But Zane insisted that I help you tonight. He's so wrapped up in this fashion show—he and Zandra—they can't think about too much else." Miller ran a hand over her cheek and allowed her chin to rest in the palm of her hand for a moment.

"Can I ask you a question?" Brittany was still holding a purse. She set it down on the counter behind her.

"Sure."

"Do you two get along okay? You and Zandra, I mean?"

Miller chuckled. "No."

Brittany smiled, her dark face contrasting with the whiteness of her teeth. "I didn't think so."

"I'll be glad when I can convince Zane to either move out or move her out. But she. . ."

"She?"

"I know they're twins, but she sort of controls him. I don't think it's natural."

"Really?"

Miller waved a hand. "I shouldn't be telling you this. . ."

Brittany laughed again. "Why not? We've talked about everything else tonight!"

Miller laughed too, just as the front door bell indicated a customer had entered the store. "We have, haven't we? Listen, I'm going out the back. Can you handle the customer okay?"

"Sure I can."

Brittany watched Miller leave by the back door, then walked to the front of the store where Marcy was standing over the accessories table. "Hey, girl," she greeted.

Marcy looked up. "Do they allow you to greet patrons like that?"

The lilt in Marcy's voice brought a smile to Brittany's lips as she walked to the other side of the table. "No, way. But when I saw it was just you. . ."

"Oh, sure. I should report you, you know."

"I hear you. Shopping alone tonight?"

Marcy picked up the scarf Katie had fondled a few days before. "Katie liked this, and I thought I would surprise her with it."

Brittany took the scarf. "Right this way, Madame. I'll be happy to gift wrap that for you. . ."

"Your home is lovely," Katie remarked to Zandra as she entered the apartment located on Seventh Avenue and glanced about the foyer and visible rooms beyond.

Zandra, looking more exotic than ever in a dark red, silk pants set, closed the door behind Katie. "Thank you. Zane decorated it. He's wonderful, don't you think?"

Katie slipped out of her coat, folding it across her arms. "I am very impressed. I'll have to keep him in mind if I ever want to redecorate my apartment."

"May I take your coat and purse?"

"Thank you." Katie handed over her coat and clutch.

"I'll take this into my bedroom where you'll be changing, so you'll have it close by when you're ready to leave."

Katie heard a door to her right open. She glanced over to see Zane exiting a bedroom. He closed the door behind him, smiling warmly. "Katie. How lovely to see you." He approached her; kissed her on each cheek. "Allow me to show you into the drawing room."

Zane extended his arm forward, indicating that Katie should walk ahead of him. She nodded once then stepped across the foyer into the drawing room. "This whole building is incredible," Katie noted.

"It was originally built in the early 1900s."

"Really?"

Zane indicated one of two light blue Louis XVI chairs angled near the fireplace. Katie sat, crossing her legs comfortably as she did so. "It was a cloak and suit factory," Zane continued, sitting in the twin chair. "It was only recently renovated for residential living." He tilted his head toward one of the windows behind him. "If it were daylight, you could see the courtyard below. Beautifully landscaped."

Zandra rejoined them, sitting across from them on the plush white sofa. "Zane, drinks?" she said.

Zane stood. "Katie? Wine?"

"I'd like that, yes."

Zane moved toward a doorway leading to what—in the dim lighting—Katie made out to be a dining room. Zandra turned to look at her brother. "Oh, Zane. Make it the Cabernet we purchased in SoHo at the festival."

Zane stopped long enough to smile at her, then moved into the dining room. Katie watched his shadowy figure being swallowed by the darkness, then illuminate as he pushed through a swinging door into a well-lit kitchen. She turned back to Zandra, who was watching her intently. "How is Brittany doing at the boutique?" she asked.

Zandra nodded, her face somewhat expressionless. "Very well. She's there tonight with my sister-in-law."

Katie felt somewhat ill at ease. Zandra was difficult to talk to simply by virtue of her beauty. "Zane tells me this building opened for residency last year. Where did you live before that?"

"We had an apartment near Central Park West."

"Oh?" Katie briefly wondered how two struggling entrepreneurs could afford to live as they did, but dismissed the thought immediately when Zane re-entered, carrying a small silver tray with three glasses of wine.

Over the next few minutes the trio talked lightly of business. . .the holidays. . .and the immediate concerns of the fashion show. At the final topic, Katie set her half-consumed glass of wine on a nearby table and stood. "Well, why don't you show me where I can go to change into my first to-die-for outfit?"

Zandra stood and walked away from the sofas and toward the foyer with Katie just behind her. "My room is here to the left," Zandra told her. She opened the door, revealing an unusually decorated bedroom. Against the far wall, painted in a warm coffee-tinted hue, was an antique French campaign bed. A large leather and brass trunk served as a table in the center of the room, flanked by a uniquely shaped chair. The walls were accented with black and white prints of New York City. A small end table, adorned by a single silver-framed photograph and a bust of a Grecian lady, remained in a corner by itself. Katie thought the room was as unusual as the woman who slept there. "How do you like it?"

"I do!" Katie exclaimed, then swerved slightly, bringing her hand up to the wall to steady herself. She laughed lightly. "Forgive me. I'm feeling a little lightheaded."

Zandra smiled. "Surely you are not tipsy from the wine?"

"Oh, no. A half a glass?"

Zandra didn't answer. She walked over to a closet, opened it, and pulled three designs from the rack. "Here you go. Try this one on first," she said, indicating a black, tight fitting, beaded full-length dress.

"It's lovely," Katie breathed, reaching for it.

"You'll be lovely in it." Zandra laid the gown across Katie's outstretched arms. "I'll leave you to try it on. If this one doesn't fit, we have several others to choose from."

Katie held the dress to its full length. "I think it will fit like a glove." She lightly fingered it. "When we're done with the show, this goes home with me."

Zandra smiled from the door. "Music to my brother's ears. Just come out when you're ready."

Katie nodded, watched Zandra close the door behind her, then walked over to the bed and draped the gown across it. She had worn a matching platinum silk georgette skirt and V-neck tunic to the McKenzie's because it was both chic and easy to get out of. She slipped the skirt from her slender hips with the palms of her hands, stepping out of it and laying it across the bed next to the gown. She reached for the hem of the tunic, pulled it over her head, and placed it on top of the skirt. She felt herself growing dizzy again, reached for the bedpost and held on to steady herself.

Katie placed her fingertips to her forehead. "I must be coming down with something. . ." she said to no one. She closed her eyes and, feeling better, reopened them. The room spun once, then stopped. She took a deep breath, reached for the gown, slipped it off the hanger and over the top of her head. It melted over her body deliciously, the cold satin lining sending shivers down her spine. She looked around for a mirror and when she couldn't find one, went to the wall mirror in the adjoining bath.

Zandra's bath was as exotic as she. The room—even in the florescent light Katie had switched on—was stark and white. The tub was inset in marble, adorned with a silk plant and two white urns. The vanity held none of the usual cosmetics one would expect. Rather, a small vase of fresh flowers stood alone and to the left of the basin. Over it, a large mirror enabled Katie to study her reflection.

She squinted her eyes; her vision had blurred a bit. She blinked and she came back into focus. She stepped closer to the mirror, turned slightly, smiled at what she saw. The gown was lovely, and she liked the way she looked in it. It was the perfect outfit for the upcoming company social gathering.

She stepped out of the bathroom, flipping the switch as she exited, and noted the glint of light bouncing from the silver frame near the bed. The photograph was of a man, and Katie nosily wondered if it were Zandra's boyfriend. She stepped over to it—she would only glance at it so she could ask Zandra about it later—and took it into her hand. Again, the face was blurry, but blinking her eyes brought it back into view.

What she saw horrified her.

She was looking at a photograph of David Franscella.

Marcy followed Brittany into the back room of the boutique where the wrapping paper was stored. "Wrap it special," she said.

Brittany looked over her shoulder. "Of course."

They stopped in front of the wrapping counter. "Do they have any little cards I can sign while you're wrapping?"

Brittany jerked her head toward the front of the store. "Next to the cash register."

Marcy left Brittany to her tasks, walked back into the front of the store and over to the cash register. She searched the counter, but didn't see anything. "Did you say they were next to the cash register?"

Brittany walked to the door. "Yeah, right. . ." She stopped. "Where did they go? Maybe we've used them all. . ." She walked behind the register and opened several drawers in search of stored cards. On her third attempt, she smiled. "Here we go. A whole stack of cards. We've got Happy Birthday. We've got Get Well Soon. We've got Happy Anniversary. . ." Brittany shuffled the cards as she spoke, laying them on the counter between her and Marcy. "And we even have some generic ones with pretty little flowers on them."

"No Merry Christmas?"

"No, sorry."

Marcy frowned. " 'Just 'Cause You're My Friend'?"

Brittany smiled, showing large white teeth. "No."

Marcy pretended to be more than a little upset. "Okay, then. Let me see the blank ones with the little flowers."

Brittany slid one of the cards across the counter. Marcy took it in her hands and glanced at it briefly. "Do you have a pen?"

Brittany pointed to a crystal bowl filled with them. "Right there."

Marcy reached for one, then jerked her attention back to the card. "Wait a minute! Where have I seen this card before?"

"He was my lover."

Startled, Katie spun around, dropping the silver frame to the floor. Upon impact, the glass shattered. The room came in and out of focus. . . once, twice. . .then settled into view again.

"You didn't know that, did you?" Zandra continued, walking slowly toward her.

Katie took a step back and gripped the poster of the bed. "What is this all about?"

Zandra stopped and smiled sardonically. "Don't you know? It's about revenge. It's about you taking David away from me and me taking you away. Period."

"Who are you?"

"Zandra McKenzie."

"Is that who you really are?" Katie glanced over Zandra's shoulder to see Zane entering the bedroom with them.

"Zane and Zandra McKenzie, yes," he answered for her. "Sorry, Katie. If it were up to me, we wouldn't be doing this, but my sister. . ."

Katie felt her breathing slow in its pace. "You've drugged me, haven't you?"

Zandra stepped closer to her and for the first time she noticed that she was holding her wine glass. "Yes, and if you'd been a good little girl, we wouldn't have to get so dirty with this."

"*You* sent the gifts?"

Zane smiled. "We couldn't afford much more. The necklace was quite a setback."

Katie shook her head. "What was the *point*? If you want to kill me, why not just kill me? Why the gifts. . .the store. . ."

Zandra ran her teeth over her bottom lip. It was almost provocative. "Knowing you thought you would get your man back. . .this brought me such delight. Knowing I wouldn't get mine back. . . ." Zandra paused for a pregnant moment. "Do you know how hard it is to come from nothing, to gain everything, then to lose it all again? I worked my whole life toward the things David could give me with a snap of his finger. He loved me and I loved him. He adored me really. With him, I could finally achieve all I'd ever wanted to achieve." She turned to look at her brother briefly. "We both could."

Katie took in several deep breaths, trying to focus on what her new captors were saying. Not so much the words. The words she could grasp. The reasoning, she could not. "How were you connected with Bucky Caballero?"

The twins looked at one another, then back to Katie. "Who?" Zane asked.

A giggle of irony escaped Katie's lips. "Timing," was all she said.

"Enough of this!" Zandra stomped a foot. "You know enough, and that's all you need to know!" She looked at her brother. "We have a lot to do if we are going to carry this out to plan."

Zane shoved his hands in his pants pockets, drawing out several feet of thin cord. "Let me see your hands, Katie."

"No."

He came closer. "I'm afraid so. Don't fight. Don't make this uglier than it has to be."

Katie's eyes darted to the open bathroom door. Before anyone could move to stop her, she bolted into it, slammed and locked the door behind her. She took deep, necessary breaths in an effort to stay alert enough to fight. She stumbled to the basin, turned the cold-water faucet on full blast, purposefully keeping her focus away from the slamming at the bathroom door. Cupping her hand into the spray of water, she splashed it on her face several times. A loud thud against the door caused her to turn suddenly.

If she didn't do something quickly, they would kill her.

"What is the point of all this?" she screamed. Her body was erect now, arms stiff and hands down by her side.

"You killed David!" Zandra yelled from the other side. "Do you know how much I loved him?"

Katie noticed a bombe chest against the wall nearest the door. She moved to it quickly and using all the strength left in her, began to push against it, forcing it in front of the door. Several beads popped off the dress and spilled onto the bathroom floor, rolling like miniature marbles in a pinball machine. "*He* was going to kill *me*!" she yelled back, just as she got the chest in front of the door. Another thud and the wood of the door seemed ready to crack. "You can't possibly think you'll get away with this? Too many people know I'm here!"

Katie turned to look around the room. Her hair had fallen into her face and with both hands she pushed it away. This bath didn't have a window. Calling or crawling out wasn't an option. Even with a window, the apartment the McKenzie twins shared was too high from the ground. She would have to find something in the room to protect herself with until. . .until when, she wasn't sure.

Katie reached for the drawers of the vanity in search of a homemade weapon, slipped on one of the dress's rejected beads, and fell to her knees. She grabbed for the edge of the vanity and pulled herself up. "Dear God, how am I going to get out of here?" she prayed.

"What are you saying?" Phil yelled into the phone. He had been at One Police Plaza nearly all day, and a new level of exhaustion was setting in.

"I'm saying I think Zane and Zandra McKenzie are our phantom gift givers."

"Why would you think that?"

Marcy stood in the back room of Jacqueline's with Brittany standing guard in the front. "I don't have time to go into details, Silver. You've got to trust me. Katie is over there now!"

Phil Silver sighed deeply. "All right. All right. Do you know where they live?"

"No, but Simon is with her. We can call the limo. . ."

"Do you have the number?"

"I'm sure Maggie has it."

There was a pause before Phil said. "Get it. Call Simon and then call me right back. Do not. . .let me repeat myself. . .do *not* go over there alone! In fact, you stay put!"

Marcy held the hand piece of the phone away from her ear and frowned at it. Bringing it back, she said, "See you later, Silver."

Simon sat in the darkness of the limousine. The engine was running, the heat keeping him warm in the sub-freezing temperature. He had hooked up his laptop just moments after Mrs. Webster had entered the Chelsea Mercantile for her appointment. Waiting for it to boot up, he glanced at the card she had given him earlier. Zane and Zandra McKenzie, it read, followed by the Seventh Avenue address. He wedged the card between the letter keys and the number keys, glanced out the window and up and across the breadth of the building. It was most assuredly an impressive structure.

The computer came to life. Simon opened the downloaded program—Cyber Detect—designed for personal searches of anyone. . .anywhere. . .

Simon shifted comfortably in his seat, typed in the name: *Zane McKenzie.* He frowned at the information on the screen. Other than the usual stuff—name, DOB, SSN, address, work history—there was little other information. Information as to his one-time ad-modeling career brought a chuckle. He had seen Zane McKenzie. He was certainly good-looking enough to be a model, and the agency he'd modeled for and companies who'd used him were impressive enough. What was he doing selling clothes in a small boutique in a hotel with a mug like that?

Simon cleared the screen, typed in ZAND. . .when the car phone rang. He turned from the laptop, reached over the back of it and lifted the phone to his ear. "Simon," he answered.

"Simon, it's Marcy Waters."

Marcy Waters sounded out of breath and anxious. The hair on the back of his neck prickled against the starched white collar of his shirt. "What can I do for you, Mrs. Waters?"

"Simon, are you still with Mrs. Webster?"

Simon looked out the window again. "She's upstairs with the McKenzie's."

"Simon, listen to me. Katie may be in danger. What is your exact location?"

"We're at the Chelsea Mercantile on Seventh Ave in Chelsea."

Simon heard Marcy repeat the address to someone, followed by, "Do you know where that is?" A female voice answered, "Yeah, I know. . ."

"Mrs. Waters, what's—"

"Simon. Call the number I'm about to give you. It's for Mr. Silver. Then get to Katie as fast as you can. . ."

Simon typed the phone number into his computer where he had been typing in Zandra McKenzie's name. "Got it," he said. "I'll call right now."

"I'll see you shortly," Marcy answered, then disconnected the line.

"There are too many people who know I'm here!" Katie repeated from her place before the vanity. She had opened several drawers, revealing makeup, cotton balls, toothpaste, a toothbrush. One deep drawer held a variety of brushes and expensive styling products.

Pounding against the door answered her exasperations. "We've taken care of all that," Zandra called back. "Do you think we are stupid?"

"Zandra, shut up and help me," Katie heard Zane order. "There's a meat cleaver in the kitchen. Go get it."

Katie's head jerked and she looked over her shoulder at the door, then back to the drawers in the vanity. She squatted to open the bottom drawer on the right, revealing a hodgepodge of items, including several makeup bags, personal hygiene items, and a pair of scissors. Her fingers grasped the scissors. She brought them up to her face, breathing heavily, aware that she was growing weaker. She stood, steadied herself, then turned on the water again and splashed herself with one cupped hand while the other held onto the very item she prayed she didn't have to use.

Phil sprinted to his car, parked in the parking garage of One Police Plaza, located in South Manhattan. "Call." He ground his teeth together, looking down at the cell phone in his right hand. White condensation puffed from his lips and blew back into his face. As he reached his car, the phone rang. He answered it immediately, shifting it to his left hand. "Silver." His right hand dug into his pant's pocket, searching for his keys.

"Mr. Silver. This is Simon—"

"Where are you, Simon?" He pulled the keys from the pocket.

"The Chelsea Mercantile. . ."

"Seventh Ave?" Key shoved into lock, twisted and opening the door.

"Yes, Sir. What's going—"

"Stay put. I'll be there—" Phil panted, sliding behind the steering wheel of his car.

"No, Sir."

Phil reached for the door handle and stopped. "Excuse me?"

"No, Sir. Not if Mrs. Webster is in any danger. I'm going in there. . ."

Phil slammed the door and cursed under his breath. Simon was as obstinate as Waters. . . "Simon, I'm calling this in right now. You need to stay put to show the officers where she is!" He turned the ignition. "Do you hear me, Simon? I'm calling this in now. Stay put!" He disconnected the line, dialed 9-1-1, and prayed he wasn't too late.

Using the ceramic bust, Zane managed to force a hole in the center of the bathroom door. Through the opening, he saw Katie Webster, pressed against the side of the vanity. Her face was dripping with water. One hand gripped the side of the counter while the other was hidden behind her back.

Zandra ran in behind him just then, panting, "I couldn't find it!"

"I don't need it, *hermana*. We're in." He reached his arm into the hole, grasping for the lock on the other side. He could see their reflection in the mirror behind Katie and was aware of the chest in front of the door. "Oh that's good, Katie," he said sweetly, smiling at her as he spoke. "You're a smart woman. I like that. In fact, I like you. Be a good girl and open the door for me." Zane's arm dangled inside the bathroom, his hand struggled to reach the half-moon lock.

"What is she doing?" his sister asked behind him.

Zane ducked his head a bit, his eyes focusing on the woman barricaded inside. She took a step toward him. "That's right, Katie. Come on. The easier you make this for me, the easier I make this for you. Don't make me have to hurt you." He looked back into the mirror, angling himself just so, trying to see what Katie Webster held behind her back.

Suddenly she bolted toward him, exposing the hand, brandishing a pair of scissors. Her arm came down. He felt the searing pain of ripping flesh before he comprehended exactly what she had done. He screamed;

felt the scissors enter his arm again and again. Expletives and spit slung from his mouth. Behind him, Zandra screamed as well, calling his attacker vile and hateful names.

Katie couldn't believe what she had done. Not only had she stabbed Zane McKenzie's arm once, she had done it three times. Blood soaked the fine silk shirtsleeve he wore and began to drip onto the top of the bombe chest. The wounded arm recoiled and through the hole he had made, Katie could see Zane backing up several steps, clutching his arm with his good hand. Explosively, he ran toward the door, forcing his weight into it. The wood—broken and weak—began to fall away in pieces, exposing the two rooms and three enemies to one another. Zane staggering backward, while Zandra—screaming in Spanish—pushed the bombe chest so forcefully, it slid across the room toward the enclosed tub.

Katie backed up, looked behind her for a breath of a second, then grabbed one of the vases on the tub with her left hand. She smashed it against the brass faucet, revealing jagged edges. She was now armed with a broken vase and a pair of bloodied scissors. It may not be enough to save her, but she wouldn't go down without a fight. From somewhere in the recesses of her mind, she was aware of sirens screeching in the city streets below. *Were they coming for her?*

Zandra wildly flung herself toward her. Katie jabbed the vase at her, hoping to scare her off. She pushed herself against the vanity, rubbing along the side of it, trying to make it to the door. Her eyes cut to it and she saw Zane—irate and seething—his chest heaving up and down. She surged toward Zandra, pushing her with all her weight, felt her slipping, then jumped back as the small woman fell against the tub, popping her head and slumping over, unconscious. The sound of beads rolling about the floor continued even after the fall was complete.

Katie turned back to Zane, who hurried to his sister's inert form. He screamed profanities, kneeling beside her, followed by, "Mother Mary, full of grace. . ."

Katie looked from the twins to the door and back again. This might be her only chance. She moved as quickly as she dared, away from the verbal assault and the danger; away from the dishevelment of the room that held her captive. As she reached the door leading into the hallway a force pushed against her from behind and she fell face forward to her stomach. She twisted her torso; Zane held firmly to her calves and feet. Still in heels, she began to kick at his chest, one time spearing him in the cheek of his face. He screamed, bent down and bit her leg, causing her to kick all the harder. She realized she still held the scissors tightly in her right hand. She jerked herself around, sitting up abruptly and sliced into his shoulder blade.

Zane McKenzie's body contorted. His face was a mixture of hatred and agony. Katie kicked one more time, sliding away from his grip. She spun around to her knees and stood, running toward the front door. She heard a scream from her own lips, involuntarily escaping in the panic of the moment. "Help me! Help me!" she shrieked.

"Mrs. Webster!"

Katie began to fiddle with the lock of the door, aware of the sound of her name beyond it. She stole a glance behind her, saw Zane struggling to rise, then returned her attention to the lock. With a final flick of her wrist, she unbolted the door, swung it wide, and ran straight into the protective arms of her chauffeur. She felt him pulling her into the hallway, heard scrambling and yelling behind him, and turned her head to look. A half dozen police officers stormed into the McKenzie apartment.

"Katie!"

Simon held her more firmly, helping her to turn at the sound of Phil's voice coming up the stairs. Her hand flew up to her mouth, and she began to sob.

Katie sat in the limousine, wrapped in a police blanket, shivering despite the heat coming from the car. She stared out the half-lowered window, watched as emergency workers loaded Zandra into the back of one ambulance and Zane into the back of another. Curious observers gathered in clusters along the sidewalks illuminated by red and blue rotating lights as well as the overhead street lamps. Phil stood several yards away, speaking quietly and authoritatively to several officers and investigators. She smiled at the scene. *God love him*, she thought, *he was made for this work.*

Marcy, who had arrived moments after the excitement had begun to fade, stood quietly next to him. Katie knew the forced silence was killing her friend, and she was proud of her resolution to behave and not interfere.

"You okay, Mrs. Webster?" The question came from Simon, who stood outside her door, guarding her like an old stone soldier. Katie looked up and out the window at his stoic face looking down upon her. She nodded. Yes, she was okay. For now.

She returned her attention to the group of law enforcement officers and Marcy, who had now broken away and walked toward the car. She stepped around the back of it, opened the opposite door from where Katie sat and slid in, closing the door behind her. "How ya doin' there, kiddo?"

Katie looked at her friend. "Okay."

"You put up quite a fight."

"I suppose I did." The two sat in silence for a moment before Katie continued. "How did Phil know?"

"I called him and told him."

Katie looked at her friend with surprise. "How did *you* know?"

"I went into Jacqueline's to buy you a little gift. . ."

"You did?"

"Yeah. Brittany and I found the generic cards used in the floral arrangements."

Katie turned to look straight ahead, trying to comprehend it all. "I see. What about Zane's wife?"

"I just heard Phil say they'd picked her up. From what the cops over there are saying, she didn't know anything about what they were planning to do. From where it stands now, she thought she was innocently sending you some flowers from her husband. She said he told her he didn't want you to think they were brown-nosing."

Katie laughed lightly. "Are they buying that?"

"I guess they'll know more later."

"I suppose so." Katie looked down at her hands, remembering the feel of the scissors. . .the sound of flesh tearing under the blades.

"Katie."

Katie looked over to Marcy. "Hmm?"

"There's one other thing you need to know."

"What?"

"One of the officers told Silver they found the body of a girl they believe to be Xi Lan Tso."

Katie's head fell back against the leather of the seat and her eyes rolled shut. "Oh, dear God. . ."

Marcy reached for her hand. "I'm sorry."

"Do they know who did it?" Tears slipped down her cheeks.

"No. Not yet. But Phil seems to think it's tied to the address on the pad and Sharkey." Marcy slid closer to Katie, wrapped her arms around her. "Let it out, Katie," she whispered. "Let it all out."

With that, Katie broke down and sobbed again. "I tried so hard. . ." she wailed. "I tried so hard. . ."

"I know you did."

Katie doubled over the supportive arms that held her, leaned over and rested her head against Marcy's shoulder. "Take me home," she whispered.

"Okay. We'll go home now. And you know what else? I'll even let you sleep in my bed again tonight."

"Just like old times?"

"Just like old times."

CHAPTER FORTY-FIVE

"Where are you, Mrs. Webster?"

"Hmm?"

"I asked you where you were. . .walking along all starry eyed and dreamy."

The dream had begun again. . .Katie recognized it instantly as being just like the one she'd dreamt just days before. . .subconsciously told herself it was *déjà vu* and asked why she was dreaming it again. . . *"Somewhere between reality and the place where dreams are made."*

Everything remained the same. . .the path they walked, the sunlight spilling through the trees, the way Ben kissed her. . .gently at first, then more amorously. The same burst of sunlight winked at her from beyond the tree branches.

"Where did you learn to kiss like that, Mr. Webster?" she asked.

"What was her name?" he teased, as he had done before.

They laughed, then Ben told her about the chalet in France. "As it turns out, a friend of mine has the most charming little chalet near the Lötschen Valley. . ."

"Where is that?"

"It's part of the Swiss Alps."

Katie again felt as though she were about to burst. "Are you serious? You're taking me to the Swiss Alps for Christmas?"

"Don't forget about the little chalet."

Katie stopped in their walk again and turned to face her husband. "Ben, I know you. When you say 'little' it's big. But, I don't care about that. I've never seen the Alps." She clapped her hands for effect. "I'm going to the Alps! I'm going to the Alps!"

Ben laughed again. "Okay, hold my hand and walk with me. I'll tell you the truth."

Katie frowned. "The truth? You aren't taking me to the Alps?"

"Yes, Sweetheart, I'm taking you to the Alps. I want to tell you the truth about the little chalet."

"Oh."

They began to walk—just as they had done before—and Katie listened to her husband as he described the place he would be taking her. "You'll be so impressed. It truly is perfect. Perfect for healing from emotional bruises and things like that."

"And Christmas holidays?"

"Most especially Christmas holidays. It's very French Country. Stone fireplaces and hearths and polished stone floors with scattered rugs. Louis Philippe furniture. Fantastic tapestries and a kitchen filled with lots of baskets hanging from the ceiling."

"I love it already."

"You will love it more when you see it. The countryside is breathtaking, Katie. In the morning, if we wake up early enough, we can sit outside and sip on hot French coffee and watch the sun rising over the lake behind my friend's place."

"A lake?"

"A fantastic lake. Mist on the water. . ."

"It sounds magical."

"It is. In the distance, you can hear the cow bells echoing up thru the valley."

Katie stopped walking and turned to her husband. "Take me

there, Ben. Take me there, now."

She closed her eyes. Cupping her face in his hands, Ben kissed her again. Again and again and again until she was breathless from the sheer pleasure of it. His lips traced a line from her mouth to her eyes and finally to her ear where he whispered something to her in French. . .something she couldn't quite make out in the feathery softness of it.

She kept her eyes closed as she asked, "What?" Her voice was nearly inaudible and—this time—her heart pounded, desperate to understand what she was being told.

He said it again.

"I don't understand," she whispered back, tears spilling down her cheeks.

"Yes, you do." He spoke into her ear, nibbling here and there as he made love to her with his words.

"No. No, I don't understand."

"Listen. Listen with your heart, not your ears."

He released her face, took a step back from her, said the words a third time, and then fell silent. Katie's breathing was slow and steady as she tried to decipher the words. "I don't know," she whispered again, then became aware of the stillness and silence around her. She opened her eyes.

He was gone. He was gone, and she stood alone on a small country lane leading nowhere.

Katie sat up with a gasp.

Marcy sat up just as quickly. "What? What?" She looked around the room as though someone were there with them, then reached for the lamp on the bedside table.

Katie grabbed her hand, turned a tear-streaked face toward her, and said, "I know what he said!"

"Who?" Marcy winked one eye, trying to adjust to the invasion of light in the dark room.

"Ben. In the dream."

"You had the dream again?" Both eyes opened.

"Yes."

"What? What did he say?"

"Cherche-moi toujours."

"Help me out here, Katie. My French is rusty."

"It means," Katie took a breath before she went on. "It means, never stop looking for me. Never. . .stop looking for me. . ."

EPILOGUE

Dark Asian eyes, set perfectly against a honey complexion, peered through the bare windows and onto the French countryside beyond. The woman behind them leaned against the window frame. Before her—through the glass panes—the gentle hills were covered in snow, glistening like white diamonds in the early morning sunlight. Behind her, the living room of the warm and inviting chalet—decorated heavily in floral and stripe chintz, winter floral arrangements, and worn quilts—was homey and bright. She sighed heavily, looking upward. From the looks of the sky, it would snow again today. Another day, unable to leave this place. Another day spent with the man she had lived with platonically for nearly two years. . .the man she loved. . .the man who she feared would never love her.

She closed her eyes and allowed herself to remember how they had come to be here, then shuddered, opened her eyes, and pushed herself away from the window. It was nearly time for breakfast, and he would be hungry and wanting her to sit with him at the table where they would sip the strong coffee she made and speak about what they would do with the day.

She left the brightness of the living room, walked through the dark stone and panel dining room and into the cozy and rustic simplicity of the kitchen. She had set the table the night before, using a faded, floral cotton tablecloth she purchased the first part of the week at a local flea market. She hoped it would make the day a bit cheerier. . .brighter. . . happier. It certainly enhanced the scarred, pine tabletop that had come with the rented chalet.

On her way to the counter, where coffee brewed atop the stove and a waffle iron stood hot and ready next to an old, farm bowl half-filled with batter, she stopped briefly at the table to adjust one of the china teacups that hadn't set quite right on its saucer and to shift the center-piece of dried flowers slightly to the right. Next, she poured the coffee, a cup for her. . .a cup for him. The intoxicating scent of it reached her nostrils on the cloud of steam rising from each cup. No sooner done than she heard him walking into the room behind her. He smelled of soap. She turned her pretty face slightly and smiled. "Good morning."

"Good morning." He inhaled deeply. "Coffee smells delicious. Did you sleep well?"

She returned the coffeepot to the stove and began to prepare their waffles. "Yes. And you?"

It was the same every morning. The same routine. . .the same questions. . .the same answers.

"Fairly well," he answered, sitting at the table.

"Did you wake at all?"

She heard him sipping his coffee; return cup to saucer. "Once. Maybe twice." She turned to look at him, resting her slender hip against the counter as the waffles were cooking. He was buttoning the cuffs of the long-sleeved black shirt he wore under a gray and white sweater. "Do you think I'll ever know what these dreams mean?" He turned and looked up at her, thin and boyishly handsome.

She turned back to the waffle iron, opened it, and lifted the waffles from the griddle and onto a waiting plate. "I'm sure you will, one day." She brought the plate over to the table, sat across from him, and dropped a waffle onto his plate and then one onto hers. She smiled. "When your mind is ready to understand, you will."

He reached across the table and took her hand. "I can never thank you enough for being here for me. You've been like an angel who dropped from a cloud in the sky."

"No need to thank me." She slipped her hand away from his, and reached for the small jar of syrup she'd placed on the table earlier. "Your friendship has been payment enough."

He didn't speak. He leaned back in his seat, crossed his arms over his abdomen, and looked out the window beside him, contemplating something. . .she could see that. . .but it was something she couldn't quite read in his eyes. She picked up her fork and knife and began to cut her waffle. "What are you thinking about so serious over there?"

He shook his head, no.

"No? No, what? No, you don't know or no, you aren't telling?" She slipped a forkful of the warm waffle into her mouth. It was light and deliciously sweet. "Mmm," she said, hoping to encourage him to eat as well. The man hardly ate enough to survive.

He turned his eyes back to hers. They seemed mysterious and yet, at the same time, bewildered. "If I ask you a question, will you be honest with me?"

Her eyebrows raised and she swallowed hard. "Haven't I always been?"

He nodded. "I think you have, yes."

"Then, of course, I will now." She felt her fingers gripping the utensils they held.

He leaned over, rested his forearms against the table, and looked intently into her eyes. "Do I know a woman named Katie?"

Andi Daniels took a deep breath, blinked twice—looking out the window once, then down to her waffle. When her eyes finally met his, she whispered, "Yes."

THANK YOU. . .

- . . .to our families and friends who have put up with us while writing this manuscript. A special thank you to Promise Press: to Susan and Greg for choosing this work; to Paul and Kelly for managing the work; to Robyn for such an incredible cover; to Shannon for outstanding public relations; and to Mike for. . . well, being Mike! Thank you to our agent, Bill Watkins of William Pens. A huge thanks goes to Linda Rooks for her guidance and to Ramona Richards, who sees beyond the words and gets right to the meaning.
- Thank you, Linda Urichko, for having the courage to do what most people never think to do, or should they think to do it, don't. You are an amazing example of salt and light in our community.
- Thank you to all our New York City contacts, especially Danielle Lavelle, Robert Marino, and Kaye Noble. L'il Chocolate, Misty, Michelle, Tony, and the others who remain nameless, *Thank you*! Thank you AWSA & CLASS! You're the best!
- Most of all, thank you Heavenly Father. . .for allowing our souls to dance. . .

THE AUTHORS

Eva Marie Everson is author of the Promise Press books *True Love: Engaging Stories of Real-Life Proposals* and *One True Vow: Love Stories of Faith and Commitment,* and co-author of *Shadow of Dreams* with G. W. Francis Chadwick. She and her husband have four children and three grandchildren and live in Florida.

G. W. Francis Chadwick, who also co-authored *Shadow of Dreams* with Eva Marie Everson, writes a financial trading advice column which is syndicated worldwide, teaches seminars for experienced investors, and specializes in stock trading systems and strategies. He makes his home in Atlanta, Georgia with his two dogs.

COMING SOON FROM
PROMISE PRESS
An Imprint of Barbour Publishing

Operation: Firebrand by Jefferson Scott
ISBN 1-58660-586-0

Former Navy SEAL Jason Kromer is appointed leader of Operation: Firebrand, a covert operations team specializing in non-lethal missions of mercy. Its first challenge: a winter rescue of orphaned children made homeless by Russian rebels.

Time Lottery by Nancy Moser
ISBN 1-58660-587-9

After twenty-two years of scientific research, three lucky individuals will receive the opportunity of a lifetime with The Time Lottery—to relive one decisive moment that could change the course of their lives.

Interview with the Devil by Clay Jacobsen
ISBN 1-58660-588-7

Investigative journalist Mark Taylor has landed the story of his career—an interview with Ahmad Hani Sa'id, the coldhearted leader of a new terrorist network stalking the United States of America.

Vancouver Mystery by Rosey Dow
and Andrew Snaden
ISBN 1-58660-589-5

Just days after Beth Martin's long-awaited facelift operation, Beth Martin is found dead—and her cosmetic surgeon, Dr. Dan Foster, finds himself playing amateur detective after being framed for the killing.

Suggested retail: $11.99 each

Available wherever books are sold!